PENGUIN BOOKS
NO MORE MEADOWS

Monica Dickens, great-granddaughter of Charles Dickens, has written over thirty novels, autobiographical books and children's books, and her works are beginning to be adapted for television and film. Her first book, *One Pair of Hands*, which arose out of her experiences as a cook-general – the only work for which her upper-class education had fitted her – made her a best seller at twenty-two, and is still in great demand.

Although her books arise out of the varied experiences of her life, she has not taken jobs in order to write about them: working in an aircraft factory and a hospital was her war work, not research. When she joined the Samaritans, it was the work of befriending distressed fellow human beings which she found compelling, although her novel *The Listeners* came from that experience.

She set up the first American branch of the Samaritans in Boston, Massachusetts, and lives nearby on Cape Cod with her husband Commander Roy Stratton, who has retired from the U.S. Navy, and her horses, cats and dogs. She has two daughters.

MONICA DICKENS

No More Meadows

PENGUIN BOOKS

in association with Michael Joseph

Penguin Books Ltd, Harmondsworth, Middlesex, England
Penguin Books, 625 Madison Avenue, New York, New York 10022, U.S.A.
Penguin Books Australia Ltd, Ringwood, Victoria, Australia
Penguin Books Canada Ltd, 2001 John Street,
Markham, Ontario, Canada L3R 1B4
Penguin Books (N.Z.) Ltd, 182–190 Wairau Road, Auckland 10, New Zealand

—

First published by Michael Joseph 1953
Published in Penguin Books 1970
Reprinted 1972, 1977

—

Copyright © Monica Dickens, 1953
All rights reserved

—

Made and printed in Great Britain
by Cox & Wyman Ltd,
London, Reading and Fakenham
Set in Monotype Times

Times are changed with him who marries; there are no more bypath meadows where you may innocently linger, but the road lies long and straight and dusty to the grave.

R. L. STEVENSON

Chapter One

THE sun was shining, and a small breeze was spicing along Piccadilly when Christine came out for her lunch.

She usually came out at midday, even when it was raining, instead of going up to the store canteen. You could never get a table to yourself, and whoever sat with you always wanted to talk grumbling shop about the customers or the management.

Everyone at Goldwyn's seemed to have a grievance of some kind, although it was one of the best London stores to work for, and many of the men and women had been there for years and years – some of them long past retiring age – for the management was good to its old faithfuls and let them stay on even when they were really past it, like poor old Miss Mattee in Model Gowns, who was always trying to sell people lace dinner dresses that were much too old for them.

Christine herself had been in the book department for more than four years. She had started as a junior, knocking over piles of books and breaking the till about once a week in her efforts to serve customers briskly. Now she was head saleswoman and moved calmly about the alleys between the bright new paper jackets, knowing that book customers liked to take their time, unlike the thrusters who stampeded through the Haberdashery with never a moment to spare.

She knew every book in the place, and all about the new ones before they came out. She was said to be Mr Parker's right-hand man – and heaven knows he needed one – and was sometimes asked in to take coffee when a favoured publisher's representative was in his office.

She liked her work, as much as one can like any job that imprisons one from nine until five-thirty. She liked Goldwyn's, but she was always glad to get away from it at lunch-time, even though it meant queueing for a table at any of the restaurants and teashops that fed the West End workers, who ate with one eye on their watches and a partiality for things like macaroni and suet pudding which were the most filling for the least cost.

She was wearing her grey flannel suit today. She thought it

made her waist look trim, although it made her stick out farther in front than she cared for. A generation ago she would have been admired as buxom. Now she was a little too plump, and streamlined salesgirls tutted at her in fitting-rooms when they could not close the zipper of a dress that was the right size for her height.

She was thirty-four. She had silky brown hair that would not stay set unless she pinned it up every night, and a full creamy face with a smile that seemed to have been carved on to it from birth.

She was often teased about being too plump, and because her face reposed in a smile even when she was not smiling inside, she was supposed not to mind the teasing.

Sometimes, when life seemed hardly worth going on with, as it does to women when they are tired, she saw herself as a figure of tragedy, like those pictures of veiled French widows walking behind their husbands' coffins at important funerals; but her face could never look the part, and people still thought of her as Good Old Christine. Always cheerful and good-tempered. Quite a tonic.

Christine liked the grey flannel suit because it gave her a good waist. She had been liking it for a long time, because she had accepted her aunt's advice that it was better to buy an expensive suit that would last than to keep buying trumpery-smart cheap suits that looked very dashing for the first few weeks, until they began to wrinkle at the elbows and sag at the seat. The good grey flannel had been what the tailor called a Classic, which meant that nobody would even turn round in the street to look at it, but it would stand having its skirt taken up or let down according to the swings of fashion. It was up at the moment, because the 'New Look' was already old, and women were no longer walking bell tents.

The book department, partly due to Mr Parker's *laissez-faire* administration and partly because it was cultural, which put the assistants on a closer level to the customers, was the only department in Goldwyn's where you did not have to wear black. With so many women going shopping without hats, this led to some confusion as to who was an assistant and who was a customer, but that occurs in all book shops, and accounts for the distressed look of people who have picked up a book they want and are afraid they are going to have their elbows grasped by the store detective before they can find someone to take their money.

With the suit, Christine wore a grey felt beret which had been sold to her cheaply by Mrs Arnold in Millinery, because it had a mark on the back and no customer would buy it. Women were absurdly fussy when they had money to spend. When they were walking along Piccadilly they were just ordinary women, quite meek, and obeying the policeman at the St James's Street crossing; but as soon as Goldwyn's commissionaire, who bought his medals at the Surplus Supply stores in the Strand, had pushed open the swing doors for them, they became customers, and that made them arrogant.

Christine had easily removed the mark on the hat with some lighter fluid. Any woman could have done the same; but to have noticed the mark with a shrewd mouth, to have refused to buy the polluted hat made them feel *recherché*. They knew what was what. They demanded the best, and so they bought a hat which did not suit them nearly so well, were borne down one floor in the lift when they easily could have walked, and sailed out of the shop in a glory of ego, thinking that the false smile of Mrs Arnold, who was in charge of Millinery, meant: There goes a lady who knows what she wants.

So Christine had got the hat and was glad. She always felt safe when she wore this suit and hat. Unexciting, but correct. Even when she hazarded the supreme test of catching herself sideways in shop windows, she looked all right. It would not matter whom she met, as it would if she were wearing the green coat with the collar like a run-over cat, which her aunt said was quite good enough to go to work in and need not be given to the nuns until next year.

Not that she ever did meet anyone in her lunch-hour. Alice, who was her junior, was always meeting people and having small adventures at lunch-time. Even if it was only a man who had picked up her glove in the cafeteria, she made it sound exciting, like an adventure. Alice and the other junior, Helen, were always giggling in the classics section where customers did not go so much. If Christine came along they would stop giggling and pretend to be straightening books. Christine thought this should have made her feel very old, but it didn't. She was much happier now than she had been at the giggling age. She liked her authority in the book department. Sometimes, outside, she inexactly did not know how she stood in relation to the rest of the world. At Goldwyn's she was someone.

Crossing Piccadilly and going through the narrows of Half Moon Street, sinister with bachelors' chambers and the brass plates of Indian doctors, she was nobody except a short plump girl who looked younger than her years, walking across Curzon Street and up Audley Street to have Welsh rarebit in an Oxford Street snackbar. She did not want adventure. She wanted just to walk in the sun and get the scent of hyacinths that someone had planted in the window-box of a little white house on the corner of South Street.

A young woman in a camel-hair coat passed her pushing two small children in a pram. Christine appraised them with interest to determine whether or not they were twins. She wondered, as she often did, what it would be like not to go to work, but to be married and not have to leave your house all day unless you had to take the children out or do some shopping.

When she looked into the future Christine was a little troubled about not being married, but ordinarily she did not worry very much about it. Her friends did that for her, even the ones who were not happily married themselves and secretly envied her independence. She would like to be married, but not as much as her friends thought when they introduced her to loveless bachelors.

Her aunt, who liked to have Christine at home, said that there was plenty of time and the right man would come along soon enough, but as he had waited thirty-four years to do it Christine was beginning to wonder whether he ever would. She had her dream man, of course, with whom she stood at the altar sometimes when she was in bed at night and fancied she was prettier than she was. She knew the way he looked and the things he said. She would recognize him immediately if he came along, and then her life would start to be quite different.

In Grosvenor Square the trees were hazed with curly bright young leaves. The grass was impeccable and knew no foot, and

10

tulips like red and white United States Dragoons were drawn up round the base of the Roosevelt statue.

People looked happier today. The women did not look as if their feet hurt, and here and there someone raised a smiling face to the sun, which had the first real warmth of the year. In the square there were girls with magazines and books and cakes in paper bags, as well as the old men who sat there hopelessly, whatever the weather. The old men did not look at the girls, but the girls sat at the far end of the benches and drew their skirts close.

There were only one or two old men colonizing in the Little America that Grosvenor Square had become since the war. Stately families had long since abandoned the tall houses that once broke the hearts and backs of servants, and nearly every door carried the plate of some Government department. Besides the flag-flaunting Embassy, there were American offices on all four sides of the square. Roosevelt was in his right place in the middle of it all. He stood alone, as he never could in life, cloaked and immortal, and English people were surprised that some of the Americans they met did not think him as great as they did. When an Englishman meets a Republican he is as surprised about Roosevelt as an American is when he meets a Socialist who criticises Churchill.

Christine walked to the north end of the square and saw that clouds were encroaching on the pale spring blue overhead. After lunch the sun might have gone in, so she decided to sit for a moment in its warmth and think about what she could possibly do with the neckline of the dress she would have to wear at the dance tonight. The green was at the cleaners and the black had torn away at the zipper last time she tried to step out of it instead of pulling it over her head. She and her aunt had been saying for days that they would mend it.

So it would have to be the spangled blue, which did something funny at the collar. It would be all right if she could wear an orchid or a rose to cover the fault, but Geoffrey did not bring you flowers – he thought it was honour enough to go out with him – and although Christine could have afforded a corsage, it would have made her feel pathetic to have to buy it for herself.

She did not feel pathetic as she sat on a bench and widened

11

her smile to the sun. She could not worry about the dress. It was not worth it, for although Geoffrey liked to talk as though he was a connoisseur of women, he never noticed what you wore.

Two American women in red and yellow duster coats and hats like jockey caps were photographing each other against the Roosevelt statue. Three others, fur-coated and expensive, walked down to the Dorchester for lunch. Expatriates, sated with the incomprehensible sleeping age of the Tower and Westminster Abbey, they came here to reassure themselves with the knowledge that this American garden was the cleanest square in London, and to recharge their vitality with the sight of the monstrous shining beetles parked all round, which dwarfed the few English cars among them into insufficiency.

They also liked to see the uniforms. You could not see English uniforms unless you went to the Trooping of the Colour, or were lucky enough to be in the Mall when the faceless Lifeguards jogged by with scarlet cloaks and burning helmets, their black horses catching at the jingle of their bits as if they knew that so splendid a sight must be accompanied by music. But in Grosvenor Square the American officers came out of the naval headquarters on the corner of North Audley Street all glamorous in dark blue and gold, with chestfuls of rainbow ribbons that did not necessarily mean a hero.

One of them walked past Christine. She narrowed her eyes to see whether, by blurring her focus, she could make him look like an Englishman. Coming towards her he could have been, but going away no Englishman could have owned that small round bottom, each side rising independently as though moved by wires from his shoulders. It was the walk that became so familiar during the war, when G.I.s in short battle-jackets proclaimed by the tilt of their bottoms that they had come over to pull England's chestnuts out of the fire once more.

The two girls in jockey caps finished their roll of film and moved away laughing, because one of them would send the pictures to her father and he would ask visitors: 'Did you know my Eileen was once photographed with F.D.R.?' and then scatter their astonishment by showing them the picture of the girl and the statue.

A robin hopped on the grass like a marionette. Christine

thought about the Welsh rarebit she was going to seek as soon as the sun reached that waiting cloud, and the American naval officer, who was evidently out for his health, completed his tour of the square and sat down at the end of her bench, breathing deeply through his nose.

'Would you care for a cigarette?' He had taken one out for himself, and before he lit it he held the packet towards her. If he had been in America he would have slid nearer to her along the bench, but as he was in England he kept his distance. English girls were always either suspecting you of evil designs or being frustrated because you did not have them. It did not occur to him that in Grosvenor Square she might be an American girl. Perhaps it was her shoes.

'No, thank you. Very much. I don't smoke,' Christine added, to show she was not snubbing him.

He did not notice anything about her except the creamy skin, which English girls got free and American women spent hundreds of dollars vainly seeking.

'Nice day,' he said, nodding conclusively at Grosvenor Square.

'Isn't it?' she answered, thinking, as she always did when she talked to Americans, that her voice sounded mincing.

She noticed about him that he had black, rather saturnine eyebrows that needed combing, and a mouth like James Stewart's that looked as if it might be going to blow a little bubble.

The sun went behind the cloud. Christine stood up, thinking of food. Had they talked enough for her to say Good-bye?

He solved that for her by throwing away his match and saying: 'Good-bye', giving it an extra little sing-song syllable that sounded like a secret smile.

Walking towards Oxford Street, Christine thought: Now Alice would make an adventure out of that. Then she wondered whether that big cameo brooch would do anything for the neck of the blue evening dress, and then she thought: But then if I'd been Alice I'd probably be having lunch with him by now. In the snackbar, opening her book and putting her knife into the still bubbling Welsh rarebit, she was glad that she was not.

Half-past five took a long time to arrive. Some days it was

upon you almost before you had time to turn round. On other days, when you were not so busy, it was a point in eternity, certain as death, but just as remote. In the middle of the afternoon Christine brought out a pile of books that were not selling, and told Miss Burman and Mrs Drew and Alice and Helen to push them on to anyone who vaguely wanted just 'a novel'.

Mr Parker had made a mistake about these books. He had bought too many of them, against Christine's advice, and when he found they were not selling he had said to her peevishly: 'What's the matter with all you people? You're letting that *Black Monkey* book hang about too long. You know what I always say – keep the stock rolling. Keep it moving. Make way for the new stuff.' He picked up pens and moved things about on his desk, as if he were playing draughts.

'We'd have sold it out,' Christine had said, 'if you hadn't ordered too many copies. I told you not to, but you had to know better.'

Because he was rather old and rather foolish, she often spoke to him as if he were an aged parent or a troublesome child. He did not mind. He had a daughter at home who spoke to him in the same way, and sometimes he thought he liked Christine better than the daughter, because although she bullied him she backed him up when he had committed himself and tried to put right his errors.

Both women often said to him: 'I told you so.' The daughter would leave him to stew in his own mistakes, but Christine worked to help him out of them. So this afternoon she brought a pile of *Black Monkey* novels out of the storeroom, blew a little dust off them, arranged them at the front of one of the fiction counters and told her assistants to sell them.

The reading public would be surprised to know how often it is sold books it does not want. Because it is allowed to wander round a book department, picking up and putting down and not being bothered unless it asks for help, it thinks it is not subject to the more obvious salesmanship of the other departments. But it is. A good bookseller can get rid of almost any book he has overbought, and Christine was a good bookseller.

By the end of the day she and Miss Burman between them had sold more than a dozen copies of *Black Monkey*. Miss Burman was also an old hand, well known to regular customers, who liked to call her by name, and responded, when she said: 'Now this is a book that *you* could appreciate, madam', like lambs to the slaughter.

Beginning to tidy up at five o'clock, Christine heard Helen say to a dithering customer with a neckful of martens. 'Oh, you *would*, madam. Everybody's reading it. In fact, we've just had to reorder.'

Alice, tossing her pageboy bob around the place, did not sell any copies of *Black Monkey*. She did not try to. Alice was self-engrossed and unco-operative. She would not last long in the book department, but would soon find herself in Art Jewellery, where she would be much more at home.

Going into Mr Parker's office with the special autographed copies of *A Golden Journey to the East*, which he insisted on locking in his safe at night, although it is doubtful whether they would have interested a burglar, Christine said: 'That Helen. She's coming along nicely. I think she'll be quite valuable to us soon.'

'She's awfully spotty,' grumbled Mr Parker.

'It's her age. So was I when I was nineteen.'

'Were you?' Mr Parker peered at her through the top half of his bi-focals. 'Come to think of it, so was I. I hated being nineteen.'

Christine tried to picture him with all his hair, and a gawky body with red wrists dangling out of his coat sleeves. He was so hunched now into the acceptance of old age, slow and precise and sparing of his waning vitality, that it was hard to believe his juices had ever run copiously enough to force an overflow in pimples.

'Well, we got *Black Monkey* moving for you,' she said. 'It might be almost cleared by the end of the week.'

'I told you it would,' he said, taking the leather-bound books from her and stooping to fiddle with the combination of his safe. 'I told you it would sell.'

'You told me to sell it, you mean. Here, let me.' Although he never changed the combination of his safe, he sometimes had difficulty in finding it. She opened the door and put in the books. There was no money in there, because the takings were delivered

15

to the chief cashier every day, but there was a mess of papers, a bottle of cheap brandy, and a tumbler.

'In the war,' Christine said, 'when I was a nurse, we used to drink the brandy from the medicine cupboard on night duty and fill the bottle up with water, but I don't see why you want to lock up the glass as well.'

'So I can be sure of finding it,' Mr Parker said.

Outside the office, Helen came up to Christine flat-footed, pushing at her spectacles.

'I don't know what to do, Miss Cope,' she said earnestly. 'That man over there has been reading the *Lives of the Saints* for nearly half an hour and he doesn't look as if he'd ever stop.' She looked at her watch, which was a man's watch with an aluminium case and a telescopic band. She did not trust the store clocks, although they were synchronized to Greenwich time.

'Tell him we're closing in five minutes,' Christine said. 'He should have read enough of the saints by now to avoid having to buy the book.'

'But, Miss Cope, you always tell me not to disturb customers when they're looking at books.'

'Oh, don't be so literal. Get rid of him.' Christine turned away, irritated by Helen's smugness and the way she drew down her mouth at the corners when she was worried.

Helen gave her a hurt look and went towards the customer, massaging her stubby hands, and Christine thought: Oh well, perhaps she's like that because she's plain and has no eyebrows or eyelashes and thinks she'll have to make a success as a career woman, if nothing else.

Actually, however, Helen had a passionate, perspiring young man who thought she was quite beautiful and was going to marry her when he had finished his military training. She did not tell anyone about him in case they asked his name. He was called Steuart Begwater, and it embarrassed her to say this.

At five-thirty the juniors put on the dustcovers, Alice in haste, because she had a date with the new young man in Cooked Foods, Helen sedulous as a priest. They all collected their handbags from the shelf under the humorous books. Miss Burman took out the bag of lemon tarts which she had bought in the bakery to take home to her mother, who could not get her teeth into anything except Goldwyn's pastry, and looked anxiously in her pot-bellied handbag to see that she had got the receipt.

If you bought anything in the store you had to show the receipt for it as you went past the timekeeper at the staff door, to prove you had not stolen it. This practice had been instituted during the war when all kinds of assistants who were not really Goldwyn's type had to be taken on. It was a source of great effrontery to the old-timers, especially when it was rumoured through the store one day that Mrs Darby in Toys had actually had her handbag searched.

Mr Parker tracked out of his office wearing his overcoat and the turned-down black hat that made him look as if he were the violinist from a German band. The other department managers usually left before closing time, but Mr Parker never did. As it was a trial to him to go down the stairs to the basement and up again to the staff door, the commissionaire kept one of the revolving doors open for him.

'Good night all,' he said vaguely. 'Have a nice weekend.' On his doctor's orders, he did not come in on Saturday mornings. He did not see how they could possibly manage without him, but they did.

'You look after that cough now,' said Miss Burman, who, from years of mothering her mother, had the instinct to mother Mr Parker too.

Christine went down to the cloakroom with Mrs Drew, who was her friend. Margaret Drew was nice-looking the second or third time you saw her, although at first you did not notice it. She was always strictly neat. Her short black hair was like a glossy elf's cap, her nose never shone, even on a summer working day, and if she broke a shoulder strap she sewed it at once, instead of keeping it pinned for days. She worked in the book department because her husband did not earn enough to keep them both and keep their son at a preparatory school. She hated Goldwyn's and often said so.

She said so tonight as she and Christine walked together to Green Park station. The warmth of the day had gone down in a thin green sunset and people were hurrying, pressing along in a crowd, unconscious of each other, because there was always a

17

crowd every night and they were thinking only of getting home.

'I'm fed up,' Margaret said, as they waited to cross Piccadilly. 'I'm fed with customers who can't make up their minds I'm fed with old Puritor, I'm fed with poor old Burman calling me dear and wanting to have lunch with me, and I'm fed with the idea of going home and cooking liver and bacon for Laurie's supper.

'I'm also fed,' she said, as the traffic stopped and they moved off the pavement like sheep in a flock, 'with seeing disgusting unmade beds when I get home, and having to make them.'

'Why don't you make them before you come out?'

'Haven't got time. Laurie always wants a hot breakfast, and he insists on me sitting with him while he eats it, and pouring his coffee and buttering his toast, as if I were a leisured wife in a flowered housecoat with nothing to do all day but my nails. He doesn't like me working, and so he clings to these last vestiges of a civilized marriage.'

Christine was surprised. She had been to Margaret's home many times, and admired her husband's constant need of her. He did not even want to go to the corner for cigarettes unless she came too, and at a party he always spent some of the time talking to her, unlike most husbands, who treated their wives as total strangers from a party's beginning to its end. But was being loved then such a bore?

She imagined how it would feel to be going home to a husband instead of to an aunt and a father. You would look forward to getting home, surely. But then Christine did not know the husband she was imagining, which made him exciting. Margaret had known Laurie for twelve years, and Christine had seen her sometimes quite unaware if he touched her.

Christine lived with her father and her Aunt Josephine in an ugly red house, redeemed by ivy, that stood on the edge of Barnes Common. The house had once been a rectory, and looked it. The downstairs rooms were high and large, and upstairs there were a lot of odd-shaped rooms which had once been nurseries for the families of prolific rectors.

It had been cold then with a holy chill, and it was cold now, except in the bathroom, which housed a boiler and a monstrous hot cupboard and was too hot to support life for long.

Christine did not like living in Barnes, which was neither in London nor out of it. She hated the never-ending bus ride down Castelnau, where the once grand houses nursed their shame of conversion into private hotels and apartments. But her father liked to be able to walk out of his front door on to the common and swing his stick among the disheartened gorse bushes. In summer, when he could not walk without stumbling over writhing couples, he would write wordy letters to the local paper, insisting that the common be cleaned up.

People coming to the house for the first time, travel-weary after the long, hopeless ride from Hammersmith Bridge, would say brightly: 'Why, it's just like the country!' But they did not mean it.

Christine's mother had died in this house when Christine was fourteen. The night after the funeral Christine took ten shillings from her father's dressing-table while he slept and ran away to Eastbourne, to the landlady of a small hotel where she and her brother had spent several holidays when they were little. The landlady gave her a breakfast of cornflakes and two boiled eggs, bought her ticket back to London and sent her home. Aunt Josephine, who was now in charge of the house on Barnes Common, gave her another breakfast, and nobody scolded her except her brother, who would have liked to go to Eastbourne too.

Christine got off the bus and walked down the sandy side-road to her home. The house was called 'Roselawn', but Aunt Josephine had let Christine's mother's roses go to ruin because she had not time for them, and the lawn, recovered from the scars of Christine and Roger's cricket pitch, had now succumbed again to Roger's children, who came there at week-ends to play.

In the middle of the lawn was a small enclosure, crudely made from wire-netting bent round sticks pushed askew into the ground, and covered with a piece of sacking. Christine lifted a corner of the sacking. A round-headed, black-and-white puppy stood up clawing at the netting and bumped her face wetly.

Neither the puppy nor the wire-netting had been there when Christine left for work that morning. She shook her head and smiled as she replaced the cover. The puppy squeaked and bounced up and made bulges in the sacking, but it was too little to get out.

Christine did not go into the house by the front door, because she had lost her key. Her father said the police should be notified. He believed, like many people of his age who were not brought up from scratch on the engineering marvel of the Yale key, that anyone finding it would easily discover which front door it fitted. Even if they had, Christine did not think there was anything in the house worth stealing. If a burglar had come after the unwieldy old silver or the incomplete sets of china in the cabinet, he would not get past her father's cantankerous alsatian, who hurled himself against the front door at the meekest knock, and had been terrorizing postmen for years.

So Mr Cope went on saying that the police should be notified, and the key went on being lost, and nobody did anything about telling the police or getting a new key cut.

Christine went in by the back door, past the dustbins and the coalshed, whose door had long ago been burst by an overflow of coke, and the bucket of garbage that Aunt Josephine put out for the man who kept chickens. The man did not really need the garbage, although Aunt Josephine insisted that she should help him, so he did not collect it too regularly, and the bucket smelled.

With eggs so scarce in the shops, Christine's father and aunt were always saying that they should keep chickens themselves. Eggs had been scarce since early in the war, so as it was now 1950 they had been saying it for ten years.

Aunt Josephine was in the kitchen, cooking supper and writing letters at the same time. She wrote hundreds of letters to her relations on thin paper, with the writing criss-crossed on the back. The Cope family was large and scattered all over the globe, and Aunt Josephine made it larger by discovering second cousins in New South Wales and step-grandchildren of Copes who had long ago emigrated to Canada and lost touch with family and home.

Aunt Josephine kept them in touch with unexciting news of who had married whom, and titbits about the royal family, and tidings of the death of people they had never known existed. She was a great one, too, for graves. She kept a little notebook with the place and date of burial of anyone remotely connected with the family, and, if geographically possible, would stumble there at the anniversary on her large turned-over foot to lay some flowers on the grave and scold the cemetery gardener for neglecting it.

Once, a long time ago, when she had taken a trip to India to see her sister, she had discovered that a very distant cousin had been buried at sea in the Indian Ocean. She took a wreath on the ship with her, made the captain tell her when they reached the exact longitude and latitude, and cast the now withered wreath upon the sea, to the edification of passengers and crew.

While she wrote at the kitchen table with her feet twisted round the legs, she had an alarm clock standing by the stove. It shrilled as Christine came in. Aunt Josephine cried: 'My pie!' and hurried to the oven, knocking papers off the table and smudging her forehead with ink as she pushed back her hair, which was like a thick, flecked off-white wool that she was still knitting into seaboot socks, because she did not see why merchant seamen should be neglected just because the war was over.

She was a tall, ungainly woman, who moved with bent knees and elbows stuck out. Her gestures were large and uncontrolled. She was always knocking things off mantelpieces and catching her heel in lamp flexes. She and the alsatian, who swished his muscular tail among the lower furniture, caused quite a lot of havoc in the house, which was one reason why there was nothing much left to burgle.

'Not done!' cried Aunt Josephine in disgust, pulling the pie out and pushing it in again with a shove that nearly sent it through the back of the oven. 'I can't understand it. I set the clock so carefully, but things are always either raw or burnt.'

'It would be easier if you watched them, really.' Christine took off her beret and shook out her short hair. 'The gas pressure's always going up and down these days, so you never know.'

'It's the Government,' said Aunt Josephine bitterly. 'Well, they needn't think I'm going to hang over my stove just to please a lot of Socialists. I've got far better things to do.' She

21

reset the alarm clock and went back to her letters, treading on one of the cats, which screeched and ran under the stove.

Another cat, a smug tortoiseshell, crooned on the window-sill among Aunt Josephine's plants and pots of chives and parsley. Two love-birds heckled each other in a cage on the wall, goldfish swam idly in a glass bowl on top of the refrigerator, and a very old snuffling fox-terrier slept on a blanket by the stove. Some cheese rinds and half a bun lay near his nose, but he either did not know they were there or could not be bothered to eat them.

Christine's own dog, which had watched for her in the road and come in with her, snatched up the cheese and the bun, rolling his eye at the fox-terrier, which would snap at him if it woke. He was a mongrel, a formless, brown-and-white wriggler, who was more like a long-legged spaniel than anything else. Sometimes you thought he would have looked better if his tail had been cut at birth. Sometimes you thought that would have made him look worse. He loved Christine with spaniel eyes all the time, and loved Aunt Josephine with drooling jaws at mealtimes.

Aunt Josephine often grumbled and muttered about having to feed and look after all these animals, but it was she who was responsible for the presence of the cats and the birds and the goldfish and the fox-terrier, and she who had bought the mongrel for Christine when he looked at her through the bars on one of her roving visits to the Battersea Dogs' Home.

The alsatian was not her doing. She fed it, and let it in and out every time it wanted to go and rave in the garden at innocent passers-by, but she did not like it, because its selfish, belligerent nature reminded her of her sister's husband, who had finally drunk himself off the map in Australia. It was her brother's dog. Ever since he came to this house he had always had an alsatian as a protection against the wild barbarism of Barnes Common.

'Well, I see you got another child,' Christine said. 'What's that out there on the lawn?'

'My goodness, I forgot all about her.' Aunt Josephine ran her long tongue over an envelope flap and banged it down with her fist. 'The poor little thing will die of cold. Run out and get her, there's a dear. I haven't got my shoes on.'

She was wearing the black leather slippers, like coffins, which she always put on as soon as she came into the house. Since she had to clean the floors, she saw no sense in bringing dirt in from outside for herself to sweep up and take out again.

She was illogical in her care of the house. She was particular about the floors. She could not bear to see dirt on them, and yet the furniture was covered with dogs' hairs, the mirror in the hall gave you a foggy reflection, and the telephone was thick with dust and so clogged with raw pastry from times when she had left her cooking to answer it, that you could hardly dial a number. At week-ends Christine was sometimes stirred to do some cleaning, but she got no thanks from Aunt Josephine, who liked to be the sole motive power of the house, with everybody else as passengers.

'It's a sweet little thing,' Christine said as she came in with the puppy, slapping down her own dog, which was trying to jump up and smell the newcomer, 'but do we really need another dog?'

'It wouldn't hurt,' her aunt said, 'but it isn't ours, so don't get excited. The Grahams have gone away for the weekend, so I said I'd look after it for them.'

'You said you'd look after the Fishers' cat over Christmas,' Christine said. 'That was four months ago, and it's still here.'

'I forgot, I can't think how. And by the time I remembered, it didn't want to go. You can't blame it. The Fishers don't know how to look after animals. They expected it to live off the mice it caught.'

'If you didn't feed ours so much they might catch some mice. There's one in my bedroom cupboard.'

'Well, you shouldn't keep biscuits in there.' Aunt Josephine made some flourishes over the paper and started another letter.

'I get hungry.' The alarm shrilled, Christine's dog barked and the puppy wriggled out of her arms and plopped on the floor. The dog and one of the cats chased it into a corner, where it stood at bay while introductions were performed.

Christine stopped the alarm, looked at the pie and turned off the oven. 'You only have pie when I'm going out,' she complained.

'Oh dear, are you going out?' Aunt Josephine looked up, her thick eyebrows drawn together in disappointment. 'I thought

23

we'd finish that hand of Canasta. I kept the cards on the table. Bruce knocked them off with his tail, but I put them back again.'

'With all the wild cards in your hand.'

'Naturally. And I'd planned a nice dinner for you, because I thought you'd be tired. The sales,' said Aunt Josephine vaguely, beginning to write again. 'I know what it is.'

'The sales were two months ago,' Christine said. 'You live in a world of your own. I'm sorry, but I told you I was going out. To that dance with Geoffrey.'

'Dreadful creature,' said her aunt. 'He has no sex.'

'That makes no odds. He's my cousin. Oh dear,' she said dutifully, as Aunt Josephine raised her head and made her face look stricken. 'I'm sorry. Have I hurt you?'

Aunt Josephine was supposed to have been engaged to a first cousin forty years ago. The cousin had spurned her and married a girl with money, and this was Aunt Josephine's 'tragedy', sacred in family history, a thing to be respected; not unmentionable, because however great her distress and shame at the time, she was now proud of it. Her blighted love was one of her treasured possessions, like her amber beads and the family Bible which her father had entrusted to her instead of to her brother. You could refer to it, but you could not speak of it lightly.

'I'm sorry,' Christine said. 'It was different with you, of course.'

'Yes.' Aunt Josephine fetched up a sigh. 'It was different with me.'

'Well, anyway – ' Christine changed the subject before her aunt could start off about: I remember the dress I wore that night he told me . . . 'Well, anyway, I'm discouraged about what to wear. Did you by any chance mend the zipper of the black velvet?'

Aunt Josephine clapped her hand to the side of her head with a sound like wood-chopping. 'My darling, I forgot! How could I have forgotten?'

She was always forgetting things. Names, telephone numbers, engagements slipped through her mind like water. If you particularly wanted her to do something, you had to write it down on the pad that hung in the kitchen, called 'The Housewife's I MUST', but she forgot to look at the pad.

Christine and her father were used to her bad memory, but Aunt Josephine herself was constantly surprised by it, although she had been forgetting things for as long as Christine could remember.

'I'll have to wear the blue then,' Christine said, 'and I look like a milk-churn in it. Not that it matters with Geoffrey. He's too busy thinking about what he looks like in his midnight-blue dinner jacket.'

'Then why worry?' said Aunt Josephine comfortably.

'Oh, but then, you know – ' Christine turned her head away. 'Other people see you, and one ought always to . . .'

Like any unmarried girl – and some married women – she was never without the idea, at the start of any party, that this time, tonight, she might meet someone who . . .

Party after party went by, but she never did. Sometimes she thought she had, but they always turned out wrong.

But the ritual of bathing and dressing and grooming yourself for a party excited you all over again to the possibility of someone who . . .

She fiddled about for a long time with the neck of the blue dress, pinning it this way and that, trying the cameo brooch in different places until the draped collar was marked by pin-holes and a smudge of lipstick from her little finger.

The front-door bell rang while she was still fiddling, and the alsatian rushed through the hall with his booming bark, his nails rattling on the polished boards. Christine was getting desperate about the dress, beginning to think that she would have to make some excuse to Geoffrey and tell him she could not go. The bell rang again. Geoffrey was always punctual. He was a stock-broker, successful, according to his views, and he attributed his success to things like being punctual and knowing head waiters at the right places, instead of to the fact that he had inherited a ready-made job in his family firm.

The bell rang a third time, the alsatian nearly went mad, and Christine's father called out: 'Front door!' although he was in the drawing-room, only a few yards away from it.

'Let him go,' said Aunt Josephine, coming into Christine's room. 'He behaves as if he had a staff of servants. Why, my dear, how beautiful you look.' She loved Christine and was as biased about her appearance as if she were her own daughter.

'Oh, I don't,' wailed Christine. 'This dress looks awful. The neck has always been wrong, only I hadn't the guts to walk out of the shop after trying on so many.'

'Let me lend you my spray of roses. You could catch it up underneath them and it would look all right.'

'Oh, I can't. I mean – artificial flowers – well, I know they're awfully pretty, but I – '

Aunt Josephine went away to get them. She liked artificial flowers, and the fact that young people thought you could not wear them did not shake her. She came back and held the floppy red silk roses against the neck of the blue dress.

Christine wriggled and then stood still, surprised to find that the roses did not look at all bad. They looked obviously unreal, which was their saving grace. The taboos of girl friends and odd quirks of prejudice culled through the years died hard. You could wear Woolworth pearls and get away with it, but you could not wear artificial flowers. Or could you?

'I'll wear them,' she declared. 'I think they look all right.'

With her tongue between her teeth she pinned them on. Aunt Josephine went away sighing, because she had offered a favour by lending the roses, but Christine seemed to be doing her a favour by accepting them.

Geoffrey was in the drawing-room with Mr Cope when they went down. Aunt Josephine was carrying the puppy, to protect it from the other animals. It nuzzled against the flat woollen bosom of her dress and licked the red V of her skin.

Geoffrey was sitting in an armchair by the fire with his fingers laced and one leg swung loosely over the other. He was a tall, thin, sandy-haired man with obtrusive glasses and a little hedge of moustache over his pink upper lip, which hung slightly over the lower one. His hands were long and dainty and his evening shoes sharply pointed. He was not effeminate, yet he was as un-masculine as it is possible to be without being a woman.

He stood up when the two women came in and said: 'Greetings', to Christine, and: 'I hope I see you well', to Aunt Josephine.

Christine's father was standing before the fire with his hands in his pockets and his trousers stretched tightly over his fat little stomach. He was a short, irritated-looking man with a pushed-out lower lip and dark shadows round his eyes. One side of his thin hair was long, so that it could be brushed over the bald top of his head. He grunted at Christine, because he had not seen her yet today. He had been working when she came in, and he did not get up until after she left in the morning.

He turned and looked at the six-hundred-day clock, which swung its leisured pendulum of four gilt balls in a glass case on the mantelpiece. 'What about dinner, Josephine?' he asked. 'This working man is hungry.'

'But Geoffrey has only just come,' his sister said, stroking the puppy. 'He must have a glass of sherry before he and Christine go out.' Her tone reproached him for not having thought of it before. She was his elder sister and had been reproaching him all his life for this and that. He did not mind.

Geoffrey said: 'Thanks very much, Aunt, but I don't drink sherry.' He meant: Not the kind of sherry you probably have in this neck of the woods. He thought Christine's family very suburban, and only asked her out when he could not get anyone else.

'Well, then, we'll have gin,' Christine said. 'Go and get me some ice and I'll make martinis.' She went to the squatting bow-fronted cupboard where bottles were kept among piles of old gramophone records, and began to pour gin and vermouth into a shaker.

Geoffrey went out to the kitchen, made a face at the cats and half raised his foot to kick the growling fox-terrier. He got out some ice cubes, with concern for his dinner-jacket, and went back into the drawing-room, where his aunt and uncle were having some kind of a small argument.

Christine dropped ice into the shaker and put on the top.

'For God's sake!' said Geoffrey. 'What are you doing? You never shake a martini.'

'Why not?' she asked, still shaking.

'Because you don't. You just stir it with a spoon or a rod. You should make it in a glass jug, anyway.'

'Geoffrey, you're so sophisticated,' said Aunt Josephine damningly.

'Don't be silly,' Christine said. 'They taste just the same. They're mixed now, anyway. Here, try one.' She poured three glasses. 'Daddy?'

'No, thank you,' he said, glancing behind him again at the clock. 'It would spoil my dinner.'

'They're supposed to give you an appetite,' she said. She brought her glass and her aunt's over to the fireplace and they all sat down.

Aunt Josephine raised her glass, which looked very fragile in her large rough hand. 'God bless us all,' she said.

'Cheers,' said Geoffrey uncheerily. He sipped at his drink with questing eyebrows, to show he knew the difference between a good martini and a bad one.

His uncle and aunt continued their argument. It was something about the standing charge on the water rate, and had been going on at intervals for days. Argument was their main form of conversation. They both enjoyed it, and neither of them ever won, because the other would never accept defeat.

Geoffrey finished his drink and stood up. 'I think we'd better get weaving,' he said. He had been in Air Force public relations during the war. 'I booked the table for eight-thirty.'

'We must finish what's in the shaker.' Christine went over to the cupboard, taking short steps, because the blue dress was too long. She hoped she would be able to dance in it.

Aunt Josephine put her glass down on the edge of a table, where it teetered and dropped just as Geoffrey put out his hand to catch it neatly before it reached the floor. 'Fielded, sir,' he told himself.

'Thank you,' said his aunt, unconcerned. 'No more for me, Christine. I had better go and eat, since your father's so fidgety.'

'I am not fidgety,' he said. 'I merely like to get my dinner at the proper time, which, God knows, seems to be an impossibility in this house.'

'You are fidgety,' said his sister decisively. 'Come and get my key from me, Baby dear, before you go. I'm not going to get up to open the door at the foolish hour you young things will probably come in.' She sometimes had the fancy to treat Christine as if she were nineteen instead of thirty-four. Ordinarily

Christine did not mind, but with Geoffrey there it made her feel silly.

Her father and aunt went out of the drawing-room, their voices raised in the hall, because the alsatian had scrambled the rugs in his infuriated attack on the front door. There were always disputes about the animals.

When they were in Geoffrey's car, humming along towards the river, Geoffrey driving with hands low on the wheel, non-chalant, and flipping the smooth gears through with the crook of his fourth finger, he said: 'There's always so much argument in your house. It must be damn dull to live with.'

'It's just a habit,' Christine said. 'I argue, too, like mad, when I can be bothered. So does Roger. Daddy says that Granny died arguing with the doctor about whether she was going to die. You must be a throwback to one of our Quaker ancestors.'

He did not answer. He was in his high-flown, rather distant mood. Christine did not think she was going to like him much this evening.

They made desultory conversation during dinner. Geoffrey raised a lot of fuss about whether the sole was fresh and the champagne cold enough. He paid more attention to the waiters than he did to Christine.

After the champagne they had a glass of brandy and then another, and Christine liked herself better. All the drink in the world could not make her like Geoffrey very much, but it could make her feel gay inside, so that she would be able to enjoy the dance and feel a shining part of the music and the assured women and the dresses and chatter.

The dance was at Geoffrey's club in St James's Square. He did not leave her at the door while he parked the car, but made her go with him to find a place for the car and then walk back. After all, she was only his cousin. She meant nothing to him except a presentable partner to take to the dance. He had asked two other of his scant female acquaintance before he asked Christine.

As they went through the entrance, which looked more like a station hotel in the Midlands than one of the best clubs in London, he was at pains to impress her with the honour of being allowed to enter by these portals, instead of having to use the

29

ladies' entrance at the back, as she would on every other day of the year.

'Isn't that wonderful?' Christine said. She was directed past some notice boards and match, inns for a dark room behind the staircase, which was being used as a ladies' cloakroom. Her coat was taken across a trestle table by a depressed woman in black, who had a small gas fire on her side of the table. The rest of the room was very cold, and full of goose-fleshed women eyeing one another and trying to see in the shadowed mirror.

Christine resettled Aunt Josephine's roses and combed her hair, which had blown about walking from the car park. She looked rather nice. It seemed a waste.

Upstairs, where the club's president and his overstuffed lady received them on a marble landing, it was also cold. It was an interval between dances. They went through to the bar, which was in the members' library.

There were to be two other people in Geoffrey's party. 'Sure to find them in the bar,' he said. 'When in doubt about old Hubert, always look in the nearest bar.'

Sure enough, old Hubert was drinking champagne with a skeleton-thin girl in a steel-grey dress which she never would have bought if she had seen her bare back view in it. Her shoulder-blades stuck out like wings above her knobbled spine. Her hair had grown raggedly, from what might once have been a petal cut, and she had cold, fanatical eyes. She was introduced as Miss Something. Christine never did find out her name all evening.

It was a very dull dance. Geoffrey danced well, and so did Christine, but you could not hear the band at one end of the long narrow ball-room, there were too many people on the floor, and Christine's dress was too long.

'What's the matter with you?' Geoffrey asked, hanging his upper lip down at her. 'You keep falling over your feet.'

'It's not me, it's you,' she lied. 'You shouldn't try fancy steps if you don't know them properly.' She tried taking her left hand off his shoulder and holding up the skirt of her dress, but that made her feel like a dowager, so she put the hand back again. She had used too much hand lotion and some of it had come off on Geoffrey's coat. She hoped he would not notice.

Supper was the best part of the dance. They had lobster and chicken and peach melba and a lot more champagne. Christine remembered pre-war Commemoration suppers at Oxford, and the night people threw pellets of bread at her and Jerry, because they would not talk to anyone else at the table. When she got home she would be silly and look again at that dreadful picture of the dance guests taken after sunrise on the lawn of Magdalen College. She looked all right, being only nineteen, but Jerry looked rumpled, shadowed with beard in the six-o'clock light.

Geoffrey hardly talked to her, except to ask why she took a second helping of lobster when she was already too fat. He was bored with her and thought it was a waste to spend all that money on a ticket for just a cousin. He and Hubert talked to-gether most of the time. Christine made one or two abortive attempts to talk to Miss Something, but she appeared to be in-terested only in the works of Christopher Fry, and was eating as if she had not had a square meal for weeks, which was what she looked like.

Afterwards, they went to the ladies' room together. Christine wished that her make-up would last the whole evening, as other women's seemed to. She put on more powder, and Miss Some-thing, who used no make-up except a purplish lipstick which had come off on her teeth during supper, stood by and watched her coldly, a bead Dorothy bag dangling uselessly from one skinny arm.

Christine began to wonder when it would be time to go home. She danced once more with Geoffrey, but then he got on to whisky and the serious business of drinking and could not be persuaded to leave the bar. She sat in a leather chair and thought about having to get up early to go to work. An ancient friend of her father's took her away to dance. He joggled her round the room and his breath smelled of catarrhal old man.

When she got back to the bar Geoffrey said, loose-lipped and goggling behind his glasses: 'Come on, we've been looking for you everywhere. Go and get your coat.'

But they were not going home. They were going on to a smashing night-club, where good old Hubert had a bottle of the best. Christine started to murmur that she had to work tomorrow, but Geoffrey thought it was silly that she was a shop girl, and paid no attention.

They were all in Geoffrey's car, and his driving showed that he was fairly drunk. Christine's foot kept shooting out to brake on the floorboards. This annoyed him and made him screech his tyres more than ever.

The night-club was a small cavern, with listless people drinking at tables in the dark, or draped against each other on the dance floor, which was made of lighted glass bricks.

Geoffrey's party sat at a sofa table, and Hubert's bottle was produced after a lot of delay and argument with the perspiring waiter. Christine did not like whisky, but there was nothing else to do but drink it and watch the half-dozen girls who came on to the floor wearing a few ostrich feathers to kick their legs and thrust their naked navels about.

While a woman with false bosoms was crooning, Hubert announced that Miss Something did not feel well and was going to be taken home. He got up with her in the middle of a song and people shushed at the disturbance they made.

Geoffrey did not want to go. He was slumped against the back of the seat with his receding chin on his crumpled shirt front, and might or might not have been asleep. When the cabaret was over Christine pinched him and suggested going home. He sat up, said: 'God no, the night is young', took a gulp of whisky and slumped back again. Christine felt too tired and hazy to stir him up again. She sat in the dark with her elbows on the table and a lot of smoke in her eyes and let her thoughts drift. Presently she was aware that a man at the next table was talking to her.

She smiled and shook her head, not hearing all that he was saying to her. He had dark, ungreased hair and the kind of small wrinkled face that never properly matures, but looks at any age only like a boy grown old. He was wearing a grey flannel suit and an Old Harrovian tie. He looked like hundreds of men you might meet in London, and quite safe.

Geoffrey's mouth fell open. He was asleep. The man in the Old Harrovian tie put his hand on Christine's knee. She removed it. She did not know how it came about, but then they were on the dance floor, and the man did not dance very well, and he held her in an excited way and laid his cheek against the side of her head.

He kissed her hair. Was it rather romantic? Christine wished she had not drunk so much, because she could not decide whether it was romantic or not; but if she had not drunk so much she would not be dancing with an unknown, excitable man and not really caring what happened next.

When the music stopped, the man took her hand and pulled her off the floor into the dim little lobby where the stairs led up to the street. 'Wait there, my sweet,' he said, and disappeared through a door.

Christine leaned against the wall and thought that when you were a little drunk it was your will-power that went first. You were a tool of fate, content to slide along with the drift of events. When the man came back she stared through him without recognition, because it had been dark at the table, and on the floor, where it was lighter, she had danced so close to him that she had never properly seen his face. He was smaller than she expected. He came close to her, and she recognized his touch and the texture of his suit. Ah yes, there was the Old Harrovian tie. She was static, waiting to see what would happen next.

'Let's go out and get some air,' he said. 'Come on. Please, darling.'

Was this the way a great love affair started? Christine wondered, making the usual mistake between love and alcohol. But I don't really do this kind of thing, she thought, following him obediently up the stairs. Perhaps it's time I did.

In the street, he said: 'Let's go on up to the Blue Angel. It's much more fun than this joint.' It had been raining. He put his arm round her waist and they walked along Oxford Street with the lights pooling red, yellow, green all down the vista of wet road, and scarcely any traffic to obey them.

He was not much taller than she was. His voice was clear and arrogantly typical of his class, but with a throbbing undertone of excitement that was communicating itself to Christine. Here I am, she thought. Picked up, and in for an adventure, perhaps.

The shop lights were all turned off. Suddenly, he pushed her into a doorway and kissed her as gracefully and successfully as if they had been before a film camera.

She did not mind. But that was dreadful of her. What was she doing? What was happening? He moved in on her and a doorknob pressed into her back. He kissed her again with less finesse and more intent, and she broke free, pushed past him out of the doorway and ran back towards the night club, her head going faster than her feet, so that it seemed she must topple forward. The man did not follow her.

When she went down into the cavern again they were still playing the same rumba that had been clicketing in her ears when she followed the man up the stairs. Geoffrey was still sitting in the same position. He had not noticed that she had been away.

'Let's go,' she said, waking him up. 'Let's go home, Geoffrey. It's terribly late.'

He felt better after his sleep. He went quite amiably out with her, collected his coat and the excessive black homburg that he wore in the middle of his small head, and did a little senseless joking with the hat-check girl, who had to earn her living in black net tights and a top-hat. Christine tried to hurry him, because she was afraid the man would come back. In the street, she looked quickly up and down before she darted across to the car, although even now she did not know that she would recognize him if she saw him.

She got into the driver's seat, not trusting to Geoffrey, but he got in at the same side and pushed her over. 'My dear cousin,' he said.

He drove quite carefully out to Barnes, grumbling all the way about the distance. He was such a bore. Christine wished now that she had gone with the man in the Old Harrovian tie. She often wished that she were the sort of girl who had adventures. Now she had turned one down. But it had been a small adventure, all the same, something to tell Margaret about. Margaret was not shocked at things that other people did, even though she would not have done them herself.

She would share with Margaret the fact that someone had found her attractive enough to pick up. Not being a natural pick-up, she did not know that you did not have to be especially attractive – you just had to be a woman – to get picked up by a half-drunk man in a dark night-club.

She felt excited when she thought about what might have happened to her that evening. She had missed her chance – of what? She sighed. Her bosom felt large and voluptuous and her waist very small. She wished she were driving with someone who would make love to her when the car stopped. Geoffrey was surely the biggest bore in the world. When he was in his car he thought of nothing else. Not that she would let him kiss her if he was silly enough to try. The thought made her giggle.

'You drank too much tonight,' Geoffrey told her censoriously.

'So did you.'

'My dear child.' He sighed. 'When you can hold your liquor as well as me, you'll have something to be proud of.' He turned in at the soft side-road that led to 'Roselawn' with a skidding sweep.

'The outposts of Empire,' he said as he stopped outside her home.

'Coming in for a drink?'

'No, thanks. I've got miles to go back,' he said, trying to make her feel bad about living so far out. His side of the family, with their money and their house in Regent's Park, had always rather looked down on the Copes, and been known to explain them away at parties as 'my suburban relations'.

The Copes thought Geoffrey and his excitable widowed mother very silly, and explained him away as 'he can't help being like that'.

He would not see her to the door. He never did. Christine said good-bye to him in the car, and then remembered.

'Geoffrey, I haven't got a key. I forgot to ask Aunt Josephine.'

'You'll have to wake her up then.' He switched on the ignition.

'What time is it?'

'Three o'clock.'

'Oh, I can't. She hates being woken up, and Daddy probably wouldn't answer, even if he heard me. He'd think it was burglars

35

at last. Come with me and let's see if there's a window open somewhere.'

'You don't need me. You know the house better than I do.'

'I can't go prowling round on my own. Suppose a policeman came? Look, you must. One doesn't just leave a girl to break into a house by herself.'

The man in the Old Harrovian tie would have thought it fun to do it with her. They would have crept about in the dark holding hands, and he would have pressed her against the wall of the house and kissed her. She could imagine the ivy cushiony and damp at her back.

She shivered. 'Please, Geoff, come and help me.'

'Oh, all right, all right.' Grumbling, he twisted his long legs out of the car, stood up and stretched in the sandy road and yawned vastly at the night.

'Shut up,' said Christine, taking his arm. 'You'll wake the dogs, then there'll be hell to pay. Come on.'

He staggered a little going up the path. He was not as sober as he thought. He followed Christine all round the house on exaggerated tiptoe, cursing when he put his foot into a flower-bed. They tried the back door and all the lower windows with no success.

'The landing window,' Christine whispered, looking up from the front door. 'The one half-way up the stairs. They sometimes forget to lock that. Look, if I stand on your shoulders I could reach it.'

'Damn,' said Geoffrey, tripping over an iron hoop that was meant to keep dogs off the bulbs. 'My God no, a great girl like you. You'll break my back.'

'You're so rude,' said Christine. She giggled. This was rather fun. She kicked off her shoes, made Geoffrey clasp his hands in front of him, stood on them teetering, with his face pressed into her skirt, put one foot on his shoulder and tried to put the other foot up as well, holding on to the ivy and the tiny gable above the front door.

He staggered, crumpled and collapsed to the ground with her on top of him. He pushed her off roughly and stood up, brushing off his clothes. The situation affronted him.

'This is ridiculous,' he said. 'I'm going to ring the bell.'

He looked sillier than ever with his oiled hair standing up in spikes.

'No, please – ' She caught his arm. 'Don't. If Aunt Josephine wakes in the night she never gets to sleep again, and then she'll have a headache all tomorrow, and it's her day for the Putney Incurables.'

'As if they hadn't got enough to bear without that crazy old woman –'

'Shut up,' said Christine, 'and do something. If you put your foot on that bit of iron sticking out of the bricks there, you could stand up and reach the window.'

'So could you.'

'I'm not tall enough. You are. Or don't you think you could make it? You're afraid you'll tumble down, I suppose.'

'God damn it,' said Geoffrey, his voice in his nose, 'I am not afraid. I'm just bloody well fed up with fooling around here with you when I ought to be in bed.'

He was so cross that he wrenched off his coat and threw it on the ground without worrying whether it got dirty. He put one narrow shoe on the rusty iron peg which once supported the wistaria that Christine's mother had loved, clutched the gable, hoisted himself up with a grunt that was more like a squeak, and got his hands on the window-sill. He stood there, one foot waving behind him in the air, and his body flattened against the house.

'Can you open it?' asked Christine, wanting to laugh.

'I could, if I could let go with one hand,' he gasped, clinging on desperately.

'Of course you can. It's easy.'

'Oh, it's easy, is it? All right –' He shifted his weight, raised one hand to the bar of the sash window, and at that moment there came a swelling roar from inside the house and the alsatian hurled itself, all teeth and claws, against the inside of the window. Geoffrey shrieked, waved his hand wildly, leaned backwards and fell with whirling arms and legs at Christine's feet, half on the path, half in the flowerbed.

When the bolts and chains of the front door shot back and Christine's father and aunt appeared in the light from the hall, he holding the alsatian by its chain collar, she holding a torch and the front of her peignoir, Christine was kneeling on the gravel, dabbing at the gaping cut on Geoffrey's eyebrow with the skirt of her dress. She felt cold with fear, yet resigned already to the emergency that life had suddenly become. It had happened. Something awful had happened. Geoffrey was unconscious and badly hurt, and the night was broken into crisis and cries and all sorts of breathless, bustling things to do.

They got him inside and laid him on the sofa. He was like a figure stuffed with sawdust and his silly face was leaden. Aunt Josephine was stanching the wound with pillowslips from her mending basket, her big face noble, as if she were saving a bleeding soldier hero with strips torn from her petticoat.

Mr Cope wanted to do something. He got out the brandy. Christine came back from telephoning the doctor just in time to see him trying to force the neck of the bottle into Geoffrey's dead-looking mouth.

She had never noticed that Geoffrey had false teeth. He must have a very good dentist, she thought absently, as she pulled back her father's arm. 'Don't give him that!' she cried.

'First aid,' he said, surprised. 'Always give 'em brandy. I thought you'd been a nurse.'

'The only thing I remember from it is that you never give stimulants to a patient with a head wound. He may have a fractured skull or compression of the brain or something. Oh Daddy, isn't it awful?'

She wanted to be comforted, because it was her fault. She put her hand on her father's arm, which felt soft and fat under the silk of his pyjamas.

He stiffened, as he always did if you tried to caress him. He turned away and poured a glass of brandy for himself. 'God knows, I need it,' he said, as if he were the only one who had had a shock.

The alsatian was still snarling and prowling round the room, giving off sudden throaty barks, to show that its outrage was not yet appeased.

'Can't you shut that animal up?' Christine asked, coming back with a hot-water bottle to put under the rug that covered Geoffrey. 'It's all his fault, anyway. He made Geoffrey fall.'

'He was only doing his job,' said her father, 'and I must

say, apart from what's happened, I'm glad of the showing he made.'

'You're glad!' Aunt Josephine looked up. 'When here's that poor Geoffrey bleeding to death on your sofa.'

'He's not bleeding to death. You've stopped the blood, like the sensible woman you are. And he's coming round now, anyway. Look at him.'

'No wonder, with the noise you and that dog are making. Go up and put on your dressing-gown before the doctor comes.'

'I will not go up. I'm perfectly decent.'

They were still arguing when the doctor arrived; not their own family doctor, but a cavernous, monosyllabic man, who had just been climbing wearily into bed after a confinement when the summons from 'Roselawn' caught him.

Geoffrey was fully conscious by now, not fussing, but appearing to accept the situation without surprise. The doctor took some things out of his bag, went away to wash his hands and came back to take scissors and needles and silk out of the sterile cases that Christine opened for him. She tried to do things for him without being asked, efficiently, to show she had been a nurse, but it was not like it had been in hospital. It was quicker and more casual. In hospital there would have been a tremendous boiling-up of sterilizers, and people rushing about with trolleys and sterile towels and kidney dishes. The doctor simply threaded a needle, squared his elbows and bent over Geoffrey. He had not even taken off his overcoat.

'You're not going to stitch him up without an anaesthetic?' asked Aunt Josephine.

'He won't feel it. He's drunk as a goat.' Geoffrey grinned foolishly, as if at a compliment. Aunt Josephine looked startled, and then stared at Christine and gave her one of her awkward winks that did not fit in with her long solemn face.

Mr Cope said : 'Oh', and walked away. He was more shocked at Geoffrey being drunk than at him being stitched up without an anaesthetic. He did not watch the stitching. The other two did, and while they were getting Geoffrey to bed in the spare room that looked over the garden at the back, Mr Cope went to his own room and locked the door loudly, as a sign that he cared for no more disturbance *that* night.

'You've had quite a lot to drink too, haven't you?' Aunt Josephine asked Christine, looking across the bed as they tucked the blankets round Geoffrey's cold feet.

'A bit.'

'Did you have a nice time?'

Christine looked at Geoffrey. He was asleep. 'Not very,' she said.

'Well, I never thought you would. That's the finish of that dress, anyway,' said Aunt Josephine, looking at the blood on Christine's skirt. 'I'll take my roses now, if you'll just unpin them.'

Christine looked down guiltily. 'Oh, thank goodness,' she said. 'They're not spoiled.' She gave them to her aunt.

'Yes, thank goodness,' said Aunt Josephine, carrying them carefully out of the room like a bridal posy. 'They escaped disaster. They looked lovely on you. You shall wear them again some time if you like.'

Christine kissed her aunt on the landing. She felt she should say something. 'Sorry,' she said brusquely, jerking her hand towards the spare-room door. 'Sorry about all this.'

'Gracious me,' said Aunt Josephine easily. 'It adds a spice to life.' She went into her room and Christine heard her talking to the puppy which was sleeping on her bed.

In her bedroom, Christine did not feel tired or sleepy. She stepped out of the ruined dress, threw away her laddered stockings and dawdled over creaming her face and doing her hair. What a night, she thought. What a night. She sat up in bed and went over the events of the evening, and she remembered the kiss in the doorway more clearly than the details of what had happened with Geoffrey.

She had forgotten to look at the picture of herself and Jerry at the Commemoration ball at Oxford. She got out of bed again and took out the picture from where it was rolled up with her old school photographs in the bottom drawer of her desk. Kneeling, she spread it on the floor and put a hand on each end to keep it flat. There he was, Jerry, rumpled and unshaven.

When you kissed me, in those days, it wasn't anything like tonight in the doorway. You were so innocent, only I didn't know it, because I was too. None of those other Canadians in the ice-hockey team can have been like you were. When you got a bit carried away, like that time in the hay barn at Jennifer's, you used to say afterwards: 'Forgive me, darling' and be afraid that I minded.

Christine smiled, rolled up the photograph again and put it away with the pictures of herself in the cricket team and the swimming eight, and the panoramic photograph of the whole school and all the mistresses making funny mouths, taken with a slowly turning camera on the tennis courts in Jubilee year. She got into bed and turned out the light. The room was not dark now and she shut her eyes and began to worry about having to get up in a few hours' time, and what she would feel like at work.

She was late getting up in the morning. A weight pressed on her eyes and her mouth was dry as sandpaper. When she went downstairs she could hear Aunt Josephine in the hall, telephoning to Geoffrey's mother. Christine went into the kitchen, where her aunt had put coffee and toast and half a grapefruit on the table for her. The butter was under a plate, because of the cats.

When Christine had a hangover it always made her hungry. It seemed a long time ago that she had eaten dinner with Geoffrey, and much had happened since then. She finished the grapefruit and the toast and was cutting a slice of bread when Aunt Josephine came in. She wore a net over her yellow-grey hair and a stiff new flowered overall that looked like the loose cover for a sofa. She sat down at the kitchen table and poured herself a cup of coffee. A cat mewed against her leg.

'How did Aunt Lottie take it?' asked Christine.

'Badly. Being woken so early gave her a sense of calamity. If she would get up at a reasonable hour like we do she wouldn't take things so ill.'

'My hour isn't so reasonable,' Christine said. 'I'm dreadfully late, even worse than usual. Mr Parker doesn't mind, but sooner or later someone's going to find out I'm never in on time, and then I shan't be the estimable Miss Cope any more.' The manager had once called her that at a staff conference, and the family had never let her forget it.

'You won't have time to get my wool then,' said Aunt Josephine sadly.

'Oh Lord, I'm sorry, no. I'll have to go straight to my own department. I'll go early on Monday and get it. I promise.'

'I could have done two or three of those pilches over the weekend.'

'Well, the Balkan Orphans can wait a few days. They're in bad enough shape as it is.'

'That's just the trouble.' Aunt Josephine leaned on the table despondently. She bore the world's troubles on her back. She saw all the babies from all the ruined homes behind the Iron Curtain running about freezing to death because Christine had not got up early enough to buy her some wool to knit drawers for them.

'I tell you what,' she said, brightening. 'Why don't you take Geoffrey's car to work?'

'He'd never let me. It's his treasure.'

'Don't ask him.' Aunt Josephine levered one side of her face into her brand of wink. 'I don't want him wakened, anyway. You'll be back with it when he goes this afternoon. His mother's coming to take him away after lunch – "in the Rolls," she informed me, as if I didn't know she had one.'

The idea of driving comfortably to work in Geoffrey's car instead of waiting on the windy road at the corner of the common for the bus and then joining the battle for the train at Hammersmith Broadway was so tempting that Christine did not let herself think twice about it. She took the car and got to Goldwyn's early enough to buy Aunt Josephine's wool from the flushed woman in Art Needlework, and get to her own department in time to hustle the juniors over their dusting.

'I say, Miss Cope, you do look rough this morning,' Alice said gaily. 'Aren't you quite the thing?'

'I'm fine, thank you.'

'Had a night out, I expect,' Alice said. 'I must say that's the only thing I'm glad I'm so young for. It doesn't show on me.'

Christine went away to tell Margaret of the night's adventures. Since Mr Parker would not be in this morning, they went into his little jumbled office and lit cigarettes, with one eye for shadows coming up to the stippled glass partition.

Saturdays were usually fairly quiet. Most people were busy buying food, and the chief customers were college students looking for technical books and children clutching five shillings in an agony of choice. Christine and Margaret usually had a cigarette or two on a Saturday morning. Even if you did not especially want one, it was enjoyable because it was illicit, like smoking in the ward bathroom on night duty, when Night Sister might come round on rubber soles at any time and catch you.

Margaret enjoyed the story about Geoffrey, whom she had disliked ever since Christine had brought him to a party at her house and he had criticized the colour of the curtains. The story of the man in the Old Harrovian tie fell rather flat. She was not shocked. She listened without comment, but in the telling it became, not a romantic adventure, but something quite sordid.

Margaret suddenly got up and went to the door. 'I'm going to have a baby.' She threw it out casually, not looking at Christine, as if she were almost embarrassed about announcing a baby after twelve years.

'Darling Maggie, how wonderful!' Christine looked at her, intrigued by the secret changes unguessed within the familiar neat exterior. Margaret seemed suddenly remote. Pregnant women lead an introverted life that no one else can share.

'I think it's terribly exciting!' Christine was over-enthusiastic, as always at news like this, to smother the little jealous stab that wished it could be her. 'Isn't Laurie pleased?'

'Well, I suppose so. He's surprised. He treats me as if I were a phenomenon, producing at my age. It makes me feel terribly old.' Margaret went briskly off among the books. Miss Burman came up to Christine with a muddled query about encyclopaedias, and the morning went on.

Since they were not busy, Christine had time to feel tired and a little sick from last night. She was buoyed up by the thought of driving home in Geoffrey's car. If she could come to work in a car every day, life would be a fine thing. Her father never let her take his stolid black car, which had been laid up with bricks under the axles during the war and had never run properly since.

Christine overtipped the car-park man, because Geoffrey's

grey coupé made her feel grand, and drove rather showily among the westbound traffic, looking without pity on the lines of people at the bus stops, who might have been herself.

Miss Burman, who was getting a lift to West Kensington, squeaked and exclaimed and leaned forward, holding on to the door. She was gratifyingly though sickeningly impressed. If only she would not keep saying: 'My stars! I don't get a ride in a car from one year's end to the next', one might be more sorry for her.

'Here's where you get out,' said Christine. 'I'll stop for you while the lights are red.'

Miss Burman had dropped her handbag on the floor and could not find it. She had difficulty getting out of the car, and by the time she had staggered to the pavement with her hat askew, leaned in to tell Christine once again how surprised Mother would be to see her home so early and shut the door without latching it properly, the lights had been green and were now red again.

Christine turned on the radio and opened the window so that the man in the old car next to her could hear that she had a radio. The car made her feel superior. Ordinarily, she did not have much to be superior about. After Hammersmith Bridge she let Geoffrey's car out far over the speed limit and arrived home feeling happy.

Aunt Josephine met her at the door with a face that wiped some of the smile off Christine's. 'The doctor's been,' she said hollowly.

'How's Geoff?'

'It's bad news, I'm afraid.' Aunt Josephine bent to straighten the rugs that the alsatian had scattered when he heard the car stop.

'What do you mean? Is it a fractured skull? Is he dying or something?'

'Heavens, why should he be? He'll be all right, but the doctor says he can't be moved for at least a week.'

'Oh gosh,' said Christine. She looked at her aunt. Her aunt looked at her. With Geoffrey ill upstairs, it would be unkind to say what they thought.

Aunt Josephine made a face. 'I shall look after him like my

44

own child,' she said theatrically and went away to dish up lunch.

After lunch Christine followed her aunt into the kitchen and said: 'I'll do the washing-up, if you want to get off to the Incurables.'

'I'm not going,' Aunt Josephine said in a martyred voice, rolling up her sleeves and turning on taps.

'Of course you are.' Aunt Josephine went every week to read to the inmates of the Putney Home for Incurables. They loved her. Other visitors read what they thought was good for the Incurables. Aunt Josephine read them what they liked, which was love stories and thrillers.

'They'll die if you don't go,' Christine said.

'They're dying, anyway,' said her aunt gloomily. 'I can't go, with that body upstairs to look after.'

'I'll look after Geoffrey. Don't be difficult. Here, get away from that sink and let me get on with the dishes.'

Aunt Josephine put on a heavy coat like a travelling rug and a red felt toque which she clung to in the teeth of all opposition, and went off to Putney. When Christine had put away the plates and silver she made coffee and took a cup into her father's study. He was working, crouched like an ape over the big varnished desk under the window which looked over the neglected lawn.

Since he retired from his job in the Ministry of Pensions he had occupied himself by translating French novels into rather stilted English. It was not very lucrative work, and he was slow at it, because, although he had been brought up in France, his French had rusted over the years and he spent more time consulting dictionaries than actually writing anything, but it kept him busy and he enjoyed it. It made him feel that he was part of the literary world. When he had to enter his occupation on any form, he did not put 'Retired Civil Servant'; he put 'Author', and he behaved as temperamentally about his work as any creative writer.

Christine took another cup of coffee up to the spare room. Geoffrey was lying in twilight with the curtains drawn. He had been sitting up, but when he heard the door handle turn he slid down under the bedclothes and lay flat with his eyes closed.

45

'How do you feel, Geoff?' Christine asked, coming up to the bed.

'Got a headache.'

'Poor dear. I'll just take your tray. Oh, good, you've eaten your lunch. That's fine.'

'Well, I just had a taste of soup,' Geoffrey grumbled without opening his eyes. 'What was it made of? Bones the dogs wouldn't eat?' But the bowl and the plate of toast were empty, and Christine had seen the amount of soup Aunt Josephine had taken up.

She knocked against the bed as she picked up the tray, and he gave an irritable exclamation and opened his eyes, which were pale and unfamiliar without his glasses. With the bandage low on his forehead, he looked like Suzanne Lenglen in her bandeau. His hair stuck up in points above the bandage.

'I thought I heard my car a while ago,' he said. 'You haven't been driving it, have you?'

Aunt Josephine had said that he was not to be excited. 'How could you possibly hear it from this side of the house?' Christine hedged. 'Quite a lot of cars go along our road.'

'I'd know the sound of mine anywhere.' He closed the eye under the wound and looked at her with the other one. 'Have you been driving it? I wouldn't put it past you.'

'Of course not.' Christine put down the tray and went to the window to move the curtains.

'Well, in any case,' he said sulkily. 'I want you to take it to a garage today. It can't stand out all the time.'

The nearest garage was far away. If she took the car there she would have to walk back right across the Common. 'But, Geoff,' she said, coming back to the bed, 'it wouldn't hurt. It's quite warm and it isn't going to rain. Why, Americans leave their cars out all the time, even in winter. Hardly any of them have garages.'

'I don't care what the Americans do!' he said loudly, raising himself bolt upright like Lazarus in his coffin. 'Horrible people. It's my car, and it's all your fault that I'm lying here, and the least you could do –'

'Whatever is going on?' asked Geoffrey's mother, surging into the room all furs and bags and umbrellas. 'Geoffrey, my

46

darling boy!' She hurried to the bed and dropped magazines and flowers on his feet. 'You're dangerously ill and you're supposed to be kept quiet, and my goodness, how uncomfortable you look! Christine, whatever are you thinking about, and you a nurse!'

Echoes of the remark made so often to Christine by so many irate ward sisters. 'How did you get in, Aunt Lottie?' she asked sulkily. 'I didn't hear the bell.'

'The front door was open, in your usual charming country style,' said Aunt Lottie coldly. She swarmed over the bed. She was a large woman, and she gave forth a lot of voice and perfume and a kind of invisible ectoplasm of high-pressure living that took up a lot of space in the air around her. 'Oh, my poor Geoffrey,' she said. 'This is surely a terrible thing. I don't for the life of me see how it could have happened. Tell me *all* about it.'

'It was all the fault of that damned dog,' he began, putting on the whining tone of a small boy with a doting mother.

'I knew it! All those animals. I knew they'd be the ruin of this family some day. The house is like a menagerie. Why, when I came in a great brown-and-white monster came at me with slavering jaws, and if I hadn't run for my life up the stairs –'

'That was my dog,' said Christine. 'Timmy wouldn't hurt a fly. If he was slavering, it was because he can smell his dinner cooking.'

Aunt Lottie ignored her. She hovered with voluptuous exclamations over Geoffrey, who lay back, looking quite flat, like a typhoid patient sinking into the mattress.

Christine brought a chair up to the bed. 'Let me get you a cup of tea, Aunt Lottie.'

'I don't care for any, thank you. I've just had my lunch, but I dare say Robbins would be grateful for a cup, if you would invite him into the kitchen. Don't you bother about me. I just want to talk to my son. Now tell me, Geoffrey. I want to hear all about this dreadful accident.'

Dismissed, Christine went downstairs and brought Aunt Lottie's chauffeur into the kitchen and gave him tea and cake and talked to him about murder trials, while she mixed scones

47

to surprise Aunt Josephine when she came home from the Incurables.

She had her hands in the dough when the spare-room bell rung.

'Just as if I was a servant,' Christine said.

'I know, miss,' said the chauffeur with feeling. 'Wouldn't it drive you off your natural.'

'Something always happens when you start to make scones.' Christine scraped the dough off her fingers into the bowl, washed her hands and went up to the spare room. Aunt Lottie was winding herself into her blue foxes.

'I'm ready to go now,' she said. 'Geoffrey wants to sleep, and the poor boy must have all the rest he can. I only wish we could have got him home.'

'So do I,' said Christine. 'I mean – you'd be happier to have him with you.'

'Please have Robbins go to the front door for me,' said Aunt Lottie, as if she were ordering her carriage and pair round to the door.

She was coming down the stairs as Christine came back from the kitchen. 'Geoffrey has told me the whole story,' she said. 'I wouldn't embarrass you, Christine, by saying so in front of him, but I consider it was foolhardy of you, very foolhardy indeed. Rash of Geoffrey, of course, but he was only trying to be gentlemanly.'

'He would have left me to get in by myself,' Christine protested, 'if I hadn't absolutely made him help.'

Aunt Lottie's attention was diverted by the large cardboard box of clothes and toys which Aunt Josephine had put out for the nuns to collect. She poked at it with her umbrella.

'You never know what you'll find standing about in the hall of this house,' she said, and went out, raising her suède-gloved hand to Robbins as if she were hailing a cab.

When Roger arrived on Sunday morning, the first thing he saw was his sister walking through the hall with a tray of dirty bandages and bloodstained cotton wool.

'Ha!' he said. 'The estimable Miss Cope. What's happened? One of the tykes been fighting?' He always called the dogs the

Tykes, just as he called his father The Aged Parent, or The Aged P., and his wife The Little Woman. He seldom called anything by its right name, because he liked to make a joke about everything in the world, even the war, which he referred to as 'that small scrap we had with the Nastys'. He called Aunt Josephine Jo Jo the Dog-faced Boy, or simply Dogface, and his two children, who bore the lyrical names of Clement and Jeanette, were always known as Champ and Boots.

The children followed their mother into the hall, round-eyed, looking for trouble. They opened the door of the grandfather clock and played with the weights, while Christine unfolded the story of Geoffrey.

Roger roared with laughter, but his wife Sylvia frowned and said: 'I don't think it's funny at all. Poor Geoffrey might have been killed.'

'The little woman wasn't born with our sense of humour,' Roger said. 'Now, kids, don't let your grandfather catch you messing about with that clock.'

'Oh, he won't mind,' said Jeanette. She meant: He will mind, but we don't mind if he minds. The elder Cope so seldom spoke to them without censure that it bothered them no more than a fly on the window-pane.

'Well, anyhow, run along and muck about somewhere till lunch-time,' their father said. 'Champ, your flies are undone again. That boy! He'll be arrested yet. Where's Dogface? In the galley, I suppose.' He went down the passage past the stairs to the kitchen.

He was a large man with too much energy and no acquaintance with relaxation. The house was noisy and restless on Sundays when he was there. His wife was quiet and unobtrusive, perhaps because she had long ago given up hope of competing for attention. Christine supposed that she loved Roger because he was her brother, but they had never been close. Ever since she could remember, he had always laughed at her, and she had never been able to share her emotions with him or take him her problems.

'There's a new puppy,' she told the children, who were now exploring Aunt Josephine's box for the nuns. 'She's out on the lawn. You can take her out of the run if you don't let her get on to the road.'

The boy and girl looked at her with delight, then looked at each other with secret faces, making the idea that a grown-up had given them entirely their own.

'Jeanette is growing out of all her dresses,' Sylvia said, as they ran out of the door, with Christine's dog scrambling after them. 'I wish I had another daughter to put into them.'

'Why didn't you?' asked Christine.

'You know I couldn't, after Clemmie.'

'Oh yes, of course, I forgot. Why didn't you adopt one then, if you wanted another child?'

'Well, we did and we didn't.' Sylvia took off her coat and hung it on the hall stand, which was piled with old coats and hats that nobody wore any more. 'And an adopted child – I don't know that it's too satisfactory. They nearly always suffer from emotional insecurity.' She was quoting something that she had read.

'Not if you treat them properly,' said Christine, holding the tray of dressings on her hip. 'I've always thought that if I don't marry I shall adopt a child.'

'You couldn't,' said Sylvia, smoothing down her dry reddish hair in the mirror that was partly obscured by all the clothes that hung on the stand. 'Single women aren't allowed by law to adopt children.'

'I'm sure I could if I really set about it,' Christine said, irritated by Sylvia's submissive acceptance of everything she was told. 'There were two women won a case about it some years ago. Don't you remember? I'd manage it somehow, and if I had a child –'

'Well, don't let's stand about in this cold hall all day,' said Sylvia, going towards the drawing-room. 'Don't you want to go and get rid of that tray?'

Christine had wanted to continue the conversation where she was, with the unappetising tray of dressings balanced on her hip. The most interesting things never cropped up when you were sitting comfortably in chairs. It was always in transient places like halls or staircases or bathroom doorways that the really important things started to be said and you had to discuss

50

them then and there, because the mood was lost if you moved away to a more suitable place.

Some of the major events of her life had come to her when she was passing through this wide chilly hall, with its grandfather clock that told the months and days of the week, its loaded hatstand, and its huge gilt framed print of Queen Victoria's coronation. It was here that her father had come from the telephone and told her that her mother had died in the nursing-home. It was here that Maurice had plucked up courage on his way out of the front door and looked back over his shoulder to ask her to marry him, and here that she had stood in her nightdress and read the letter from Jerry, which said that he was on leave in England.

But Sylvia did not like halls, and she was not interested in the problems of a woman who loved children, but had no husband to give them to her. She went into the drawing-room and poked the fire, and Christine took her tray out to the kitchen and then came back to pour sherry for all the family.

The Sunday was like so many other Sundays. It started off with everyone friendly and glad to see each other, and ended with a dyspeptic bickering, after they had eaten too much lunch and tea.

At one o'clock Mr Cope came in from his study, rubbing his eyes to show he had been writing.

'Hullo there, aged P.!' called Roger from the fireplace, where he was straddling to warm his behind. 'How's the *magnum opus*?'

'Pretty fair. I make slow progress though, and the publishers want it in a month's time. They never will realize that translating is a highly meticulous art and can't be rushed.'

'Philistines, all of them.' Roger shouted his laugh, which went: 'Ha-ha-ha!' on the air, like a bubble coming out of the mouth of a character in a comic strip. 'What are you on to next? Why don't they give you something Parisian and sexy for a change? It would warm the cockles of your old age. Get the old glands gushing again.'

His father ignored this. He did not think Roger should talk like this in front of Sylvia. She was a favourite with him. He considered her one of the few really nice girls he knew.

She played up to him. She called him Copey, and made a great point of fussing over him and paying him respect, as if she did not think he got enough of it from his family. She brought him his sherry now, and settled him in an armchair, telling Roger to move over so that his father could get some of the fire.

Aunt Josephine came in from the kitchen with her face and hands red and some of the hairpins slipping out of her heavy hair. Christine went out to fetch the children, who had already got themselves dirty. She helped them to wash in the little lobby under the stairs. If she left them alone they would just hold their hands under the cold tap and wipe some of the dirt off on a towel, so she washed their hands in her own, liking the feel of the strong clutching little paws in hers.

She washed their faces with the corner of a wet towel, and they shut their eyes and pursed their soft mouths. She looked in the mirror over the basin and imagined that she was their mother. When she was drying Jeanette's face she bent and kissed her.

'Why do you do that?' asked Clement with interest, swinging on the towel rail. 'You always kiss us.'

'Don't you like it?'

'Oh, we don't mind.' His face shone and his black hair was combed wet and flat to his round head.

'It's because I love you,' Christine said, untying Jeanette's bow, which was slipping off the end of her forelock. 'Doesn't Mummy kiss you?'

'Not too much,' said the boy. 'She says it's unhygienic.'

'She often has a cold, you know,' said Jeanette seriously, admiring herself in the mirror. 'She suffers terribly with her sinuses.'

Sylvia always did sniffle a bit. Her small coloured handkerchiefs were often at her freckled nose, and her voice had a slightly nasal pitch.

At lunch Roger carved the roast beef at the sideboard, and the children took the plates to Aunt Josephine, who added vegetables and gravy.

Mr Cope said, as he said at every Sunday lunch: 'It was a relief to me when you got old enough to carve, Roger. The carver

52

never gets a chance at his own food before people are wanting second helpings.'

'You hardly ever carved,' said Aunt Josephine. 'Catherine used to do it when she was alive, and after that I did.'

'Isn't there any more horse-radish?' he asked, digging in the bottom of the jar. 'This stuff is growing mushrooms.'

'You know there isn't,' said Aunt Josephine. 'We had all that out at supper last night.'

'At school,' Jeanette said, going carefully round the table with a plate, 'we aren't allowed to have seconds, even when there's heaps left.'

'They don't starve you,' said Roger. 'And don't say seconds.' He pointed the carving-knife at her with a threatening grimace.

'Why not?'

'Because it's common, dear,' said Sylvia, patting her mouth with a napkin, although she had eaten nothing yet.

'Well, everybody says seconds,' persisted Jeanette, 'and everybody isn't common, or you wouldn't send me there.'

'Quiet, Boots,' said her father. 'You don't know what you're talking about.'

'I'm afraid she does,' said Aunt Josephine. 'Cut me a nice thin slice for Geoffrey, will you, Roger, and someone can take up his tray.'

'Let me, let me!' clamoured the children. They did not like Geoffrey, but now he was exciting, because he was in bed behind a closed door and they had been forbidden to go in.

'No, troops,' said Roger. 'You'd drop the tray.'

'You can come up with me if you like,' Christine said, 'but you must be very quiet.'

'I don't approve of all this getting up and running about at meals,' said Mr Cope. 'We never get a peaceful lunch. Let those children sit down and get on with their food.'

But they were already out of the door after Christine. They tiptoed into the spare room and stood at attention at the end of the bed, staring at Geoffrey. He did not speak to them, and so they did not like to say Hullo.

Christine rearranged the pillows and put the bed-table across his knees. He had been smoking, and there was ash on the sheets and on the front of his pyjamas.

53

'The doctor said you weren't to smoke yet,' she told him.

'Might as well be dead,' he said. 'What's this?' He poked at the food with a fork. 'I don't know that I want any.'

'Now, you've got to eat that all up,' ordered Christine, to save his face, because she knew that he really wanted to eat it, but was afraid that he would not be thought ill if he did.

She went out with the children, and they asked her eagerly on the landing: 'Is he dying?'

'Not yet,' she said, 'but he has a terrible big wound, you know. The doctor had to put eight stitches in it.'

She knew that they would enjoy hearing about the stitching, and they did. She told them about it as they went downstairs, and about how much blood there had been. They would retail it to their mother when they got home, and Sylvia would disapprove.

Christine suspected herself of trying to curry favour with the children by telling them things that they would not hear from other grown-ups. She knew she should not try to make them find her better company than their parents, but she could not help it. She was jealous for their affection. Once, Jeanette had said to her in one of her rare moments of clutching warmth: 'I love you better than Mummy!'; and although Christine had said: 'Hush, of course you don't', she had exulted in her heart.

After lunch she played cricket with the children on the lawn. They screamed and yelled, and Geoffrey kept ringing his bell to complain about the noise. The family had tea too soon after lunch, because Roger and Sylvia had to get back to Farnborough. Aunt Josephine had made cakes and scones, and everyone ate them, although they were not hungry.

Sunday was a day of eating and lying about in chairs with the Sunday papers. It was a day of earned indulgence, but it made you feel unhealthy.

The family had said all the fresh things there were to say after a week's separation. Local gossip had been exchanged on both sides. Aunt Josephine had given Sylvia her new recipe for icecream without cream. Sylvia had told what the doctor had said about Clement's ears, Roger and his father had discussed the Budget, and now there was a lull, when they were all a little tired of each other.

The children had been careering about all day, missing their usual afternoon rest, and were ready to quarrel with each other or anyone else. Clement reached for the jam, Jeanette slapped his hand in a prissy way, and he spilled his milk on the carpet. His father shouted at him to go and fetch a cloth and his face dissolved in tears.

'I wish you wouldn't shout at him,' said Sylvia mildly.

'If it wasn't for me,' Roger said, 'there would be no discipline at all in this family. You're much too soft with them.' Jeanette watched him narrowly, nibbling the icing of her cake.

'It's all very well for fathers,' Aunt Josephine said, scenting a quarrel, and entering battle with alacrity. 'They're out all day while the mother copes with the children, and then they come back and behave like God Almighty for an hour or so, until the mother takes the children away and has the trouble of trying to get them to bed after the father has upset them.'

'You're right, Aunt Jo,' said Christine. 'Men are an awful nuisance in a family.'

'Without the men,' said Roger, guffawing, 'there ain't going to be no family. Isn't that so, Aged?' He dug his father in the ribs. Mr Cope edged his chair away.

'I think men are hell,' said Aunt Josephine placidly.

Sylvia frowned and shook her head. She did not like words like hell used in front of the children.

'Just because you could never get one for yourself –' began Mr Cope and stopped himself before he could commit sacrilege on his sister's far-off broken romance. 'This tea is abominable.' He drained his cup. 'I don't believe you ever boil the water before you make it.'

'If you know so much about it,' said Aunt Josephine, 'why don't you sometimes come out to the kitchen and help me? Slave, slave, slave for you, and all I get is criticism.'

'Destructive criticism at that,' put in Christine. 'The worst kind.'

'Now don't you all be mean to poor Copey,' said Sylvia. 'He's the easiest man I ever –'

'Don't be smug,' said her husband. 'Sucking up to the old man, as if he had something to leave you. I suppose you're trying to imply that I'm difficult.'

They argued on, half joking, half disgruntled. Jeanette sat on the edge of her chair and looked uncertainly from one to the other. The alsatian lying by Mr Cope grumbled in his throat, and the two love birds in the cage by the window began to shuffle up and down their perch and squawk in accompaniment to the voices.

Clement came back from the kitchen still whimpering and began to mop up the carpet. Christine and Aunt Josephine both noticed that he had brought a clean dishtowel, but said nothing.

They bickered on for a while, keeping the argument going for argument's sake, and when it was time for Roger and his family to go they were all quite pleased that Sunday was over. Aunt Josephine wanted to clean up the kitchen. Christine wanted to listen to a programme on the wireless, Mr Cope wanted to go to sleep, and Sylvia wanted to get back to her tidy polished house where, even if Roger did make a lot of noise, no one answered him back.

In the hall, Clement tried to put on his sister's coat, and Jeanette screamed and hit him. He screamed louder than she did and fell on the floor.

'Overtired,' said Aunt Josephine crisply. 'Take them away, Roger.'

'Boots! Champ!' he bellowed. 'Stow that, and get on out to the car. We're sick of you.'

The children went out looking very small, with their hats pulled too far down on their heads. They walked far apart from each other down the garden path. Christine wanted to run after them and kiss them good-bye, but Sylvia might not like that, and the children were in no state to like it either.

Everyone kissed in the hall, and said how lovely it had been, and almost meant it. It had been like most other Sundays, and Sundays were always supposed to be lovely, with the family all together.

'I'm going to close my eyes for five minutes,' said Mr Cope, as Aunt Josephine waved from the door and shut it as the car drove off. 'Don't anyone come into the drawing-room.'

Christine said good-bye to her wireless programme and went upstairs to see how Geoffrey was.

He was hot and cross and complaining about crumbs in his bed, although he had put them there.

'Those children are the noisiest ever,' he said, sitting huddled in a chair while Christine made the bed. He was wrapped in an eiderdown, and with his bandage askew and two days' growth of beard on his yellow skin he looked like riffraff saved from drowning. 'I'd just got to sleep this afternoon when they started raising the devil in the garden.'

'I'm sorry,' she said, making a beautiful mitred corner with the sheet, and wishing that Sister Ram, who had always said her beds were the worst in the ward, could have seen it. 'I'm afraid that was my fault. I was playing with them out there. I must remember I've got an invalid in the house now.'

'Yes,' he said, hitching the eiderdown round him like an old woman, 'you must.'

Chapter Two

As Geoffrey's condition improved he grew more demanding. It meant that Christine and Aunt Josephine could never be out of the house together, because Mr Cope would not answer the spare-room bell, even if he heard it.

They nursed him as kindly as they could, but it was very trying having Geoffrey in the house. Christine was glad to get off to work after she had washed him and made his bed in the morning. She had taken his car to the garage on Sunday night when it was raining, and walked back with Timmy across the Common, cold and wet and feeling martyred, and hoping Geoffrey would pay the garage bill. She did not drive the car any more.

Margaret was away from Goldwyn's all that week, which put more work on to Christine. Stocktaking was drawing near, and Mr Parker was working his old bones up to a small panic about it. He would call Christine into his office a hundred times a day to ask her something she had told him six times already.

On Wednesday, while she was searching through the shelves at the back of the department for an old novel that had not been wanted for years, a man came diffidently up to her. He was wearing a light raincoat over tan-coloured trousers and his face looked vaguely familiar.

When he asked her if she had got a book called *Communism is Amongst Us*, she was not surprised to hear him speak American. It was mostly Americans who wanted that kind of book. English people were tired already of reading about the Communist menace. They hoped vaguely to deny its existence by ignoring it, but Americans wanted to probe it out of its terrors.

'I'll get it for you in just a moment, sir,' Christine said. 'As soon as I've finished with this customer.'

Then she remembered who he was. He was the American naval officer who had sat beside her on the bench in Grosvenor Square and offered her a cigarette the day Geoffrey cut his head.

He looked more insignificant out of uniform, narrow-shouldered and lightweight and a little lost, standing in people's way between the counters, looking about him with his black brows drawn down. She watched him while she was wrapping up the novel for the customer before him, and wondered whether to risk reminding him that they had met.

When she found him the book about Communism, he said: 'Thanks a lot for your trouble', and was so pleasant about it that she said, before she had time to feel shy: 'I saw you in Grosvenor Square the other day, didn't I? We sat on the same bench.'

'I know it,' he said, watching her hands as she made up the parcel for him. 'I was wondering if you would remember.'

Christine found herself wishing that she were not wearing the old skirt and jumper which was all she could be bothered to put on this morning after Geoffrey had been captious about his dressing. Her hair needed washing. She knew it.

The American talked to her for a few minutes about nothing very much, and then she saw a customer walking about helplessly with a book, and said: 'Excuse me. I'll have to go.'

'O.K.,' he said lightly. 'I'll just wander around for a while. This is quite a store you have here.'

'Better than Saks, Fifth Avenue?' It was the only American shop she knew.

'Well, I suppose not, but –' He meant: Pretty good for London, but did not say it. He was a very polite man, and more at his ease than most of her English male customers, who were apt to be brusquely embarrassed in the act of buying.

Christine went away, and the naval officer stayed in the department, looking at books with the critical and slightly dissatisfied air of all Americans in shops, on the defensive against the salesmanship that pursues them all their lives. Christine saw him looking at her once or twice, and then he went away and out of her life, as customers did.

She told her aunt about him when she got home, and Aunt Josephine said: 'Romance! A meeting in Grosvenor Square. It sounds like a film with Anna Neagle and Michael Wilding.' Aunt Josephine loved that kind of film. She loved Ivor Novello, too, and had seen all his shows two or three times, swooning a little in her upper-circle seat.

'Not romance,' said Christine. 'He wasn't particularly

59

attractive. It was just funny though, meeting him that day, and then him coming into the shop.'

'Think you could get any nylons out of him?' Aunt Josephine, though careless about the rest of her appearance, favoured her legs, and saved up to buy sheer silk stockings for them, which she laddered, kneeling to polish the floors.

'Alice would have, if she'd seen him first,' Christine said, 'I was slow. I missed my chance, and I shan't see him again.'

He was back the next evening, just before closing time. He looked better in his uniform. He stood looking around, and Alice pranced pertly up to him, but he saw Christine and went over to her. It was nearly five-thirty, and the last customers were being hustled gently out of the department. Christine was tired and wanted to hurry home, because Aunt Josephine was waiting to go out.

'Can I help you, sir?' she asked briskly. 'We're just closing.' She was piling up books as she spoke, and then she was sorry that she had been offhand, because he looked down at his shiny black shoes and said: 'Oh, I wasn't going to trouble you for a book. I just wondered, if you had the time, whether I could take you for a cup of coffee or a drink, or whatever you'd want.'

Christine was surprised. He was looking at her expectantly, with his cap under his arm and his narrow head with the clipped black hair tilted to one side, like a bird. His mouth was pursed up, judging her reaction.

When she said that she was sorry but she had to hurry home, he looked crestfallen, and a little regretful of having asked her. With the clock at five-thirty and the commissionaires beginning to lock the doors, she could not embark on an explanation about Aunt Josephine and Geoffrey, and she was afraid that he thought she was making an excuse because she did not want to go out with him.

If Aunt Josephine had known about it, she would have said: 'Don't come home. You might get some nylons', but that would have meant telephoning and all sort of complications, and, anyway, she had said she could not go.

'I'm sorry,' she said, feeling a lift of the soul because he had liked the look of her enough to come back. 'Look, you'll have to go if you don't want to get locked in.' She began to move away, but he still stood there looking at her with deep-lidded eyes that were peculiar because they did not blink.

'Could you come out another day?' he persisted, like a man who has set himself a task and means to carry it through. 'Tomorrow maybe?'

'All right,' said Christine, even more surprised than she had been the first time he asked her.

'Thanks a lot. I'll look forward to it,' he said. 'Good-bye now.'

He went over to one of the Piccadilly doors, which had been locked by the commissionaire, who was now drawing across the iron grille outside. The American coolly tapped on the glass, as if it were part of the commissionaire's duty to let him out whenever he wished, and the man unlocked the door for him. He would have done the same for anyone who tapped on the glass, but an Englishman would not have tapped. He would have been distressed to find the door locked, asked for help inside the shop, and been shown out through the delivery entrance in Jermyn Street.

Christine set her hair carefully that night, and asked Aunt Josephine to iron her white blouse with the ruffles. She did not say why, because Aunt Josephine would have cried: 'Romance!' and it was not romance. She was just going to have a drink with an almost strange man, who would probably turn out to be a bore. He had undoubtedly only asked her because he did not know anyone in London.

The next morning she put on her grey suit with the white blouse, told Aunt Josephine that she would be late home, and looked forward all day to the evening.

She was enjoying the anticipation more than the reality. She knew that she was dramatizing something that might turn out to be quite dull, but by the middle of the afternoon she began to get a little excited, and to glance towards the street doors, although he would not come for some time yet.

Alice was often fetched from work by young men. Christine seldom was, and certainly never by a stranger about whom she knew nothing. This was something different. This was an adventure. She had quite a lot of friends, and sometimes went on to a cocktail party or out to dinner after work, but after the age of thirty all your friends seemed to be old friends. You did not live perpetually in the expectation of gathering to yourself new people, as you did when you were experimenting with life at twenty.

The American was in the store at five-twenty-five. He was wearing uniform and his rather solemn expression, which eased into a smile when he saw Christine. He did not smile easily. His small, full-lipped mouth weighed up situations before it relaxed to accept them.

'Hi there!' he said, as Christine went over to him. 'Good to see you.' He behaved as if they were already old friends, which rather damped her spirit of adventure. However, he was there. She had decided by five o'clock that he would think better of it and not come back.

'I'll have to go out by the staff door and punch the clock,' Christine said. 'Will you meet me there? Do you know where Jermyn Street is?'

'No, ma'am.' He shook his head. He wore his cap very straight, and he kept pushing at the knot of his tie, to make sure he looked correct.

It seemed funny to think of anyone not knowing where Jermyn Street was. She told him where to meet her, and shepherded him out of the department before the doors were locked.

'Who's the boy friend?' Alice asked her, while they were getting out their handbags from under the humorous books.

'What boy friend?'

Miss Burman, collecting paper bags, was listening with pin-point eyes.

'The sailor. American, isn't he? Nice going, Miss Cope.' Alice went click-click out of the side of her mouth and wiggled her hip.

'I'm off home,' Mr Parker informed them, coming out of his office with his Dr Coppelius shuffle. He always said that, as if he could possibly be going anywhere else at that time in the evening. 'Did you check those Everymans for reordering, Miss Cope?'

'Yes,' lied Christine, because he might have expected her to stay and do them tonight.

'Good girl. Good girl. Well, good night all.' He lifted the musician's hat to his women and made for the door.

Christine renovated her face in the cloakroom, put on her grey beret, took it off, put it on again and finally decided to go without it. Most of the crowd had gone by now. She imagined the American standing in uniform by the staff entrance, watching all the girls coming out and being scrutinized by them, bold because they were in pairs or groups and he was standing alone.

Miss Burman had stayed behind to tidy her locker. She pressed up the stairs beside Christine, who wished she would not stay so close. If they went out of the door together she could not introduce the American to Miss Burman, because she did not know his name. She hurried on, while Miss Burman showed the receipt for her pastry to the timekeeper, but Miss Burman caught her up and punched the clock just behind her, and was at her side as they went out of the door.

The American was waiting with his arms held a little out from his sides, one foot on the kerb and one in the road. He stepped forward with a small salute and smiled. When he smiled his eyes closed up, so that you could not see his odd, unwinking stare.

Miss Burman, who had been holding Christine's arm – she always had to touch the people she was with – let go of it. 'Oh, excuse me,' she stammered, and melted away, as if she had surprised some clandestine intrigue.

'Gee,' said the American, 'I thought you were never coming. I never saw so many girls in my life.' They both laughed, and then he suddenly saluted again, stood to attention and was very formal. 'Commander Vinson Gaegler, United States Navy,' he announced, as if his name were the most serious thing in the whole world.

'Oh – thank you. My name is Christine Cope,' said Christine, quite embarrassed by the sound of her own name, although it was far less embarrassing than his.

'Well, fine,' he said, shaking hands as if they had never met before. 'Now, Miss Cope, where would you like to go? I'm not too familiar with this city.'

She was the native and he the stranger. It was up to her to

63

suggest somewhere, but she was suddenly shy, not knowing what kind of place he had in mind.

'We could go up to the Air Force club on Park Street,' he said, 'if you'd like that.'

She would have agreed to go anywhere, since she had no ideas of her own.

'We'll get a cab.'

'It might be difficult, this time in the evening –' she began, but a taxi was already following his lifted hand to the kerb. That was her first experience with an American of being able to get anything you wanted whenever you wanted it, even in London.

It was one of the new taxis, longer and shinier and less like a horseless hansom.

'I love these funny old London cabs,' Vinson Gaegler said.

'But this is one of the newest ones.'

'I think it's marvellous,' he said, not understanding.

Christine could never ride in a taxi with her feet on the prickly mat without remembering Jerry and how painful it was to the knees when you were kissing on the prim leather seat and slipped off it. She had not kissed anyone in a taxi for years, but she rode in them little enough to think of them still as creatures of the night, their interiors dark buckets of love. It always seemed wrong to be in a taxi in the daylight.

The American sat far away from her in the corner and read out the names of streets. She asked him how long he had been in London.

'Not too long. Just ten days. The navy flew me in to Bovingdon at eighteen hundred hours, and I came to London and found they had no hotel reservation for me. I had quite a time finding accommodation that night.'

'Where did you go?'

He named a hotel in which nobody that Christine knew would ever stay. People took a room for one night, or perhaps just a few hours. She smiled, because the American seemed rather proper, and she wondered whether he had known what kind of place he was in.

'I'm not there now, of course,' he said, 'I'm at the Mount Royal.' He pronounced it wrong, with the accent on the Mount. 'I like London pretty well,' he said, 'but I plan to get out and see some of your country as soon as I get time. I never was here during the war.'

He was easy to talk to, because he gave information without you having to ask for it. All you had to do was to sit in your corner of the taxi and let him talk in his slow level voice.

'My family originally came from Birmingham,' he said. 'I'd like to get up there some time, and there are a lot of other places I should see.'

Christine wondered whether she ought to offer to take him to Stratford or Blenheim or somewhere, but it might sound too on-coming, even if she only meant it to show that English people were not all standoffish and stuffy.

'How long are you over here for?' she asked. 'I mean, are you stationed here now?'

He leaned forward to read the scale of increased fares pasted under the meter. 'I'm afraid, with regard to the section I'm with, I can't tell you that,' he said carefully, making her feel like a spy, when she was only making polite conversation. It seemed so odd, when England and America were supposed to be allies, that they were perpetually having secrets from each other and setting up complicated organizations to try and find them out.

'There are many people at your Admiralty here who would like to know just what I'm doing,' the American said, with some satisfaction.

The taxi stopped at one of the narrow houses in Park Street, which used to disgorge G.I.s with canteen mugs and tin cutlery every day at noon during the war. Inside, Commander Gaegler spun his cap on to a counter and took Christine upstairs to a lounge with an ornate fireplace, whose windows looked on to a small paved garden. It was easy to imagine it as a drawing-room in its private days.

There were two Air Force officers with sleek-haired American girls who laughed a lot, and a spectacled soldier with his wife and two small boys, who had shaved blond heads and drank Coca-Cola through straws solemnly, as if it was a rite.

Commander Gaegler put Christine on a sofa, asked her if she would settle for a martini and rang the bell. When the bar-man came to take their order, he said: 'How's it comin',

Commander'? He was English, but he had been at the club long enough to speak the language.

The drinks were very large and very strong. There was more gin in them than in the martinis Christine made. The American, however, screwed up his lips and said: 'You can't get a really dry martini anywhere in London.'

He was more sophisticated here in his own surroundings than he had been in the shop. Christine thought that perhaps she liked him better when he had been diffident and a little lost in the book department.

However, he was easy company, and by the time she had finished the martini Christine began to feel as if she knew him quite well, although she had a suspicion at the back of her mind that if she really had known him quite well, with all their personal information already exchanged, there would not have been so much to talk about.

He asked her questions about herself, and was gratifyingly interested in her answers. She told him about Goldwyn's and about her family at home and what she had done in the war. She told him about all the animals at 'Roselawn'.

'Do you like dogs?' she asked.

'Oh sure. My mother has a chihuahua.'

She did not mean that kind of dog, but never mind. He told her about his home town of Kaloomis, Kansas, and about his sister's marriage to the eldest son of one of the oldest families in town, and about his mother, who wore a badge of the Mothers of the Purple Heart, because her other son had been slightly wounded in Korea.

When Christine looked at her watch, she had been there more than an hour and had had two of the outsize martinis. Probably her nose and her cheeks were shining. She took out her compact. They were.

She powdered her face and said: 'I must go now. I mustn't be back too late.'

'I'll see you home,' said the American, getting up with her.

'Oh no, that's all right. I live rather far out, you see. It's much too far. I can get a bus right here at Marble Arch.' She admired herself for being able to produce so easily the Americanism of 'right here'. After an hour of his company it came quite naturally.

'I have a car,' he said, pleased that he had this to offer her. 'A brother officer lent it to me while he's in Germany. We'll go and collect it, and I'll run you home.'

She did not want him to take her home, because there would be the difficulty of whether or not to ask him to stay to supper, and what her father would say if he did, and whether there would be enough food, and she remembered that Aunt Josephine was making shepherd's pie tonight, which was not one of her most successful dishes.

The American had made up his mind, however, so they walked up to a garage at Marble Arch. The car was a beautiful cream-coloured Buick convertible, such as Christine had never ridden in in her life.

She felt wonderful as she drove out to Barnes with Commander Gaegler with his gold braid and his coloured ribbons, directing him and pointing out items of interest, like the Albert Hall and Olympia.

He did not know that to live on Barnes Common was inconvenient and rather suburban. For all he knew, it might have been the grandest place to live in London, and he was delighted with the gorse-scrubbed open space before the house, and with the house itself, which he called an Interesting Old Place, although to Christine it was only shabbily Victorian.

He seemed also to be quite pleased with all the animals. 'This is real homey,' he said. He made a noise like tearing silk at the budgerigars and ran his finger-nail along the bars of their cage. The cat that was asleep with its front paws over the fender would not come to him, but Christine's gregarious dog put its head on his lap, and he stroked it while Christine mixed him a martini, mostly gin, because that was how he said he liked it. She mixed it in a glass jug, as Geoffrey had told her she must, although she would not submit to doing this for Geoffrey.

Presently her father came in, and Vinson Gaegler sprang to his feet and was introduced. Christine could see that her father was a little suspicious of him. Who is this Yank? he was thinking. We haven't heard about *him* before. He wandered about the room, not looking directly at the guest, and the American

67

was very respectful to him. He offered to mix him a drink, which Mr Cope thought was not respectful, but presumptuous.

Christine got them both sitting down and tried to maintain an easy conversation. She knew that her father was worrying about whether the American was going to be asked to stay to supper. Vinson Gaegler gave him a little brisk information about the American Navy, and Mr Cope grunted in response. He used to be like this when Christine was young, and brought new young men to the house. If they dared to come again, he had been capable of greeting them with : 'Good God, you here again?' He thought that was funny, a joking reference to their persistence after his daughter, but the young men did not think so.

During a lull in the talk, when Christine was wondering what she could say to recover the easy relationship she and the American had had at the Air Force club, a piercing shriek came suddenly from above. It was followed by another, and then a reverberating groan. The house was like Nightmare Abbey in a Gothic tale. Christine and the American had sprung to their feet, but Mr Cope remained seated and said : 'It's only Geoffrey. The doctor has come to take out his stitches.'

'It's my cousin,' Christine explained to the startled American. 'He had a slight accident here on Saturday.' It sounded silly. 'Christine has had a slight accident' was what her nurse used to say when she hustled her upstairs to change her knickers.

'That's tough,' he said. 'I'll be going. I'm sure you wouldn't want me here at a time like this.'

'No, that's all right. Do sit down and finish your drink. They won't need me up there.' By the time she had seen him off and gone upstairs the operation would be over, and she would have sent the American away for nothing.

Geoffrey continued to fill the house with horrible noises. 'Good God,' said Mr Cope, getting up, 'I can't stand this. It's worse than a maternity home.'

The American looked at him, surprised that he should have come out of his monosyllabic grunting to say this. Mr Cope went out of the room, calling to his dog, and they heard the front door bang with her father's slam that sometimes brought a hat down off the stand.

Christine sat down and told the American the story of

Geoffrey, and how they had come home late without a key and tried to break into the house. Gaegler did not say much, and she wondered if he was shocked at such goings-on. He did not look the kind of man who would get drunk and cut his head open bungling an easy climb. But you never knew with people. They nearly all got drunk at some time or other and did something ridiculous. Look at Geoffrey.

The American was beginning to make the motions of thinking it was time to go, when Aunt Josephine came in with her head, for some reason, bound up in an old scarf, and a triangular tear in her cooking apron where she always bumped against the corner of the kitchen dresser.

'That Geoffrey,' she said in despair. 'If I ever saw anything like him my name is Artemus Jones. Talk about a cry-baby! You never heard such a noise as he made about a few stitches coming out.'

'We heard,' said Christine. 'Aunt Jo, this is Commander Gaegler of the American Navy.'

'An American!' cried Aunt Josephine in delight. 'Well, I am glad to meet you. Is it *the* American?' she asked Christine.

Her niece blushed and made a face at her, which she thought Vinson Gaegler saw. He moved quickly about with his springy step, offering Aunt Josephine cigarettes and chairs, but she was too restless to sit down. She tramped about the room, giving out ejaculations about the frightfulness of Geoffrey and the stupidity of the doctor, who said he must stay a few more days. The American turned his head to watch her with his unwinking tortoiseshell eyes, and Christine wished she knew what he was thinking.

'You've been drinking,' said Aunt Josephine, picking up an empty glass.

'Have one,' said Christine.

'Certainly I will. Heaven knows I need it.' She flopped into a chair and ran her big hand over her face, pushing the scarf askew on her head.

The American offered her a cigarette. 'No, thank you. I – Oh, but a Lucky Strike! The only kind I like. I haven't had one since my canteen days. Christine, you are clever to bring somebody home with American cigarettes.'

At the bow-fronted cupboard, Christine prayed that Aunt Josephine would not forget herself so far as to say something about nylons.

'Let me help you.' Vinson Gaegler came and took over the drinks from Christine as naturally as if he had been in the house many times.

When he had finished she saw that he had made a drink for himself and her as well. She did not want one, but she took it, to let him prove to her that there was nothing in the world like an American martini. Why did every man always think he alone knew how to make a martini?

His visit had been a little sticky up to now, but with Aunt Josephine in the room it became a success. She liked him and he liked her. He did not seem to think her odd, as some of Christine's friends did. Aunt Josephine was at her oddest when she had had a drink. She became dogmatic now, and started to hold forth about the Atlantic Charter, and the American sat on the edge of a chair opposite her with his knees together, and treated her as if she were the only person in the world.

Christine felt *de trop*. She hid her drink behind a vase and wondered whether anyone would notice if she picked up the evening paper.

Mr Cope came back and asked if the all clear had sounded. He was not too pleased to find the American still there, but he was hungry, and at the risk of having to invite him to the meal, he asked his sister: 'What about supper? It's long past time.'

'So it is,' she answered without getting up.

'No wonder your dishes are always either burned dry or half cooked,' said Mr Cope, 'since they never get to the table at the right time.'

Christine hoped they were not going to argue in front of the American. He would not understand.

'Shepherd's pie can wait for hours,' Aunt Josephine said. 'But why don't you go and get it out yourself, if you're so famished, though how you can be after the lunch you ate –'

'I don't want to burn my hands, thank you. I can never find a cloth in that disorderly kitchen of yours.'

'Why is it, Captain,' Aunt Josephine asked Commander

Gaegler mistily, 'that men can't stand to touch as hot things as women can?'

'I wouldn't know,' he said seriously. 'Could it be it's something to do with the pigmentation of the skin?'

'How clever you are!' said Aunt Josephine embarrassingly. 'Christine, I wish you would always bring home clever people like this. It does me good.' The American looked more than ever like James Stewart in a coy situation.

'It's the gin that's done you good,' said Christine shortly, thinking as she said it that she probably ought to be all sweetness, and flutter round her aunt for the American's benefit.

But did she really care what he thought? He had taken hardly any notice of her since they came home, and he was certainly rather smaller and slighter than a man should be, and it was doubtful whether he had a sense of humour.

It had been exciting being taken by a strange American in uniform to have drinks in an American club, but when you got him home, where you had to be just your family self and could not play at being whatever you wanted you to be, it palled a little.

'You'll stay and have supper with us, I hope, Captain?' Aunt Josephine was saying, while her brother made faces at her behind the American's back.

'Thanks a lot,' he said. 'I appreciate your offer, but I really should be going. I have a date tonight.'

No, Christine thought, he was not exciting. For all that he had picked her out and come back to the store to see her again, he seemed to have small interest in her as he took his leave in the hall and said: 'I've been so happy to meet you.' Absurd, then, of Christine to find herself thinking, as she closed the front door: Who has he got a date with? A girl?

At supper, Aunt Josephine and Mr Cope discussed the American *ad nauseam*, and when Christine went up with Geoffrey's cheese, he said: 'I hear you've got yourself a new boy friend. Congratulations.'

'I hear you were a brave, brave boy having your stitches taken out,' she retaliated. 'Congratulations on that.'

'I suffered the agonies of the damned,' he said. 'No one knows what I endured.'

71

'We all do,' she said. 'We heard you enduring.'

When she went back to the dining-room, Aunt Josephine said, folding her napkin in a way that creased it more than if she had left it crumpled up: 'Well, I liked him, Christine dear. He and I got on fine, and I hope you'll bring him home again.'

'I thought you were a bit tight,' said her brother.

'He did mix the drinks very strong,' said Aunt Josephine. 'I *like* Americans.'

'I can't see why they have to wear uniform all the time,' he grumbled. 'They have this mania for dressing up. And all those medals. It's ridiculous. Two months in the potato squad and you've got a chestful of ribbons. Fruit juice, they call it.'

'Fruit salad,' said Christine. 'Well, anyway, don't worry. I don't suppose I shall see him again.'

He rang her up on Saturday evening to ask her if she would drive out to the country with him on Sunday. He seemed to take it for granted that she was free, and because she had not expected to hear from him again, she was surprised into saying Yes at once.

'Fine,' he said. 'I'll call for you around eleven-thirty. I have to go to Mass first.' Catholics always made a point of telling you they were going to Mass, or had just been to Mass, as if no one else ever went to church.

'Eleven-thirty then,' he said. 'Good-bye now.' His telephone manner was clipped and utilitarian, as if he were more accustomed to using the telephone for business than for conversation. Except that he said, after they had said good-bye: 'Just a moment. Tell me something. Why did your aunt ask: "Is it *the* American?"'

'I can't imagine. Did she?' Christine tried to sound cool.

'Well, skip it. I just thought –'

'Good-bye,' said Christine. 'I'll see you tomorrow.'

So he had thought she had liked him well enough to be enthusiastic about him at home, did he? Christine did not think she was going to like him if he was going to be conceited.

When he arrived on Sunday, however, you could not help liking him, for he had brought, rather shyly, a large box of food

72

for them from the Navy commissary. They took the box into the kitchen and unpacked it on the table among Aunt Josephine's preparations for Yorkshire pudding. There was a ham, and tins of bacon and sausages and butter, and chocolate, and packets of Lucky Strike for Aunt Josephine. It was really very kind of him. He watched their delight as they unpacked, like a Red Cross worker bringing bread to starving war victims. He was pleased with himself for giving so much pleasure. He had brought a box of cigars for Mr Cope, and Christine slipped away into the study to warn her father not to say he did not smoke them.

As she came out there was a violent banging on the front door. She opened it, and Clement and Jeanette fell into the hall.

'There's a super American car outside the gate! It's huge! Absolutely super! Come out quick, you must see it!'

'I have,' she smiled, wanting to kiss them, but unable to catch their darting, exciting bodies. 'I've been in it too. It can go more than a hundred miles an hour if it wants, and you don't have to change gear.'

'Gosh!' they breathed, as if they had glimpsed heaven.

'What's occurred, Chrissie?' asked Roger, coming up the path and jerking his head towards the Buick. 'Got yourself a rich boy friend at last?'

She wished that they could have seen Vinson Gaegler first in uniform. Roger and Sylvia were so critical, and he looked better in uniform than in the overpadded tweed jacket and smooth-textured slacks that he wore today.

The introductions went off quite well. Americans always knew how to make conversation to new people straight away, without standing about awkwardly. The children were already well disposed to him because of the car, and he pretended that he had brought candy just for them, although he could not have known they would be there.

'Candy means chocolate and sweets,' said Jeanette, who had an American airman of her own at Farnborough. 'I know.' They rushed off to the kitchen, jostling their grandfather as he wandered in from his study.

Having been warned by Christine, he did not say: 'Good

73

God, you here again?' but: 'I have to thank you for the cigars. It was extremely kind of you, Captain er –'

'Gaegler,' said the American, not correcting him about the rank.

'Of course. Excuse me. I've been working. Just an absent-minded author. You know what writers are.'

Everyone laughed, as they always did at Mr Cope when he became literary, and the American looked from one to the other wishing to join in the joke, but not understanding.

The children were cross because Christine was going out for the day. 'Just when we come,' they said, sucking at bars of chocolate marshmallow and kicking the furniture. 'And you said you were going to teach us how to bowl a legbreak.'

'Christine was captain of the eleven at school,' Sylvia explained to the American, which left him more mystified than before.

She and Roger were also disappointed that Christine was going out to lunch. 'Got something better to do this Sunday, eh?' said Roger, when she came back from getting her coat. 'Well, I don't blame you when the chap has a car like that. Cuts out the English boy friends a bit, doesn't it, Miss Cope? Well, so long, you two. Don't do anything I wouldn't do – and that gives you plenty of scope.' He winked at Vinson Gaegler, who laughed with him, eager to join in the fun and be one of the family.

'Your folks are swell,' he told Christine, as he started the engine and turned the car on the sandy road, his thin, knuckly hands grappling the big steering-wheel.

'I'm glad you liked them,' she said. 'I feel bad in a way about going out, because we're usually together on Sundays. Poor Geoffrey was a bit peeved too, because I'd promised to finish a chess game.'

'You're very good to your family,' he said. It was his first personal comment about her.

'Not really, but we get along all right.'

'I like to see a family all together,' he said, taking a corner on the wrong side. 'My goodness, will I ever learn to drive on the left? My parents are divorced. It doesn't help.'

'I thought you were a Catholic –?'

'Yes. My father is, but he didn't think too much of it when it came to going off with a chippy. That broke up the home somewhat. And to tell you the truth, none of us are too close. I think it's wonderful to be in a family home like yours.

'You must come another Sunday and have lunch with us,' Christine said politely. That was the sort of invitation you could throw out, and not have to abide by if today did not go well.

'I'd appreciate that very much,' he said.

They drove down the Portsmouth road. The American wanted to go to a hotel that another officer had recommended. He expected that she would know of it, and she felt that she ought to. It felt odd to be piloted through one's own country by a foreigner.

When they turned off the main road he knew the way exactly. He had looked it up on a map before he started out, and drawn a little chart for himself. He was evidently a methodical and efficient man. He drove fast but well, and slowed down strictly through towns and villages.

'You're the first person I've ever driven with who's stuck to thirty miles an hour in built-up areas,' Christine said.

'But that's the speed limit. I've got a book of your traffic laws.'

'I know, but no one ever does it. If the police do stop you, you can always say you didn't see the sign. They don't believe you, but they let you off the first few times.'

He thought that funny. 'Gee,' he said, 'back home the cops are tougher than that. They'll fine you right on the spot without a trial. You don't fool with them if you want to keep out of jail.'

He sounded as if he admired that, and he had laughed at the English police, so Christine said: 'Sounds like the Gestapo to me. I suppose America has to have police like that, to stop them going back to the lawless jungle we discovered.'

'Now don't let's be like that,' he said, looking straight ahead. 'We're supposed to be friends, remember?'

She did not know whether he meant he and she, or England and America. 'I was only joking,' she said. 'I like Americans awfully. I always have.'

75

'It's odd,' he said. 'You know it? Plenty of English people say that, yet they can't be with an American more than a certain length of time without starting to goad him. Same thing happens the other way around. I suppose it's because we're each trying to disguise the fact that we admire each other a hell of a lot.'

The hotel was a converted country house, standing by itself in a rolling park that had been partly ploughed up for crops during the war and would never get back to its mellowed pasture again. The formal garden had been maintained, and there was a putting course on the lawn in front of the gravel sweep. The interior was gracious and not too chintzy, attractive to the American, but a little sad to an English person who could imagine it as the private home it could never be again.

He took her straight to the bar, which was in what used to be the gunroom. A few rifles and an old blunderbuss still stood in the racks to make the bar picturesque, and two stags' heads and an assortment of stuffed game stared frozenly from the walls.

The American ordered drinks quickly. Alcohol seemed very necessary to him, and he did not speak until drinks came. He looked critically at the size of the glass, downed half his drink and then looked round more happily.

'Chuck was right,' he said. 'This is quite a place. All the atmosphere you want. I wonder if the family left these hunting trophies behind when they sold the place.'

'Oh, that isn't hunting,' said Christine, wishing to enlighten rather than correct. 'Hunting is only what you do with hounds. Foxes and hares and otters, and drag hunts with aniseed. This is shooting.'

'Mm-hm.' He did not pay much attention. In America, shooting was called hunting, and that was that.

An elderly manageress in creased black silk, with a tilt to her hennaed head that hinted at better days, came to ask them if they were taking lunch, because it was quite ready. She meant that if the kitchen staff did not get off on time they would give notice, but the American ordered another drink and they stayed in the bar for quite a time before they went into the dining-room.

It was a dignified, high-ceilinged room with panelled walls and

76

french windows leading to the rose garden. The small restaurant table and wooden chairs looked as out of place as village children at the annual party in the baronial hall.

There were only a few people lunching, because the season had scarcely begun. One of the couples had two small boys, evidently on a day out from a local boarding-school. They were very little boys, with button noses and slicked-back hair and dangling legs that would have looked more at home in shorts than in their long school uniform trousers. Their parents were too old for them. The father looked bored and the mother ate carefully, having trouble with her teeth and the rhubarb pie.

An elderly couple were obviously residents, for they had sauce jars and a packet of crispbread and a bottle of medicine and a half-empty bottle of Empire wine on their table. The two other people in the room were young and meekly self-conscious. They spoke in whispers, not watching each other eat, and trying not to look as if they enjoyed the food. They might be honeymooners, adventuring into more expensive places than they were used to, but secretly regretting that they had not stuck to the teashops where they had done their courting.

Christine did not know whether the American would enjoy watching and commenting on people in restaurants, so she said nothing, while he studied the menu.

'The chicken sounds the safest,' he said, with the experience of one who has spent two weeks in England. 'How would that suit you, Miss Cope?'

'Please don't call me that. It reminds me of the shop.'

'All right, Christine,' he said. 'Soup then, and the chicken? And we could try their apple pie.'

The waitress was setting tables for dinner at the other end of the room. He finally caught her eye; and when she had taken the order, Christine asked: 'What shall I call you then? Vinson is a sort of difficult name. I couldn't call you that.'

'It's a family name,' he said a little stiffly. 'I'm proud to bear it.'

It was another of these rather difficult moments when one of them unintentionally offended the other by having a different point of view. An American did not see anything odd in being called Vinson. Their minds went away from each other, but he brought them together again by saying: 'Some of my friends call me Vin. I wish you'd call me that.'

'Sounds like a bath cleaner,' she said and laughed. 'I like it,' she added quickly before her laugh could push the friendliness away again. 'Well, here's to you, Vin.' She raised the glass of water which he had asked the waitress to pour.

'Here's to *us*,' he said, and she dropped her eyes in sudden dismay before the brown-and-amber gaze of his. Don't try and tie me down, her thoughts fluttered. Don't let's start all that. We'll never be anything to each other, and I can't be bothered to play the game of pretending that we might.

When she looked up his eyes had moved away, and after that he was friendly and quite casual towards her. They had coffee in the sunny drawing-room and looked at magazines, and Christine tried to explain the jokes in *Punch* to him. The manageress, who roamed uneasily through the house like a family ghost, came in and told them a long story about when she had been to America with her husband, now, alas, passed away with the full glory of a military funeral.

They escaped from her and went out to the putting course. Vinson started by letting Christine win the first two holes, but when he saw that she was quite skilful he competed seriously against her and was pleased when he won.

They stopped for tea on the way home. The evening was warm and smelled of summer. Cresting a hill, they saw London lying before them in a clear sea of sunset, remote as a mirage.

When they reached streets and people again, Vinson said: 'You'll come and have dinner with me, won't you, Christine?'

'I can't very well. I'm not dressed for it.' She was wearing a tweed suit with a yellow sweater, which would not be suitable for the kind of place he might want to go.

An Englishman would have said: 'What does it matter?' scarcely noticing what she wore, and leaving her to bear any embarrassment that might arise; but the American, trained to take women seriously, said: 'I see your difficulty. We'll go to the club then. I can get you a steak there, a real steak like you can't get anywhere else.'

It sounded better than going home to family cold supper and the remains of the day's washing-up to be done, and Geoffrey disgruntled because he had not had his game of chess and Aunt Josephine did not make his bed tightly enough.

'All right,' she said, 'but don't think I'm accepting only from greed. I seem to have done nothing but eat all day.'

'It's been a good day, hasn't it?' He turned to look at her with his black eyebrows raised.

She said: 'Oh yes, lovely,' and he seemed relieved, and said: 'I'm so glad you enjoyed it. I wanted you to.'

It was too early to eat, so Vinson suggested that they should go up to his hotel room, where he had a bottle of whisky. If Christine said no, it would have looked as if she feared he had designs on her, so she went up to his room with him, hoping that he had not.

He was very proper. He poured out whisky and showed her his colour photographs and made it seem so unlike a bedroom that she did not have to avoid looking at the bed, but could even sit on it and take off her shoes.

They talked for a while. They were friendly together. Vinson suddenly said: 'You're very kind to me. Why are you so kind?'

'Why? Because I like you, I suppose.'

'Do you? I certainly hope you do.' He was standing in the middle of the room, poised on the balls of his feet, and she thought then that if she had given the smallest sign he would have come over to the bed. She got up, pulling down her skirt and wanting to hitch her suspenders.

'Well, I'm hungry,' she said. 'What about that steak?'

He took his eyes off her and went quietly to get her coat.

The steak was enormous. It was so big and garnished with so many fried potatoes and onions that it had to be on an oval dish instead of a plate. When it was set in front of Christine she thought it was for the two of them and began to cut it in half, but another oval dish the same size was set in front of Vinson, who attacked it without surprise. Christine was left with half the steak on her plate, and she said that she wished she could put it in a paper bag and take it home for the dogs. Vinson laughed, to make sure that this was only meant to be a joke.

The roads were empty when he took her home, and he drove fast, enjoying the car and not speaking much. When they stopped outside the badly hung gate of 'Roselawn' and he said he would not come in, she thought, as she turned to him to say good-bye: Oh dear, now he will try to kiss me, and I don't want him to. I shan't know whether he is only doing it because he thinks he ought, and I've got indigestion.

He did not try to kiss her. He got out of the car, came round the back and opened the door for her. He shook hands and accepted her thanks politely. She was glad that he had not kissed her, but when he had gone she felt a little deflated. As she went into the house she realized that he had not contemplated kissing her, had not wanted to kiss her, and the sunny day fell away behind her in discouragement as she went to the kitchen to find the bicarbonate of soda, tiptoeing past the drawing-room, so that Aunt Josephine should not call out: 'Come and tell us about your day!'

On Tuesday afternoon Vinson came into the shop and said that since he was just passing by he had come to see if she would care to meet him for a drink after work. Christine had to refuse, because Geoffrey was to be allowed his first outing tonight, and she was to take him. He would not be driven in Mr Cope's car, so she would have to hurry home and get his own car from the garage.

When she told him this, Vinson did not register disappointment. He dropped the invitation quickly, as if he had never made it.

They talked for a while rather stiltedly, as if they hardly knew each other, and Christine found it hard to believe that she had spent a day in the country with him and had sat on his bed chatting and drinking whisky. He asked dutifully after her family, and was carefully solicitous about Geoffrey's health, although he had never met him.

The book department was busy, and she did not want to stand talking to him. He was in uniform, and the eyes of her assistants were on him, Christine excused herself, and he went away without smiling, briskly, as if he were bent on going to find someone else to have a drink with him.

After that he did not telephone, and he did not come back to the shop. Alice said: 'What happened to that handsome sailor of yours, Miss Cope? We don't seem to see so much of him these days.'

She rattled on. Alice was always talking. You could not stop her. When she could not talk to the other assistants she talked to the customers, and they did not always like it.

'You given him the chuck, Miss Cope?' she went on. 'I'll have him, if you don't want him.'

'He's gone away,' said Christine.

'Oh dear, what a pity. I thought it was so nice for you.' She looked down on Christine from her height of nineteen years and a different boy friend for every day of the week.

Margaret was back at work now, pale and disappointingly reluctant to discuss the baby. Christine always told her everything, but she found herself not telling her about Vinson Gaegler, in case Margaret should ask what had become of him.

Christine often wondered what had become of him. She wondered for two weeks, and then decided that he had gone back to America.

Geoffrey went home at last, wearing a broad piece of sticking plaster rakishly over one eye.

'Chaps in the office will think I've been in a fight,' he said, not displeased that he should be thought the young devil he was not.

He was delighted to go home, which was natural enough, if a little ungrateful. His good-byes were brief. He had never learned how to say thank you properly, but the next day roses arrived for Christine and an azalea plant for Aunt Josephine, without a card, but from the most stylish flower shop in London, which would obviously be Geoffrey's choice.

'Well now, you see,' said Aunt Josephine, fussing delightedly over the plant and trying it in half a dozen places in the kitchen to see where it would be happiest, 'perhaps you have maligned poor Geoffrey after all. This is really very pleasant of him.'

'It was you who was always maligning him, and saying you would rather nurse a wardful of old men with bladder trouble,' Christine said. 'Why don't you put that plant in the drawing-room where everyone can see it?'

'It's my plant and I want to see it, and I'm more often in the kitchen than anywhere else, with the drudging life I lead.'

'Look here, Aunt Jo, you know I'd help you more if only you'd let me, but you always think no one can do anything right except you.'

'Nor they can,' said Aunt Josephine, pushing a questing cat away from the azalea. 'You never clean your saucepans.'

'Oh, I do! It's you who always leaves the sink piled up with pots and pans until finally you've nothing left to cook with.'

'I won't argue with you,' said her aunt. 'Answer the bell, there's a good girl. That will be Rhona, I expect. Did I forget to tell you? She telephoned this afternoon to say she was coming to see you.'

Rhona had been Christine's crony at school. Unlike most of her other school friends, who had disappeared soon after into the limbo of marriage to dull men and chit-chat about the price of baby foods, Rhona had remained close when they were first grown up and even after her marriage to an ambitious and rather common man, whom Christine and Rhona used to laugh at when they were single girls together.

Christine did not laugh at him now, because he was Rhona's husband, but Rhona still laughed at him, mainly for that reason.

When they had talked to Aunt Josephine for a while, they went upstairs to ruffle through Christine's wardrobe to see whether there was anything that would do for Rhona. They were about the same size, which comforted Christine, for Rhona did not look too fat, and was much admired.

They had been wearing each other's clothes for years, and before Rhona was married they often shared boy friends as well, and had to be careful that they did not both wear the same dress with the same man. Not that it would have mattered, because Christine's clothes looked different and smarter on Rhona than they did on her, and she could not wear Rhona's jaunty dresses with the same *élan*.

Rhona pulled out a paisley silk dress that Christine had no intention of letting her have, and squirmed before the mirror, trying to see her back view in it.

'You don't want this,' she stated.

'I do. You're not having it.'

'I look better in this thing than you ever did.'

'I like it, and I've only had it about a month –'

'You'd look far nicer in that green of mine with all the buttons. I'll swop it for this. Dan says the green is the wrong colour for my skin, and he does know about clothes, if nothing else.'

'How is he?' asked Christine. 'Look, you can have this red blouse if you like. I'm sick of it.'

'Thanks.' Rhona had her head in the wardrobe again. 'Dan? Oh, he's much about the same. That's his trouble. He's got nothing left to surprise me with any more. Even when he's being mean I know just what he's going to say.'

She turned round, holding a white organdie evening dress against her. 'Look, here's this old thing. I always try it on and it's always too big. Must be for you too. Lord, we must have been fat sows in those days, and we thought we were such sirens. Why don't you give it to Aunt Jo for her nuns? They would make it into nightdresses for fallen women or something. I always loved it on you, though. You wore it at Oxford the year before the war. I wore that red-and-yellow topless number, and that dreadful spotty friend of Carl's said I looked like a tulip. It seems centuries ago. My God.' She sat down on the bed with the white dress crumpled on her lap. 'What's happened to us, Chris? I feel dreadfully old.'

'We did have fun,' said Christine, remembering. 'We were silly, but I wish it had lasted longer.'

'Was it us, was it us,' mourned Rhona, 'you and I, who drove up to Oxford in that dear little red car of mine, cutting such a dash, with a gramophone in the back playing "Goody Goody"? Now that you can have radios in cars it isn't fun any more. Was it us who danced all night and didn't go to bed for days on end and drifted about on the river and cruised from party to party and thought those awful callow young men were so exciting? Have you still got that picture taken after breakfast at the Magdalen dance? No, don't bring it out. I don't think I could bear to look at it. You keep it because of Jerry, I suppose. There you are. That was really romantic. You and Jerry. Things like that don't happen when you get older.'

'I sometimes wonder,' Christine said slowly, standing with her back to the dressing-table and looking at her friend, whose bright face had become harder and bolder through the years of marriage to an unsubtle, successful man, 'whether we were really so happy then as we think we were, looking back on it now. I don't think I'd like to go back to being eighteen. I was awfully shy, and I used to care too much what people thought. It's probably better being thirty-four. I don't mind about parties now. If I don't like them, I go home; but in those days, if you didn't like a party, you thought there was something wrong with *you*, not the party.'

'Well, I wasn't shy,' said Rhona, smiling. 'Better if I had been, perhaps. I'd never have ended up at Bow Street with that awful Italian. Remember how we worked to keep it from Father? I'd love to go back to being eighteen again, though, mind you, I'd handle things a bit differently.'

She lay back on the bed and stared at the ceiling. 'And I sometimes wonder where it's all gone to, all the things I thought life was going to be for me. Of course it's different for you.' She turned her head to look critically at Christine. 'You didn't get married. I wish you would, though,' she said illogically, and then switching back, closing her eyes: 'Oh, you know, Chris, I do really envy you, having a room to yourself. You can read all night if you want to, without someone keeping waking up and looking at his watch and cursing. Dan's so *big* to have around. I don't know. And he won't stick to his dressing-room, and you know what? I just hate the smell of men's shoes.'

'I'm sure you'd hate far worse being a spinster,' Christine said lightly. 'Come on, try on that awful hat if you want to, and let's go down and feed the dogs.'

'Yes, I suppose I would hate it,' said Rhona with a sigh, swinging her legs off the bed and feeling for her shoes. 'Poor Chris. It must be dreadful for you really. I wish you'd get married and have lots of children and I'd be their godmother. Isn't there anyone you could possibly . . .?'

They reviewed the list of Christine's men friends, which was not extensive and not very satisfactory.

'You know,' said Rhona, 'I often wish you'd married that Maurice. He wouldn't have given you any trouble. Except that it would have been sort of uncomfortable if he went about being so embarrassed all the time. Haven't you got anyone new on the *tapis*?' she asked, making a disgruntled face at her reflection under the benighted black hat which Christine had bought hastily for a funeral and never worn since. 'What about that American Aunt Jo was talking about?'

Aunt Josephine was always talking about Vinson Gaegler. He had made a great hit with her. Whenever she put any of the food he had brought on the table, she would say: 'By courtesy of the U.S. Navy', and Mr Cope would say: 'I don't know that I like being treated like a distressed person', and attack the ham or the American bacon with gusto.

'Well, what about him?' repeated Rhona, throwing down the hat and stopping to rifle Christine's sweater drawer. 'Does he give you nylons? How did you meet him? Can I have this yellow cardigan? What's he like? Tell me all.'

Christine told her. It was often easier to tell things to Rhona than to less frivolous people. 'He was quite nice really,' she ended. 'His mother lives in Kaloomis, Kansas. But he was evidently only ships that pass in the night. I've written him off.'

'Oh, but you mustn't!' cried Rhona, who never wrote off the possibilities of a man until he was dead. 'Look here, I've got two tickets I don't want for the Royal Command film show. Ask him to that.'

'He's probably gone back to America.'

'Well,' said Rhona patiently. 'Ring up the hotel and find out.'

'But I don't think I could ask him, Ro. He'd think I was chasing him, and I'm not. He's not so fascinating.'

'He's an American, and that's something different from the stuffy old Empire builders you and I plug on with,' said Rhona, speaking as if she were still as unattached as Christine. 'Let's be thankful for that.'

'Well, but I couldn't –'

'Of course you could. Most natural thing in the world. You'll be just kindly offering to show him the sights of London. He's bound to come if he thinks he's going to get a look at royalty. You know what Americans are. I'll send you the tickets, and don't you dare take Aunt Jo. Don't tell her, or she'll want to go, because it's a Stewart Granger film.'

When her aunt and father were safely in the drawing-room, Christine went to the telephone, which had been first installed in the draughty hall years ago and had never been moved to a more convenient place.

Nervously she half hoped to hear the hotel operator tell her that Commander Gaegler had left, but while she was waiting for her to say that, Vinson came on the line, using his clipped telephone voice.

When she told him who she was, he sounded friendly. 'Hello there,' he said. 'Good to hear your voice after all this time', although it was his fault that he had not heard it before. He accepted the invitation with pleasure, noted the time and place to meet her, and rang off without further conversation.

As the film show was too early for Christine to have time to go home and change, she took her paisley silk dress to the shop and changed into it and did her face in the cloakroom after work. Some of the other girls were also getting ready to go out, changing into clean blouses, or adding scarves or jewellery to brighten up their black work dresses.

Alice, with her tongue in the corner of her mouth, was sitting in her petticoat, tacking a large square of lace collar on to her dress, which a woman's magazine had told her was 'a cute trick for busy girls to turn day into night with that little black dress'.

'Going on the loose, Miss Cope?' she asked. 'That's ever such a pretty dress; though, of course, I always say prints are trying. Excuse me, dear.' She leaned forward. 'You've got a blotch of powder on one side of your nose.'

Christine took out her puff again and fluffed it off. The light in the cloakroom mirror was too dim to do your face properly, and she did not think she looked very nice this evening. She had washed her hair last night and changed the side of the parting, in the innocent hope that this might make Vinson find her more attractive than before, and it kept trying to flop back to the other side.

She told him to meet her in the bar of a hotel near the shop, and he was there waiting for her with two martinis and more potato crisps and salted nuts than anyone else on the little round table before him.

He jumped up and fussed over settling her coat on the back of the chair. As they sat down, Christine wondered why she had worried about not hearing from him for more than two weeks. He had not enough substance for a man, and his face, in spite of heavy black eyebrows, was inconsequent, with its short, incurious nose and small chin. His eyes were unusual, however: dark when he looked away, but seeming light when he looked at you, staring, as he often did.

He stared at her now as they drank their cocktails, and made a flattering comment on her dress. Christine thought that was just his polite American habit, and brushed it aside.

'Why don't English women know how to take compliments?' he said. 'If you tell an American girl you like her dress, she'll say: "Thank you", and look pleased, but an English woman just mumbles: "Oh, this old rag? It isn't really."' His attempt at an English accent was so funny that Christine laughed, and he laughed too and spoke some more English, and they began to have a good time together.

They waited in the crowded foyer of the cinema to see the royal family arrive. Christine was excited to see a few English film-stars, the women making the most of small bosoms in strapless dresses, and the men smaller than heroes should be, with bad complexions. She pointed them out to the American, but he had not heard of them. He was intent on trying to stay near the door, so that he could get a good view of royalty.

Several other people were intent on the same thing; and when the uniformed ushers and the thin officious men in tail-coats began to push them back to clear a lane through the centre, the scented, well-dressed crowd jostled and battled almost as violently as the street crowd outside battled behind the arms of the amiable policemen.

A cheer began to murmur down the street, swelled to a growing roar, and became a clamour of distinguishable shouts and cries as the royal car slid up to the end of the red carpet. Peering over the furred shoulders of the woman in front of them, who smelled of exotic boudoirs, Christine and Vinson saw the Queen cross the pavement and step into the foyer in a lilac-coloured crinoline, with a pleased smile for the photographers.

After her, into the sucked-in murmur of: 'Isn't she lovely?' stepped Princess Margaret in white with a white fur, looking as if she felt as attractive as she looked.

'The *Prin*cess!' breathed Vinson Gaegler, visibly moved. 'My, she's a honey. I wish I had my camera.'

Christine was glad he had not, although flash-bulbs were popping all round.

'Is that the King?' he asked, as a tall man with a white carnation in his tail-coat followed the Princess and her mother into the cinema.

'Of course not, silly.' Christine shushed him, because he had spoken loudly, and people looked at him. 'That's just someone who's with them, same as that other girl in black. She's a lady-in-waiting.'

'Well, who are they?' he persisted, wanting to miss nothing of the show. He was surprised that she did not know the names of all the British aristocracy in the royal entourage. The Queen and Princess stayed a few minutes, shaking hands with the line of film personages who were waiting to be introduced, and he stood on tiptoe and stared intently, with his throat working.

'Gosh,' he said, sinking back on his heels with a sigh as the royal party disappeared. 'That's a thing I shan't forget. Those two lovely women, and all the dignity and homage. It's the finest thing your country has to show a foreigner.'

'I'm glad you like the royal family,' Christine said, as they moved slowly with the crowd to find their seats. 'Some people pretend they think it's silly to make such a fuss of them, although they probably read everything about them avidly in secret.'

'I like it fine,' he said. 'For your country, of course. It wouldn't do for ours.'

When they were in their seats, waiting for the lights to dim, Christine said: 'Why wouldn't a monarchy do for the States? Americans always get so excited about the King and Queen. Why wouldn't they like to have a pair of their own?'

'Americans,' he said seriously, 'swear allegiance to the flag, not to any one person. We admire your royal family as emblems of the old world, but they would have no part in ours. When people talk about a closer tie between the two countries – absorbing Britain right into the United States – they forget that there's one major reason why it could never work. We wouldn't accept your monarchy, and you wouldn't relinquish it.'

Christine could think of several other reasons why England could not be absorbed into the United States, but a roll of drums brought everyone to their feet as the orchestra laid down the first challenging notes, and the Queen came smiling to the front of the royal box to accept the swelling anthem of God Save the King.

When the film was over and the royal party had left, they had to wait in the foyer while the police settled a minor riot outside, in which a male film-star lost his tie and coat buttons to the shrieking crowd. There would be pictures of it in the papers tomorrow, and Christine would be able to talk about it at work and say she had been there.

At last they managed to push their way out on to the disorderly pavement, where a host of women who should have had something better to do were still milling about in and out of the gutter, exchanging badinage with the policemen.

Coming out of the cinema, Christine hoped they would think she was somebody, but all the film-stars had gone now, and the crowd was not interested in the people coming out. They were just interested in being a crowd, which would not be moved on before it felt like it.

Vinson took Christine to dinner in an underground restaurant with a dance floor. He had not booked a table, and they were stowed away at a tiny table in a corner, where they did not get good service, but Vinson thought the waiters were just being English, and did not seem to mind.

He danced well, holding her lightly, and his steps were easy to follow. It was the year of scarcity of good new tunes, and the band, like bands at Broadcasting House and all over the country, were playing old tunes from the thirties. When they played 'Love is the Sweetest Thing' he sang it softly in her ear as if he meant it, but when the music stopped and they stood apart, he looked round the room at the other dancers and seemed to have forgotten her.

When they were dancing after dinner he laid the side of his head against her cheek, and the short hair above his ears felt bristly, and his skin smelled nice, but it did not mean anything. It was just his way of dancing.

When it was time to go and he had paid the bill, with a large enough tip, Christine was glad to see, because foreigners sometimes did not work it out right in a strange currency, he put both hands on the table and said, staring at her: 'Did you like the flowers I sent?'

'Flowers? You sent – ? Did you? I'm afraid –'

'Roses,' he said, 'to go with your cheeks. And a plant for your aunt.' The rhyme sounded funny, like ants in your pants.

'My goodness,' said Christine, 'were those from you? We thought they were from Geoffrey.'

'Oh, I see. Well, why not?'

'There was no card with them.'

'No,' he said, getting up. 'I thought perhaps you'd guess.'

He was silent on the drive home, and Christine thought that she had hurt him, but it was his own fault. How could she guess? And suppose she had thought they were from him . . . How awful if she had thanked him, and they were not.

When he stopped the car outside her gate he switched off the engine, got out and opened the door for her. He took her hand, and they stood for a moment by the car, looking at each other without speaking.

'Christine,' he said, 'I'm going to pay you a compliment. I'm not going to kiss you. I like you too much, and respect you for what you are.'

This was not as flattering as he meant it to be. Christine said: 'Oh', and turned towards the gate, and he squeezed her fingers and said: 'Good night, Chris*tine*', accenting the last syllable of her name in the way he did.

After that he took her out quite often. They went to the theatre, and he took her to dinner at the Air Force club again, and one Saturday she took him out to Luton Hoo, where he insisted on looking at nearly every one of the hundreds of treasures, which exhausted her.

He had boundless energy. He was never tired, and when they were out together he was always looking at his watch to see if they could fit in one more thing than they had planned. When they went sightseeing in London it was not enough for him to see just the Tower and Westminster Abbey, which to Christine

90

was a day's work, but he insisted on stopping off at St Paul's, and then dragging her up the hundreds of steps of the Monument in Billingsgate. He went up in front of her, swinging his neat little bottom up the spiral stone steps and flattening himself politely against the grubby walls, where despairing climbers had scrawled their names, when he met anyone coming down. When Christine reached the top he was already studying the map on the parapet and trying to identify every church spire.

She leaned against the parapet, looking out over the sooty view with a singing head and watery legs.

'Come and look at the map,' he said, staring out into space like a captain on the bridge, his clipped hair unruffled by the wind. 'It makes it much more interesting.'

'I can't. I'm out of breath. I'm too fat for such a climb.'

'You're not fat,' he said, without looking at her. 'I like your shape. And when you climb up all those steps it makes your cheeks glow. Your complexion is beautiful. I like that too.'

'Do you?' She looked at him, wishing he would look at her.

'Oh sure. It's odd, there's a domed church over there I can't seem to identify.' He dismissed the subject he had started, as he often did if you took him up on a personal note.

Although he would seldom talk intimately, she was seeing him often enough to learn quite a lot about him. He talked to her about his early life in Kaloomis, Kansas, and about how fine it had been at Annapolis, where he was a Star Man, and he told her about his career in the Navy, of which he was proud. He was always saying: 'Look, I'm a professional naval officer', to qualify an opinion about the American Navy, or the war, or the navy of any other country.

He knew that the American Navy was the finest in the world. Christine knew that the British Navy was the finest in the world, but she did not argue about it. She was learning to avoid Anglo-American arguments, which were frustrating and got you nowhere. He was American. She was English. Nothing could alter that, and so, if you wanted to be friends, you had to accept the differences of opinion caused by an accident of birth.

With this growing realization that they must always be different in so many ways, she did not worry so much about who was right and who was wrong. He used his knife and fork in one way, she in another. He pronounced certain words differently, and said things like 'hospitalization', but who was she to criticize? He might just as well have criticized her for saying 'going to hospital'. As she began to like him increasingly and to feel a friendliness in his company, she began to be just slightly shaken in her ingrained belief that because whatever you did or said was English it must be right.

He came to lunch at 'Roselawn' one Sunday, bringing another parcel of food and chocolate, and got into an argument with Roger about Marshall Aid, which made the meal boring for everyone else. They were both opinionated, but Roger, being a Cope, took the argument in his stride, while Vinson took it seriously and wanted to go on with it after Roger had tired of the subject and everyone was talking about something else.

Roger had said: 'You Yanks think you're the only people who know how to live, but really you're the only country in the world which hasn't begun to know what life's about.' Christine knew that Vinson was hurt by this, but she could not rouse herself to his defence. The Copes always banded together against outsiders, and it took more than her courage to champion the wrong side, because the family would have said to themselves: 'Here, here, what's all this? She *is* interested in this chap.'

None of the family except Aunt Josephine seemed to like Vinson very much, but Christine went on asking him home, because she knew he liked it. He was envious of her family life. He wanted to be part of it. He liked her best when she was at home, moving about with trays, or sitting quietly with some sewing in the drawing-room, while the men talked. Although he came from the New World, he was old-fashioned in many ways, and he liked to think that she was old-fashioned too.

He gave courteous attention to her father, whom he admired as a literary figure. There were so many overpublicized new authors in the States that every American at this time was thinking he would like to write a book; and to get something published, even if it was only a translation of someone else's work, was to Vinson a marvellous thing. He tried very hard with Christine's father, but even when he talked to him about his work, Mr Cope was still suspicious of him as a foreigner and would not react properly.

Vinson also tried very hard with the dogs and cats, which were such a centre of interest and conversation in the house. Christine's dog would go to anyone, but the cats were wary of him and would not go to him to be petted. This was the only thing that caused any doubt to Aunt Josephine. She set great store by the opinions of her cats.

Christine continued to see Vinson Gaegler quite often, and it was not long before the family were referring to him as 'Christine's boy friend', and making insinuating remarks which they thought were funny. If she had told them that he had never kissed her they would not have believed it.

There came quite suddenly a very warm day, when spring was summer before its time. All day, moving about the book department, Christine had seen the sun flooding the pavement beyond the glass doors, and had looked with jealousy at the women who came in from outside, caught unawares by the sudden heat, wearing last summer's dresses.

Mr Parker, shut in his stuffy little office, did not know whether it was Christmas or Easter, but all his assistants were restless, and longed to get out for their lunch-hour.

Christine had told Vinson that on the next sunny day she would walk up to Grosvenor Square and sit with him on the bench where they had first met. She was in the cloakroom getting ready to go out when Margaret Drew came down and found her by the grubby washbasins.

'I changed my lunch-time,' Margaret said. 'Old Burman wanted me to go with her to that awful teashop that smells of fish, and I just couldn't bear it. Let's buy sandwiches and go and sit in the Park. I never see anything of you these days. You never come to supper any more. You're always out with that little American with the funny name.'

Margaret knew about Vinson Gaegler by now. Everyone in the book department knew about him, because he sometimes came to fetch Christine at the shop, where he was known as 'Miss Cope's American', as established as he was at home as 'Christine's boy friend'.

93

Because Margaret had said: 'You're always going out with that little American with the funny name', Christine could not tell her that she was planning to meet Vinson now, so she put him out of her mind and went up the stone steps into the sunshine with Margaret.

They bought twice as many sandwiches as they needed, because ever since the war, sandwiches had one side that was just plain bread, so you had to throw away the dry bread side and put two spread sides together to make them edible. They walked down Piccadilly to Green Park and found two empty chairs among the crowd of lunch-time workers who had come to open out like crocuses to the sun.

Margaret ate her sandwiches quickly and wished they had brought more.

'It must be wonderful to be able to eat as much as you want without worrying about getting fat, because you know you're going to get fat soon, anyway,' Christine said. 'What's it feel like, having a baby?'

'Queer,' Margaret said. 'You get breathless if you talk too much. And it's not so much fun being able to eat a lot, because there are so many things you can't face. Laurie always wants to have salami and liver sausage, and I can hardly sit at the table with it.'

'Why don't you tell him? He wouldn't eat it. He's always so sweet and considerate.'

'I don't want to make any more fuss than I have to. It's bad enough for him as it is.'

'Bad? I should think it was marvellous for him having a baby after all this time.'

'That's the trouble. By this time we've got organized into being able to manage fairly comfortably, just the three of us, and keep Bobby at the school the Drews have always gone to, and not have to give up that silly old big house, which Laurie adores. But now there'll be all this expense with the baby. Laurie insists on me having a private room. He says no wife of his is going into a public ward, though it's silly when I've been paying five shillings a week all this time to let the Government have my baby for me.'

'I'd like a public ward,' said Christine, 'except for the communal bed-pans. I'd like to lie on my side and discuss symptoms with the woman in the next bed.'

'So would I, but you know what Laurie is. And then there'll be all the clothes to get. I gave away all Bobby's things years ago. And after this one is born I shan't be able to work, because of looking after it, and I just don't see how we're going to manage. I tell you what it is, Chris. We just can't afford to have a baby.'

'Oh, Maggie, don't. No one says that.'

'Well, I don't, but Laurie does. He sat looking at me the other night, at the spot where I can't do up the button on that yellow housecoat any more, and he said, with a face as long as a boot: "We can't really afford to have this baby."'

'He said that to you? Oh, poor Maggie –'

'Well, why shouldn't he?' Margaret shrugged her shoulders. 'It's true.'

'But one just doesn't say those things to a wife.'

'My dear Chris, when you've been married fourteen years you say the truth to each other. After all that time you're like one person, so if it doesn't hurt you, you don't think it will hurt the other.'

Christine was shocked, not only at Laurie's remark, but by Margaret's cool acceptance of the dreadful thing he had said. How little one knew about one's married friends – the happily married ones who did not quarrel in public and seemed to have made a natural circumstance of the fusing of two lives. One knew nothing really about their marriage, because it was only significant when they were alone together. That was when the important things happened.

Walking back to the shop, Christine thought about the mythical, romantic marriage that she sometimes imagined for herself, and tried to picture it reaching the stage when you were so used to each other that one could say a hurtful thing without the other minding. But, like the magazine stories, her imagined marriage never got much farther than the wedding day and the picture of herself in a frilly apron waiting for his key in the lock in her bright little kitchen. It did not embrace the realities of familiarity. The dream would lose its charm if it did.

At a quarter past five Vinson came into the shop with his cap set perfectly straight on his head and his eyes narrowed to a gleam under his black brows.

Christine was busy with a customer. Out of the corner of her eye she saw him waiting impatiently, pretending to look at books. When she was free he came quickly up to her and caught her arm above the elbow, pinching a nerve against the bone.

'Why didn't you come to Grosvenor Square at noon?' he asked, his voice strangely uneven and rough.

'I'm sorry,' Christine said. 'I went out with Margaret. I hope you didn't wait too long.'

'I waited an hour for you, that's all, and didn't get any lunch,' he said, sticking out his lower lip.

'That's a shame.' He was cross, so she spoke lightly, trying to make him not cross by pretending not to notice it. 'But we hadn't exactly made a definite date, had we?'

'You said you would meet me there if it was sunny,' he said. 'Well, it was sunny today, and you didn't come.'

Christine apologized again, but he would not be appeased, and because he continued to be cross she ceased to feel sorry. She drew him behind the bay of the classics section, where no one could see them.

'Look here,' she said, 'you're being silly to make such a fuss. If I couldn't come, I couldn't, that's all. Don't behave as if you owned me.'

'When I make a date with a girl I expect her to keep it. You said you'd be there and you weren't, and that's no way to act.'

'Don't lecture me.'

'I will, goddamn it, if you need it.'

They had quite a quarrel there behind the rows of collected editions. They had never had a real quarrel before, and Christine did not like it. Vinson was petty and petulant, and Christine thought that if he was going to be like this it was not worth while having anything to do with him.

'You just didn't take time out to think whether I'd be waiting for you,' he said. 'It doesn't mean a thing to you. You wouldn't care if I went back to America tomorrow.'

'Probably not,' she retorted. 'Why? Would you?' Her voice

was rising with his, and then he suddenly spoke softly and pulled them both down to normal, as a telegraph pole seems to pull down the rising wires as you pass them in a train.

'Yes, I would,' he said very sweetly, and he smiled at her and her own easy smile spread quickly, because he had made it all right.

'I really am sorry, Vin,' she said, touching his arm. 'Margaret gets a bit low these days. You know, she's going to have a baby, and so I thought –'

'Don't start on explanations,' he said. 'Forget it. You should never try to hold post-mortems after a quarrel's been stopped. Don't you know that? Let it drop, and forget the excuses.'

She liked him when he told her how to behave. She liked to think that he was wise and knew more about life than she did, so she readily became complaisant, and when he said: 'I've only got an hour, because we've got a late conference coming up, so go and ask if you can get away now,' she went obediently to seek Mr Parker's permission, and hurried out to meet Vinson at the Jermyn Street door.

They drove up to Regent's Park and walked a little way over the grass. A bushy hedge made an angle of retreat from the open space where people were walking home across the Park, and he took her hand and made her sit down there, and then he kissed her.

When he had been kissing her for a little while, and putting his hands on her body, Christine realized that she had been wanting him to kiss her for a long time.

'Why didn't you do this before?' she asked, pulling away from him and lying back on the grass, which was fresh and new and not yet soured by the treadings of a hundred picnics.

He turned, resting on the flat of his hand, and looked at her. He had lipstick on his mouth, but it looked all right. 'Did you want me to, Christine?'

'No,' she lied, 'I never thought about it.'

'Well, I did. But I didn't think you'd care for it too much. I didn't know – I don't know – whether anyone else had more right than I to kiss you.'

'No.'

'I thought maybe your cousin – you'd been going to parties

with him, and there was that day you wouldn't come out with me because of him, and you thought he'd sent the flowers.'

'Geoffrey?' Christine laughed and sat up. 'Oh, Vin, if you could see him! Fancy thinking that. Men are funny.'

'Yes,' he said. 'They are funny like this. They like to do this.'

He was extremely nice to kiss, and, oddly, it felt familiar and right, as if he had been making love to her for months. Time stopped, and there were only two of them in the world. It seemed like that to her, but he suddenly raised his head and looked at his watch and stood up, brushing grass off his uniform. A naval officer is never late for a conference. Even love comes second to the United States Navy.

'Stick around in town,' he said, 'and meet me later and we'll drive out to the country and find somewhere nice to eat.'

'I will,' she said, sitting on the grass and dreamily tidying her hair, 'if you'll kiss me again afterwards.'

'Why, Christine, I thought you were so proper,' he said, looking pleased.

'I am really. You'd be surprised.'

'We shall see.' He pulled her to her feet, and Christine thought: I could stop this now, or let it go on; but she did not have any will to decide, and it did not seem to matter.

She put her arms round him. 'Don't go for a moment,' she said, but he did not move close to her. Looking back on this, long afterwards, she saw that this was the first of all the many times she had said to him: 'Don't go', and he had put the Navy first, until soon she began to hate it.

Things were changed after that. Christine went out with Vinson nearly every night. He let her have the car, and she would drive herself home after she had been with him, come to work in the car in the mornings and then fetch him at the naval headquarters after she came out of the shop.

She thought that when he had gone back to America she would never again drive down North Audley Street, past the red-brick corner building where the transient American sailors, loosely hung together, waited with white seabags, and the neat naval wives came out of the commissary store with huge brown-paper bags, without remembering Vinson. Whether she would remember him with or without regret, she did not know. She could not tell how this affair would end, and she was content to live in its present, without troubling about its future.

One night, when they were out dancing and had had quite a lot to drink, Vinson said: 'I love you.' Christine did not let herself say: 'I love you too', having learned long ago the folly of letting alcohol say that for you when you were not sure you meant it; but when he breathed deeply and said: 'Come back to the hotel with me', she hung her head and said that she would.

The night porter looked at her shrewdly, but she did not mind. He did not know her. Vinson lived at the hotel, and the censure, if any, would be on him.

When they were in the room together he kissed her violently – he was stronger than he looked – and then he sat her on the bed and sat down quietly beside her and took her hand.

'Christine,' he said, 'forgive me. I'm a little plastered right now, but I know what I'm doing. I shouldn't have asked you to come here. My wife doesn't go to hotel bedrooms with me.'

Christine stood up, with a chill on her heart. 'I didn't know you were married,' she said, with her back to him, trying to sound casual.

'I'm not. I'm asking you to marry me.'

She did not know what to say. She hesitated, still with her back to him, and before she could answer he got up and went over to the wash-basin, where he began to mix drinks for them.

In the silence, Christine looked at herself in the mirror on the wall and wondered why anyone should want to marry her. There came into her mind all the proposals she had imagined from a dream husband, but none of them had been like this. In her dreams she had always known what to say, and had said it well, because the man gave her the right cues; but what could you say to a man who was bending over the basin trying to make the water run cold enough to mix with whisky, and who, when he turned round, wore an impersonal face, as if he had already regretted or forgotten that he had asked you to marry him?

'Drink this,' he said, handing her the glass she did not want. 'You'll feel better.'

'I feel fine, thank you,' she said, and then she saw his eyes, and they were not impersonal at all, but staring at her with a naked appeal not to be hurt.

'Oh, Vin,' she said. 'I –' And because it seemed so unkind not to buy you at once, she hedged with the excuse of: 'I don't know that I could live in America. I've never been there, and I –'

'Christine,' he said. 'Look at me. I'm not asking you to marry America. I'm asking you to marry me.'

Christine was silent. It was better to say nothing than to say the wrong thing, and her thoughts would not collect themselves. She was excited. If he had put his glass down then and taken her in his arms and kissed her, she would probably have said yes, but he did not move towards her. He took a long swallow of his drink, walked to the window, turned and said judicially: 'I'm not asking you to give me an answer right now. I can understand you may want to give the matter some thought.'

Why, oh why, she thought, standing in the middle of the green carpet with the untasted whisky in her hand, why be so sensible and level-headed about this? This is an emotional matter, and it should be settled emotionally. This is all wrong.

'I think I'd better go, Vin,' she said unhappily.

If he had protested she would have stayed, but he said: 'All right, my dear. If you want to go away and think about it, I'll be happy for you to do that.'

Christine did not want to think. She wanted to be swayed irretrievably one way or the other. She wanted to accept him with joy and passion, or reject him with sorrow and a few tears, but he was already picking up her coat. When she had put it on, she said, wanting some contact with the man who had asked her to marry him and then withdrawn into himself: 'Aren't you going to kiss me good night?'

'No,' he said, looking noble. 'I don't want to influence you in any way. I want you to be free to make the right decision. This is real, Christine. You haven't got to make a mistake.'

But it isn't real, she thought. It doesn't seem to be happening at all. In the little lobby of the suite, he held open the door for her, and when she looked seriously into his eyes he smiled.

Oh, you fool, you fool, she thought. How can you ask me to marry you when you don't know how to treat me? If you would only take me back into the room and kiss me, and make me love you, of course I would say yes. You fool. She hated him suddenly, because he had spoiled it for both of them.

'Good night, darling,' he said gently. 'I'll be waiting.'

Well, wait on, she thought furiously, as she went down the endless hotel corridor, her whole body aching for the embraces he had not given her.

Driving home in the lovely American car, which answered your touch like a thoroughbred horse, she thought, as she out-stripped two other cars at the traffic lights: If I told Rhona that Vinson had asked me to marry him, she would probably say: 'My dear, of course you must, if it means driving about for the rest of your life in cars like this.'

Christine laughed aloud, with the moving air through the open window lifting her hair, and felt suddenly happier. Perhaps life was not such a grim business after all. Perhaps Rhona's way of picking a husband was the right one. She had professed to marry her husband for no better reason than that he kept a motor-launch on the Thames.

Christine parked the car, closed all the windows and locked all the doors and went into the house, savouring experimentally the important feeling of being engaged. It would be fun telling all the people who had been saying for so long that she ought to get married. It would be exciting to take Vinson round and introduce him as My Fiancé. He was not the best-looking man she had ever seen, but there was nothing wrong with his ap-pearance. It would be exciting to go to American parties with him and be introduced as his fiancée. It would be something new to give up work and buy a lot of clothes and have a wedding day, with herself as the central figure.

But when she was in her room she did what she had been afraid she would do ever since Vinson had said: 'I'm asking you to marry me.' She knelt to the bottom drawer of her desk and took out the photograph taken after the Magdalen College dance, and allowed herself to think of Jerry.

Jerry had been drunk the first time she saw him, drunk on beer at a party in someone's rooms at Oxford. Christine was twenty, too plump, and unsure of herself, overshadowed, as she was by most of her girl friends, by the casual Jennifer, with whom she was staying at the manor house a few miles out of Oxford.

Oxford was Jennifer's happy hunting ground. From the age of seventeen she had been running through a succession of undergraduates at every college, and scarcely a party was given without her. She was Rhona's friend first, and then Christine, who was Rhona's inseparable, began to be asked for weekends too, and to be taken to parties at Oxford and left to sink or swim.

Rhona and Jennifer swam with the crowd of sloppily dressed young men and precocious girls, but Christine sometimes sank, because she could not keep up with the slick conversation. She was sinking at this party where she first set eyes on Jerry. She could not drink a lot of beer. Her throat rebelled against swallowing it, but no one else's did, and girls were sitting on laps, and someone was playing the piano in the middle of a roaring crowd who thought they were singing.

A thickset boy with brown hair falling into his eyes sang a descant in a pure tenor, waved his mug of beer and sat down in a heap on the floor.

'Who is that?' Christine asked the man sitting next to her on the sagging sofa. She had been trying to think of something to say to him for some time.

'Oh, that,' he said, 'That's one of the Canadians. He's in the ice-hockey team. That's about all they're good for. Toughs all of them.' He was an intellectual young man, with earnest glasses and a mobile Adam's apple. He got up and left her and Christine sat alone, wondering where Rhona was. Jennifer was among the group round the piano, but Rhona had disappeared with a long young man with a head like a snake.

Christine could not remember how that party had ended. Dinner somewhere, she supposed, and then driving home too fast, with Rhona and Jennifer busily disparaging the young men who had kissed them.

The next night they went to another party. Almost as soon as they arrived, the drunken Canadian, quite sober now, with his hair slicked back and a slightly tidier suit, came up to her and said: 'You were at Porgy's party last night. You were sitting on the sofa. You had a yellow dress. I noticed you.'

'You were drunk,' Christine said, her tongue loosened by the happiness of someone having noticed her and remembered.

'Sure,' he smiled, 'but not too drunk to think you looked pretty swell. Come on, I'll get you a drink and let's talk.'

That was the beginning of it. That was the beginning of Oxford with Jerry, and being in love, and writing to each other every day, and going to all his ice-hockey matches in London and sitting at the edge of the rink, wishing she could tell the people sitting by her that the burly, padded figure who was always being turned off the ice for fouling was hers, and would take her out alone somewhere afterwards, while the rest of the team went on to beat up the town.

Jennifer was all for love, although she did not believe in it for herself, and Christine was asked to stay more often. Jerry had a dreadful little car with flapping celluloid windows, and he would come out and spend whole Sundays at Jennifer's house, and unless they were wanted for tennis or billiards, no one minded what they did.

That was when they used to go into the hay barn, and Jerry said: 'Forgive me, darling.' It was not until long after that, after the Commemoration Ball, where Christine had worn the white organdie dress and people had thrown bread at them at supper, that Jerry came down to Cornwall, where she was staying with Roger and Sylvia; and in the little inn bedroom with the Old Testament pictures and the uneven floor, he did not say: 'Forgive me, darling', because they both knew there was nothing to forgive.

That was the end of August. When war broke out Jerry went back to Canada to enlist, and Christine's loss was lightened by the thought that when the war was over she could go out to Canada and marry him. He wrote to her often from the training camp, and at first he talked about how they would marry, but after a while he did not mention it, and then gradually he wrote less and less, until he did not write at all, and Christine did not know whether he had gone abroad or whether he was alive or dead.

After a while Christine's hurt grew less. She went into a

103

London hospital as a probationer nurse, and soon had neither the time nor the energy to remember too often that she had a broken heart. When the other nurses wrote letters to army post offices, and showed pictures of what they called their fellows, Christine would show them the photograph of Jerry taken in a canoe on the Cherwell, which got lost when the bomb blew in all the windows of the nurses' home one night, and they were not allowed to go back to their rooms until the debris had been cleared.

His letter came when she was having her day off. She had come home the night before, dog tired, because she was on the Theatre, and it had been Mr Trellick's tonsil day, and she had gone to bed intending to sleep late. But the habit of the six-o'clock alarm was not to be broken by one night's freedom from it a week. She woke at exactly six o'clock, turned over to look at Nurse Jones sleeping beside her in the black iron bed, discovered that she was alone in her own room at home, and felt wide awake, as she never did at this hour in hospital. She lay for a while enjoying the thought o ˙ the others crawling out of bed and fixing caps and aprons with sleep-numbed fingers, and then she went downstairs in her nightdress and bare feet to find something to eat.

As she stepped down into the hall she heard the scrunch of feet on the gravel path, and then the letter-box flapped inwards and three letters fell on to the doormat. One was for her, from Jerry. He would be on leave in London in two weeks' time, and he insisted, without thought that she might be working, that she should keep the four days free for him.

She had not seen him for three years, and it was two years since he had written to her, but as she stood in the hall reading the letter over and over, with her bare feet turning to ice in the draught under the front door, all her pushed-away emotions came flooding back, and she was in love with Jerry as radiantly as she had been in the far-away summer at Oxford.

She had only had one week's holiday this year. She had another week due to her. At nine o'clock the next morning she put on a clean apron, checked her stockings for ladders, and waited with the line of criminals and petitioners outside the door of Matron's office.

'What do you want to see the old girl for?' asked Nurse Broderick, who stood next to her.

'Holiday. My boy friend's coming home on leave,' said Christine, wanting to tell all the world.

'Lucky cow. I'm going in to get slayed for being late in again last night. That lousy new night porter saw me climbing in the eye clinic window and reported me. Damn conchie. Look, you'd better go in before me, because the old girl will be in no mood to give anyone a holiday after she's dealt with me.'

She changed places with Christine, but the Matron was already in a bad temper when Christine went meekly in and stood before the desk with her hands behind her back and her toes pointing straight forward.

'Ah, Nurse Cope,' said the Matron, louring at her from under her pinnacle of cap. 'Thermometers again, I suppose.'

'No, Matron, I haven't broken one for weeks. I just wanted to ask you – I have a week's holiday due. Could I possibly have it the week after next?' She did not say why. If the gossip about Matron's sex-frustrations was true, that would be fatal.

'It's odd you should ask that, Nurse,' said the Matron, brightening up, 'because the answer is no.'

Odder still, thought Christine, if the answer had been yes.

'You're going on night duty next week, on the gynaecological ward, so, you see, your holiday will have to wait a bit.'

She smiled. She only smiled when she had said something nasty to you. The gynae ward, of all places! On most of the other wards you got a little peace while the patients slept, but women who had had female operations kept you running about all night.

After a week of night duty among the gynae women, Christine was almost too tired to worry about Jerry. She was crawling into bed one morning after a night when she had an emergency Caesarean, a disastrous haemorrhage and five women to prepare for operations, when the maid pounded on her door and shouted: 'Telephone, Nurse Cope!'

Hell, thought Christine, flapping down the night nurses' corridor in her dressing-gown and slippers; but it was Jerry. He was in London. His voice sounded just the same, and her heart went out in love to him.

She could not bring herself to tell him yet that she had not been able to get her holiday. She explained that night nurses were not allowed to go out before five, but she would meet him then at a hotel near the hospital. He began to grumble about her being a nurse, but she rang off hastily and went along the corridor to Nurse Fletcher's room. Nurse Fletcher was in bed, reading yesterday's papers.

'Fletcher,' said Christine, 'you've got three nights off tomorrow, haven't you?'

'Praise the Lord,' said Nurse Fletcher, without looking up.

'Be a love and let me have them. Night Sister won't mind, and you can have my nights off at the end of the month. It's terribly important to me. Please do.'

'Why should I?' asked Nurse Fletcher with narrowed eyes. She was a mean character.

'If you do, I'll give you my electric fire. Give, not lend. The one you can boil a kettle on as well.' Electric fires were treasures in the chill cells of the nurses' home. They were not allowed, but you could hide them in a suitcase under the bed when you were out of the room. Christine had burned the bottom out of a suitcase when she had to put the fire in it red hot one evening when the Assistant Matron made a surprise raid.

Nurse Fletcher was tempted. 'You can have the kettle as well,' Christine said, and, grudgingly, she fell.

Jerry was waiting in the lounge, looking handsomer than anyone who had ever come to that stuffy Victorian hotel. His uniform was not smart – none of his clothes ever had been – but his eyes were bluer than Christine remembered, and his face was brown and firm. He looked ten years older instead of three.

He tried to sulk when Christine told him that she had to go back to the hospital in an hour, but when she said that after tonight she would be free for three days he looked at her with love and said that he would take a room at the most expensive hotel he could find, and they would have a honeymoon.

She did not ask him why he had not written to her for two years, and she made up her mind that she would not mention it unless he did, so as not to spoil any of their time together. She could not have a drink with him, because the gynaecological women might smell her breath. They ordered tea, but they

106

hardly touched it. They sat in the lounge among the old ladies and provincial business men, and held hands until it was time for Christine to go back to the hospital.

He was waiting for her outside the nurses' home at ten o'clock the next morning. Christine had ploughed through another gruelling night, and was so tired that, as she forced her weary limbs to go through the motions of dressing and packing her case, she had almost hoped that he would not come, so that she could just roll into her bed and sleep.

But he was there, and he was very bright and gay, and although he knew she had been up all night, he expected her to be bright and gay too. The sun was shining and he wanted to walk, so she tagged along with him, stumbling over kerbstones, but trying to match her spirits to his, in case he thought she was not happy about their honeymoon.

They went to the hotel to leave her bag, and when Jerry left her to go down to the hall for cigarettes Christine stopped in the middle of unpacking her case, lay down on the bed and went to sleep.

When she woke it was dusk outside the hotel windows. She was alone, and she was quite sure that Jerry had gone away in disgust, and she would never see him again. She cried for a while, and then decided that she would sleep a little longer and then get up and pack her things and go out of the hotel, inquiring at the desk: 'Has my husband paid the bill?'

She could not go to sleep again, because she was still crying. She was crying when Jerry came into the room and lay down on the bed beside her, but then everything was all right, and everything about their time together was as wonderful as it had ever been at Oxford, or in the fishing inn in Cornwall.

It was soon after that that the bomb fell near the nurses' home and Christine's photograph of Jerry in the canoe was lost, so she never had any picture of him except the tousled one of him standing behind her with his hands on her bare shoulders after the Magdalen ball.

Much later, after she had written to his mother in Canada, and his mother had written back to say that Jerry had been killed, she wrote again to ask for a picture of him, but Jerry's mother had never sent her one.

107

Christine rolled up the photograph again and put it back in the drawer. It was no use looking at it, and asking Jerry whether he would mind if she married Vinson. The dead did not mind if you committed sacrilege on their memory by pretending to love someone else. They just shrugged their shoulders and left it to you to decide. The dead would not help you. All they would do was make it more difficult for you by not letting you forget them.

At three o'clock in the morning, when she was sure she would not sleep, Christine went into Aunt Josephine's room. The night-light was by the bed, because Aunt Josephine, who was afraid of no man, had been afraid of the dark all her life. The night-light flickered in a pool of wax, and by its wayward light Christine could see her aunt's head tied up in a net, the mouth open and the nose pointing vastly to the ceiling.

At the foot of the bed the old fox-terrier slept like a heap of corrupted flesh, his brown-and-white patches bleached into his off-white senility, his fat haunch twitching to dreams of a Nimrod youth. When he twitched, one of Aunt Josephine's legs twitched too, as if she were dreaming with him.

The opening and closing of the door had not woken her. Christine stood by the bed with her hands clasped, and said desperately: 'Aunt Jo. Please wake up, Aunt Jo.'

Aunt Josephine's thick eyelids quivered, her mouth closed, champing on the empty gums, and then suddenly she sat up gaping, her eyes wild. 'What – what? What's the matter? Is it a fire?'

'It's all right.' Christine put her hand quickly on the big rough hand that trembled on the bedclothes. 'It's all right, Aunt Jo. It's only me. I'm terribly sorry to wake you, but I just had to.'

Fully awake, Aunt Josephine became her solid self. She switched on the bedside light and sat up, blinking and yawning hugely. 'What's the matter, child? You look like the wrath of God.'

'I feel like it. Aunt Jo, I'm awfully sorry. I know you hate to be woken up, but I just had to talk to you.'

'Well, just let me get my grinders in,' said Aunt Josephine, never averse to a chat at any hour of the day or night. 'I can't talk properly without them.' She fumbled at the toothglass, where her large yellow teeth nestled in cloudy water, thrust them in, worked her jaws for a moment, and sat upright, staring at Christine with bright eyes.

Christine sat down on the bed and passed a hand over the bloated side of the fox-terrier, which growled in its sleep. 'I'm in a terrible worry, Aunt Jo,' she said. 'I can't sleep, and I can't get things straight, and I felt I should go mad before morning if I didn't discuss it with you.'

'Fire away,' said Aunt Josephine, hitching the eiderdown up to the neck of her woollen nightdress. 'What's your worry? I may not know the answer, but I'll force advice on you just the same.'

'I want you to. I want someone to tell me what to do, instead of having to decide for myself. He wouldn't help me decide –'

'He? That young Gaegler, I suppose.'

'He's not so young. He's thirty-eight.'

'That's all right for you. I suppose he's asked you to marry him?'

Christine nodded, fiddling with the bedclothes and not looking at her.

'I knew he would. He asked me what I thought about it some time ago, and I said: "Go ahead and ask her. It's no affair of mine."'

Christine was disappointed that Vinson had spoken to Aunt Josephine before he risked asking her. It seemed Victorian, and rather cowardly.

'What did you think I'd say?'

'I hoped you'd say yes. Chrissie, he's nice. There are a lot worse men than him in the world, and a lot worse people than Americans.'

'Yes; but, Aunt Jo, you don't marry someone because they're *nice*.' Suddenly, she was bored with the whole thing. It was too much bother. She wished she had not come into Aunt Josephine's room and made Vinson's proposal important by talking about it. She wished she were just the estimable Miss Cope again, calmly asleep until seven-thirty, when she would get up to go to the shop with nothing on her mind except the day's work.

'I don't love him,' she said irritably.

'Oh – love,' said her aunt. 'When you're as old as I am and have seen as many people passionately in love one year, and suing for divorce the next, you'll learn to get cynical about that word.'

'Don't,' said Christine. 'I did love Jerry. I still can't think of him without loving him.'

'Jerry is dead,' said Aunt Josephine harshly. 'You're morbid. I never should have read *Great Expectations* to you at an impressionable age.'

Christine felt that she was going to cry. No one could understand about her and Jerry, no one had ever had anything like that since the world began.

'I dare say you think you'll never love anyone like you loved poor Jerry,' said Aunt Josephine. She reached for a packet of Lucky Strikes, shook out a cigarette and lit it, coughing alarmingly. Since Vinson had kept her supplied with American cigarettes she had taken to smoking in a big and choking way. 'And you're right. You never will. He'd never have married you, though.' She knew the whole story of Jerry, and had formed her own opinion. 'But most people marry without being in love like that. Look at your mother. She seemed quite happy, poor thing.'

Christine could not think of marriage as applied to her mother, that unreal figure of fading memory, who was so often ill, and seldom much more to her children than the smell of washed wool bedjackets, and injunctions from nurses and maids not to make so much noise on the landing. She had never questioned whether her mother and father loved each other. It was impossible to think of her father in a relationship with any woman, and one just did not think about what one's parents must have done before one could be born.

'If you'd never known Jerry,' Aunt Josephine went on, 'you'd be able to think you loved that Gaegler enough to marry him.'

'I don't know whether I love him at all.'

'You must, or you wouldn't even contemplate marrying him. You'd come to me and say : "Ha, ha ! That Gaegler asked me to marry him. Have you ever heard of such a thing?"'

'I wish you wouldn't call him That Gaegler.'

'You wouldn't mind if you didn't like him.'

'We do get on pretty well,' Christine said doubtfully. 'But I don't know. It would mean living in America, and I –'

'My dear baby, the man comes first, not the place. That just goes with the man.'

'That's what he said.'

'Then he's a man with more sense than I credited him with. Oh, I know you think you couldn't leave dear old England – wave the flag, and all these jolly red buses and everything – but you'd get on all right in America. They tell me it isn't *all* like the films.'

'Would you mind if I went?'

'That's not the point,' said Aunt Josephine shortly. 'I should mind like hell, if you want to know. So would your Pa, I suppose, though he might not be able to say so in so many words.'

'Well, then, how could I –'

'Look here, Chrissie,' said her aunt sternly. 'You're thirty-four. You don't want to be a spinster all your life, do you? It's all right now, because people want you, but think about when you're fifty. Who wants a single woman then? She's just a nuisance, who everybody tries unsuccessfully to find a widower for. You love children. Well, it's all right now being Aunt Christine, who's more fun than Mummy, but later on other people's children won't want you. Clement and Jeanette will have to be told: "You must go and see Aunt Christine", or "You really must write to the old girl. She doesn't have much to live for."'

'But, Aunt Jo,' said Christine in distress, 'you shouldn't say that. Everybody wants *you*.'

'Like hell they do,' said her aunt cheerfully, lighting another cigarette from the stub of the first one. 'I'm useful, because I run your Pa's house, but I'm a bit of a nuisance, you must admit, and people say: "There's that crazy old woman with all her dogs and cats."'

'They don't!' said Christine, remembering the times when she had heard people like Geoffrey say something like that.

'Don't worry. I like them to. I like to be that crazy old Aunt Josephine. If I can't be desirable I can at least be renowned as an Old Character. I have my niche.'

111

Yes, she had her niche. She had her letters to the family abroad, and her cats and dogs, and her charities, and her pilgrimages to cemeteries. Christine gave a little shiver, seeing herself in thirty years' time as that crazy old Aunt Christine.

'You're cold,' said Aunt Josephine. 'Marry that Gaegler and have a nice warm double bed. It'll do you a power of good.'

'But then, about Daddy,' Christine said, imagining what Vinson would look like in pyjamas. 'I've been at home so long, and Roger isn't really any use to him except to carve the joint on Sundays. Ought I to leave him and go so far away?'

'Don't you worry about him. I'll look after him, same as I always have. He won't mind too much. I know he doesn't like that Gaegler much, but then he won't have to see him often if you're in America.'

'That's another thing,' Christine said. 'Everyone is so stuffy and insular. Just because Vin doesn't like beer and went to a school that they've never heard of, no one likes him except you and me. What will Roger and Sylvia say if I tell them I'm going to marry him? They'll be crabby.'

'I'll tell them,' said Aunt Josephine, 'I'll settle them. Don't worry.'

'Aunt Jo,' said Christine, bending to kiss her, 'you're marvellous. Do you know, I believe I really might get married.'

'Of course you will,' said Aunt Josephine briskly. 'And now go down and get us something to eat for the Lord's sake. I'll never go to sleep again, and I'm starving. Let's have the wedding here, shall we? What excitements. I shall wear a feathered toque and a blue satin dress with a dipping hem and a bow on the hip. I see it all.'

Much later, when Christine came out of Aunt Josephine's room with the empty plates and cups, they had made so many plans that she felt as if she had been engaged for months and was almost as good as married.

It was exciting. It was important. She was someone with a definite status, someone at last to whom something really noteworthy had happened. Then it occurred to her, with some surprise, that it had not happened yet. She knew that she was going to marry Vinson, but he did not. He had probably lain awake all

112

night in a torment, chewing his nails, She knew that he bit his nails, because she had seen them.

It would be unkind to keep him a moment longer in suspense. It was only six-thirty, but Christine went down to the hall and dialled the number of his hotel. They had to buzz his room for a long time before there was a click and a grunting 'Hello.' He always said Hello, instead of Hullo, as English people did.

'Vin,' said Christine eagerly. 'It's me.'

'Oh, hi there,' he said without enthusiasm. 'What's the matter?'

'Nothing's the matter. Everything's all right. I will marry you, Vin.' There was no answer. 'I mean – if you still want me to?'

'What's that? If I want you to? Oh, sure, sure. Don't be ridiculous, Christine. I'm a bit dopey, that's all. Haven't had my eight hours yet. You're calling pretty early.'

'Well,' said Christine drearily. 'I thought you'd be anxious to know.'

'Oh, sure, honey. It's marvellous. Look, you go back to bed now, and I'll call you later, hm?'

She had a feeling that he was asleep again almost before he put down the receiver. He was more interested in getting his sleep than in knowing whether Christine would marry him. She almost rang him back to say: 'I've changed my mind', but if she woke him again he might not listen properly, and her anger would fall flat.

At breakfast she disappointed Aunt Josephine by refusing to carry on with the plans they had started the night before. She would not talk about Vinson. Her pride would not let her tell how he had hurt her.

When Aunt Josephine, putting her coffee on the table with a joyful gesture that spilled some of it into the saucer, said: 'Well now, baby, here's a happy day for you! Aren't you glad your crazy old aunt persuaded you to do the right thing? You see, I do have some sense after all', Christine stirred the coffee and muttered: 'Perhaps not as much as you think you have.' And she bit her aunt's head off when she asked if she might tell her brother about his daughter's engagement before Christine got home.

'Don't interfere, Aunt Jo,' Christine said, as she went to the car. 'You're always interfering.'

Doubting and worrying, she tried to give her mind to work that morning. She snubbed Alice and snapped at Helen, and avoided Miss Burman, who followed her about trying to tell her about her mother's birthday party, with eight big candles and two little ones. With a rush of business that came in the middle of the day, Christine was glad to have to take her mind off Vinson and occupy herself with the customers.

She had to go up to the accounting department about a mail order, and when she came back Margaret said: 'Your boy friend rang up, but I told him not to hang on, because I knew you'd be hours with those muddlers upstairs. He wants you to ring him back as soon as you can.'

Well, I won't, thought Christine angrily. Let him just see, that's all. Let him just see.

But let him see what, she was not quite sure. She did not know whether she would marry him or not. Aunt Josephine had made her think she would, but it ought to have been Vinson, not Aunt Josephine, who had persuaded her. She did not know what she could say to him.

Mr Parker called her into his office to hear a publisher's representative talk about an epoch-making new book. She glanced through the book and did not think much of it. All this firm's books were epoch-making. The representative was a bouncing young man, who was always saying: 'In confidence, I'll stake my reputation on this one', and was quite unabashed when Goldwyn's did not do well with it.

The telephone rang and Christine answered it, holding it well away from her ear, because the receiver was dusty. It was nobody's job to dust Mr Parker's office, and since Mr Parker did not want it done, because he was afraid that things would be moved and he would not be able to find them, no one was going to make it their job.

It was Vinson. Christine could not say: 'I've changed my mind. I can't marry you', with Mr Parker and the bouncing young man listening. She was non-committal, and so was Vinson, because he was not alone in his office either. She thought that the least he could do would be to go out and make

114

the call from a telephone box when talking to the girl who a few hours earlier had said she would marry him. They had a sterile conversation. Vinson wanted to see her, but she said that she must go home first, and he could ring her up there and they would make plans for the evening. She wanted to talk to Aunt Josephine and get assurance before she saw him.

When she rang off Mr Parker, who had been waiting, tapping a pencil, said mildly: 'I don't know that you ought to make your private calls here, Miss Cope', and the publisher's representative said archly: 'Ah well, we all know Miss Cope is a young lady much in demand. I'm sure there are many people, Mr Parker, who would like to get her away from you.'

If he imagined he was going to increase Goldwyn's order by that, Christine thought, he had another think coming. When he had gone she persuaded Mr Parker to reduce the order for the epoch-making book from a hundred copies to seventy-five.

Five-thirty came slowly. When at last it was time to go, Christine hurried out of the shop, and fretted and fumed at the traffic which kept the Buick crawling nearly all the way to Barnes Common. She wanted to talk to Aunt Josephine. Aunt Josephine would make her feel that whatever she decided to do was right. Aunt Josephine would help her, as she had helped her, erratically but lovingly, ever since she had taken over the job of mother, and been more to Christine than her own mother had ever been.

She stopped outside her home, thinking that if she gave up Vinson she would have to give the car up too and go to work by bus and underground again, and hurried up the path and through the front door, calling: 'Aunt Jo! Aunt Jo! where are you?'

Aunt Josephine usually came out of the kitchen wiping her hands on a dirty tea-towel when Christine came home and called her. Today, no one came out of the kitchen, but Mr Cope came out of the drawing-room with bent knees, a newspaper dangling from his hand.

'Chrissie,' he said, 'thank goodness you've come home.'

'Why shouldn't I?' she began, but she stopped, seeing his face. The smudges under his eyes were darker than usual, and his mouth was slack.

'It's your aunt,' he said in a dead voice. 'She's had a stroke,'

115

he added abruptly, concerned less with breaking the news gently than with unloading his own troubled thoughts as quickly as possible.

Aunt Josephine, robust Aunt Josephine, who everyone thought was as strong as a horse and could do her work day after day and never be spared, had fallen down while she was carrying a tray of books to the back door to pack up for hospital. She had clutched at the dresser and broken some plates as she fell. The pieces of china and the books she was carrying still lay scattered on the kitchen floor, where the cats were mewing for their dinner.

Mr Cope did not want to go to the hospital with Christine. He did not like hospitals. Aunt Josephine was still unconscious, and he had seen her unconscious on the kitchen floor, had watched her there for a long time until the ambulance came. He did not want to see that any more. But Christine made him go with her. Aunt Josephine might come round, and she would want them. As they went out of the house the telephone rang. It was probably Vinson, but she did not go back to answer it. He was like a dream that did not matter any more.

Driving to the hospital in the Buick, which he did not like, because the seats sloped farther back than in his own car and made him feel uncomfortable, Mr Cope kept saying: 'I heard the crash, you see. I was working, but I came out at once, and there she was, lying on the floor with her mouth open. I was working, but I came out at once,' he kept saying, as if to justify himself that, whatever had happened, it was not his fault.

Christine hardly heard him. She drove automatically, knowing the way well, for she had often driven Aunt Josephine down these roads with books and bundles of clothing for the hospital. All she could think of was that she had been unkind to Aunt Josephine this morning. When Aunt Jo was so eager about the engagement, Christine had said: 'Don't interfere. You're always interfering', and Aunt Josephine's big face had looked like a gun dog disappointed of a walk.

She could not forget that long-chopped, fallen face. If Aunt Jo died, was that how she was doomed always to remember her?

'I was working,' Mr Cope said, 'but when I heard the crash in the kitchen I came out at once. I did what I could,' and

Christine kept seeing Aunt Josephine's hurt, triangular eyes, and remembering that she had banged out of the house without saying good-bye to her.

Aunt Josephine had had a stroke. They were driving to her bedside, but Mr Cope and Christine were thinking less of her than of themselves; he trying to justify his own part in the affair, she struggling with the bogy of regret. She thought with shame of the fickleness of human sympathy. You could only be really sorry for someone if what had happened to them did not make you sorrier still for yourself.

When they went round the screens in the ward where Aunt Josephine lay, Christine forgot everything except the log-like figure, whose toes reached to the end of the high iron bed. They had taken the pillows away, and Aunt Josephine was lying flat on the mattress with one side of her face slipped backwards, and drunken snores coming from the twisted cavern of her mouth.

Mr Cope looked at her dutifully and then looked away, pretending to examine the dish with the tongue forceps and spatula that stood by the bed. Christine gazed and gazed, trying to see beyond this strange and horrifying façade and find Aunt Josephine. She must be there, her spirit unchanged by the blow that had befallen her body, needing help, asking for help perhaps, from the limbo where she was confined; needing help and not getting it.

Christine had nursed many unconscious people. Like the other nurses, she had learned to look on them as no more than bodies, needing routine care and watchfulness, making a lot of work, almost perverse, it sometimes seemed, when their beds needed changing just when you were most busy. Relations had come and gone, had wept, or looked in silence, and stroked the stubbornly still head that did not know or care if it was touched by a mother's hand or a nurse's.

There was a boy who had been unconscious for three weeks before he died. The doctors had said he would never regain consciousness, but his mother had come every day and held his hand and talked to him, and Christine had marvelled that she could without effort see beyond the wall of coma to her son, and treat him as if he knew she were there, and could respond.

'He does know me,' she told Christine, smiling quite cheer-

117

fully. 'I know he knows I'm here.' But when Christine had asked the Ward Sister: 'Could he?' Sister had said: 'Of course not. Use your sense, Nurse – and you must tell his mother she'll have to go now, before the surgeons' rounds.'

Standing by Aunt Josephine's bed, Christine knew that the Ward Sister had been wrong, and that she herself had been wrong when she treated unconscious patients as impersonally as if they were already dead. Aunt Josephine gave no sign, but Christine felt that she knew she was not alone.

Her father muttered: 'We'd better go. You heard what the nurse said. They don't think she'll come round. We can't do anything here. We'd better go.'

'No, I don't want to,' Christine said. 'I want to stay with her.' But the Staff Nurse came round the screens, drawing a turnip watch from under the starched bosom of her apron, and said: 'I'm afraid you'll have to go now. I have to close the ward.'

They took the screens away from Aunt Josephine, so that the Night Nurse could see her when she sat at the desk in the middle of the ward. The patients in the other beds peered over at Aunt Josephine, and peered at Christine and her father as they went away down the polished length of floor, their heels making too much noise.

Alone together, each needing comfort from the other and not getting it, Christine and her father were almost like strangers. Their intimacy of thirty-four years was not deep enough to absorb this crisis. Before, when anything had happened it was always Aunt Josephine to whom they turned. She was the apex of the triangle, they the two points at its base, now left looking at each other across the space that divided them.

There was a lot to do. Christine prepared supper for her father and tried to eat with him, and then she cleared up the books and broken china in the kitchen and fed the dogs and cats, who wandered about uneasily all evening and would not settle anywhere.

She rang up her brother. Roger was out, and Sylvia dealt with the news with studied calm, thinking that she was being of great practical help. 'Now, you're not to worry,' she said. 'You should take a Veganin and try and get a good night's sleep. I don't want you to worry.'

'Sylvia says we're not to worry,' Christine told her father caustically. Aunt Josephine would have laughed at that, but Mr Cope nodded and said vaguely: 'Kind girl. She's a good, kind girl.' When Christine said: 'They're coming up tomorrow, I'm afraid. I couldn't stop them', he said: 'That's right. The family should be together at a time like this.'

Christine did not want them to come. They had never been particularly nice to Aunt Josephine. Roger had tormented her and disobeyed her consistently when he was a boy, and since he married he and his wife had looked on her chiefly as a useful solution to the problem of his father, who might otherwise have had to live with them.

When Vinson rang up and Christine told him what had happened, he said he would come down to her at once, but she did not want him either. People always wanted to rally round you, even though they could do nothing except talk round and round what had happened, and you did not want the bother of them. Certainly she did not want Vinson. He was outside her trouble, and she still could not think what she was going to say to him. Only Aunt Josephine could help her with that.

She promised him that she would ring him up in the morning, but in the morning she went off to the hospital and forgot about him. She had telephoned to inquire for Aunt Josephine three times during the night, and a busy Night Sister had told her briskly that there was no change and likely to be none, and no need to inquire. She would be informed of any change, the Night Sister said; but when she and her father reached the hospital, Aunt Josephine had been dead for two hours, and no one had told them.

It did not seem worth making a fuss about that. There was nothing to do but collect Aunt Josephine's clothes from a harassed probationer and go home.

As they went down the corridor, Sylvia and Roger came out of the lift and walked towards them. 'How is she?' they asked, making their faces concerned. 'We came as soon as we could.'

When they heard that Aunt Josephine was dead Roger pressed his father's arm in a manly way, and Sylvia's ever-fluid sinuses began to overflow at the eyes and nose. Seeing her sob and sniffle and flush loosened the stricture in Christine's throat and she no longer had to fight to keep herself from crying. If Sylvia, who had not loved Aunt Josephine, was going to weep for her, Christine did not feel like crying.

They all went into the waiting-room and sat down on the wicker furniture. Mr Cope told over again the story of how he had been working and had heard the crash in the kitchen and had come out at once to find Aunt Josephine lying on the floor.

'What I can't understand,' Roger said, 'is how she could have been taken like that without ever having any symptoms. She always seemed so strong. I don't see how she could have had a stroke,' he grumbled, as if aggrieved that Aunt Josephine had pulled a fast one on him. 'I don't see how she *could* have had a stroke.'

'Well, she did,' said Christine. 'It's no good keeping saying that.'

'Take a hold on yourself, Chris,' said Roger, narrowing his eyes at her. 'It's no good getting cross with me. It wasn't *my* fault.'

Why was everyone so concerned with proving that it was not their fault? It was not anybody's fault; and if it had been, fixing the blame somewhere would not bring Aunt Josephine to life.

Nor would talking about it, but they talked on and on in the overheated waiting-room, and Sylvia snivelled and Roger wore his heavy, serious face, and Christine listened to the ticking of the radiators and tried to make herself understand that Aunt Josephine had not just taken the leading part in a dramatic episode, but had gone away for ever and would take no more part in anything.

It was a scene in which Aunt Josephine should have participated. She had always been there at family conferences. She had always been the loudest voice, and given at the same time the sanest and the most startling opinions. She should have been there. She would have pulled them together and given the scene some point. Christine kept thinking that she should be there, and having to make herself realize that if Aunt Josephine were there the scene would not be happening at all.

A woman came in with a composed little boy, who carried a fibre suitcase and had evidently come for admission to one of the wards. They sat by the window and whispered, and presently a nurse came in and said: 'Is this the Tonsils for Mr Bishop?' and asked the Copes if they were waiting to see someone.

'No, thank you, we're just going,' they said, and they all stood up, as if she had dismissed them. Roger and Sylvia wanted to get back to the country. Arrangements had been made about the funeral, and there was nothing more to be done or said.

'Thank heaven for you, Chris,' Roger said, as they went out. 'We needn't worry about the aged P. with you there to look after him.'

'Do you think you'll be able to manage, Christine?' Sylvia asked. Manage was one of her favourite words. It applied to everything from a child's tantrums to a dinner-party without enough matching plates. There were two kinds of people in the world: those who managed, and those who did not, and it was only possible to be one of those who did.

'I could ask my Mrs Hatchett to come up for a few days if you like, to help you get straight. I'll manage without her,' Sylvia said. 'You may find it rather difficult at first to manage both house and your job. Until you find a Woman, that is. You'll have to have to get somebody in. I'll give you the address of that agency I always go to.'

In the slow lift, which was long and narrow to accommodate stretchers – or mortuary trolleys – she went on about Daily Women and Mother's Helps and two-and-six an hour. Christine let her talk; and when the gates slid back and they stepped out, she said: 'I'll be all right, thank you. I'm sure I'll manage perfectly well.'

'My little girl's going to look after me now, aren't you?' said her father, drawing her arm through his in an unwonted gesture of affection, and Roger said: 'Good old estimable Miss Cope. I don't know what we'd do without you.'

No, thought Christine bleakly, but without bitterness, as they walked across the gravel space outside the hospital to their cars. I don't know what you would do without me. Aunt Jo solved the problem of Daddy before. Now I do.

They took it for granted that her lot in life was now to stay at home and keep house for her father. Unknowingly, they had decided for her what she should do about Vinson. Perhaps, in that far-away time which was only yesterday when Aunt

Josephine was still alive, she might have married him. Now she could not, and the idea of it was already a senseless dream.

Roger was more cheerful now that he was outside the hospital. 'Still got that pansy car, I see,' he said, as Christine went towards the Buick. 'That Yank must be pretty far gone to hand that smashing job over to a ham hand like my sister.' He wanted to make jokes now, to resume his position as master of the family, and shake them out of their trouble.

'I'll be giving it back,' Christine said. 'He's going away soon.'

'Oh well,' said Roger, 'they come and they go. I don't suppose he'll be much loss to you, apart from the car. I must say, for one awful moment, we were afraid you might be going to marry him, weren't we, Syl?'

'Hush, dear,' she said. 'You're making too much noise.' She did not add: 'with Aunt Josephine only a few hours dead', but that was what she meant.

Roger became grave again and helped his father dutifully into the Buick. Mr Cope had not spoken much since the nurse had met them at the entrance to the ward and they had seen through the glass doors the bare springs of the bed from which the mattress had gone to be fumigated, and the lost, empty look had come down on his face and settled there.

He was not irritable any more. He was not sarcastic or fidgety or self-centred. He was not even sad. He was just nothing. He muddled through the days, doing whatever Christine suggested, but she suspected that when she sent him into his study to work he spent most of the time staring out of the window.

Their tragedy did not bring them closer. They were two people together in the overlarge house, but alone, with nothing to say to each other. Christine had not yet been able to find anybody to come and help her in the house, and she was busy all the time she was at home. She and her father rarely sat together, except at meals, which he did not enjoy, because she could not cook as well as Aunt Josephine.

Mr Parker had offered to give her a week's leave, but she refused. She did not want to stop working. It was all she had left of her old life, and there were people to talk to at the shop. She could not bear the thought of being at home all day, and so she struggled on, with the house growing dirtier and more untidy, the animals getting out of hand, Aunt Josephine's possessions still unsorted, and herself getting more and more tired and discouraged at the idea of the future, which promised to go on like this for ever.

Sooner or later she would have to see Vinson. She put him off with one excuse after another, but a few days after Aunt Josephine's funeral he arrived at 'Roselawn' one evening when Christine was sitting in an overall in the kitchen, trying to sort out the tradesmen's bills.

Vinson came in by the open back door, as he had learned to do since he became a frequent visitor to the house. Christine got up, pushing back her hair and conscious of her bedraggled appearance as he put his arms round her and kissed her.

'What's the matter?' he asked, when she did not respond.

'You know what's the matter.' She turned away.

'Sure. I'm terribly sorry about this. Christine, why wouldn't you see me before? You know how sorry I am for you, but it doesn't make any difference to you and me. I'm still there, honey. You can put your head on my shoulder and cry if you want to.'

The arrogance of him. The typical male arrogance, which thought that a loss could not matter to you as long as he was there. 'I don't want to cry,' she said quite crossly. 'I finished crying some time ago. I don't need to howl all the time to show how much I mind about Aunt Jo. I wish you hadn't come. Please take the car and go away. I don't want to see you.'

As soon as she said this she was afraid. She had seen Vinson angry once or twice, and she did not like it. He became different and quite frightening, his slight body tense, and revealing the strength it did not normally seem to have.

She looked at him cautiously, but he was not angry. He was evidently going to humour her and treat her gently, and she despised him for it. She would have preferred his anger.

'Now then,' he said, putting his arms round her again. 'Now then, darling. You're all upset, I know, but you mustn't be that way. It's all right. Everything will be all right when we're married.'

'But we're not going to be married!' Christine pulled herself away and went to the stove, where she began to stir the dogs' horsemeat furiously. 'I can't marry you, Vin. I know I can't.'

'Look here,' he said calmly. 'This isn't good enough. You told me several days ago that you'd marry me. I believed you. I believed you meant it, and I'm holding you to your promise. I expect you to keep faith with me as I shall with you.'

'Oh, don't be pompous!' she said, resisting a theatrical desire to stamp her foot. She went on stirring, and the steam from the boiling horsemeat made her eyes smart. She would not turn round in case he thought that she was crying.

'I'm not pompous,' he said. 'I'm damned mad, if you want to know.'

She risked a look at him, and he was angry now, his brows down and his mouth set. He looked like a Sicilian with a knife in his palm.

'What do you think you're playing at?' he asked roughly. 'One day you'll marry me, and the next you won't. This is a hell of a way to treat a man, and you'll have to learn you can't play that game with me. Come away from that goddamn stove. Come here.'

'I won't,' she said, hearing her voice rising. 'I've changed my mind. I told you. I can change my mind, can't I?'

He dropped his voice. 'I suppose it's because you think you can't leave your father now,' he said, and because he had guessed most of the truth Christine turned round and said furiously: 'Can't you understand – are you so conceited that you can't understand that I just don't want to marry you?'

'I see.' He picked up his uniform cap from the table and went out of the kitchen. Christine heard the Buick start, turn round and roar away, and she knelt on the floor and laid her face against the silky cheek of her dog, who always came to her when she was crying.

She cried several times during the next few days. She cried for Aunt Josephine, because she was tired and discouraged. Aunt Jo had always been the one to go to when you were tired, or could not cope with something you had to do. Aunt Jo would say comfortably: 'Leave it. It'll keep. Do it *domani*, like the Italians do.' And she would put you to bed with a hot-water bottle and a bowl of soup, or take you out to see a silly film, either of which worked equally well.

Margaret was away from work again. She had been ill and nearly lost her baby, and it was doubtful whether she would ever be able to come back to the shop. Mr Parker, who hated new people in the department, clung to the idea that she would, and did not ask for anyone to replace her.

Helen was on holiday, and Christine was sometimes too busy even to take her lunch-hour. When she did she could not be bothered to go out. She trailed up to the canteen and ate what they called Vienna steak, and listened to the futile complaints of the people who were always saying that they were going to tell the management, and never did.

In what she already thought of as The Old Days, when she came home from the shop, Aunt Josephine had always wanted to hear about her day and about the funny or irritating things that had happened. But her father did not want to hear. He was not interested in Goldwyn's, and if she said that she had had a hard day he would say: 'Well, why don't you give it up? You know I've never liked you being a shop girl', although he could not possibly go on living in that absurdly big house on the little money his translations brought him, if Christine gave up Goldwyn's.

Now when she came home tired from the shop, dreading the thought of having to cook supper and do a mountain of ironing and clean the silver or wash the kitchen floor, or tackle any one of the hundred jobs that were piling up on her with no hope of ever getting done, there was no Aunt Josephine to make her go to bed early and say: 'Do it *domani*.'

She found a woman to come and clean in the mornings, but she made a noise banging her brush against the stairs when Mr Cope was working, and he fired her before Christine came home. She found another woman with a long wet nose and weak ankles, who brought with her a misshapen four-year-old daughter, who ate all the cakes and biscuits and broke a valuable vase. Christine forgave this, and the woman and child disappeared one day with the last of Vinson's American hams, a bottle of sherry and the orphanage box full of pennies, and were never heard of again. Christine did not have the time or energy to look for anyone else. She struggled on alone.

She went to bed exhausted, and woke still tired. For the first time in her career she began to make mistakes at work. Alice, catching her out in a muddle over the cash register, said: 'You must be in love, Miss Cope. That's what it is.'

In love! If only she was . . . When she had been in love with Jerry she had been vague and unpractical, living only for the weekends when she could get up to Oxford, but it had not mattered. When you were in love the world conspired to help you, to take the boring practicalities of life off your hands so that you could get on with the charming business of being in love. Loving glorified you and gave you an unfair advantage over other people.

Rhona was in love again, with a Hungarian film director, with whom she was occupying herself while her husband was in Brazil. She came down to see Christine and was horrified by the mess and drudgery in which she found her. She took a duster and sat down at the kitchen table to help Christine with the silver, but she soon pushed her chair away from the table and forgot about the silver while she talked about the Hungarian.

She was fond of Christine and warmly sorry for her, but at the moment she was more interested in the Hungarian.

'It's really love this time,' she mooned. 'I know now that it was never the real thing before.'

'Oh, you always say that, Ro. It's always the one and only real thing – until the next time.'

'Don't be horrid. You wouldn't say that if you knew Lajos. You must meet him.' Rhona tipped her chair back against the dresser. 'He's wonderful. I tell you he's made a different woman of me.' All Rhona's new men made a different woman of her.

'He's so brilliant. He's much cleverer than me, which is such a relief. I'm sick of men who pretend to think I'm cleverer than them, and sit around waiting for me to say something witty. With Lajos, you know, I sort of – sort of feel almost like a peasant girl.' She laughed, looking less like a peasant girl than it was possible to imagine.

126

'He dominates me, you see, and it's wonderful. It's exciting. You know, Chris, I believe that's how women really want to be treated.'

'You might try it with Dan some day,' Christine said, thinking of Rhona's husband, who was a ball of fire in the business world, but a trained seal in his own home.

'Oh, Dan!' Rhona said. 'That's different. Don't let's talk about him, or I might start feeling guilty. Let's talk about Lajos. Let's have an evening together soon and you'll see what I mean about him. You bring someone and we'll go dancing.'

'Oh, Ro, I don't think I can go out. Daddy doesn't really like being alone in the evening, and, anyway, I've got too much to do here.'

'Nonsense,' said Rhona, 'you're getting warped. We'll have a party. Who'll you bring? Why don't you bring that American you took to the film? What about him, by the way? How's that coming along?'

'It isn't,' Christine said. 'It didn't work.'

'Oh well, too bad,' Rhona lost interest, because she had looked at her watch and seen that it was time to go and meet the Hungarian. 'I'll find you someone else, Chris darling. When I'm in love I always want everyone else to be in love too, and you can't go on playing at being a Victorian daughter for ever. You look ten years older already.'

'Thanks. That's a big help.' Christine kissed her at the door and Rhona drove away, taking her light and excitement with her.

Christine went back to the kitchen table and the pile of heavy old silver, which made her its slave instead of being a slave for her use. It was Saturday afternoon. Her father had announced at lunch that he had invited a friend for dinner, and presently Christine would have to go out with her shopping basket and find something for them to eat.

After dinner her father and Mr Wilson, who dropped cigarette ash on his waistcoat and constantly cleared his throat, would sit and talk about the Labour Government, and Christine would wash the dishes and darn her father's socks. It would go on like this for years and years, and she would grow to look as drab as she felt now, and people would say what a good daughter she was, and call her That poor Miss Cope, who never married.

She wanted to cry, but what was the use of crying if you had no one to be upset that you were upset enough to cry? If Rhona cried she would have the Hungarian to comfort her. There would be some point for her in crying, because it would stimulate the Hungarian to emotion too, and they could have quite a scene together. But you could not make a scene all by yourself.

When Vinson came in at the back door she was still sitting with her hands among the silver, doing nothing.

'Hullo,' she said. 'I look awful.' Usually, you only said this to a man when you knew that you did not. Christine knew that she looked awful now in a sweater that had shrunk in the wash, with her hair straight because she had been too tired to set it last night; but Vinson was out of her life, and it did not matter.

'That's O.K.,' he said, not denying it. He was in civilian clothes, with a striped tie that no Englishman would have worn unless it was his Old School colours, and he looked more at home in the kitchen than he did when he was in uniform. He sat down opposite her at the table, picked up a spoon and began to polish it carefully, as if that were his only interest in the world.

'I told you not to come here again,' Christine murmured, feeling that she ought to say that, although she was glad that he had come.

'Oh, sure,' he said, starting on another spoon. 'I only came to see if you had the monkey-wrench from the car. I can't find it.'

'Oh yes. We used it when we were trying to unstop the waste-pipe in the bathroom. Aunt Jo must have put it in our toolbox. I'm sorry. I'll get it.' She got up. Nowadays, when she got up from a chair, she had to push herself up with her hands, and he noticed it.

'Don't bother now,' he said. 'It can wait. Let's you and me have a drink together first, what do you say?'

'A drink?' She looked at the kitchen clock, made like a fry-ing-pan, which she had bought for Aunt Josephine last Christmas. 'It's not five o'clock yet.'

'So what? You British never raise a thirst before six o'clock because the law says you mustn't, but an American can raise a thirst any time. Can I go fix one for us?'

'All right. You know where everything is. My father's out walking his dog.' They both knew that Mr Cope would disapprove of the cocktail cupboard being unlatched at this hour.

Vinson took out some ice, and when he had gone through to the drawing-room Christine hastily went to her bag and powdered her nose, put on lipstick and combed her hair. He caught her at the mirror when he came back with two strong whiskies on a tray. He always carried drinks and food as neatly as if he were a trained parlourmaid.

'That's better,' he said. 'You're so pretty, Christine, you mustn't let yourself go. You've got thinner,' he said, as she came over to the table, where he had cleared aside the silver and put the glasses down.

'Have I? That's a good thing then. I was too fat before.'

He did not answer this. He did not seem inclined to talk much. He sat there sipping his drink and smoking, and left it to her to make the conversation. She did not know what she should say.

'I can't stay very long,' she told him. 'I've got to go out and get some food. Daddy has asked a friend for supper.'

'You've got too much to do,' Vinson said.

It was the first time anyone had said this to her since Aunt Josephine died. She had drunk half her glass of whisky, and it made her unable to resist saying: 'Oh yes, Vin, I have. It's awful. I can't get anyone to help, and I just can't cope, and Daddy doesn't want to leave this house and get a flat, and I just don't know how I'm ever going to get straight. I can't see it ever getting any better.'

'You're pretty unhappy, aren't you, Christine?' he said, looking at his glass.

She paused, and then she said on a sigh: 'Oh, Vin, I am.' She knew she should not say this to him; but although he was there in the kitchen with her he was out of her life, and so perhaps she could admit it.

'It's awful. I miss Aunt Jo so much, and I'm so tired, and it's so dreary because Daddy and I – well, he never wants to hear about the shop or anything. He doesn't like it if I go out, and I don't really want to, but I've got nobody to talk to. I've got nothing.'

She held herself from making the noises or the facial expressions of crying, but tears began to run down the side of her nose and into her mouth, and she kept her head down as she said: 'Aunt Jo was always here, and she was my friend. But it's all so different now. I've got nothing.'

'You've got me,' Vinson said quietly. It sounded like a line from a play, facile and just right, but when she looked up at him she saw that he meant it.

'You've still got me,' he said, and a warm flux of comfort began to flow through her as she let herself drift for a while on the tide of all the things he began to say to her in a quickened voice. He leaned across the table, twisting his empty glass round in his narrow hands, and told her that she was the sort of girl he had been looking for all his life and never found, and how his friends would be jealous of him, and how he would make her happy. He told her about America and the home they would have there together, and how wonderful it was, and how she would get to love it more than England. . . .

'No,' she interrupted. 'I could never do that.' But she was only speaking theoretically, because she knew she could not go to America with him.

She did not tell him that, because she did not want to abandon just yet the illusion of relief and escape which he was offering her. To be looked after . . . to have someone who cared about what you felt and did . . . She shook herself out of the dream and stood up.

'Don't go on, Vin,' she said. 'I must go out now and get some food before the shops close.'

'To hell with the shops,' he said, getting up and coming round the table to her. 'Forget it. I'll take you out to dinner.'

'I can't. There's Daddy and Mr Wilson –'

'We'll take them out too. Give them a bang-up meal. Take them to the club if you like, and buy them a steak. I've got to get in right with your father.'

'Why?'

'Because I'm going to marry you.'

She smiled. She thought that he would kiss her then, but he just patted her shoulder and turned to the table to pick up the glasses. 'I'll go get us another drink,' he said.

Telling Roger and Sylvia was the hardest part. Her father had been quite easy. So that he could not make a fuss, Vinson had told him in front of Mr Wilson, who sat at the table in the Air Force club gorged with food, with his eyes popping out. Mr Cope was more concerned at the time with worrying about whether he was going to be able to digest the food he had eaten than with worrying about Christine going away to marry in America; but when he and Christine talked about it alone at home afterwards he realized that she meant it, and he began to say:

'What will happen to me? And what is going to happen to me?'

'You knew I might get married some time.' Christine steeled herself against feeling too sorry for him. 'You must have thought of that. It happens to nearly all fathers. It's just because I've been at home so long that you . . . But you'll be all right,' she said briskly, determined not to be held back by pity. 'You'll be fine. You know that Roger and Sylvia will be glad to have you, and you'll have a lovely home with them. You know you like Farnborough, and it will be wonderful for Bruce. There'll be hundreds of places you can take him for walks.'

She was trying to persuade herself as much as him. She still had to persuade Roger and Sylvia.

When Mr Cope's dog was mentioned they seized on that and made it a point of issue. They could not very well say that they did not want Mr Cope, but they could hint at it by quibbling about his dog. They held up the more important plans by objecting to details, and they were like that all through the talk which Christine had with them when she took a Saturday morning off and drove down to Farnborough to tell them that she was going to marry Vinson.

They did not like it. In common decency, they could not object to the larger aspects of the case. Christine had a right to get married, and her father had a right to expect that his son and daughter-in-law would give him a home. Whatever they were thinking, they could not deny that in so many words, and so they tried to unsettle Christine by cavilling at details.

It was a horrid interview. It might to be so wonderful to go to your family and say: 'I'm going to be married', and to be kissed and wished happiness. Sylvia did kiss her, with her nose cold and wet against Christine's cheek, but all she could wish her in the way of happiness was: 'I hope you're not making a mistake, Christine. No doubt you know what you want.'

It was made more difficult for her because Vinson had been recalled to Washington. If he were there Roger and Sylvia would not have been able to talk as they did, but Christine had seen him off from the airport two days ago, and now she was alone, and the confidence she felt with him was ebbing.

They had lunch, a dull, overcooked lunch served laboriously by a slow maid. When the maid had gone out of the room, Roger began again to try and undermine Christine's assurance.

'Look here,' he said. 'We don't know anything about this fellow. He's obviously a first-class chap – don't get me wrong – but aren't you rather rushing into this without knowing anything about his background? We don't know who his people are, and so on. I mean, you've only seen him over here as a naval officer, and you never can tell about Americans, anyway. They all sound the same to me.'

'You mean you think he's common.' Christine stabbed at a brussels sprout with her fork. Sylvia was the sort of housekeeper who aggravated the horrors of having to have brussels sprouts in season by having them out of season as well, when there were other vegetables to choose from. 'Don't be a snob, Rodge. Vin isn't common, though it wouldn't matter if he was. Our family's not such great shakes. What about Uncle Willie and the pawn-shop? Anyway, nobody's common in America. The word doesn't exist.' She had gathered that from Vinson's mystification when she had used the word to him in describing someone.

'Must be what's wrong with that country then,' said Roger complacently, slathering mustard on his meat. 'But honestly, Chris, you're going to find it awfully different over there. I wonder if you'll like it? I know I wouldn't.'

'I'll love it,' said Christine. 'You're so beastly insular. I think it's exciting to be starting out all over again in a new country that has the future of the world in its hands.'

She was quoting Vinson, and Roger said: 'God help the world, if that's the case.'

'Of course you'll be living in the land of plenty. It will be very different from what we have to manage with over here,' said Sylvia gently but accusingly.

'I'll send you food parcels,' said Christine, determined not to be confounded by them. 'And chocolate for the children, and I'll send you nylons.'

'I'd have to pay duty on them.' Sylvia quickly found fault. 'But you mustn't worry about us. You'll have your own life to lead over there, and we'll manage all right, no doubt, though I must say I wouldn't have expected you to spring this on us just now, so soon after Aunt Jo –'

'She liked him!' cried Christine violently. 'She liked Vinson, and she wanted me to marry him.'

'Oh, so you discussed it with her?' Sylvia raised her thin gingery eyebrows. 'I must say I think it's a little funny that we never heard anything about it.' Funny was another of her favourite words.

'Why should I tell you when I knew you'd be like this? Aunt Jo was the only one who cared whether I was happy or not. She wanted me to marry Vin. She said so, and I don't care what you or anyone thinks –' She paused blindly at the unappetising food on her plate, and Sylvia said in very English French: '*Pas devant la bonne*', as the maid trod heavily back into the room with a plate of blancmange.

The children had been lunching with a neighbour. When they came back Christine told them her news. She thought that they would be pleased and excited, as children were by any new turn of events, whatever its implications. Even death was something new to marvel at; but instead of being excited about Christine they looked at her in dismay and said: 'What about us? You're going away to America and we shan't ever see you again. What will happen to us?'

Jeanette clung to Christine and began to cry, and they both put on a ridiculous act, crying: 'What shall we do without you;

oh, whatever shall we do?' as if they had a cruel mother and father, and she were their only hope in the world.

It was almost as if their parents had put them up to behaving like this. Everyone was conspiring to make Christine feel bad about following her perfectly natural desire to be married and have a life of her own.

When she left, Roger made his final shot. 'Well, we shan't be calling you the estimable Miss Cope much longer,' he said amiably enough, as they went down the path between the neat box hedges, which were one of the reasons why Sylvia did not want to have Mr Cope's dog, 'but I don't see how you can face the thought of being called Mrs Gaegler. That's no kind of a name. My sister, Mrs Gaegler.' He shook his head and snickered. 'I can't see myself saying that with a straight face.'

It was not much better at the shop. Christine's outside friends were pleased when she told them. Rhona was ecstatic, and began making plans to come to America and stay with her, and Margaret and Laurie were unselfishly delighted, although they would miss her. But in the busy book department, where the estimable Miss Cope was so much needed, the congratulations were shadowed by the unspoken reproach that she was letting them down by going away so suddenly before anyone could be trained to take her place.

'Of course I'm glad for you, my dear,' Mr Parker said, 'but if only you could have stayed just a little while longer and helped me to organize the department under a new head saleswoman. I don't know who they'll send me. The personnel is so poor these days. Mrs Drew could have taken over, but I doubt she'll come back now. She seems to have deserted us too.'

'She's going to have a baby. Surely she's allowed to do that.'

'I know, my dear, I know. I'm not complaining, but to lose the two of you ... Miss Burman will never amount to much, poor old soul, Alice is being moved next month, and Helen – well, she's a worthy enough girl, but she hasn't your experience. Oh dear, Miss Cope, I just don't see how I'm going to manage without you. You've been indispensable to me, but your young man must come first, I suppose.'

He managed a brave smile, which flickered out of his face

134

almost at once. Christine agreed with him. She did not see how he was going to manage without her. She knew that she had held him together in his uncertain sway over the book department. Even if he got efficient new helpers, they would not cover up for him and look after him as she had done.

She worked like a beaver in her last few days at the shop, to try to make amends for her desertion. She brought the stock list up to date and checked the order book and rearranged untidy sections, but Mr Parker, in his distress at losing her, was already becoming more futile than he had ever been, and she dreaded to think what muddles he would get into when she was gone.

Now that she knew she was leaving the shop she wanted it to happen quickly, but at half past five on her last day she did not want to go. She remembered only the nice things about working at Goldwyn's, and none of the things she had grumbled about.

Mr Parker, Miss Burman, Alice and Helen, and even the new assistant, who had a fluting voice and cut-away nostrils, had clubbed together to buy her a silver ashtray with her new initials on it: C.M.G. They gave it to her with some embarrassment after the shop closed. Christine wanted to cry. Miss Burman did cry, and Mr Parker shook her hand feebly and shuffled away in his black musician's hat to the door which the commissionaire was holding for him. It was very distressing.

Just before she left England Margaret told Christine that she had had Miss Burman to tea, and Miss Burman had told her, with many indrawn breaths, that Mr Parker had resigned his post. 'Though given the sack,' Miss Burman said, 'would be more my way of putting it.'

Then there were the animals. Mr Cope's dog was going to Farnborough, under Roger's half-joking threat that he would shoot it if it gave any trouble. Christine had wanted to take her dog Timmy to America with her, but Vinson said that they would be living in an apartment, and dogs were not allowed. Even if they moved away from Washington, he said, they would not want to be trammelled with a dog when they did not know where they might be sent.

When he wrote that to her, Christine almost wrote back to say she would not come to America. Vinson had pretended to like dogs when he first came to 'Roselawn', but now that he was safely engaged to her she saw that he did not. If only they could have talked it over, he might have reassured her, but three thousand miles was too far to make contact over things like this. Christine's letters were warm and impulsive, the sort of letters she would like to get; but Vinson's letters to her were carefully composed and a little stilted, and did not reveal his feelings. Even his love messages sounded as if they came out of a book. Christine thought that she would mind leaving Timmy more than anyone in England. Margaret was going to take him for her, and two days before her boat sailed she took him over to the Drews' house. It would have been terrible if he had been sad and pleaded her with his eyes not to go, but it was even more terrible that he settled down quite happily, ate a large meal and was too busy with a bone in the garden to notice when she went away.

The goldfish were given to Sylvia's children. She struck at having the love-birds, and they were given to a pet shop, whose owner would not pay anything for them, because he said they were too old.

The oldest cat had to be destroyed because Christine could not find anyone who would take it. Two of the others had run away after Aunt Josephine died, and the remaining cat was given as a parting present to Miss Burman, who might not have been so delighted with it if she had realized it was expecting kittens.

There remained only Aunt Josephine's decrepit fox-terrier. Christine had been looking after it as well as she could, even letting it sleep on her bed, although it did not like her.

'Have to be put down, of course,' Roger said robustly. 'Put it out of its misery as it should have been long ago.'

'But Aunt Jo loved it,' Christine said. 'It seems so mean to her to let it die.' But no one would have it, and there was nothing for Christine to do but to take it away to be destroyed. When the vet carried its soggy old body away, with one leg dangling down under his arm, it looked at Christine with eyes of deep distress.

When her father said good-bye to her at Waterloo she looked

out of the window as the train pulled out, and saw in his eyes the same look that the fox-terrier had when it was carried away to die.

She had let everybody down by going away. No one was pleased that she was going to be married. No one was happy for her, and she could not feel happy for herself. A bride going to her lover should have gone with shining eyes and an eager heart, but Christine sat miserably in the train to Southampton and would not look out of the window. When people exclaimed about the buttercups, she would not look at the fields. She did not want to leave England.

'Look,' said the man next to her, leaning over. 'There's our *bateau*. Quite sizeable, isn't she?'

Christine turned her head, and there was the black-and-white hull of the liner rising, it seemed, right out of the flat fields, as the train slid past it and into the customs shed.

Chapter Three

WHEN she was on the boat Christine began to feel better. She had only been to sea before on a Channel steamer, huddled under coats on the windy deck because people were being sick below, and this was a completely new world to her. This lazy, luxurious liner life of eating and sleeping and making friends with people you would never see again was really the start of the tremendous adventure to which she had committed herself when she said that she would marry Vinson, and the excitement of it revived her flagging courage.

She began to feel like a different person, which was what she wanted. She could not see the old Christine as a suitable wife for Vinson. The old Christine was an unambitious small-time person; attaching too much importance to a trifling job in a book department, slow to make new friends, happy with people who expected no more from her than cheerfulness, content with her own company and slightly ill at ease with sophisticates, and altogether unfitted to the challenge of being an American wife.

She did not think that Vinson knew what she was really like, but with his help she could learn perhaps to be all the things he would want her to be, just as she was learning to act the part of a first-class passenger on one of the world's biggest liners.

She had not wanted to travel first class, but Vinson said that a commander's wife did not travel any other way, and so she had drawn out her savings to obey him. At first she had to keep reminding herself that she had paid a fantastic amount for her ticket and was entitled to the attention and service she was given. Being waited on did not come naturally to her. She made mistakes, like folding her table napkin and making her own bed, which brought her a gentle reprimand from her stewardess: 'There's no need for that, madam. It's very kind of you, but I'm afraid you didn't make it quite right.'

She wore her new clothes and never went out of her cabin without doing her hair and face as carefully as if she were going to a party, but she thought that people must guess that underneath there was only Christine Cope, and think her an impostor from the Tourist decks. Before long, however, her diffidence was eased away by the insidious luxury of a transatlantic crossing. She was accepted at her ticket value. She began to make friends and to be asked to meet people for cocktails in the bar. Gradually she felt herself learning to be this new person, this first class passenger who was being borne across a well-behaved ocean to marry a commander in the United States Navy. She began to enjoy herself.

As the slow days went by and the unseen miles slipped past she thought less and less of what she had left behind and more about what was in front of her. The cable from Roger and Sylvia saluting her departure was less real than the cable from Vinson saluting her approach. She had a picture of him on her dressing-table. Her stewardess dusted it reverently every morning and took a pleasing interest in hearing about Miss Cope's young man, although no doubt it was only one of her duties to make the passengers feel that they mattered to her.

Other stewardesses were called in to view Vinson, and to see the dress and hat which Christine had bought to be married in. The photograph was much admired, and the bath stewardess said that Vinson looked like Tyrone Power. That must be the eyebrows. He was in uniform, wearing his professional naval officer look, with the mouth set and the eyes slightly narrowed. Christine said Hello to the photograph every time she came into her cabin, and wondered if Vinson did the same with her picture she had given him.

It was hard to imagine what he might be doing in that unknown map-shaped country to which the liner was faithfully ploughing through the days and nights. If it had not been for the photograph, she would have found it difficult to remember what he looked like. When she lay in bed at night she could not see his face, although she knew what his voice sounded like when he said Chris*tine*. She knew so little about him; but whoever knew enough about the man they married? If Jerry had come back from the war and married her, she would not have known enough about him, except that she loved him.

She did not know whether she loved Vinson. Looking at herself in the mirror and thinking of the pictures she had seen of

139

gorgeous American girls, she did not see why he should love her. He must think he did. Surely a man would not embark on the risky enterprise of asking a girl to marry him unless he felt he could not live without her.

A man could live without a woman. Why should he saddle himself with a wife just for the sake of being married? A woman might do that, because there was not enough in life for a woman who did not marry. Towards the end of her journey Christine dared to ask herself whether that was what she was doing.

She looked at Vinson's picture and wished violently that he were there to kiss her. She remembered the night in his hotel room when she would have stayed there with him if he had let her. Surely it was all right. She wanted to marry Vinson, with the emphasis on Vinson and not on marry.

She liked him better than any man she knew. He loved her and was good to her; and when he made love to her, she had for him a feeling that must surely grow into a real love as soon as they could be together all the time.

She began to get excited about seeing him. People on the boat conspired in her excitement. She sat at a table in the dining-saloon with two American couples and a desiccated English widower who was being lent to the Atomic Energy Commission. They were thrilled when she told them that she was going to be married the day after the boat docked. One of the American women said it was darling, and the other said it was the most romantic thing she had heard of since the lovely *Prin*cess was betrothed to Phillup. The American men folded their hands over their little paunches and said it was a fine thing for the cause of greater understanding between anti-Communist nations. That was not why Christine was marrying Vinson, but she felt proud.

The English scientist did not say much, but he joined with the others in calling her The Bride, and they all teased her gently and made her feel important. On the last night there was champagne and the dinner was in her honour. Everyone kept toasting her and wishing her luck, and the Americans told her what a wonderful life she was going to have, and what a clever thing she was doing in marrying an American.

She sat in the place of honour in her new white evening dress

140

and felt happier about marrying Vinson than at any time since that Saturday evening in the kitchen at 'Roselawn' when he had said: 'Because I'm going to marry you', and she had not denied it. She was a girl who was going to be married, a girl who was loved enough to be sent for across three thousand miles of Atlantic, and she felt that this was what she must have been waiting for all her life.

She did not sleep much that night. She woke early and went on deck to see that the shore buildings of New Jersey were already sliding by. She did not know what she had expected America to look like. It looked big, and there seemed to be a lot of factories and oil tanks on it.

She had planned to write home about her first glimpse of the Statue of Liberty and the New York skyline, but she stayed so long in her cabin packing and doing her face and changing her mind about which suit to wear for Vinson that she missed it all.

When she went up to the promenade deck all she could see was the end of a great black shed. A rope mat hung on the corner of the concrete jetty that surrounded it, and the idea was evidently to lean the side of the liner against the mat and swivel it round into the dock. It took a long time. Nothing happened for half an hour, and Christine hung out of a window in company with other passengers who had already said good-bye to each other at breakfast and now had to fill in the anticlimax by saying it all over again.

'You're excited, I guess,' said one of the Americans, who was wearing a wide-banded hat of some consequence and an overcoat that looked as if it had been cut for a pregnant woman. 'This is some day for you. Your boy friend be here to meet you?'

'He said he would. Perhaps we'll see him in a minute.' Christine leaned out of the window as a few people appeared at the open end of the shed, looking up at the liner and waving. Surely one of them would be Vinson. The pit of her stomach was hollow with suspense. It had been easy enough to look forward to seeing him during the trip, when he could not appear. Now that the moment she had been waiting for had come, she did not not know how it would be. What would he look like? What should she say to him? Excitement and apprehension panicked her into a sudden wish that the liner would back away from the dock and never cast her up on New York.

A sailor with a white cap and a square collar was standing among the people on the end of the jetty holding a bunch of flowers. 'Is that your young man?' the American asked. 'I thought you said he was a commander?'

Christine laughed, but she was disappointed that Vinson was not there. If a sailor could wangle his way out to the jetty, why couldn't a commander? She did not know the American Navy then.

He was not there waiting with the group of people at the end of the gangway when the liner finally swung round the corner and inched up to her berth. Passengers on board were waving and calling out: 'Hi, there!' to their friends and relations on the dock, who were wearing thinner clothes than the people who had waved the liner good-bye from England. Christine leaned out of the window and stared and searched, examining quite unlikely men, in case she was wrong and Vinson did not look like she expected.

Shipboard acquaintances kept coming up and asking to have him pointed out to them. She felt ashamed that he was not there. Perhaps they would think that she had invented the story of a fiancé to give herself glamour. Or, what kind of a fiancé was it, they might think, who was not standing tiptoe on the dock to greet his bride?

She felt let down and deserted. He had not come to meet her. Perhaps he was not even going to marry her. She would be stranded alone and penniless in New York, like those G.I. brides you heard about after the war, sailing out to marry men who were either in prison or already married.

In the huge, bewildering customs shed she at last found her luggage and sat on it, waiting for someone to come and help her. When an official came up he was coloured. Christine had never spoken to a coloured man, except once when a drunken negro had tried to snatch her bag in Tottenham Court Road, and she was afraid.

Everyone round her was talking American. She could not see any of the English people who had been on the boat. When she

142

told the customs officer what she had to declare, her voice sounded silly to her and she was afraid he would not understand what she said. He asked her to open all her bags, but he made only a show of looking into them. He kept glancing away from her abstractedly, as if he did not care whether she came into America or not.

He wanted her to open her hatbox, which had nothing in it but her wedding hat. 'Must I?' she said. She did not want his great black hand fumbling about among the veil and delicate flowers.

'Look, lady,' he said, 'I'm sorry, but you picked a bad day. It's a check-up. I'm not inspecting you. They're inspecting me.' He nodded towards a pillar, where a blue-jawed man in uniform with a huge shining badge stood watching him as sternly as the recording angel.

The coloured man smiled, showing the pink inside of his mouth, and Christine felt better. As he helped her to shut her bags, she told him that she did not know what to do because she could not find Vinson.

'You'll be O.K., ma'am,' he said. 'The party will be waiting down there behind the ba'ier.'

Christine looked, and saw the crowd pressing and peering and waving beyond the wooden barrier at the end of the customs hall. Abandoning her luggage, she hurried over and stood irresolute, searching among the faces. She heard Vinson calling: 'Christine!' before she could see where he was.

Suddenly he was there, right at the front of the crowd. He looked smaller than she remembered, and he wore an unfamiliar suit, a bluish sharkskin with a long double-breasted jacket which made his legs look too short; but his face was just the same and she wondered how she had ever forgotten it, and when he kissed her awkwardly across the barrier his skin smelled just as she remembered. She was safe.

She came out to him through the gate and he kissed her again and gave her a corsage of roses, which she tried unsuccessfully in her fumbling excitement to pin on to her suit. He would send a porter for her luggage. He had taken over, and everything was all right.

'Oh, Vin,' she said, taking his arm as they went down to the

143

street in the lift, 'I was so worried when I couldn't see you. I thought you hadn't come to meet me.'

'Not come to meet you? Not come to meet my girl? What do you think I am, darling? You've got an American to look after you now.'

'Well, but,' said Christine, ignoring the slight on Englishmen, 'there were people waiting on the dock. There was even an ordinary sailor, and I thought you'd sure to be there.'

'You have to wangle a pass,' he said. 'I don't believe in pulling rank to get these privileges. Wait here, honey, while I get the automobile.'

He left her on the kerb at the edge of the cobbled space where taxis and cars were coming and going. Coloured porters with square red caps were calling and pushing each other about like children, and policemen were stamping in the puddles, waving their arms and shouting at cars in what seemed to be a permanent state of fury. Not the hysterical, hopping fury of Paris policemen, but a resigned and bitter resentment against everything in sight, as if anyone outside the Force must be regarded as a potential criminal, from whom nothing could be expected but trouble.

The rain fell soft and straight like anywhere else in the world. A bridge-like structure of girders, carrying a road or a railway, rose just ahead, so that Christine could see nothing of New York. It might have been Southampton or Liverpool or Calais or any dockside, and yet, even without the gaily-coloured taxis which were bigger than most English cars, the coloured porters and the policemen looking as if they were extras in a gangster film, you would have known you were in New York. The very air smelled urgently of America. Christine, sensing it for the first time, recognized it with an answering urgent excitement. She was here. It was true. She was in America.

Vinson's car was a black sedan, not as dashing as the Buick he had driven in England, but still impressive by Christine's standards. He said it was only an old jalopy and they were going to get a new one soon, but it had gears on the steering wheel and a radio and all sorts of post-war gadgets, and Christine wondered what Vinson must have thought of her father and his 1939 Vauxhall of which he was so proud.

They drove away from the docks among traffic that terrified Christine. Huge lorries as big as railway engines, in which you could not see the dwarfed driver high above, bore down on them, or raced alongside, threatening to crush the car with their shining chromium sides. She tried not to show Vinson that she was frightened. Once in England, when she had flinched and gasped at a near-accident, he had said: 'Don't tell me you're one of those women who panic in cars', so she was determined not to be.

She did not want him to be disappointed in her in anything. She wanted to be what he would have been expecting while he waited for her to come to him across the Atlantic. He would have been looking forward to showing her America, and expecting her to be impressed, and so she made enthusiastic comments about everything she saw, from the dresses of women on the streets to the advertising balloon which rode in the sky, although she was still too bewildered by the noise and size of everything to take in America properly.

They swept into the Holland tunnel with a change of noise and an increase of speed. It was an endless yellow tube, with cars and deafening lorries all racing along in the same direction, and policemen immured like nuns in little glass boxes at intervals along the tiled walls.

'What do you think of this?' Vinson asked, as proudly as if he had bored the tunnel under the Hudson River himself.

'It's incredible,' Christine gasped, raising her voice above the increased noise of the car. 'I've never seen anything like it.'

'I thought not.' He patted her hand. 'I thought this would thrill you. There's so many things to show you, and I want you so much to like it all. I want you to like America.'

'Oh, I do, Vin,' said Christine, gazing with relief at the pinpoint of light ahead, which showed that the monstrous tube must come to an end at last. 'I think it's wonderful.'

He kept asking her what she thought of America and how she liked her new country, and she kept answering that it was wonderful and she loved it, although she was not sure yet. Driving south from New York, it takes a long time to shake off the soiled fringes of the city. It was ugly, ugly; and although she

145

told herself that all America would not be like this, her thoughts flew back to England.

They were driving on a great highway that rose above the flats of wasteland from which came a vile smell, which Vinson said was the refuse of New York burning.

Vinson drove fast, much faster than he had in England. Christine could not object, because everything else was going at the same speed. She sat tense, clutching the edge of the seat under her skirt, so that Vinson could not see. The traffic went in three solid lines, and all the cars raced along as if they were travelling without thought for anyone else on the road. Time and again it seemed as if the black sedan must scrape the side of another speeding car, and time and again it did not. After a while she began to accept the fact that American drivers knew what they were doing – they must, if they wanted to stay alive five minutes in this traffic – and she relaxed and uncurled her fingers and stopped driving with her eyes, and sat back and looked at Vinson.

His face was set, as it always was when he was driving. His neck went straight up from his spine, and his heavy eyebrows met in a cleft of frown. Now and again he turned to smile at her, but when he turned back to the road his smile disappeared at once. He took his driving very seriously. In England that had seemed to her unnecessary. Over here, where it seemed that you had an even chance of being killed at any moment she thought that probably he was right.

'Vin,' she said, 'I'll never learn to drive over here.'

'Yes you will. My wife can do anything. Besides, you'll have to, if you want to go anywhere in the daytime. The buses aren't too good out at the suburb where we live.'

'I'll never do it. I'll just have to sit at home and wait for you.'

'That's a nice picture. When I'm working I'll like to think of you sitting at home.'

'What shall I be doing?' She could not visualize her married life at all.

'Well, you'll be busy around the apartment, and then there's the radio, and there'll be plenty of women neighbours for you to make friends with. There are about five hundred apartments in this development. That will be nice for you.'

'Yes, I expect so.' She would be like the women in magazine advertisements, having coffee in her trim kitchen with Mary Lou from next door, who had dropped in to exchange cake recipes.

Concentrating on the car, Vinson did not talk to her very much. He pointed things out for her to admire, but they were going so fast that the things had usually gone by before she could see them. She was excited when she saw her first motel, which was called 'Paradise', and had neon signs and a row of little huts like a Butlin's holiday camp, but by the time they had passed motel after motel, each bearing some unsuitable name like 'Ye Olde Manor House', 'Tumbleweed Haven', she began to get blasé and was not surprised by them any more.

The traveller to America expects to be surprised, and for the first hour or so he is. But the most surprising thing about the whole country is the short time in which it ceases to surprise you. The first miles of the road are full of marvels, but too soon you become sated. You cannot be amazed any more. You find yourself sitting back and accepting without question the recurring beads of hot-dog stands, Bar-B-Qs, chromium diners shaped like railway carriages and churches topped by neon crucifixes that are strung along the necklace of the eastern seaboard roads.

By the time they stopped for lunch Christine was beginning to feel as if she had been in America all her life. She was hardly shaken by the size of the roadside restaurant, which had a long snack counter, where people mused over towering sundaes, dozens of plastic-topped tables in booths and a menu better than any West End hotel.

Vinson ordered for her, because Christine did not know what to choose. He was a little offhand and arbitrary with the waitress, who wore a lace handkerchief ruffled on her bosom like a flower. He had been like that sometimes with waiters in England, where it had not got him anywhere. It occurred to Christine that all the American principles of democracy and the pursuit of happiness were not as strong as the principle that in a land of producers the customer is king.

A mammoth red jukebox stood near the restaurant door, and you could put a nickel in a slot on the wall by your table and press a button for the record you wanted. Christine asked

147

Vinson for a nickel. She wanted to press the button marked 'Stardust', but he would not let her.

'Why not? You're meant to. People must like the music, or they wouldn't have that thing there.' As if in answer, the machine leaped into amplified life with a sobbing rendition of 'You darling'.

'There you see, Vin. Someone else has put a nickel in, and now I'll have to wait for mine. If they can do it, why can't I?'

'It was those high-school kids over there. That's all right for them. Look, Christine, this is a good place for us to come and eat, but you and I don't play the jukebox.'

'I can't see why not.' If he were going to put all kinds of taboos and snobberies on her in America, she might as well have stayed in England, where at least she knew what the snobberies were, without having to learn them.

It was a long drive to Washington. In England, such a mileage would have been a tremendous undertaking, with maps and tuning of the car and advice from the A.A., but over here, where the big cities were farther apart and you could average almost twice the speed on the one-way roads, it was a mere afternoon's work.

Christine was asleep with her head on Vinson's shoulder before they got to Baltimore. He had woken her up when they were crossing the bridge over the Delaware River, and she had marvelled dutifully at its span and slept again.

She woke again when they were crawling with the traffic through endless narrow streets, where you could guess what the occupants of the houses were like by the state of their front steps. Rows and rows of thin red terrace houses, some of them with imitation landscapes painted on drawn blinds. Rows and rows of front doors, painted, peeling, or varnished like a coffin, with imitation graining. Set after set of four steps up from the street; some shining white, some dirtied beyond the trouble of an occasional hearthstone; some made of rickety old wood, others replaced by funereal marble; some steps tumbling with negro babies, some a forum for a gang of small boys with pistols and eclipsing cowboy hats; one with a girl in a lavender dress waiting for a boy, or for something to happen; one with an old crone knitting; some with a dead potted plant waiting for the trash collector; some with a young couple to whom the steps were something more than the hundreds of others like them in the row.

'What town is this?'

'Baltimore. Hell of a place to drive in.'

Christine raised her head, afraid that it was in his way.

'Don't take your head away. I like it there. Christine,' Vinson said, as he stopped the car at red traffic lights, 'I'm so glad you've come. I've longed for this.'

'So have I. Oh, Vin, are we really going to be married to-morrow? I can't believe it. Everyone on the boat thought it was awfully romantic to be married as soon as I arrive. And it is, isn't it?'

Her voice was dreamy, but his was practical as he answered: 'It's the best thing. You'd have had to stay in a hotel otherwise, and that would be a waste of money.'

'Wouldn't you have let me stay with you at the flat – apartment, I mean – even if we couldn't be married tomorrow?' Christine asked sleepily, as the lights changed to green.

'In Washington? I work there, don't forget.'

'I wouldn't have minded.'

'The Navy would –'

'Oh, the Navy –' Christine went to sleep again.

It was dusk when they came into Washington down a broad avenue that shone with tramlines, coloured electric signs and the lights of an endless stream of cars. Christine's first impression of the city was that there must be some sort of gala tonight. Nearly every house had its porch lamp turned on, the square glass canopies outside the cinemas were a dazzle of jewel-massed lights beating on the pavement like an insufferable sun, and strings of glaring white electric bulbs outlined the open spaces where used cars were drawn up for sale.

'No,' Vinson said. 'It's just an ordinary evening. I guess it's always like this, but of course this is your first sight of an American city by night. What price Piccadilly Circus now? This is a bit brighter than the dear old Dilly, isn't it?' He sometimes used expressions which he thought were English slang.

'All those second-hand cars.' Christine could not get over

them. 'Why, in England it's almost as difficult to get a second-hand car as a new one. And all these look so shiny and new. Who buys them? And why do they leave them out in the open like that? Don't they get stolen? Perhaps they leave the lights on all night. But that would be awfully expensive. Do they have a man to watch them?'

Vinson did not know. He was not interested in the problems of used-car dealers. They had passed two mammoth churches and were going down a hill now between huge blocks of flats with plate-glass entrance doors and flowering shrubs and ever-greens artistically planted, and he was pointing them out as being swank apartment houses.

'But this is the best address of all,' he said, as the hill steepened and they were among shops again. 'This is George-town,' he said reverently. 'Each side of this avenue. Gee, I wish we could live here.'

'Well, why don't we?'

'We couldn't get near it on my pay. It's mostly diplomats and politicians who live in Georgetown.'

'Well, who wants to live among them?' she said, but he would not be consoled.

'The best address in Washington,' he said regretfully. 'I'd sure like to have it on my notepaper.'

Christine was about to say that she did not see that it mattered, but fortunately, before they could start another of those small dissensions that crept upon them sometimes out of their different points of view, Vinson turned down a side-street and said: 'I'm going to take you past the church where we're going to be married tomorrow. That's why I brought you this way, though it's not the quickest route to the hotel.' He was always much exercised about knowing the shortest way from place to place.

'Is it the church where you always go to Mass?'

'No, but it's a smart place to be married. All the best people come here.'

Christine thought that they should have been married in Vinson's parish church, but she was discovering that the secret of keeping a man happy was not to tell him the things he did not want to hear, so she said nothing.

It was a dignified white church with pillars. Christine was pleased with it, and thought she might look quite well being photographed on the porch after the ceremony, with Vinson in all his gold braid.

'Of course we can't be married actually in the church,' he said. 'It will have to be in the rectory.'

'Why?' Her visions of walking down the aisle in her new dress faded.

'Because it's a mixed wedding. They don't allow non-Catholics to be married in church in this diocese.'

'Well, I think that's pretty stuffy. Aren't I good enough for them?'

'Look, honey' – Vinson moved the car on as a driver behind them sounded his horn an unnecessary number of times – 'we haven't had a religious argument yet. Don't let's start one now. You don't mind my being a Catholic. You said so.'

'At least you go to church, which is more than most men I know do.'

'You see what I mean about Georgetown?' he said, as they drove down a street of pretty little houses which were no two alike; some white, some coloured, some soft red brick snug with creepers, and some with painted shutters.

'Some of these houses are a hundred and fifty years old,' he said, with the same awe he had given to Westminster Abbey.

The houses were charming, and there were trees everywhere, in the streets and in the gardens of the houses. Some of them were lit theatrically by street lamps where insects clustered, and she was reminded of the gilded leaves of London plane trees on a summer night. When she leaned out of the window she smelled the familiar summer city smell, which at the same time endears you and makes you long for the country.

'I think I like Washington,' she said.

There were trees everywhere all over the city. Trees and broad avenues, and then they were driving between the great white State Department buildings, with their clean lines and bold carving.

Christine was genuinely amazed at America now. She did not have to assume admiration to please Vinson. People had told her that Washington was the most beautiful city in America, but although she had lived all her life in London she did not like towns, and she had not believed that any city could be beautiful.

But this was different. She had not expected the Washington Monument to be glowing with light and to rise up serenely from a sea of grass, and although she had seen pictures of what the Capitol dome looked like she had not expected its floodlit, majestic beauty. It soared above the hill like a heavenly body, as if dissociating itself from the machinations and intrigues that went on below.

Vinson drove her around the buildings on Capitol Hill. 'Now, doesn't this make you proud to be an American?' he asked her, sitting very straight behind the wheel, as if someone had waved the Stars and Stripes at him.

Christine pulled her head in through the window. 'I'm not an American.'

'You will be after tomorrow, darling, whatever your passport says. All this will be yours,' Vinson said, waving his hand at the imposing steps of the Senate. 'The government belongs to the people here, you know, not the people to the government.'

'It's beautiful,' Christine said. 'It's sort of depressing, though, to think of all the rubbish that must have been talked here by men with string ties and mouths full of teeth since this building was put up.'

He did not laugh. Perhaps she should not have said this. He could joke about American institutions when he was with his own countrymen, but with her, who was a foreigner, he took his country seriously. She could understand that, because that was how she felt about England. Perhaps after tomorrow, if he thought that marrying him made her an American, she could make jokes about the government.

The hotel was a towering place, with most of the ground-floor walls made of plate glass, so that the people in the lounge and the cocktail bar were like goldfish in a bowl. If Christine had been a down-and-out, she would have come and flattened her nose against the glass to make the hotel guests feel embarrassed.

Vinson's mother, who sounded like something of a hypochondriac, had felt unable to make the trip from Kansas for the wedding, but his sister and her husband had come from Wil-

152

mington to keep the family flag flying. Vinson had assured Christine that they were easy people to get on with, but she dreaded meeting them. What would they think of her? The sister would be sure to be smart. Even with her new clothes, Christine did not think she would ever be smart in the way Americans were. What would they think of Vinson marrying an English girl? Would they say, as she had heard one Wave say to another at a cocktail party Vinson had taken her to in England: 'Isn't an American girl good enough for him?'

The receptionist told them that Mr and Mrs Lamm were waiting for them in the bar. Christine followed Vinson, and a small woman with a monkey face and a mad hat with butterfly antennae stood up and smiled and waved.

She was nice. She went on smiling after she had been introduced to Christine. She told Vinson that she was cute as Christmas and a typical English girl, and when Christine called her Mrs Lamm she said at once: 'Oh, you must call me Edna. You and I are going to like each other.'

Her husband, whose name was Milt and who had a head like a jumbo grade egg and trousers straining across stout thighs, was sold on Christine from the first moment he saw her. Christine conquered the suspicion that it was part of his act to be sold on every woman from the start, and enjoyed hearing him tell Vinson: 'Where did you find her? Now just where ever did you find her? But, Vin boy, she's lovely. She's just the loveliest thing . . .'

Christine did not feel very lovely after a six-hour drive with no chance to do her face or change her wrinkled skirt, but perhaps the light in the goldfish bowl was flattering. She sat back in the red-leather chair, which was shaped like a cut-away barrel, and sipped the strange new taste of bourbon, which she was told she would like and didn't, and wondered if people looking in from outside would envy her for being a frequenter of the Capitol-Carlton Hotel.

Vinson and Edna did not seem to know each other very well. He had told Christine that his family were not close, but she was surprised that he talked so politely to his sister, asking about her trip from Wilmington and whether she was satisfied with her room at the hotel. If Roger had talked to Christine like that, she

153

would think he had gone mad, or had found some new form of humour to try on her.

Everyone seemed to be very polite in America. When Edna suggested that she should take Christine up to her room, the two men immediately sprang to their feet and pulled back the women's chairs and handed them their bags. When they went into the lift a man who was in there took off his hat and held it against his chest, and when they reached his floor he made quite a ceremony of excusing himself to step out past them.

Christine's room was all windows on one side, which would have been nice if the glass had not been very dirty and covered on the outside by grimy wire screens, which kept out the air as well as the flies.

When she spoke to Edna about this, Edna said: 'Don't worry. The hotel has air conditioning.'

'Well, but wouldn't it be much simpler if they just got air in through the windows?'

'Listen, honey,' Edna said, 'you don't know Washington in summer. In about a month there'll be no air to come through the windows, and what there is is like a Turkish bath.'

'I shan't mind. I like the heat.'

'Not this sort you won't. It's frantic.'

'Well, don't put me off,' Christine said. 'I'm looking forward to being married and living here.'

'Sure you are, and I'm very glad you're marrying my brother.' Edna took off her hat and prodded at the heavy coffee-coloured knot of hair that was lodged precariously in the nape of her neck. Although she wore a mad hat and an expensive-looking dress, Christine was relieved to find that she was not a smart kind of person at all. She wore the wrong shade of yellowish powder on her crinkled monkey face. Her hair was untidy and full of unconcealed pins. Her nails were square and unvarnished and looked as if she did all her own laundry, and she walked with an odd little sideways stoop, which made her clothes sag.

'I've been glad about you and Vinson ever since he wrote us the news,' she said, sitting on the bed and kicking off her shoes. 'You'll excuse me, won't you, but I bought new shoes for your wedding and they kill me. Vinson needs a wife. He should have gotten married long ago, though I want to tell you I'm glad he didn't do it, because that girl was a tramp.'

Christine did not ask: 'What girl?' She was not going to admit that Vinson had never told her.

'Why does he need a wife?' she asked, exploring the room, which had spindly modern furniture and a bed made up to look like an upholstered couch. 'Oh, look what a lovely bathroom I've got.'

'Kinda small,' said Edna, squinting towards the bathroom door. She screwed up her face a lot, working it about as she talked as if it were rubber. 'Why does he need a wife? Well, honey, what man doesn't? But particularly in the Navy. There's so much entertaining' – Christine's heart sank – 'and then, you know, Vinson has been so much among other Navy men that he's gotten to be – you'll forgive me if I say it – just a little narrow.' She screwed up her face very tightly and looked at Christine from under the loose puckered skin of her eyelids. Sometimes she looked about thirty-five; sometimes she looked fifty. She might have been any age.

'How do you mean?' Christine went to the window and rubbed on the glass, but the dirt was on the outside. Seven storeys below, a sprinkler had just gone by, and the endless cars were going swish, swish, swish along the wet black street.

'I mean that he's a little given to thinking that life begins and ends with the United States Navy,' Edna said. 'He's lived nearly forty years, and he knows a lot about his job, but not too much about what goes on outside it. He needs someone like you from a completely different world to freshen up his ideas a bit. Maybe I shouldn't be talking to you like this when we've only just met, but we are practically sisters-in-law, and, anyway, I've never believed in two people wasting time walking around each other like a couple of dogs before they can get to know each other.'

'I'm glad. I like you, Edna,' Christine said, not feeling as shy as she would have if she had said this to a comparative stranger in England. 'It's a bit difficult, you know, getting married without any girl friends or anyone to back you up.'

'You're telling me,' Edna said. 'I ran away from home to marry Milt. He was in Kansas City, Missouri, and I don't know

155

a soul there. I tell you, I never was so unhappy. I cried like a fool on my wedding day.' She laughed. Her teeth were white, but prominent and badly spaced. It seemed odd in this land of export dentistry that they had not been properly fixed when she was younger.

'I shall be terrified on my wedding day,' Christine said. 'I shan't know anyone at my own wedding.'

'You'll know Vinson,' Edna said. 'I guess that's about all that matters. You'll be all right, hon. He's a pretty nice guy. You love him, huh?'

'Oh yes. I'm marrying him.'

'Swell. He and I have never known each other as well as we should. I guess he told you we were separated a lot after my parents were divorced, but I know enough about him to like him a whole lot, and I like him even better now that I see he was smart enough to pick someone like you.'

There was a knock at the door and Vinson came in. 'Hi, girls,' he said. 'What are you yattering about?'

'We're talking about you,' Edna said, 'and saying how smart you were to pick Christine.'

Vinson's face, which was more quick and tense in America than Christine remembered it in England, relaxed into one of its most loving smiles.

'I think I was too,' he said. He came over to Christine and put his arm round her shoulder and kissed her. 'How do you like her, Edie? Don't you think she's marvellous?' He rocked her back and forth, and Christine hung her head and smiled foolishly, feeling like a child being shown off to visitors.

'She's a honey,' Edna said. 'I've been telling her she's much too good for you.'

'I know it.' Vinson kissed Christine again, and Edna said: 'Well, I'll be going, kids.' She struggled into her shoes and picked up her hat. 'What do you say we eat in about half an hour, Vinson? Milt's on a new diet, and he has to space his calorie intake exactly, so don't be later than you can help.'

When she had gone, Vinson turned Christine round and kissed her long and properly for the first time since she had come to America. When he kissed her like this she knew why she had come three thousand miles.

After a while he said: 'If you're going to change your dress, Christine, you'd better get around to it, or we'll be late.'

'I will in a minute. Edna won't mind. She's awfully nice, Vin.'

'You'd better get changed now.' He went to the mirror and straightened his tie and smoothed his hair. 'It will be impolite to them if we're late.'

Christine, brought up with Roger, did not see how you could be impolite to a sister. The word in its social sense had no place in her family vocabulary.

'You've had your hair cut again, darling,' she said. 'Why do you wear it so short?'

'Of course, I've had it cut for my wedding. A naval officer doesn't go around looking like a bear.'

'It could be a bit longer without looking like a bear. It's awfully short. You've got a nice shaped head, and you ought to make the most of it.'

He glanced sideways at the mirror to see the shape of his head. 'This is regulation length,' he said. 'My goodness, I'd like to see the Admiral's face if I turned up at my wedding with it any longer than this.'

'Oh,' Christine said. 'Is the Admiral coming?'

'I believe he might,' said Vinson, with reverent hope.

At dinner he talked to Edna about the wedding plans. Milt talked to Christine, asking her how she liked America and applauding her unremarkable answers.

When the food came he poured tomato sauce all over his steak and said: 'This is a bit different to English austerity, isn't it? You ever see anything like this before?'

'If we did, it would be the week's ration for two people,' Christine said. She had discovered on the boat that this was always a sure-fire statement to interest Americans.

'If they'd only pull their socks up over there they could eat like this any day of the week,' Milt said. 'Look at the Germans. The British could take a lesson from them in recovery.'

Vinson had been half listening to their conversation while he

157

talked to Edna. He was conscious of Christine all the time when they were with other people. 'Watch your step, Milt,' he said. 'Be careful what you say about England.'

'Don't worry,' said Milt. 'Christine and I are friends. I think she's just the most wonderful person I've met in ages. You don't mind anything I say, do you, Christine? There – aren't you cute? Of course you don't. Let me tell you, I think Britain's just the finest country.'

He seemed only to have superlative adjectives in his vocabulary. Everything was the finest he had ever seen – the food, the wine Vinson had chosen, Christine's dress. She wondered if he was like this at home. Did he tell Edna all the time how wonderful she was? And, if so, did it sound more sincere than all the praise he was throwing around now?

She also was conscious of Vinson all the time. Accepting the encomiums with which Milt sought to make up for his criticism of Britain's post-war effort, she was half listening to the conversation between Vinson and his sister.

'Oh, not Aunt Felice,' she heard him say. 'She can't come to the wedding.'

'She must, Vinson. She wants to come, and she'd come, anyway, whatever anyone said.'

'Oh no, I can't have Aunt Felice there.' Vinson frowned.

'Why not?' Christine asked.

'Well –' He spread his hands and laughed self-consciously. 'Well, she – she's not quite the type of person one should ask one's guests to meet.'

'He means she's nuts,' said Edna, biting crisply into cole slaw.

Christine did not see that it mattered. Nearly every family had at least one odd relation. If she had been married in England there would have been Great Aunt Isobel, who would have had to be kept from the champagne, and probably that weird, hymn-singing housekeeper of Uncle Leonard's, who everyone thought was his wife, and should be, if she wasn't.

Vinson was quite put out about Aunt Felice. He brooded until the dessert, which was pie with ice-cream. Milt wanted to eat it, but Edna would not let him. He did not tell her that she was the most wonderful woman he had ever met. He told her that she was a goddamn interfering woman, and Edna laughed and told him that he was no better than a greedy hog. Christine liked that. She was used to that kind of amiable family abuse. It was the way her father and Aunt Josephine used to talk to each other.

Vinson did not like it. Christine took his hand and said: 'Don't worry, darling, I won't ever talk to you like that. You shall eat all the pie you want.'

'Vinson doesn't have to worry about his front. He has just the loveliest figure I've ever seen on a man,' Milt said, and Vinson cheered up and squeezed Christine's hand.

After dinner they went for a nightcap to the cocktail bar, where a woman was aggravating the drinkers by playing on a Hammond organ. Sometimes she played on the organ with one hand and on a near-by piano with the other, and that was worse. You could not talk against the organ, and Vinson soon suggested that, in view of the wedding tomorrow, it was time to retire.

He went up with Christine to her room. 'I mustn't stay long,' he said. 'You've got a big day ahead of you.'

'I wish you could stay all night,' Christine said. She liked to shock him, because now that she was his bride, and English to boot, he thought that she should be so proper.

The upholstered couch had been miraculously made into a bed, and they sat on it and began to talk seriously, suddenly realizing what they were approaching tomorrow.

'Are you sure you're not making a mistake?' Vinson kept saying. 'Are you sure you love me? Do you love me more than any other man you've ever known? *Have* you ever loved another man, Christine? We've had so little time together, you haven't told me these things.'

'What does it matter?'

'It does matter. Tell me.' But when she began to tell him about Jerry he did not really want to hear. He dismissed it as: 'Romantic sentiment. You were just a kid. Don't try and make me jealous of a dead man.'

'I'm not. You asked me.' Christine stood up. Her tears for Jerry were finished long ago. This was no time to have them brought out again from the grave where they were buried with

159

him. She took a deep breath and turned round, making herself smile.

'Well, anyway,' she said, 'what about that girl you nearly married, who Edna said was a trump? You've never told me about her.'

'I'd have gotten round to it,' he said. He told her about the girl to whom he had once been engaged. He told her at some length, although she did not want to hear. It was long dead and buried, and it did not sound as if it had ever amounted to very much, but he took it seriously. Apparently he could have a romance in his past. Christine could not.

She grew tired of hearing about the girl, whose improbable name had been Amarella. She came back to the bed and took Vinson's tight-skinned face in her hands and kissed him. 'Never mind about Umbrella,' she said lightly. 'I don't expect you to have reached the age of thirty-eight without being in love with other women besides me. You can tell me about the others another time.'

'Make a nice topic for evenings at home,' he said, looking up brightly, and they both laughed, and kissed again and liked each other. When he left her she went to bed and slept untroubled by the misgivings that are supposed to assail every girl on her last night alone as a single woman.

She did not see Vinson the next morning. She wanted to see him, but he was very strict about the bridegroom not seeing the bride before the wedding.

'No one will know,' Christine had said. 'You could just come along to the hotel and say hullo.'

'It wouldn't be right. I'll see you at the church, darling.'

On the morning of her wedding Christine wanted Aunt Josephine very badly. How Aunt Jo would have enjoyed bringing her a special breakfast in bed, passing a warm iron once more over the little veil of her hat, helping her to dress, dashing at her with a needle and cotton for last-minute adjustments.

The chambermaid was in and out of the room, because she was old and forgotten and a bride excited her, and Edna came in to help Christine to dress, but it was not the same. At this last moment of leaving her old life she wanted someone from the old life to cling to.

Edna was very kind. She was wearing a brown printed silk dress which matched her complexion, and her face looked more creased than ever. It was one of those faces which take a long time to recover from sleep. She helped Christine to pack, she fluffed out her hair at the back under the little white hat, and said that her blue-and-white dress was just darling.

Christine had learned from Vinson not to say: 'Oh, it's nothing much', but: 'Thank you. I'm glad you like it.' She still felt conceited saying it, however.

Vinson had sent her gardenias to wear and a posy of gardenias to carry. She pinned on the flowers and held the posy in front of her, and stood in front of the long mirror behind the cupboard door and thought: A bride. Well, I suppose I look it.

All her life, ever since she was old enough to read fairy tales, she had imagined herself as a bride and dreamed the dream of being dressed up and acting the part of the central figure on the greatest day of her life. Now that the day was here at last the reality was not as real to her as the dream had been. She was too nervous to take in everything that was going on. After the short ceremony, when Vinson kissed her on the church steps for the photographers, she found that she had hardly noticed what had happened in the flower-filled room of the rectory. She would like to have it all over again so that she could pay proper attention to the responses she made, and to the injunctions the bald, spectacled priest laid on them. She could not remember what he had said. All she remembered was Vinson's cool hand holding her hot one, and being suddenly afire with shame when she thought he was going to stumble over a response.

They posed for a group photograph, with Milt wearing his huge buttonhole and sweating at the forehead and Edna in a surrealistic hat, and Art Lee, the best man, with a crew cut, a rigid stance, and hands clenched by the trouser seams.

Christine smiled for the photographers and hoped that Vinson was smiling. She hardly dared to look at him now that he was her husband. He had suddenly become someone else. He had taken over the place of her own independent self on whom she had always had to rely. The Catholic Church had made him a part of herself, and she was as shy of looking at him as one is of seeing oneself in the mirror when one is not quite sure how a new dress will look.

They stood by the door of the hotel reception-room and shook hands with some hundred people who all looked the same to Christine. The women looked at her curiously, and the men, who were mostly in naval uniform, clapped Vinson on the upper part of his arm and said something hearty. It was like a wedding in England, except that none of the guests were shy. They all knew what to say to the bride. They said: 'I'm so happy to meet you', or: 'I'm certainly glad to know you', as if they meant it.

The Admiral did not say that. Admiral Hamer was a small, pouchy man with a domed bald head and irritable eyes, who spoke only in grunts. Vinson saw him coming three couples away in the receiving line, and became distrait and could not concentrate on the guest he was speaking to. When the Admiral arrived before them grunting, Vinson almost fell over himself with deference. Christine was afraid for a moment that he was going to bow from the waist.

The Admiral appeared to be cross at having been dragged to a wedding on a Saturday morning. He did not look at Christine. His wife did, however. She looked her up and down, her eyes calculating behind her long-toothed social smile. She was a spare, unyielding woman, with a hard black straw hat like a Gilbert and Sullivan sailor, and a complexion that looked as if she had spent more hours on the bridge than the Admiral.

Vinson was delighted that they had come; although for all they contributed to the gaiety of nations, Christine thought they might as well have stayed at home. When she was beginning to enjoy herself, drinking champagne and talking to Vinson's friends, who were all very nice to her and very easy to talk to, Vinson kept telling her to go and talk to the Admiral's wife, who was standing in a corner with an untasted glass of champagne, holding court among a few sycophantic women whose husbands were worried about their promotion.

'Must I?' Christine said. 'I don't want to. I shan't know what to say to her.'

'It doesn't matter. Just be charming. I want her to like you. She can matter a lot to our future, you know.'

'I didn't know wives ran the Navy. Though I suppose if the Admiral can only grunt, someone has to do the talking.'

Vinson shushed her, and Art Lee, who was standing near, said: 'Wait till you've been in the Navy a while. You'll see what Vin means.'

'Cut it out, Art,' Vin said. 'Look, Christine, you go and ask Mrs Hamer if you can get her another glass of champagne. I want her to enjoy herself.'

'She hasn't finished the one she's got,' Christine said. 'I don't think she wants to enjoy herself.'

'Now, honey,' Vinson moved away, and Art laughed and said: 'My wife feels just like you do. I can never get her to do the right thing. It's been the ruin of my career. I want you two girls to get to know each other. You'll get on fine. Where is Nancy? I never can find her at parties.'

'I've been talking to her. She's the one with the black fringe, isn't she? She's sweet.'

'Fringe? Oh, you mean bangs. Yes, she's swell. The best. They broke the mould after they made her.'

Christine hoped that Vinson would talk about her like that to other people. She liked Art Lee, although he looked odd, with his long, big-jointed bones and his cropped red hair and his knobby face that looked crudely drawn, like a character in a comic strip.

'You're a nice girl,' Art said. 'I like you.' America was strange and bewildering, but strangers were always giving you confidence by saying they liked you.

'I'm glad you married Vin,' Art said. 'He's a swell guy. We've been buddies for a long time. He and I were classmates at Annapolis, you know.'

A lot of the officers at the reception had told her that. It seemed to be a passport, like Englishmen being at the same public school together.

After the Admiral and his wife had left, and with them a very senior captain, who was Vinson's divisional chief and caused him some unease, the party began to loosen up a little. The women got together in corners and gossiped, and Vinson and his friends got together in other corners and laid their arms across each other's shoulders and raised their voices. If it had been a film, Christine thought they would have sung 'Sweet Adeline'.

She was followed about the room by the mad Aunt Felice, whose only peculiarity, apart from wrinkled khaki cotton stockings and one drooping eye, seemed to be that she felt it her duty to try and tell Christine derogatory things about Vinson's mother. As Aunt Felice had the kind of stammer that gets hung up for a word for seconds at a time, her recital was costive. She was constantly interrupted by another guest claiming Christine, but she persevered, following Christine about, gaping for words, and even pursuing her into the ladies' room to finish the story of 'that Christmas when poor little Vinson was only five'.

Edna had quarrelled with Milt because he had had too much champagne. She rescued Christine from Aunt Felice and told her that it was time for her and Vinson to leave.

'I thought so,' Christine said, 'but I can't get Vin to go. He's having such a good time.'

'Men,' said Edna. 'They're all the same when they get together. Look at Milt.' There was nothing wrong with Milt, who was sitting quietly on a sofa, but Edna was irritated with him today and he could do nothing right. He had been stupid about parking the car, and she did not like the way he had kissed Christine after the wedding ceremony.

'You tell Vinson if you don't go soon the hotel will make you pay more. They're waiting to get the room ready for a cocktail party,' Edna said.

Christine went over to Vinson and said: 'I think we ought to go now, darling.'

'Sure, honey. I'll be with you in a moment. Jim's just finishing one of his stories.'

'Well, I'm going to get ready and have my bags brought down. If you don't come soon I'll go without you,' Christine said, and one of Vinson's friends made a joke about her being his commanding officer.

Christine went upstairs, feeling rather out of it. If Vinson were going to turn out to be one of those men who were always

164

ganging around with the Boys, she might just as well have married an Englishman who always wanted to get into a corner with his friends and talk about golf.

Vinson came into the room while she was powdering her nose. He put his arms round her waist and laid his head against hers, looking at their faces together in the mirror.

'Have a good time at your wedding?' he asked.

'It was lovely. I enjoyed it. Did you?'

'You bet. I'm so glad the Admiral and his wife came. It was just all it needed.'

'Vin, I don't think Aunt Felice is so mad,' Christine said, changing the subject, because she could not share his enthusiasm for the Hamers. 'She's just annoying. She kept trying to tell me things about your mother. Did she really turn your father out of the house one Christmas and refuse to even let him come back for his razor?'

'I don't remember it. Aunt Felice wanted him for herself at one time. That's why she talked that way.'

'Well, she didn't give any trouble. I think everyone enjoyed themselves, don't you? I like your friends, darling. Was I all right? They were very nice to me.'

'I thought Art was being a bit too nice to you,' Vinson said, moving away and flicking at the shoulders of his uniform. 'What were you talking about all that time?'

'Oh, I don't know. Vin, don't be silly. You can't be jealous of your wife at her own wedding.'

'This town is full of wolves. You've got to watch out.'

'Not Art. Darling, he's your friend. You can't talk about him like that. It's ridiculous. I hope you're not going to be jealous of every man I talk to.'

'I've had too much champagne,' he complained.

'I know, darling. Come on, let's go down now and get away on our own, and then you'll feel fine.'

It was exciting running out through the hotel with the people in the lounge staring and standing up to see them, and having confetti thrown over them by the wedding guests as they got into their car. They had not driven more than a block away before a tremendous blowing of horns behind them announced that some of Vinson's friends were following them through the

165

traffic, and when Christine looked out of the back window she saw a shoe bumping along on a string behind the car.

All up Connecticut Avenue they were pursued by the noise and the shoe, and people on the pavements stared and waved, and a traffic policeman grinned and saluted and did not seem to mind the noise.

Christine enjoyed it. 'I feel like a queen,' she said, taking off her hat and shaking out confetti.

'It's tough,' said Vinson, 'but it's just one of those things that happen at weddings. I'll get down a side-street and try and shake them off.'

'Oh, but I like it.' Christine laughed excitedly. 'I want everybody to know I'm coming and that I'm Mrs Vinson Gaegler.' It still sounded an odd name to her, but she was getting used to saying it.

When he had left his hooting friends behind he stopped the car and got out to untie the shoe. While she waited Christine heard another weirder noise swelling towards them.

'Oh, quick, darling,' she leaned out of the window. 'Hurry up. Someone else is after us.'

'Silly,' he said, getting into the car. 'That's not for us. That's only an ambulance or a fire truck.'

'Only!' she said, as the noise grew to a hideous wail of sound and passed by them unseen on a parallel street. 'It's the most awful noise I've ever heard. Worse than the sirens in the Blitz. Why do they have to do it?'

'Gets the traffic out of the way. You hear it all the time.'

'I've heard it on the films, when the cops are chasing gangsters, but I didn't know it happened in real life.' Things were always happening in America that made you feel you were in a film.

Before they got to the country hotel where they were to spend Vinson's few days' leave, he stopped at a filling station and had the confetti brushed out of the car, and went into the men's room to brush off his uniform.

'Oh, why?' said Christine. 'I like our confetti. I don't care if people at the hotel do know we're honeymooners. They're bound to, anyway. I'm sure we look like it.'

But Vinson did not want to look like it. While they were at the hotel he behaved most circumspectly to her in public. When they were alone together he was not circumspect. He was everything that she could wish for in a lover, and she came back from her honeymoon far more in love with him than before.

Chapter Four

It was hard to say when Vinson ceased to be a lover and became a husband. The transition was so gradual that Christine did not notice it happening until one night, when she could not sleep, she kissed Vinson awake and turned him over to her, and he was annoyed that she had woken him.

It was the most hurtful thing that had ever happened to her in her life. When she had stopped crying enough to be able to talk, she said: 'You wouldn't have been like that on our honeymoon.'

'Look, honey,' he said, 'I love you like crazy, but I'm a man with a job of work to do, and I need my sleep. Marriage isn't all honeymoon, you know.'

'I suppose you're right,' she said into the pillow. 'I was silly to think it could be.'

After that she did not make the first advances to him again. He still came to her often as a lover, especially at week-ends when he did not have to get up early, but it was not the same. Hers became the more passive and submissive role, depending on his love rather than hers for its stimulation, just as in ordinary things she was learning to be as dependent and compliant as he wanted her to be.

He was a demanding, sometimes a didactic husband. Having gone her own way all her life, Christine found at first a certain pleasure in playing the part of obedience. It was nice to belong to somebody, and a relief to have the burden of initiative taken from you. Vinson discussed things with her, but it was always he who made the decisions. When they both wanted different things she gave in and let him have his own way. She knew that she was encouraging him to be selfish, but he was selfish by nature, anyhow. She could not change that, and so the smoothest course was to allow it. He did not like it if she pitted her will against his, and so, to keep him happy, she crushed her family tendency to opinionated argument and tried to be the kind of wife he wanted.

She was a good wife. She took a lot of trouble with the apartment, she tried not to be extravagant, and she was always there looking nice when Vinson came home at night.

It was fun to have her own little home to do as she liked in. Housework, with her bright modern kitchen and all her gadgets, was a very different matter from the hopeless drudgery of trying to keep 'Roselawn' from degenerating into a shambles. At first she was very busy, but after a while, when she had done everything she could think of to soften the apartment out of the bachelor habits it had acquired when Vinson lived there alone, she found that marriage had not given her enough to do. There were days when she was bored, bored, bored, and longed for her busy working day at Goldwyn's and for the friends she had left behind in England.

Christine liked most of the women she met, and she had made friends with Art Lee's wife, but Nancy, like most of the naval wives, had children and was busy in the daytime, so Christine did not have anyone to go out with unless she was with Vinson.

She missed Timmy painfully. It was terrible not to be able to have a dog. She came home from a pet shop with a kitten one day, but Vinson said that cats were not allowed in the apartments either, and she had to take it back. She changed it for some goldfish, and they swam moodily round in a coiled glass tube fixed to the kitchen wall, poor company when she was lonely.

Her apartment was on the fourth floor of the building, which had stone stairs and a cold painted iron banister and a row of little letterboxes by the entrance, because postmen did not climb stairs in America. You had to go down and unlock your box with a key. Sometimes Christine lost the key for a few days at a time, and Vinson would be cross, although the letters that came for him were mostly bills. There were a terrible lot of bills. Things like rent and the telephone had to be paid every month, and the month's bill was almost as high as it would be for a quarter in England. Everything in Washington was fabulously expensive, especially when you made the mistake of translating it into terms of English money.

All the apartments had ultramarine painted doors with brass knockers and nippled rubber mats outside. As you climbed the stairs you could hear what was going on behind every door. A baby crying, a saucepan lid falling, a radio commentator declaiming about a political scandal or an airplane disaster. The news never seemed to be about anything else. Christine's door was like all the others, except that when you pressed the bell dulcet chimes sounded on the other side of it. That worried Christine, but Vinson seemed quite happy about it.

Inside the door was a little square hall with the bedroom and bath on one side and the sitting-room on the other. The wall between the sitting-room and the kitchen did not go to the end of the room, and the space where the kitchen merged into the sitting-room was used for dining, which was handy in some ways but awkward in others, for guests sitting at the table could see what kind of chaos your kitchen was in.

The nicest thing about the apartment was the screened porch which led off the sitting-room. It had a tiled floor and cushioned window seats, and potted plants grew there with an ease which would have delighted Aunt Josephine.

The apartments were in great red-brick blocks set up the side of a hill, with a sandy playground in the middle, which screamed all day long with the children who were too young to go to school. At the side of the apartment buildings ran a new road where the residents fought for a place to park their cars at night, and opposite was an expanse of raw earth, where the ground had been cleared for new houses.

Christine's windows faced this clay desert on one side and the playground and the back of another apartment block on the other. There was nothing beautiful to look at, and nothing beautiful to listen to. The playground resounded with children's shrieks, and the occasional scream from a window flung up by an exasperated mother. The apartment walls were thin, and all day and most of the night babies cried and radios clamoured and men and women argued, or gave parties, or knocked on things with hammers.

It was not a very nice place to live. Christine longed for a house, but Vinson said they could not afford it yet, and this was quite a good address for a naval officer to live at. Why, there was even a captain living two floors below them. That made it all right.

The Navy had to be at work by eight o'clock, which seemed

to Christine unnecessary. Other wives told her that their husbands were seldom in the office on time, since they did not have to report in until eight-thirty, but Vinson was never late. He left the apartment punctually at seven-thirty, and it seemed a very long day until he came home. Other husbands left their offices at four thirty, but Vinson often stayed late to finish some work, and she might not see him until after seven. Sometimes he brought work home, or read naval manuals for long hours after supper. He was very conscientious. One day he brought home a dictaphone and put it by his bed in case he had an idea in the night about his work. Christine was sometimes tempted to say rude things into it, but she refrained. She was a good wife, and she would help him to be made a captain, if that was what he wanted.

Christine got up when Vinson did and gave him his breakfast and kissed him good-bye by the front door. She determined that she would kiss him good-bye until the end of their days together. When you did not kiss your husband good-bye in the morning and hullo in the evening it was the end of a proper marriage. It happened to a lot of people, but how exactly did it come about? Did the kisses become cooler and more perfunctory until gradually they faded away to nothing? Or was there one terrible day when you had quarrelled and you did not kiss him good-bye, and the quarrel was still with you in the evening, and he just unlocked the door and flung down his cap and you did not get up to greet him, and that set the pattern for all the days to come, long after the quarrel was over?

Sometimes, after Vinson left in the morning, Christine went back to bed with the paper, which was about twenty times the size of the one she used to read in London. She could never find her way about the Washington newspapers, which were riddled with stories of political corruption, the names of victims of air disasters and road accidents, and society news about gay little parties given by women with German-Jewish names.

When she had had her bath and set her hair, which she could not pin up at night now that she was married, she cleaned up the kitchen and washed the supper dishes from the night before. Vinson would never let her do the dishes at night, although she always itched to get out to the kitchen after

171

supper. He wanted her to sit with him, although he usually worked or read the paper or listened to the radio and did not talk to her very much. It sometimes seemed as if they had exhausted nearly everything they had to say to each other at supper.

In England, before they were married, there had always been so much to talk about. Vinson had been interested in what she had to tell him about her day at the shop, and there was so much to discover about each other's past lives. But now that they had told nearly everything about themselves that they intended to tell, what was left? Sometimes there seemed to be a great vacuum between them, a no-man's-land across which they could not reach each other. Christine would look up from her book or her sewing to where Vinson sat dangling a house shoe from his toe, and realize in a moment of panic that she was married to him and that he was a stranger.

She wondered what other married couples talked about when they were alone. Gossip, probably, about people they both knew, but Vinson did not care for gossip. He had definite ideas about people. He either liked them and they could do no wrong, or he did not like them and he could not hear any good about them. That was that, and he was not interested in the fascinating details of their lives.

Marriage was supposed to bring you close, but sometimes, as you got to know a person better, it drove you farther apart. When you did not know someone very well, irritating habits and small disagreements were passed over in the excitement of discovering the things you did have in common. But when you were sealed within the walls of marriage for ever, small inadequacies, even tiny differences of mood, could grow out of proportion and push you both as far back into yourselves as if you had a real quarrel.

When Vinson came home feeling masculine and wanting to love her, everything was all right between them. At such times they were happy together, and in these first months of their marriage there were enough of these times to make up for the moments when Christine struggled against disappointment like a fly caught in a cobweb.

She was happy. Of course she was happy. She had wanted to

172

be married, and now she was. It would come out all right. Marriage was not as easy as it looked at first sight, and if there seemed to be anything wrong it must be her fault. She would be more loving and more tolerant and everything would be all right. Everything *was* all right. Think what some people's marriages were like! She and Vinson were lucky.

These things she told herself as she cleaned her apartment and listened to the morning quiz programmes on the radio.

There had been nothing like them on B.B.C., except perhaps Wilfred Pickles, but 'Have a Go' was only a very mild version of these programmes where people from the studio audience were made to tell the microphone the most intimate things about themselves, before they tried to answer the general knowledge questions that could bring them fabulous sums of money, or a precision-built plastic rocking-chair or a television set with a tone 'as mellow as an old Stradivarius violin'.

Whether they won or lost, of course they were given samples of whatever product was sponsoring the programme. When some colourful bearded character from the backwoods was hauled up to the microphone to tell his simple story to the amazed children of progress, Christine wondered how he felt about lugging home to his rustic retreat six giant-size boxes of Foamo, the new miracle sudsmaker that cuts dishwashing time in half, yet is mildest of all to your hands. The sponsors were usually paying his bill at a hotel in Chicago or Hollywood or wherever the programme came from, so he probably gave the Foamo to the chambermaid and went happily home to dip his tin plates in a cold mountain stream, with a hundred dollars in his pocket for knowing who was the manager of the Boston Red Sox baseball team in 1932.

There was one programme which shamelessly exploited people's misfortunes and tragedies to provide entertainment for the vast morning audience of housewives all over America. You were supposed to write in to the studio that your child was going blind, or your wife crippled from polio or your home burned to the ground with all your savings tied up in an old sock inside it. The worse you could make it sound the better, for whoever had had the most ghastly things happen to them was asked to come along to try and win money for an operation on their child, or a wheelchair for their wife, or a down payment on a new home, so that these wonderful, wonderful people could make a new start in Little Rock, Arkansas.

It was no doubt a charitable idea, besides being a good advertisement for soap, but Christine sometimes found it quite embarrassing to listen to the tales of woe told by these 'wonderful people'. Anyone who came to the microphone was automatically a wonderful person. Everyone was buddies and bursting with the milk of human kindness, but the plight of the wonderful people, telling their stories of crippling and ruin and sudden death for the sport of listeners, was reminiscent of the freak at a circus, exploiting his misfortunes for cash. Once a woman who had lost a husband in the last war and two sons in Korea broke down and had to be led away, and a man whose wife had died having their fifth baby sobbed right into the microphone and got the biggest applause of all.

It was all very embarrassing. Worse still when the unfortunates could not answer the question and had to trail back to Kokomo, Indiana, or Gallipolis, Ohio, with the fare wasted and the glittering prize unwon. If you could be very pathetic, however, a listener might call up the studio and offer to give you a piano or a half share in a garage or your fare to the sanatorium where your wife languished. That was very, very wonderful, and all the announcers got madly excited and handed out bars of soap all round. Christine often thought that if the benefactors had money to spare for plausible unknowns it might have been better to help their family or friends nearer home.

Better perhaps, but not so spectacular, for if charity began at home the listening millions would not hear about it, and be softened up for soap buying.

Whatever Christine felt about the programme, she always had to listen to it while she pushed her vacuum cleaner or watered her plants, much as one is impelled to stop and watch a street accident. When it was over she switched off the radio, made sure that she had her keys in her bag, for she had locked herself out more than once and had to take a taxi to Vinson's office, and went out to do her shopping.

It was a quarter of an hour's walk to the shops. Down a hill, under a railway bridge where there was often a puddle of

174

muddy water which cars splashed on to your stockings as they sped unheeding by, and up a winding hill on the other side, past house after little suburban house with awnings on the windows and cutely planted evergreens and sometimes a light by the gate made like a miniature street lamp.

One of the houses had a lamp held aloft by a plaster statue of a dwarf dressed as a jockey. He was fastened to the gatepost by a stout chain and padlock, although Christine did not think he was in any danger of being stolen.

Some of the houses had the owners' names painted on little white boards and stuck into the front lawn like Keep-off-the-Grass notices. It was always the people with the oddest names who had them planted there in bravado, as if to show that they were not ashamed of them.

The shopping centre, when she reached it, was all that she could wish for. There was a Woolworth's, and a hardware store that sold every kind of nail the world had ever made, a florist where she bought her plants, a drugstore with a soda fountain where she treated herself to banana splits, until Vinson told her she was getting fatter, and finally the supermarket, which she did not think she would ever cease to enjoy, however long she lived in America.

The supermarket has become one of the natural phenomena of American life. It would be a small and backward village indeed that did not have one. Children are brought up to it and never know the friendly tea and biscuit smell of a corner grocery. No one stops any more to think how wonderful it is, but to anyone fresh from post-war England the supermarket is a marvel, a cornucopia of the world's riches.

The first time Christine ventured into her local supermarket she thought she was in heaven. She took her little wire basket on wheels and pushed it round, gaping at the thousands of tins on the shelves, at the vegetables freshly washed and wrapped in cellophane, the deep-freeze locker where you could get whole meals all ready to be thawed out and eaten, and the butcher's glass-fronted refrigerator, which was a jewel case of pork chops, lamb chops, legs of veal, breasts of chicken and crimson rounds of the kind of steaks Christine had long since forgotten.

In England, when you see something unusual on the grocer's

175

shelves, you buy it even if you do not need it at the moment, because it may never appear again. It took Christine a little time to drop this habit. She kept seeing things that she had craved for years, and she bought so much that she could hardly carry it home, and then had no room for all the tins in her small kitchen.

Soon, however, she managed to get into her head that she could buy anything she wanted at a moment's notion and up to nine o'clock on Saturdays, and so she curbed her enthusiasm. She had to because she was spending too much. The prices were terrifying. When you got to the cash register at the end of the store where the incredibly quick man, who had his name pinned to his overall in a little celluloid card case, reckoned up the contents of your basket, the final sum which sprang up on the till was always more than you expected. Vinson gave her money every Monday, and she did not like having to ask him for more before the end of the week. He always gave it to her without saying anything, but she did not think he liked it.

She grew canny. She compared prices and saved a cent here and there like any Service wife. She learned not to ask for a 'joint' of meat. She had tried that and the butcher thought she meant pig's knuckles. She learned what a chuck roast was, and 'fryers' and 'picnics', although she never did discover what standing ribs might be. She learned to call a tin a can and Vienna sausages Wienies, and she tried to make herself say tomatoes with an American A. She was learning the ropes.

The suburb where Christine and Vinson lived was in Maryland. It was a long journey from there to the centre of Washington. No buses ran past the apartments, so she had to walk fifteen minutes to the shopping centre and take a bus from there to the District line, where you had to change, because the state transport systems would not run into each other's territory. You got on to what Christine had quickly learned to call a streetcar, after she had asked a man painting white lines on the road where the trams stopped, and he had straightened up and stared at her as if she ought to be in St Elizabeth's asylum.

You had to put fifteen cents into the slot just inside the streetcar door. Christine was always careful to have a nickel and a dime ready, because, although most of the drivers were pleasant, some of them were crotchety and she was nervous of asking them for change. She thought that if she had to be a tram driver and a conductor at the same time, she would be crotchety too and have the ulcers they were popularly supposed to possess.

It was a forty minute ride to the centre of the town where the cinemas and the best shops were. You stopped and started and stopped and started and jerked, and the bell clanged like a loco-motive in a switchyard, and the streetcar's radio played dance music and told you to buy a reconditioned sewing-machine for no money down and a long, long time to pay on the magic credit system. It also told you where you could borrow money on the easiest, friendliest terms in town. It exhorted you, it begged you to borrow money. It encouraged you to spend more than you earned and then pay off your debts by getting into debt to a loan company. It told you to forget that you had been brought up to think there was anything shameful in borrowing money. There was nothing wrong with it. All the best people did it. It was one of the most delightful business transactions you could make, and jolly Jim Jedwin was there at the Anacostia office to help you, and friendly Art Farmer would welcome you at the Friend-ship Heights branch. Just plain old country folks all of them, eager to give you the old-fashioned greeting of a simple, homey firm.

And so it went on. The music played. The usurer's front man rollicked on about loans, and the streetcar jerked and stopped and started and clanged, and finally Christine got off at Fif-teenth Street and dived for the pavement among the phalanx of cars that she never believed would stop for her.

She sometimes spent an afternoon walking about looking at the dresses and hats and shoes in the shop windows, but she did not often risk going inside. Vinson was particular about her appearance. He was always saying: 'You must get the right kind of dress' for this or that party, or: 'You can't go to the Henderson's without a hat', but if she spent too much his face tightened up when he went through her cheque stubs at the end of the month.

He was a great one for saving, and Christine was glad, although she had never learned how to save herself. To her, money was money, to be enjoyed when you had it and wished for when you did not; but Vinson had been saving for a long time, and soon perhaps they would be able to get out of the apartment and have a house with a garden – and children?

When they talked about having children, Vinson always stuck to his original opinion that they should wait a year or two 'until we see how things are'. He was always thinking that there was going to be another war at any moment. It was depressing. Christine wanted to have a child soon. It would give more point to her life, and make her days less lonely.

'I'm nearly thirty-five,' she said. 'I oughtn't to wait too long. Soon I'll be too old. I'm dreadfully old now.'

'Women are in their physical prime at thirty-five,' he said. He had read that in a magazine.

Sometimes, when she went down-town, she went to the cinema to while away the long afternoon. Once she went into a big book store with the idea of perhaps getting into conversation with the assistants and talking the language of her old life at Goldwyn's, but they were offhand and they did not seem to know anything about the books they sold, and so she did not try to talk to them.

Going home was a nightmare if you timed it wrong and tried to get on a streetcar when all the workers were pouring out of the shops and offices. You had to wait on a narrow wooden platform in the middle of the street with cars swishing close to your legs and sometimes the rain coming down on your head. Car after car was full, and when the driver did consent to cram in a few more bodies there was no queuing system, and it was every man for himself if you wanted to get home at all. Christine always had to stand up all the way to the District line. The only man who ever got up and gave her a seat was a coloured man. When she told Vinson this he would not believe it. He did not like negroes. He said they were the ruin of Washington and someone ought to stop the evil that Roosevelt had wrought in letting them encroach all over the town like termites.

Christine did not agree with him. She liked to see so many coloured people about. It made her feel that she was in an exotic country. She was fascinated by their high voices and by the loose, bent-kneed walk of the men, the garish clothes of the women and the way they sat about on broken chairs outside their rickety homes in the evening sun, with the hair of the stick-legged little girls pulled into tight plaits that sprung from odd places all over their heads.

She had a friend called Maxwell, who did odd jobs around the apartments. He was very black indeed and he wore a bellying cinnamon-coloured cap and had one thumb missing and a silver plate in his head from the war. She asked him to clean the outside of her windows, and Vinson came home too early and found Maxwell having coffee and cake in the kitchen and telling Christine the sins of his first wife.

Vinson was cross. 'You must learn that you can't encourage them,' he said. 'Give them an inch and they'll take a mile. I know these Shines. The next thing will be he'll be asking you for money. You'll see.'

'Oh no,' Christine said. 'Not Maxwell. He's terribly honest. He even told me when I gave him too much for the time he'd worked.'

'Softening you up,' Vinson said, 'for future benefits.'

'Oh no, darling. You mustn't be unfair. You're absolutely wrong,' Christine said, but it was not two weeks before Maxwell rang the door chimes to say that if he did not have three dollars to pay off arrears of rent he would be turned out of his house.

Christine gave him the three dollars. She did not tell Vinson, partly because it would be unfair to Maxwell, and partly because she did not want to admit she was wrong. After that Maxwell occasionally touched her for half a dollar to take his wife to the movies, but he carried her shopping for her when she met him in the street, and he unstuck windows that would not open, and told her about his method for picking up girls when he was in the Navy – 'You is on the street with a long black cigar, and you gits her eye in yo' eye and you keep it there' – and he was altogether quite a pleasure to her.

The ordeal of getting to town and back in the streetcar determined Christine to learn to drive Vinson's car and get her permit as soon as possible.

He was loath to teach her. 'It's dangerous,' he said. 'It's nothing like your London traffic. I'm so afraid you'll get into trouble and get yourself hurt, darling.'

Christine liked him to be concerned about her, but it did not deflect her. 'I drove all right in England. You let me drive the Buick, and you said I was the only woman you'd ever not been scared to drive with. But of course that was when you were courting me.'

'Could be,' he said, 'though you didn't drive so badly, for a woman. But you'll find it so hard to learn to drive on the right.'

'You learned to drive on the left in England pretty quick. I can do it if you can. Take me out tonight and let me try and I'll bet you I could go and take my test tomorrow.'

'Oh no, honey!' He did not want to think she was too efficient. 'Besides, there are all sorts of highway regulations you'll have to learn. You can't treat the Washington cops like you treated your London bobbies.'

'I'll learn. I will be careful. Oh, please do take me out tonight. We could find a side-road, if there are such things in this part of the world.'

He said that she should have a learner's permit. He said that there was hardly any petrol in the car. He said that he had meant to work. Finally, when he saw how much she wanted it, he agreed to take her. Although he was selfish, his honest desire was to make her happy, although his ideas of what should make her happy were not always the same as hers. When he bought her presents, for instance, he consulted his own taste rather than hers. He bought her great purple orchids, and she did not tell him that she liked the little butterfly ones better. He thought she ought to like heavy and ornate jewellery, and he never discovered that she preferred small and delicate things.

Christine got on quite well with the car among the intricacies of boulevarding, and three-way traffic lights and one-way streets, although Vinson made her nervous by being nervous himself and shouting: 'For God's sake, watch it!' when she was doing no wrong. She was not sure whether he was afraid for her or the car.

Resigned to the fact that she was bent on driving and not being for ever the helpless little wife in the passenger seat, he got her a book which told her all the traffic rules. When she had driven with him a few more times she prevailed on him to take her up to get her permit, although he did not think she would pass the test. His possessive love for her did not embrace too great a faith in her capabilities. The estimable Miss Cope was a ghost of the past.

In the great white Municipal Building she was sent into the examination room, while he had to wait on a bench outside. He bade her farewell with glum tenderness. It was rather like going to the dentist.

It was a long room like a schoolroom, with some fifty desks at which people sat with their legs twined round the chairs, hunched forward and sucking their pens as if they were struggling with a Matriculation paper. At the teacher's desk sat a middle-aged policeman with grey hair and benevolent spectacles.

Christine found an empty desk and sat down to look at the question paper lying on it, taken back all at once to the moment of panic at the start of school examinations, when all you had studied fled from you, and you hardly dared to look at the question paper for fear that the fiends had tricked you after all and were asking that impossible one about: 'Compare the Medieval Guilds with modern Trade Unions. What was the main difference? Describe the influence of Christianity on both these movements.'

The driver's permit test, however, was more like an elementary intelligence test for backward children. There were three alternative answers to each question. They were written out, and all you had to do was to put an X in the space opposite the one you thought was right, so that, provided you could read, it did not matter whether you could write or not.

Some of the people round Christine did not look as if they could read or write. They sat at the desks hopelessly, as if they had come to the end of their powers and could go no farther. One man looked as if he had been there several days. His face was unshaven and his hair was on end from the amount of times he had pushed his pen through it. The floor round him was littered with cigarette butts. From time to time he fetched up great sighs, like a man in travail.

One or two bright boys were finishing their tests and taking them up to the policeman at the teacher's desk, looking as smug as the loathsome candidates at school examinations who keep going up for more writing paper, when everyone else is struggling to think of enough to fill the paper they have been given.

Christine determined to get full marks. The questions were mostly very simple, even if you had not read the book of traffic rules. One of them was: 'If a streetcar stops in front of you, would you (*a*) Stop and wait for the people to descend? (*b*) Blow your horn to hurry them up? (*c*) Drive on and make them get out of your way?'

Another was: 'If an automobile comes up to pass you on your left, would you (*a*) Increase your speed? (*b*) Pull over to your right to give him room? (*c*) Swerve left and crowd him out?'

The desks were close together, and Christine saw the man next to her ponder a long time over this question, and finally put his X in the space marked (*a*). She wondered if he would get his permit. He looked as if he might want to be a truck driver, and would need it.

When she had finished she took her paper up to the policeman, who glanced through it briefly, made some cryptic calculations and came up with the score of ninety-five. She did not think she had made any mistakes, but perhaps you were never given full marks, in case it looked like cheating.

The policeman covered each of her eyes in turn and made her read some letters on a chart and tell him the colours of a set of red, amber and green lights. As they were placed in the familiar order of traffic lights, you could have got it right, anyway, even if you had been colour blind. Then he told her that she had a pretty English accent, lady, asked her if she was in the diplomatic service and passed her on to a window where she waited in a line for a rattled woman with hair escaping all over a grey cardigan to take her papers.

She sat with Vinson and waited half an hour for her name to be spelled out over the loudspeaker. The rattled woman could not trust herself to pronounce any name more complicated than Smith. Then she had to go to other windows and wait for other half-hours until she was finally given a fistful of papers and sent to take her driving test. There seemed to be more red tape and forms than in Socialist England.

Vinson was inordinately proud of her for having got ninety-five out of a hundred. It was nice that he was pleased, but not very flattering that he had expected her to say that she would have mown down crowds at a streetcar stop, or pushed cars off the road if they tried to pass her.

Waiting in the big car park where the driving tests were held they watched a red-faced man in a very old Ford trying to park the car between two white posts, while policemen and examiners looked cynically on.

'Jesus,' said Vinson. 'Those markers are awfully close. You'll never make it, honey.'

'Of course I will. Just because I scraped a fender the other day by bad luck. You've never got over that scratch. Don't belittle me, Vin. You make me nervous.'

'Don't be. Just take it easy. Don't lose your head. Make a fresh try if you ball it up first time. Don't be nervous.'

'I'm not, but you're making me. Please, Vin, don't watch while I'm doing it.'

He promised not to look, but she felt that he was standing behind her watching when her turn came. It took her three tries to get the car parked properly, but at least she did not knock the poles down and run over a policeman's toe, as the man in the Ford had done.

An examiner wearing a pair of blue jeans and an old leather flying jacket climbed wearily into the car with her and said, without looking at her: 'Go ahead, lady. I'll tell you where.'

Christine had been driving for fifteen years, but with his jaundiced presence on the seat beside her and his turgid eye looking through the windscreen at the course she took she felt as if she had hardly been in a car before. It felt odd to be driving so primly and carefully, making exaggerated hand signals and letting every pedestrian in Washington pass in front of her.

With no alteration of his countenance the examiner shifted his gum to the other cheek and began to try tricks on her. He told her to turn left when there was a sign saying NO LEFT TURN. He told her to turn right when the street on the right said DO NOT ENTER. He said: 'Go on. Go ahead', when a green light changed to amber. Vinson had warned her that the examiner might play games like this, so she was careful, and he shifted his gum back to the other side, foiled.

They drove round the city blocks for about ten minutes. Christine dared not talk to him, in case it was against the rules, as if you were trying to curry favour, and he did not offer any conversation except the statement that she was British and must be in the diplomatic corps.

When they had finished the tour he got out of the car without saying anything, wrote something on his papers, gave them to her and went away without a word.

Vinson came up with an anxious face. 'I've passed!' she told him, and kissed him in front of everybody, which he did not like when he was in uniform.

Now that she could drive she often took the car into Washington to go shopping or do a little gentle sightseeing, but she soon found that the difficulty of finding somewhere to park was almost as much nuisance as the dreary ride in the streetcar. Parking lots and garages were expensive, but every space on the street seemed to be taken by people who dashed into town at nine o'clock and stayed there all day. When you did see a space it was always on the wrong side of the road, and by the time you had described a complicated geometrical figure round the block to get to it someone else's big fat car was always there.

The only empty spaces were the ones that said NO PARKING. Christine sometimes risked them, until one day she came back to the car to find a police ticket stuck under the windscreen wiper.

It was Vinson's boast that he had never had a parking ticket in Washington. When Christine got hers he was almost as upset as if it were a prison sentence.

'I knew you shouldn't be driving here,' he said. 'I knew you'd get into trouble.'

'It isn't trouble. Everyone gets tickets. Nancy Lee gets one every week. She told me.'

'What Art's wife does and what my wife does are two very different things,' Vinson said. He had never liked Nancy since she had taken Art away from him when they were sharing an apartment in Bethesda five years ago.

He wanted to go to the police station with Christine. He said he might be able to do some talking, but Christine thought she would rather do it herself. There was no talking to be done, however. She walked in and put her ticket on the high counter, an officer in shirtsleeves with his heavy badge sagging the front of his shirt said: 'Three dollars', she paid up, another officer stopped filing his nails to write her name and address in a ledger, and that was that. No muss, no fuss, as the corn-remover advertisements said.

When she wanted to use the car she had to take Vinson to work in the morning and fetch him at night. She had already driven with him on the maze of roads that surrounds that mammoth temple of Mars, the Pentagon, and she had got over her first alarmed surprise at the thousands of cars going from every direction along the roads that loop over and under each other like a fantastic model railway.

She had not known what it was like at eight o'clock in the morning, however, when half the military might of America was converging on its desks to fight for freedom and democracy. The first time she took Vinson to work at the Arlington Annexe, just above the Pentagon, she could hardly believe there were so many cars in the world, let alone merely going to work for the U.S. Government.

From the jammed Key Bridge onwards you could hardly see the road for cars. They drove in a solid mass, and when they left Rosslyn and came out on to the rolling green open space that exists solely for the purpose of containing the criss-crossing loops and swirls of roads that are necessary to get people to and from the Pentagon there were cars everywhere as far as the eye could see. Cars rushing, cars crawling, cars going in every direction like ants with an unknown purpose, and cars drawn up in their thousands in cindered car parks, as if the biggest football match in creation was going on.

She did not think she would ever find her way home. When she left Vinson at the Annexe he told her to go back the way they had come, but all the roads looked the same to her. She missed a vital turn and found herself going round and round the Pentagon with no hope of ever finding the way out. You could not stop anywhere on the road, so she drove into a car park, took a deep breath and surveyed the landscape, trying to figure out a way back to the Key Bridge. But in this traffic system the road you should take probably did not run in the direction you wanted to go. It was liable to swoop upwards in a clover leaf to get you across a bridge over another road. She ventured out again and thought she was more successful. She had the river and the bridge in sight, but the road took a sudden turn and plunge and she was back again at the Pentagon, going round in circles.

When she was a child she had been lost in the Hampton Court Maze. She remembered how she had run round and round, crying because she was lost to the world for ever. Crying and screaming had brought her mother then, but it would do nothing for her now. She went back into her car park, wondering if she would have to stay there all day until it was time to fetch Vinson.

An Army officer drove up in a green Chevrolet and told her peevishly that she was in his parking space. His eyes looked bruised and bloodshot as if he had a hangover, but he told her how to get back to the bridge, and this time she managed it. It had taken forty minutes to drive out to the Annexe with Vinson. It took her an hour and a half to get home.

She was so unnerved that she did not take herself for the drive she had planned, but parked the car with the aid of Maxwell, who was cutting grass, and went back to bed and slept for the rest of the morning.

She allowed herself plenty of time to go back and fetch Vinson. He had said to her once: 'My wife must never be late. Nothing looks worse than a man waiting around for a woman.'

'Except a woman waiting for a man.'

'You know you've never had to wait for me.' It was true. He was never late. Christine had always been late for everything all her life, but with Vinson she made great efforts to be on time. By luck she found the right road to the Annexe at the first attempt and was there much too early. She backed the car into Vinson's numbered parking space and listened to the radio until it was nearly half past four and she could begin watching the doors for her husband.

At exactly four-thirty the high glass doors opened. A woman came out, then two coloured men, a naval officer, three girls, and then suddenly a whole horde of people, who poured down the steps in a solid stream and made for the gate in the wire fence. They were also coming out of another door farther along the building, and that stream joined the stream from the main doors, until there was a floodtide of hurrying people, some white, some black; girls, men, naval officers, cripples, hunchbacks, even a neatly clad dwarf or two. No rush hour that Christine had ever seen was anything like it. It was all humanity, jammed into one building and all gushing out at the same moment as if someone had opened a sluice-gate.

She did not see Vinson at first. There were so many naval officers dressed like him, and so many with his slight build and springy walk. She had already waved to two strange men, and was wondering whether to wave to another who looked like Vinson from a distance, when his head suddenly came in at the car window, with his white teeth shining and his flecked brown eyes eager to see her.

Driving home with him seemed so easy that she wondered how she had ever missed the way that morning. She soon learned her way to the Annexe and back, but she always had to keep her mind on the road. If she let it wander while she was driving she was apt to find herself carried away on a curving branch road that might lead her back to Washington, or out to Alexandria, or descending again on the Pentagon to drive round and round that hopeless merry-go-round designed by someone far cleverer than the driver of any car.

When she did not have the car she waited in the apartment for Vinson to come home. She always changed her dress and did her face, tidied away her ironing-board or her sewing, because, although it pleased him to see her busy at domestic tasks, he liked her to be unemployed when he came home, and ready to open the front door as soon as she heard his whistle on the stair. He had a special whistle for her, two rising notes, such as one might use to call a dog. He trained her to answer this promptly, and he got her so attuned to it that even when he whistled very softly she could hear it, as a dog will answer to a high-frequency whistle that the human ear cannot detect.

Sometimes, when they were sitting with people, he would whistle very softly from across the room and Christine would raise her head and look at him, although the person to whom she was talking had not heard. Vinson liked to show off this trick in public. It made him feel like Svengali.

Christine had to be ready in the evenings in case he came home punctually, but more often he stayed on to finish some work when the other people in his office had gone, and Christine waited, and worried whether the supper would spoil, and wondered whether, if she had a drink and cleaned her teeth afterwards, he would notice. He did not like her to drink alone. He liked her to wait until he came home and made his special brand of martini, which took a lot of trouble and pouring back and forth from different jugs, but tasted no different to her from any other.

She always looked forward to seeing him. Her days were often long and lonely, and she saved up small items of news for him during the day and planned how she would tell them to him. But sometimes, after he had kissed her and pressed her hard against the brass buttons of his tunic, when she started to tell him something she had been saving up, he made the wrong kind of answer, or interrupted her, and it fell flat. That often happens when you plan a story to tell someone, because while you are planning it you write all the dialogue yourself – theirs as well as yours – and then, of course, they don't know their part.

Often Christine looked forward eagerly to chattering round Vinson in the kitchen while he went through his methodical motions of mixing martinis, and often she was disappointed because he did not think the same things funny, or was not as interested as he should have been in what the man at the drugstore had said.

Sometimes when he told her a piece of news from his day, she heard herself making the wrong comment on it, and was immediately sorry, because he, too, might have been planning while he was driving home how he would tell it to her, and now she had disappointed him, and she knew how it felt.

In the afternoons, while she waited for it to be time for Vinson to come home, she listened to the radio programmes that she had learned to call soap operas. These were a series of domestic dramas, each lasting a quarter of an hour, during which time a set of characters with easily distinguishable voices went through a chain of emotional crises. They were supposed to represent

188

ordinary families – 'people just like people you all know' – but if any ordinary family had experienced so many ups and downs as these radio characters suffered from day to day they would all be in a psychiatric ward before long. The B.B.C. programme 'Mrs Dale's Diary' was a direct descendant of these soap operas, but while Mrs Dale and her tedious suburban family led a fairly eventful life they never experienced anything like the intrigue, murder and illicit passion in which their American counterparts indulged.

Some of the soap operas had been going on for years, but the characters in them never seemed to get any older or wiser. They were suspended in time, like the eternal Bob Cherry and Billy Bunter in the English boys' weeklies, who had been in the Remove at Greyfriars as long as Christine could remember. They had a faithful listening audience, who had followed their fortunes from the beginning and perhaps knew more about the radio characters than they did about their own husbands. At the same time, however, the script writer had to cater for the listener who might be hearing the programme for the first time and would not know who was who. A character, therefore, would have to refer, even with intimates, to 'my wife Ethel', or 'the landlady, Mrs Gooch', or 'Paula Revere, the leading lady in my current Broadway show', which struck a stilted note in an otherwise free-and-easy dialogue.

Since more and more soap operas had hit the air to sell detergents and deodorants and headache pills, it was the fashion in America to condemn them for the nonsense they were, but Christine suspected that more people listened to them than would admit it. She herself, being new on their onslaught, was fascinated, and followed the fortunes of the various sets of characters with deep interest. Sometimes she tried to tell Vinson about them, but he did not want to hear, and if the programme was going on when he came home he would switch it off, so that Christine would have to wait until the next day to know whether Joanne had finally agreed to marry Anthony (with the H pronounced) or whether Leslie (pronounced Lesslie) had freed himself from the ropes in time to go after the burglar who had stolen the secret formula for the wonder drug.

There was a programme about a poor young widow with two

children, who played out 'the eternal conflict between a mother's duty and a woman's heart'. The children were never heard from – perhaps because child actors would be in school at the time the programme was relayed – and the young widow sometimes went off for days at a time to follow some twist of the plot, without thought of her Mother's Duty, but such details did not matter in the larger drama of the soap operas. The children had probably played an important part at the beginning of the series – heaven knows how long ago – and after the script writer got tired of them no one thought of changing the announcement record about the Mother's Duty and the Woman's Heart. The public would not have wanted it changed, anyway. It was the kind of public that likes to know where it is.

There was a sinister cripple in this programme, who talked in a snarl and never threw a decent word to anybody. All the characters had to be like that – all bad, or all good, or always funny. They never said anything out of character, in case listeners should think someone else was talking.

The machinations involved to prove that the widow's boy friend was not married to the cripple's sister had been going on now for several months, and looked like going on for ever, with a fresh twist of tragedy or hope whenever the plot slackened. Of course you knew it would come out right in the end, because the widow was a Good character, who said things like: 'Whatever terrible things have happened to us, I think we shall all be better people for it.' She was also apt to tell her friends that she was looking for stars in the crown of heaven. It was very affecting.

To point up the drama in these programmes an organ was used for the incidental music. This was cheaper than having an orchestra, as its suspenseful chords could be used to make any speech momentous.

A character would say: 'We have come to a crossroads in our lives –' *Boom!* from the organ. 'There is something I have to tell you' – careening arpeggios – 'I've met someone else.' *Boom, boom, boom!* with all the stops pulled out.

A love scene could be accompanied by a tremulant rendering of 'Beautiful Dreamer', the *vox humana* could help Mom when she made another of her sacrifices to keep the home together, and the carillon dinged out at any mention of religion, for God was cast quite frequently for a minor role in the soap operas.

Each programme was sponsored by some product, and began and ended with a commercial announcement. The words of the commercial were on a record and were always the same, so that you got to know them so well that you did not hear them any more, which is one of the reasons why people are able to bear with sponsored radio. Some of the advertisements were set to music. Christine heard them so often that they printed themselves on her brain. When she was doing housework she sometimes found herself singing: 'Veeto – says No, no – to Underarm O!' or, to the tune of *Ach, du lieber Augustine*: 'Mrs Filbert's *mar*gerine, *margerine mar*gerine. Mrs Filbert's *mar*gerine – buy some today!', or 'Brush your teeth with Colgate's – Colgate's dental cream. It cleans your breath – what a toothpaste! – while it cleans your teeth!'

Such was Christine's life during these first months in Washington. When she stopped to think about herself she was surprised to find how quickly she had settled down. She had thought that life in America would be very strange for a long time. Although she was still frequently surprised by things she saw or heard, the new routine of her life was becoming so familiar that the old rhythm of her days in England was already like a far-off song, only half remembered.

She was less bored and lonely when she began to make friends with her neighbours in the apartments. The woman who lived opposite was a large and amiable hausfrau with short stiff blonde hair and a husband who could not sit down without grunting. They were called Mr and Mrs Pitman R. Preedy and they seemed to spend most of their time eating. Christine met the wife staggering up the stairs with brown-paper bags full of food, and often when the husband came home from work, he too carried a paper bag with a salami or a bottle of cream sticking out of the top.

Mrs Preedy was for ever making cakes, and sometimes she baked an extra one for Christine. In the course of a conversation across the hall from front door to front door, which was how they usually talked, for Mrs Preedy always said she had no time to step into Christine's apartment, and she never asked Christine into hers. Christine had told her that she never made cakes. Mrs Preedy did not know that this was because Vinson did not like them. She thought it was because Christine did not know how to make them, and so about once a week Christine would answer the door bell to find a large iced cake sitting on her door-mat, and Mrs Preedy retreating to the shelter of her own front door, stretching her orange-tinted lips in delight at her good-neighbourliness.

She was very sorry for Christine, because she had come from England. She thought that everyone in England was starving. The thought of the meat ration moved her almost to tears – and the toilet paper! A friend of hers had been to England, and the stories she had told her about that! She treated Christine as if she were an African native, newly come from some benighted jungle village. Once when she met Christine in the supermarket, buying quite ordinary things like milk and eggs and butter, Mrs Preedy had said: 'I think it's wonderful how you know what to buy. Do they have *milk* in England?'

Christine never knew what to do with Mrs Preedy's cakes. Sometimes she ate a piece for her lunch, but Vinson, who had liked her figure in England, had begun to notice that she was too plump in comparison with American girls, and she was trying hard to reduce although she did not think it would suit her. She usually gave the cakes to Maxwell, and once, when she and Mrs Preedy went out together to go shopping, Maxwell was sitting on the grass at the side of the apartments with the plate at his side and a large piece of cake half-way to his dusty pink mouth.

Christine did not know whether Mrs Preedy had seen, but the cakes continued to arrive outside her front door, although less frequently, as if Mrs Preedy might be having a struggle to make her good-neighbourliness overlook the incident.

Vinson did not like Mrs Preedy, although she called him Commodore and always asked politely after the Navy when they met on the stairs. He said that the Preedys were not the type of people you expected to find living opposite you, and the apartments must be going down in tone. One Saturday morning when he was at home he had heard Christine and Mrs Preedy calling loudly to each other across the hall about Mr Preedy's gastroenteritis, and he had called Christine inside and asked her if she was trying to disgrace him.

When he said things like that to her he used a voice that reminded Christine of her headmistress at school and her matron in the hospital, and it made her laugh. Then Vinson was a little sad, and told her that it was only because he loved her and was proud of her that he wanted her so much to measure up to the right standards.

'What standards?' Christine asked, still laughing at his pursed-up mouth and serious, unblinking stare. 'The standards of a commander's wife, I suppose you'll say.'

'If you like.'

'Well, don't you ever be made an admiral, Vin. I'd never live up to it.'

'I sincerely hope that I shall some day. It's the crown of every professional naval officer's career. And you'll make a fine admiral's wife. I know it.'

'Oh yes,' said Christine, making a rude face. 'I'll wear pompous hats and be a wet blanket at junior officers' parties and stand in a corner looking down my nose at all the bootlicking women whose husbands want promotion.'

'Now, honey,' said Vinson uneasily, for he did not like her to talk that way about the sacred Mrs Hamer.

'It will be bad enough when you're a captain. I don't seem able to behave like a commander's wife, but it will be worse trying to be a captain's wife. I hope I don't get like that woman downstairs.'

'Now, honey,' Vinson said. 'Captain and Mrs Decker are very fine people, and she's been very friendly towards you.'

'I don't like her. She's got a face like a crab and she's always telling me stories about people I've never heard of, and what good families they come from, and the other day she drove me to the shops when it was raining, and because I wanted to go to Woolworth's – only for just a moment – she wouldn't wait for me and I had to walk back.'

'I'd still be happier to see you making friends with her instead of some of the wives you run around here with.'

'What's wrong with them? I love old Mrs Minter. She knows

how to make tea the English way. And Nora Beckley is a dear although I know she looks a bit odd. But you needn't have been so offhand to her that time she was here when you came home. Her husband's got cancer.'

'Well, don't look at me as if it was my fault. I'm certainly sorry for her, but I do want you to make the right kind of friends, darling.'

'What's wrong with Lianne then? She's the nicest person I've met since I came to America. Life around the flats – sorry, apartments – has been much more fun for me since I've known her. I suppose you don't like me being so friendly with her because her husband's only a lieutenant in the Naval Reserve.'

Vinson did not answer. If an accusation was true he did not deny it or try to defend himself. He just ignored it, so that you never knew whether you had scored a point off him or not.

Christine had met Lianne Morgan one day when she was in the basement laundry putting her washing into the machine. A very tall slim girl with a wide mouth and a lot of flopping brown hair had come down with a basket full of dirty clothes and an even dirtier small boy in a cowboy hat covering her from behind with a couple of pistols.

'Hi,' said the girl to Christine at once. 'I've seen you before. You're the English girl who's married to the good-looking Commander, aren't you?'

'Yes,' said Christine. 'How did you know?'

'Oh, I know most things that go on around these tenements. We've been here since way back. You'd be surprised at some of the things I could tell you. Dick – that's my husband – says I'm too nosy, but I can't help it. We live in the block across the playground from you, but our laundry's full of yackety-yacketing women this morning, so I came over here. Let me dump these things – and come up and have some coffee, won't you? Quiet, child,' she said to the little boy, who was killing washing machines – bang, bang – right and left. 'He's home from school because he said he was sick, but I found out afterwards that he'd held the thermometer under the hot faucet. Pretty cute at his age, don't you think? I've got a little girl who's older, but she isn't half as smart.'

Christine knelt down to the little boy, who had a round bright

194

face under the dirt, and reminded her of her nephew Clement. 'What's your name?' she asked. The boy looked at his mother.

'He's called Perrin, poor little brute, because it's one of Dick's family names and his father insisted on it. I call him Peter, but Dick has to call him Perrin, in case we'll forget when the old man comes.'

'Well, he doesn't call me that too much,' said the little boy, mitigating the case against his father. 'Mostly he calls me that evil child.'

Christine went up to Lianne's apartment, and found it the same shape inside as her own, but looking quite different because of the state it was in. Christine's apartment was very tidy. She had plenty of time to keep it so, although it went against her nature. She had been brought up by Aunt Josephine on the theory that there was no sense in putting things away only to have to get them out again. Her father had been allowed to keep his study in a mess of books and papers, and the drawing-room at 'Roselawn' had always been littered with mending, newspapers and dog pills ready to hand. If you brought down glue to mend something, or nail varnish to do your nails in front of the fire, the bottles might stand around for days, and people would look at them as they passed and say: 'I must put that away some time.'

But Vinson did not like that kind of thing. If yesterday's newspaper was still lying about when he came home, he would take it out to the kitchen before he sat down. He was a very tidy man. He always put his clothes away and his shoes neatly in line, so Christine had to do the same. If she left underclothes lying about he was quite capable of putting them away himself, and she did not like him to do that, in case he saw that there was still a pin on her knickers where a button should have been.

The Morgans' apartment, however, was in chaos. 'Forgive it,' Lianne said, waving a hand round the living-room as they came in. 'It isn't always like this.' Christine suspected that it usually was. A child's night-clothes were thrown half on and half off the sofa, books had been pulled out of the bottom shelf of the bookcase, and one male shoe stood on the table. In the porch was a battered model railway track, which ran in and out under the chairs, some broken toys, children's books thrown down open with the pages crumpled, a litter of scrawled drawing-paper and some dirty glasses and ashtrays. Two wooden handles hung from coiled wires on the wall.

'That's Dick's muscle builder,' said Lianne pulling on them with a backward swing of her long body. 'He has to do something now that he's back in the Navy in command of a large steel desk. But he will do it out here with no clothes on. He swears he can't be seen through the screens, but of course he can. I've been outside to look. The Captain's wife who lives below you has bought herself a pair of fieldglasses.

'We had a party last night,' she said, to explain the state of the kitchen. Christine liked it. It was the first untidy kitchen she had seen in America.

'Some people over here wouldn't dream of letting you into their homes unless they'd spent all day cleaning them up,' she said.

'I know it,' said Lianne. 'Maybe I should be like that. I don't know. Are you that way?'

'Not by nature,' Christine said. 'But I try, because my husband thinks that I –' She stopped, realizing that what she was going to say might sound critical of Vinson. Lianne gave her a quick look and then turned to the cupboard to see if she could find two clean cups.

After that visit Christine often went over to Lianne's apartment, or Lianne came to hers after the children had gone to school. Sometimes they went out together in the afternoon, and once, when they had been to an affecting film, they had both cried so much that when they came out they had to go and have a drink. Lianne had told the children to go to a neighbour's apartment when they came back from school, so they did not hurry home. They had three cocktails and giggled all the way back on the streetcar, and when Christine got home she found Vinson there before her for the first time since their marriage.

He was not pleased. He did not come to the door to greet her. He sat in his chair swinging one foot, and waited for her to come to him.

She kissed him and was ready to apologize, but he pulled back his head and said in his matron voice: 'Where have you been?'

'Out with Lianne. We went to a movie. It was –'

'You could at least have left a note for me.'

'I would have, but I didn't know I'd be so late, or that you'd get back so early.'

'Why shouldn't I, when I wanted to hurry back and see my wife?'

'Please don't make me feel bad about it, darling. You know I've never not been there when you come home. I thought you'd understand, just this once. Give me a kiss and tell me you love me.'

He stiffened. 'You've been drinking, Christine.'

'Well, we had to have a drink, because the movie upset us so much. What's wrong with that? You talk as if I was a nun or something.'

'You go off drinking down-town with your trashy friends while I sit here and worry about whether anything's happened to you.'

'You make it sound so terrible. I'm sure you weren't worried. You just say that because you're cross that I was late. I'm sure Dick isn't cross with Lianne, although he's bound to have been home before she was. He doesn't work so late as you, being only a lieutenant.'

'That boy will never get anywhere,' Vinson muttered. 'He's irresponsible.'

Christine had by now got so far out of her role as humble and obedient wife that she could not get back into it.

'Well, I like Lianne and Dick,' she said, incensed now and unable to stop herself provoking him, 'even if you don't. You have your friends – and I don't like all of them. I can't bear that fat Willie who drops peanuts down the cracks of my sofa – so why shouldn't I have mine? You're jealous, that's what it is. You're jealous of my being friendly with Lianne because I can talk to her intimately. Why shouldn't I have someone to talk to? I gave up friends like Margaret and Rhona in England to come out here to you, and I don't see why I –'

'Christine,' he said, looking at her out of his odd, tortoiseshell cat eyes, 'are you trying to quarrel with me? You're wasting your breath if so, because you know I won't quarrel with you.'

'I wish you would.' She felt her face flushing. 'I wish you would quarrel sometimes, instead of being so smug.'

Even this did not rouse him. He shook his head and smiled. 'I'm not going to spoil my marriage that way.'

'Well, you'd better look out,' Christine said, almost shouting, 'or you'll find you are spoiling it!'

She ran away because she was crying. She ran into the bedroom and lay on the bed and cried and felt sorry for herself. When she had got her breath back and was lying there pouting and trying to squeeze out another tear she realized that she was having to make an effort to go on feeling sorry for herself. She was in the wrong. She had come home late. She had tried to quarrel. She violently wished unsaid those things that she had worked herself up to say because she thought it would do Vinson good to hear them.

If he would come in now – and perhaps he would, for surely he would not like to think of his wife crying in here alone – she would throw her arms round his neck and kiss him and tell him how sorry she was. He would forgive her, and she would be just a silly and emotional woman, and make him feel strong and sensible.

She sat up and reached over to the dressing-table to powder her face, so that she should not be looking unattractively tear-blotched when he came in. Then she lay back on the bed and waited for him, with one knee slightly raised, because her legs looked better that way.

He did not come into the bedroom. She waited for quite a long time. What would happen if she lay there until bedtime and he came in and undressed and let the sun go down on his wrath? That would make tomorrow as terrible as this evening. The only thing to do was to get up and go meekly into the kitchen to prepare his supper, just like ordinary evenings, to show him that it was all over and she was a good wife again.

It took quite a lot of doing, but she managed it. There was nothing else to do.

Late one afternoon, a few weeks later, Lianne rushed over to Christine and said that she had to go out to a cocktail party with Dick, and her baby-sitter had not shown up, and could Christine possibly go and look after the children for an hour or two.

198

Christine looked at the clock. 'I'd love to,' she said, 'but I don't see how I can. Vin will be home soon, and you know he hates it if I'm not here.' She had told Lianne what had happened after they had been to the cinema. Lianne had been interested, but incredulous. Her life had never encompassed a man like Vinson. Dick was casual and accommodating, and she had always done what she liked with her former boy friends.

'Please, honey,' Lianne said, pulling up her strapless brassière. She was wearing the low-cut black cocktail dress in which she never felt comfortable. 'Be a pal and help me out. Everyone else who'd do it is busy. You're my last chance.'

'You know I would if I could. I'd love to put Peter and Betsy to bed. I could finish that story I started reading to them the other day. But – it seems sort of mean to Vinson.'

'Oh, phooey,' said Lianne, hitching at her girdle. 'You're much too good a wife. You spoil that man like nobody's business. You're always falling in with what he wants to do. Let him fall in with you for a change. Do him good. I tell you, honey, you don't know how to bring up a husband. Take a tip from an old married woman. You're laying up trouble for yourself.'

That was an American wife talking. Vinson said that was why he had not married one. Christine was an English wife. Vinson said that was why he had married her.

But Lianne was her friend. She would do anything for Christine, except understand her attitude towards her husband. Christine could not let her down, and perhaps, after all, Vinson would be proud of her for being kind and helpful. She would get him to come over to Lianne's apartment, and when he saw how good she was with the children perhaps it might encourage him about having their own baby.

Lianne took off her gay little hat, put it on again the other way round, gave Christine her front-door key and rushed off, leaving her gloves and bag on Christine's bed. Christine left a note for Vinson explaining and telling him to come over to the Morgans' apartment and went across to Peter and Betsy, whom she found sitting on the floor in front of the refrigerator, eating cake.

She had a wonderful time with them. They were volatile

199

children, but affectionate, and apt to counter any serious order with: 'I *like* you!' and a football tackle round the knees. Christine gave them their bath and cooked eggs for them, because they said they always had fried eggs, although she knew they didn't. Then she chased them into bed and read to them, and all the time she was thinking how domesticated and maternal she would look when Vinson came in.

He did not come. When Lianne and Dick returned, a little tight, and Christine went back to her apartment, Vinson's cap was in the hall and his uniform neatly on a hanger in the bedroom, but he had changed his clothes and gone out again.

He came back about ten-thirty and said that he had had supper. He would not say where he had been. He had obviously not been drinking. Christine would almost have preferred him to have gone out and got drunk. If he was as cross as that it would have been more natural. He was quite polite to her, but distant, and they went to sleep without kissing.

The next morning Christine was affectionate and quite gay, to try and make everything all right between them. If he wanted to apologize for having shrugged off on his own last night she would make it easy for him to apologize now, but Vinson had never in his life apologized when he considered that he was in the right.

To clear the air Christine would readily have said that she was sorry for going baby-sitting, but when she began: 'Vin, about last night. I –' he said: 'Forget it. It doesn't matter', which was worse than if he had been cross with her, because she thought that he was still cross inside.

She was miserable all day. She did not tell Lianne about it, because Lianne would have taken her side and said: 'Phooey'; and although that would have been comforting, it would not help her to make things right with Vinson. All day she planned how she would say to him that evening, after he had had a drink: 'Please, Vin, if you're cross with me, say so. Let's have it out, and I'll say I'm sorry, and then we can love each other again and forget it.'

She rehearsed how she would say it, but when the time came, and Vinson was on his second martini, sitting on the porch with his jacket off and his tie pulled loose, Christine could not find the courage to say it. He was unapproachable. He was behaving as if nothing had happened and it was an evening like any other, and Christine took refuge in the compromise of letting well alone. They spent quite an amicable evening, but he was a stranger. She did not know what he was thinking.

That was one of the nights when she wanted him to make love to her. If he would do that, would confirm the inalienable physical tie that was between them, she knew that everything would be all right and they would be close again, but he kissed her good night and turned away from her, and either went to sleep or pretended to.

Christine lay awake for a long time. She looked at his gently moving shoulders and the bristly back of his head dug stubbornly into the pillow. You fool, she thought, and she remembered how she had thought: You fool, as she walked down the corridor that night at the Mount Royal, when everything would have been all right if he had only had sense enough to make love to her.

In the days that followed, Vinson entered into one of his periods of being particularly sweet and loving to her, and it charmed Christine into the conclusion that whatever had happened must have been her fault. She determined once more to start all over again and be the kind of wife he wanted her to be. Happiness was that way. If his ideals sometimes clashed with hers, she could not change him by opposing them, and so she might as well make them both happy by accepting them.

For days at a time, when he was loving her like this, Christine was happier than she had ever been in England. It made everything worth while. She saw the French film, 'La Ronde', and was impressed by the remark with which a husband checks his importunate wife: '*Dans le mariage, il y a des périodes qui sont calmes et puis des périodes qui sont – hm – moins calmes.*' Christine thought that was true. She was growing to believe that marriage went in cycles, with short seasons of coolness and warmth alternating rapidly, and that it would be as foolish to think that marriage could be all warmth as to think that the year could be all summer. At these times when she was happy marriage seemed such a simple affair, and she felt she could already write a book on the subject.

201

Lianne and Dick gave a cocktail party. Vinson did not want to go, partly because he did not like the Morgans, and partly because he thought that there would be a lot of junior officers there. Christine said jokingly that if he did not go she would go without him. He half believed she might, and so he consented, with a kind of *noblesse oblige* air, to accompany her.

He would not go so far as to come home early from work, however. They arrived late and the party was in full cry, with the children in nightgowns running about like dogs among people's legs, and three men already on the floor playing with the electric trains.

Vinson found to his surprise that there were two commanders and a captain present. His spirits rose as Dick's powerful cocktails went down. Christine stood close to him while they had their first drinks, because he complained that he always lost track of her at parties, although it was he who usually wandered away to a male group and left her among the women.

'That's right, darling,' she said, watching the frown slide off Vinson's face. 'You'll feel fine when you've had a couple of drinks.'

He did. He felt much too fine. He got drunk at the party, and Christine was ashamed, although one or two other people were also drunk, and nobody minded. Lianne did not mind. Vinson had always been a little stiff with her before. She was glad to see him loosening up, and encouraged him to do his imitation of Danny Kaye, to which nobody listened, so it did not matter that it was not very good.

Dick did not mind either. 'A little tight myself,' he told Christine when she said good-bye.

Christine did mind. She had seen Vinson drink too much before, but she had never seen him drunk. It was all right to see other people like that. They were funny sometimes, but when you knew your own husband's face so well it was not funny to see it unco-ordinated and blurred at the edges.

She managed to get him home, although he wanted to stay at the party, and he was extremely rude to her on the stairs going up to their apartment. She was afraid that someone would come out of a front door and see him stumbling up the stone steps dragging at her arm, but when she tried to hurry him he called her a goddamn fleabag. When she told him the next day that he had said this he did not believe it, and was shocked at her for inventing it.

When they got inside their apartment he stopped being rude to her and became amorous. Christine let him pull her towards him, but when he kissed her she found that being kissed by a drunk husband is like being kissed by a stranger, and she backed away. 'I'll make some coffee,' she said, 'and get you something to eat. Then you'll be all right.'

'I'm fine.' He lurched towards her. 'Let's go to bed.'

Christine went into the kitchen. She heard him trip over the edge of a rug as he went into the bedroom, then a crash that must be him kicking her dressing-table stool out of the way. Then silence.

When she went into the bedroom Vinson was asleep, snoring on his back, with his clothes scattered on the floor. She picked them up and put them away. It was the first time she had ever had to do this for him.

In books, when husbands got drunk, wives sometimes spent the night on the sofa in dignified reproach, but sofas in books were longer than Christine's, and she would feel silly and prudish in the morning when he woke up sober and wanted to know what she was doing there.

She undressed quietly and got into bed, well over on her side and keeping an apprehensive eye on him. He did not wake up.

In the morning Vinson was awake before her and came out of the bathroom clear-eyed and jaunty. She opened her eyes to see him sitting on the bed grinning at her.

'How do you feel?' she asked.

She expected him to say: 'Lousy', as he often did in the mornings, but he said: 'Fine. Just fine. How do *you* feel?'

'All right. Why shouldn't I?'

'Well, I thought you had quite a load on last night, honey.'

'*I!*' She sat up affronted. 'It was you. You were drunk as an owl. Don't you remember?'

He shook his head. 'Can't have been. You're making it up.' He laughed at her.

'Oh, Vin –' She took his hand. 'Please don't do it again. It was horrible. I hated it.'

203

He laughed again. 'Get up and make some coffee,' he said and went out of the room.

Christine and Vinson were going to have a party too. Not a noisy, disorganized party like the Morgans', but a small buffet supper with everything just so. They had been to many such parties at the homes of other naval officers, and the evenings had all been much the same.

Drinks first – either old-fashioneds or martinis or highballs. The children, if any, sat in dressing-gowns before the television set watching Kukla, Fran and Ollie or a cartoon programme, and everyone said how cute they were, and the children either showed off or stared coldly at the guests.

When the children had been sent to bed, still showing off or staring coldly as they went up the stairs, the hostess brought out the supper, trying not to look too proud of the dishes she had spent all day straining to make better than the dishes of other hostesses. The food and the plates and cutlery were laid out on the table and everyone helped themselves and took the plate back to a chair and ate off their laps or on small occasional tables, like a vicarage tea-party.

Since Christine was the most newly married, she was always asked to serve herself first, which was a pity, for you did not like to take too much, and then you saw other people piling their plates and wished you had too.

The food was nearly always the same – fried chicken or a pot roast with vegetables, which the hostess spent so long carefully spooning out of the casserole and arranging on the best dish that it was half cold by the time you got to it. Vinson wanted to play safe and have fried chicken or pot roast, but Christine privately determined to have lobster salad. She did not tell Vinson in case he might worry beforehand about the consequences of so daring a departure from naval etiquette.

He discussed the invitations with her, but he had already made up his mind about the guests. He wanted Art and Nancy Lee, because he and Christine had been to supper (fried chicken) at the Lees' house, and Vinson was meticulous about paying off invitations in kind. If someone asked him to supper he did not think it was enough to pay them back in cocktails, and if they asked him to a cocktail party he did not see why he should ask them to supper.

Christine did not see that it mattered, when someone was a good enough friend to be your best man. With her friends in England it had never mattered who invited whom, or to what, so long as you saw each other, but she liked Art and Nancy, so she let him put them on the list. He always made the lists in their household. Christine could never find any paper, but Vinson always carried a little notepad in his pocket, so he was the one who wrote things down. He had small, very neat handwriting, and he liked to make lists of things. He even wanted to make her shopping list before the party, but she would not let him, in case he queried the lobster.

A new captain had recently come to Vinson's division. Vinson had made Christine waste a Sunday afternoon calling on the Captain and his wife in a prissy little bungalow that smelled of new chair covers. They were very dull people, and Captain Fleischman seemed to have watered down the whisky, but now they must be asked to supper. Christine protested mildly, but Vinson admitted that he had already mentioned the invitation to Captain Fleischman, which was cheating, so down they had to go on the list.

She protested, too, about Commander and Mrs Elgin, whom she had only seen half drunk at a big naval cocktail party at the Army and Navy Country Club. Vinson overruled this objection by reminding her that most of the officers had been half drunk by the end of that party, because they had paid for their tickets beforehand and were determined to drink their money's-worth. Vinson had done the same, and Christine had spent most of the evening sitting on a sofa talking to some woman who kept trying to make her join a bridge club. It was very hot, and the woman fanned herself all the time with a paper napkin and said: 'I feel it so particularly, coming from my air-conditioned place.'

She also said that she despised Washington (Christine was discovering that it was the modish thing to affect dislike of the nation's capital) and she kept saying: 'It isn't the heat, you see, so much as the humidity', a remark which Christine had already heard many times in Washington and would hear many times

205

more. Americans talked about the weather even more than English people, and weather bulletins were given every half-hour on the radio to appease this passion for meteorology.

She was very tired of the woman with the paper handkerchief by the time Vinson came back rather unsteadily to find her. She was annoyed at being left for so long, and Vinson did not help by accusing her of being picked up by a man in a floral bow tie sitting on her other side, although the bow tie had been brooding over straight whisky and had not spoken a word to her.

So Commander and Mrs Elgin went on the list, and Christine hoped they would arrive sober. When people are drunk the first time you meet them, you are inclined to think of them as permanent dipsomaniacs; just as when a man has a cold sore on his lip when you are first introduced, you visualize him always with that blemish.

Now they must think of two other people to make up the party. Christine wished they could have some civilians, so that there could be a few other subjects discussed than how old Chuck would like his new post at Norfolk, Virginia, and why the Admiral was getting rid of this aide; but Vinson knew hardly anyone in Washington outside the Navy, and Christine had no friends of her own.

'Let's ask Dick and Lianne,' she suggested. 'They'll liven it up a bit.'

'Oh no, honey. That wouldn't be suitable.'

'Why not? What's the point of giving a party if it can't be lively?'

'I don't mean that. I mean that young Morgan is too junior. You can't ask a reserve lieutenant with senior officers like this.' He tapped the list.

'Of course you can! Why, Dick had loads of captains and commanders at his party. Don't be – '

Before she could say: 'Don't be such a snob', which she did not really want to say any more than he wanted to hear, he said: 'What have you done with that book I gave you on naval social customs?'

'I gave it to Lianne. She wanted something funny to read when that poisoned finger was getting her down.'

'A pity. It would help you to understand these things.'

'If I did all the things it told you to I might as well be dead. It says you must always wear a hat and gloves when you go visiting, and that you must never sit down at a party when the Admiral's wife is standing up. Old Ma Hamer never sits down – I don't think she can bend in the middle – so why have any chairs at all when she's around? That book do you know what it says? I learned this bit by heart. It says: "Do not engage in long clinches on the dock when a peck on the cheek would do. There is a certain dignity attached to the wearing of uniform, and nothing looks sillier than two people trying to show how much in love they are."'

'I know who we'll ask,' said Vinson, changing the subject, because he thought the book was right. 'We'll have Captain and Mrs Decker from downstairs. I'd like to get to know them better.'

'I wouldn't. I don't like them. She looks as if her corsets pinched, and he just opens his mouth and words pour out of it whether you want to hear them or not. It would be much more fun to have Lianne and Dick.'

'We've been into that.' Vinson wrote down the names of the Captain and his wife who lived in the apartment below.'There, that makes a nice little party.'

Christine thought it sounded like a deadly little party.

It was. Nancy Lee could not come because one of her children was ill, and Art had a cold and might as well not have come either, for his cold depressed him and he hardly spoke all the evening.

Captain Fleischman from the chintzy bungalow was even duller than he had been at home. The drunken Commander turned out to be even less attractive sober than he was drunk, Captain Decker from downstairs was as prolix as Christine had feared he would be, and their three wives sat in a row on the sofa and made no effort, as much as to say: 'All right. You asked us, and here we are. Now entertain us.'

Even the drinks did not get the party going. Vinson was an attentive host, but he was too stiff and formal with people he did not know well, especially when they were senior to him. Captain Fleischman, who was the head of his department, almost paralysed him with etiquette, although the Captain was an owl-eyed nervous little man, who you would not have thought could paralyse a rabbit.

Christine made a great effort to talk to the women. Captain Fleischman's wife did not want to talk. She wore a dress that looked as if it had been made up of pieces left over from loose covers at the bungalow and was quite content to sit and watch the proceedings, like an old lady at a village concert. When pressed into conversation, she would say: 'Oh, surely', or: 'I guess that's so', which was amiable enough, but not inducive to sparkling dialogue.

The Commander's wife was too smartly dressed, as if she had expected a large party. She put a wet glass down on a polished table and some cigarette ash on the carpet, and sent raised eyebrow messages of boredom to her husband. Mrs Decker from downstairs thought as little of Christine as Christine did of her, and showed it. Her flat crustacean face was all downward curving lines as her shoe-button eyes travelled round the room, taking a disparaging inventory of the curtains and furniture.

It did not help much when Mrs Preedy skipped across the hall to borrow a jelly mould. Vinson answered the door; but although he tried to block the opening, Mrs Preedy was larger than he, and everyone could see that she had her hair in curlers and an orange chiffon scarf tied in a flowing bow round her goitrous throat.

'That extraordinary woman,' murmured Mrs Decker. 'What a neighbour to have! But I suppose you have made friends with her.'

'Of course,' said Christine defiantly, while Vinson frowned at her and Mrs Decker told the company with an acid laugh: 'It's so charming the way British people will make friends with *anyone*.'

When Christine went into the kitchen to add the finishing touches to the supper none of the women came out to help her. Art Lee came out and found her furiously banging plates and knives and forks on to a tray.

'Can I help?' he asked. 'What's the matter, Christine? You look all burned up.'

'I am. Those damn women just sit there like the three witches and none of them offers to help.'

'I'll bet you hate their guts. Why do you and Vin invite such crummy people to a party?'

'Vin wanted them. He wouldn't let me have my friends because Dick's only a reserve lieutenant. I wonder he even invited you. You haven't been a commander long enough to mix with such exalted rank.'

'Vin's an ambitious boy,' said Art dryly. 'He will go far, without a doubt.'

'I hate the Navy,' Christine said. She did not mind what she said to Art. She could say things to him that she would not say to Vinson.

'So do I,' said Art. 'Let me help you. Gee, I wish I didn't feel so lousy. I feel the way those goldfish look.' He stuck out a pallid tongue at the fish, then leaned against the wall and nursed his drink and his cold and forgot about helping.

Vinson came round the partition into the kitchen to get more ice, and asked Christine why she was not in the living-room entertaining her guests.

'Well, my goodness,' she said, exasperated. 'I've got to feed them, I suppose, since I presume they only came here to get a free meal. I can't be out there and in here getting things ready at the same time.' She straightened up to look at him, passing the back of her hand across her hot forehead. He was still wearing the polite face he was using in the drawing-room. He made her feel cross.

'You should have gotten things better organized before. You shouldn't have to spend so long in the kitchen.'

'Well, for God's sake!' she exploded. 'As if it wasn't bad enough having to spend all day preparing food for these morons without you coming in here and criticizing me.' Art did not feel strong enough to stand a quarrel. He slipped his long body diplomatically past them and went out of the kitchen.

'I have to criticize you,' Vinson said, 'when you neglect your guests and spend hours out here fooling around with Art. You might at least consider what your guests will think, even if you don't mind how I feel about that.'

'Oh, if you're going to be jealous of *Art* –' Christine shrugged her shoulders and turned back to the salad bowls.

Vinson grabbed her arm and twisted her round to stand close

to him. His face was not polite any more. It was dark and almost frightening, like that evening at 'Roselawn' when she had stood stirring the dogs' meat on the stove and told him that she could not marry him after all. 'Of course I'm jealous,' he said roughly. 'I'm jealous of every man who speaks to you. Don't you know that, you little fool?'

When he spoke to her like that and kissed her so fiercely, she did not mind him being jealous, even of poor Art. Her passion leaped up to meet his, and for a moment the kitchen was the only place in the world, and the stupid people in the living-room could starve or go home for all Christine cared, but Vinson controlled himself almost immediately, wiped a hand across his lips, picked up the bowl of ice and went back among the company, with his face already polite again.

He would not serve drinks with the supper. Christine had wanted him to, but he said it was not the thing to do. Christine did not like the American habit of drinking solidly before the food and drinking only iced water or coffee with it. You either drank too much before the meal or not enough to carry you through it. Her guests had not drunk too much. They had drunk too little. Vinson had not been stingy with the drinks, but they were the kind of people who did not expect to be entertaining, so did not bother about drinking enough to make them so.

The evening came to an end at last. When the last guest had gone Christine fell back on the sofa and wanted to cry. A dull party at someone else's house can make you laugh when it is over, but a dull party in your own house can only make you weep.

Vinson came back from seeing the Deckers downstairs to their apartment. 'And now,' he said, 'perhaps you'll tell me what you said to Captain Decker that made him say to me: "Your wife is certainly outspoken. How does she get on over here?"'

Christine had been afraid he was going to ask that. 'I couldn't help it,' she said. 'He's such a know-all. I was trying to be polite and talk to him, but he was being so pompous and laying down the law about everything. He's got that disgusting wart on his nose too. It wiggles when he talks. You can't help looking at it.'

'Go on,' said Vinson, folding his arms.

'Well, he was being so silly. You know what he said? He said that England was undefendable, and in the next war it would only be an advanced target, so the only thing to do would be to evacuate all the people over here and let Russia waste her ammunition blowing England to bits. So I said: "That shows you don't know much about England. Most people would rather die there than be made to come over here."'

'Chris*tine*! That wasn't very polite.'

'Well, it's true, anyway. And it goes for me too. He needn't have been so huffy. I hope his wart turns to cancer,' she said bitterly. 'It's going a bit blue. It looks as if it might.'

'What do you mean, that goes for you too?' Vinson asked.

'If England was being bombed I wouldn't want to be sitting safely over here, rolling bandages for the Red Cross, with great care not to break my nails, and being hostess at clubs for officers who were spending the war in the Pentagon. An English friend of mine got stuck over here in the last war, and she nearly died of envy because she hadn't been through the Blitz.'

'Don't be so childish,' Vinson said. 'What good could you do? You'd only be a nuisance. Of course your place would be here. You're an American wife now, and by that time you'll probably be an American citizen.'

'Yes, dear,' said Christine, and began to collect dirty glasses and ashtrays.

She thought afterwards that if she had made her rude remark to a lieutenant instead of a captain, Vinson would not have minded, but she was glad she had not thought of telling him that at the time. It was bad enough even to find yourself thinking of remarks with which you might score off your husband.

They gave other parties, and went to many more naval parties themselves, and she was careful never to be rude to a captain. She was trying to be a good wife, and if that included sharing Vinson's unwholesome respect for rank – well, she would have to learn that.

But you could not enjoy parties if you had to think all the time about what rank people were, and could not enjoy talking to them as if they were just ordinary people. She discovered that not all admirals and their wives were like the Hamers, and not all captains and their wives were like the Deckers. Some of them were worse, but many of them were revealed, to Christine's surprise, to be quite human.

Going home after one party where she had spent a pleasant ten minutes talking to a slight, grey-haired man in a baggy suit, who looked more like a skilled carpenter than anything else, Vinson said in awe: 'Admiral Briggs talked to you for a *long* time, didn't he? I think that was wonderful of him.'

'Why shouldn't he? I'm not a leper.'

'But darling, he's a three-star admiral. And he talked to you for *ten* minutes.'

'Perhaps you'll be made a captain tomorrow,' Christine said pertly.

There were too many naval cocktail parties. You could not remember one from another, because they were all exactly the same. You met mostly the same people, and got to know the women's repertoire of dresses and hats as well as your own. If it was a high-grade party, with admirals present, the men kept their coats on, but if it was a lower-grade party, with no one higher than a captain, the men took their coats off if it was hot, and you got to know whose husband had a paunch and whose husband had retained his figure in spite of the Washington desk-sitting.

The drinks were always the same: martinis, or bourbon or scotch whisky with so much ice in the glass that it bumped against the end of your nose and you could hardly drink it. The food was always the same too. As well as the usual elaborate canapés, prepared with diabolical care by a hostess determined to outdo other naval wives, there was always a large cold ham at one end of the table and a large cold turkey at the other, from which you were supposed to cut slices and make a sandwich, which was a difficult thing to do when you had a glass in one hand and were trying to talk politely to an admiral's wife.

At the first party where she saw ham and turkey Christine was greatly impressed at such lavishness, although the hostess herself seemed to be more proud of the fact that she had provided

English mustard. 'You make it by mixing the powder with water,' she boasted, which, to people accustomed to buying their mustard ready mixed in jars or tubes, seemed to be the most exciting and progressive thing.

As she went to other parties and saw other turkeys and hams, invitingly sliced, but almost untasted by the guests who had come to drink, rather than eat, Christine was no longer impressed, but rather depressed by the waste of food and money. She was more depressed still when they gave a cocktail party themselves and Vinson insisted that they must have a turkey at one end of the table and a ham at the other. However, she had been obstructive about the fried chicken and the pot roast, so she let him have his way, and they were eating turkey and ham every day for a week afterwards until Christine finally gave the remainder to Maxwell. However, they had conformed to the quaint old naval custom. They had not lost caste.

Another quaint old naval custom was the paying of social calls, which Vinson swore was a necessity, but which seemed to Christine an archaic irrelevance. She had protested at first, and said that in England all that nonsense had gone out with Queen Victoria, hoping that the American respect for the English social code would deter him, but to no avail. In the United States Navy one paid calls, and so she had to waste many a week-end afternoon putting on hat and gloves to go and visit someone she did not want to see, and she had to try and look pleased when she was fetched away from washing underclothes in the bathroom to open the door to somebody who had come to call on her in gloves and a hat.

They had not yet called on Admiral and Mrs Hamer. Having seen them at her wedding Christine dreaded this, and kept making excuses not to go, until it was too late and the Hamers had gone away. Their default had preyed on Vinson, and now that the Hamers were back in Washington it was now preying more strongly, and Christine knew that they would have to get it over some time.

All calls made her nervous. The conversation was apt to be strained, because the people you had disturbed at their gardening or woken from their Sunday afternoon sleep wanted to see you as little as you wanted to see them. With the Admiral and his wife it would be even worse. The Admiral would grunt at them and blink his eyes, which were set in folds of rusty skin, like a tortoise, and Mrs Hamer would pass her eye up and down Christine, give her a mental percentage of acceptability and then sit back and expect homage.

She said all this to Vinson, but he was adamant. They must call on Admiral Hamer.

'All right, dear. Some day soon.' Christine was suddenly acquiescent, because she had thought of a good idea. For several days she kept telephoning the Hamers' number. If any-one answered she put down the receiver without saying anything until on a Sunday afternoon she telephoned and there was no answer.

She ran out to the porch, where Vinson was playing solitaire with his shirt off. His chest always attracted her. It was not broad, but it stood out well like a box above his flat stomach.

'Let's go and call on the Hamers now,' she urged him. 'I've finished what I was doing, and if we go now straightway we'll be back in time for you to hear that "Stop the Music" pro-gramme.'

He was pleased that she had suggested it herself. They drove out to the Hamer's house, which had fake beams and a fake antique porch lantern and a self-conscious white fence round the tiny garden. No one answered their ring at the coy set of sleigh bells which hung outside the door, so they pushed their cards through the letter-box – and they had made their call. It was as easy as that.

It was a wonderful idea. Christine wished she had thought of it before. Some day she would write a book on naval etiquette to rival the one Vinson had given her, and earn the undying gratitude of naval wives for telling them her invention for painless call-paying.

She had not escaped as easily as she thought, however. Two days later the Admiral's wife telephoned to thank Christine for having left cards and to say how sorry she was that she and the Admiral – she always called him The Admiral – had not been at home. She did not sound as if she meant it, but no doubt she meant well.

No doubt she meant well, too, when she went on to say that

214

she would expect to see Christine at the next luncheon given by the Officers' Wives' Club. It was not an invitation. It was an order.

'I shan't go,' Christine told Vinson. She had heard about these lunches from Nancy Lee.

'You must go,' he said. 'When the Admiral's wife herself invites you –'

'She didn't invite me to go. She told me to go,' Christine muttered.

'When Mrs Hamer herself invites you,' he continued, 'it's obvious that you must go. You may even enjoy yourself,' he added without much hope. 'I'll give you some money and you can buy a new dress for it. You will go, won't you, honey?' he said, suddenly nervous and almost boyish, like a child trying to persuade his mother to go to the school Speech Day.

'Yes, dear,' Christine said. She had taken to saying 'Yes, dear' lately. When she said it she felt that she sounded like a thousand middle-aged wives, but it made Vinson happy, and so she said it.

When she went into the lounge of the club where the luncheon was held, all she could see was women. Women everywhere, holding thick little glasses, and all talking. Women in white hats, women in black cartwheel hats, women in little pink hats with flowers on them. No women without hats, except Christine. She patted down her hair nervously and approached the table by the door, where three women in red, baby-blue and natural straw hats respectively sat with some notebooks and cardboard boxes and one of those little black tin money-boxes so beloved of treasurers of women's clubs.

The treasurer in the red hat took a five-dollar note from Christine and scrabbled delicately in the box for change with long mulberry-coloured nails which did not match her hat. The woman in the baby-blue hat ticked Christine's name off on a list and smiled at her with expert charm. No doubt she had risen to the exalted position of being allowed to sit behind the table and tick off lists on the strength of that smile. The woman in the natural straw hat, who looked like a carthorse dressed up for the summer, except that her ears did not stick out through holes in the top, searched in the cardboard boxes and gave Christine a place number and a little red card with her name on it and a safety-pin at the back. Christine pinned the card to her bosom as directed, feeling like a man who took your money in the supermarket.

The woman in the baby-blue hat, all charm, told her to go to the receiving line. Christine approached timidly and recognized Mrs Hamer in tubular brown silk, flanked by three or four other notable ladies, one of whom was Mrs Fleischman, still wearing the dress made of bits left over from the loose covers at the bungalow. She was the only one of the outriders who seemed pleased to see Christine. The others smiled, but distractedly, looking beyond her at the people coming up behind. Mrs Hamer did not smile. Her face was not made that way. She was very tall, with long pointed feet encased in patent-leather shoes which looked like the halves of over-ripe bananas. She towered over you, austere and all-powerful. It was like shaking hands with the Statue of Liberty.

Christine managed to say: 'Thank you so much for having invited me to come', although the invitation had meant that she had to fork out a dollar seventy-five for her lunch. Mrs Hamer murmured some regal blessing, and it was only after she had passed thankfully out of the receiving line that Christine realized that Mrs Hamer had no idea who she was.

About three hundred women were milling round the big lounge like hens in a barnyard. They were all drinking something out of the thick little glasses, but Christine could not see where they got it. With relief, she saw the black fringe and scarlet-lipped vivacity of Nancy Lee, and she edged through the crowd to her. Nancy pushed through the women who were clustered around the bar table like flies round a sore, and came back with something in a little glass for her. It was sherry, very sweet and oily and warm. Nancy and the two cheerful girls with her were wearing white name cards on their bosoms. Christine looked down at her own.

'Why is it red?' she asked. 'I feel like a pariah.'

'You're worse than that.' One of the cheerful girls laughed. 'You're a new girl. It's your first time here isn't it? You wait. After lunch you'll be made to stand up so that all the girls can look at you.'

'Oh no,' Christine said. 'I can't. I'm the only one here without a hat.'

'We've all been through it,' the other girl said. 'It's murder. You feel everyone's giving you the hee-haw; and if you're fairly newly married, all these hags take a good look to see if you're pregnant.'

'I'm going home.' Christine put down her glass.

'No, you're not.' Nancy grabbed her arm. 'Everyone's going into lunch. Come on, let's get in quick and I'll juggle the numbers round so we can sit together.'

Several other people seemed to have done that, or else they had come with friends and been given consecutive numbers at the door. Nearly everyone was sitting next to someone they knew, which makes the lunch less of a bore, but defeated its object of bringing the girls together, because the girls just talk to their friends, and most ignored the strangers around them.

The woman next to Christine had a slim taut back with a zip fastener all the way down. That was all Christine saw of her, for she remained turned away throughout the lunch and talked to her friend on the other side about all the things she was going to cite against her husband for divorce.

The lunch was as unsuitable to the warm day as the sherry had been. It was some kind of meat served in lumps, with too little gravy and a mound of undercooked vegetables. The coloured waiters were the only men in the room, and it seemed to unhinge them. They were very slow, and they argued together a lot in corners, and by the time they reached Christine's end of the table with the ice-cream it was only a cupful of white liquid.

'A dollar seventy-five for this,' Nancy said. 'Plus paying a baby-sitter. I don't know why we do it.'

'Vin made me come,' Christine said. 'Does Art make you come too?'

'He doesn't, but he *is* in the Navy, for his sins, and I feel that the least I can do is to keep in with the top brass.' She nodded towards the top table, where Mrs Hamer sat in the middle of a dozen rarefied women, who had had their ice-cream first, while it was still ice as well as cream.

'Everyone talks as if the wives of senior officers did the promoting,' Christine said. 'I can't see how they run a Navy that way.'

'It isn't exactly that, but it works the other way. If you get in wrong with one of those babies up there she'll see to it that she talks enough about you to make them think twice before they recommend your husband for promotion.'

'Well, but –'

'Hush. Something is going to occur.' Nancy sat back and closed her eyes, as the secretary of the club, a well-fed, florid woman who had given a sweaty handshake in the receiving line, rose to her feet and banged on the table with the back of a spoon.

It was just like all other meetings of women's clubs that Christine had ever attended. The minutes were read in a flat reciting voice, and no one listened to them. There was the usual to-do about who should propose that the minutes be signed and who should second the proposal. At first no one would get up, and then suddenly three women jumped up together and began: 'I wish to propose –' and then looked at each other in some confusion, apologizing and saying: 'No, no, not me', like guests at a tennis party when there is only one court for ten people.

Our sympathy was extended to an absent mother who was in hospital in Hawaii, regrets were expressed at the loss of our valued subscriptions secretary, Mrs Jowitt, whose husband was being ordered away, congratulations were offered to two ladies who had produced little future naval officers, and our sincere thanks went out to all those ladies who so wonderfully gave their services to make the wonderful Arthritis Ball such a wonderful success. Here followed a tedious list of who had helped with the tickets, the flowers, the decorations, who had lent this and that coffee urn, and who – this was a nasty one – who had promised beforehand to help and been 'regretfully prevented'.

Other people besides Nancy had their eyes closed by this time. Christine herself was lulled into forgetting the ordeal that the red card on her bosom presaged, when the secretary sat down to about as much applause as a tap dripping, and Mrs Hamer rose majestically to her feet, with her large hands spread flat on the table and her gaze raking the roomful of tables as if the rose on the front of her hat was a searchlight. Christine sat up. This was it.

'Before we hear from our social secretary' – ah, that would be it – 'I take pleasure in introducing to you Miss . . .' – she glanced down at the table – 'Miss Mavis Harbright, who comes to us through the good offices of our member Mrs Westling' – a cold nod down the table – 'to give us a little talk on how to acquire the art of charm and social poise.'

'This ought to be good.' Nancy sat up. It was, but Christine, her ordeal only postponed, was still too nervous to enjoy fully the spectacle of an overweight and overhatted woman with a fistful of rings on her pudgy fingers telling the members of the club, who were mostly young and elegant, how they could be new women if only they would do as she did.

It was soon apparent that the good offices of our member Mrs Westling meant that the overhatted woman was a friend of Mrs Westling and had prevailed on her to get her into this *galère*, so that she could advertise the deportment school of which she was proud to be the principal.

Mavis Harbright worked hard. You had to give her that. She sat, she rose, she shook hands with imaginary guests, she stood at an imaginary cocktail party with the weight balanced just so to enable one to swivel round and chat lightly to all comers. She paced up and down the room with her gloves on her head. One of the naval wives called out: 'Try that with a glass of water', but luckily, a bamboo screen by the kitchen door fell over at that moment, so no one heard her.

Miss Harbright then stood in the best position for health and beauty, telling the ladies to be sure to tilt the pelvis and lock the thighs when so doing, which brought a giggle from one of the coloured waiters, who was listening agape. Mrs Hamer's eye was still daring the screen not to fall down again. She shifted it slightly to the left and the waiter was withered out of the room like a piece of charred newspaper. Miss Harbright demonstrated how to get in and out of a car without loss of grace or poise, and one of the girls near Christine remarked audibly that if she did it like that she would knock off that darned mushroom hat. This brought the death-ray eye of Mrs Hamer round from the kitchen door and trained it down the table to where sat

219

the irreverent girl, whose husband now perhaps would never get that half-stripe.

Christine's heart sank when the exponent of poise and charm sat down at last, feeling for the chair with the calves of her legs, as demonstrated, and Mrs Hamer rose once more to call upon the social secretary. It was the lady in the carthorse hat. She glanced round the room, wet her lips like a torturer, and announced that she was going to read out the names of the new girls, who would each rise as her name was called and remain standing until told to sit down, so that all the other girls could feast their eyes.

'Mrs Adamson!' A short fluffy girl stood up, trying to look unconcerned. She did not know how furiously she was blushing. 'Mrs Adamson's husband is at Main Navy, and she comes to us from El Paso, Texas.' Everyone stared, and Mrs Adamson dropped her eyes and grew red as a beetroot, as if there were something shameful both about her husband and El Paso, Texas.

'Mrs Dooley!' Oh, heavens, they were doing it in alphabetical order. It might be Christine next. 'Mrs. Dooley!' The social secretary looked round with her mouth open. No Mrs Dooley. Poor little Mrs Adamson stood there bravely alone, like the little boy in 'When Did You Last See Your Father?'

'Mrs Dooley! Come along now, please!' Someone pinched a vague, untidy girl, and she squeaked and jumped up, laughing and apologizing and quite at ease.

Everyone laughed with her. She was evidently the buffoon, who always did things wrong. It was all right for her. People knew her and liked her and laughed with her. But what if they laughed *at* poor Mrs Gae . . .

'Mrs Gaegler!' It sounded as silly as Christine had feared it would. Nancy dug her in the ribs, and she stood up, dropping her napkin and wishing that she had held on to her handbag, to give her something to do with her hands.

'Mrs Gaegler's husband is at the Arlington Annexe. Mrs Gaegler comes to us from London, England, and' – the social secretary's voice dropped ghoulishly – 'she's a bride!'

What could one do? Where could one look? Christine put her hands behind her back, realizing too late that this made her chest stick out too far, and fixed her eyes on a ventilator high up in the wall, while female stares stabbed her like darts from all over the room, and she imagined that she could hear whisperings from three hundred female tongues about this phenomenon who was a bride, and who came from London, England, and who had not got a hat. Were they asking each other if she was pregnant?

In utter ignominy, she stood straight and stiff while other names were called and other luckless girls stood up, but Christine felt all the time that every gaze was still riveted on this spectacle who came from London, England, and who had no hat and was either pregnant or too fat.

When Vinson came home that night and asked her how she had enjoyed the lunch, Christine flung her arms round his neck and burst into tears against the hard shoulder board of his jacket.

'Here, here, what's this?' He led her into the living-room. 'What's happened? What's all this about?'

'Oh, Vin, it was terrible. It was awful. They made me stand up, and everybody stared at me. I've never felt such a fool.' She cried so much that she slipped off the sofa and sat on the floor with her wet face jammed against his khaki trouser leg.

He was very kind to her. He tried to comfort her, but she could not make him see how awful it had been. 'They wanted to have people get to know you, darling. You mustn't be so self-conscious.'

'No, no!' she wailed. 'They just want to make a fool of you. They all stared and whispered, and I was the only one without a hat, and all those awful women – millions of them – nothing but women – and if you're newly married they stare at you to see if you're pregnant.'

'Well, honey, you don't have to worry about that.'

'But I am, Vin, I am!'

She did not know why she had not told him before. She had only known definitely for two days. She was going to tell him, but, hugging her delight to herself, she was half afraid to share it with him, in case he was not pleased.

He was very pleased. He was delighted. He forgot that he had said they could not afford to have a baby yet. They were very happy together, she kneeling on the floor with her arms round his waist; but when she remembered about the lunch and began to moan to him again about it, he patted her and said: 'I'm sure there was really nothing wrong. You just feel upset and hysterical because of your condition. I'm sure they were all very kind. They're a lovely group of women.'

'Maybe.' Christine stood up. 'Perhaps you're right.' She did not think he was, but he did not want any more tears, and she did not think she could ever explain it to him.

Chapter Five

NEVER having been an expectant father before, Vinson treated Christine as anxiously as if she were going to have the baby at any minute. She was reminded of the day when she had sat eating sandwiches with Margaret in Green Park, and Margaret had complained that Laurie treated her as if she were a rare curio.

At first it was very pleasant to be told to put your feet up and to be made to sit idle in the living-room while Vinson cleared away the supper but after a time his solicitude grew a little irksome. He would settle her into chairs as if she were a frail old lady. When they crossed the street he would take her elbow and almost lift her on and off kerbs. He would sit gazing at her contemplatively, just as Laurie had done with Margaret, as if trying to puzzle out the secret thing inside her that he had brought about, and he was always asking her, with a puckered brow, how she felt.

She felt amazingly well, apart from the inconvenience of being sick every morning, and she wished that he would not keep asking. Her sickness worried Vinson so much, and she was so irritated by his standing outside the bathroom door and calling out: 'Are you all right, darling?' while she was *in extremis*, that after a while she took to getting up five minutes earlier and getting her retching over before he woke up.

He was so careful of her, so solicitous of her every whim, that when she spoke to him again about moving to a house with a little garden, which would be a more suitable place for a baby than the hot little apartment, he surprisingly agreed.

Christine had dreamed of a house in the country, but Washington was spreading its suburbs so far in every direction that there was no proper country within reasonable driving distance of Vinson's office. They bought a small house in Arlington, which was simply moving from one suburb to another. Many naval officers lived in Arlington. It was a suitable place for a commander to live.

With the down payment made out of Vinson's savings, and

the instalments on the house to pay every month, Vinson said
that they were now living too extravagantly and would have to
economize on other things. Christine did not see why they could
not use some more of Vinson's savings to pay off their bills and
to buy things she needed for the house, but Vinson was of the
old-fashioned habit of mind that thinks savings are meant to be
saved, not spent. Christine knew that she ought to think this was
wise, but she had been brought up by Aunt Josephine to look
on money as an expendable commodity, and it seemed to her a
pity not to use it until you were too old to enjoy it, or dead before you could spend it.

When Aunt Josephine had been left some money in a legacy,
she had spent it all on giving Christine and her father a long
holiday in Belgium. How sad it would have been if she had saved
it up for the old age which she never saw. How much better that
she had squandered it all on the trips to the battlefields in her
long grey linen dress, the afternoon sessions of cream horns and
grenadine at the Café du Port, her reckless flings at the Ostend
Casino, where she sometimes got so excited that she staked on
black and red at the same time, and her wild plunges at the
trotting races at Breedene, where she would back any outsider
because it had a noble face.

Vinson, however, did not see life that way. With the baby
coming, he now had an added reason for thrift, and since the
money was his Christine had to learn to follow his wishes. She
tried not to spend too much on the new house. If she made a
suggestion which seemed to him extravagant, Vinson was liable
to say : 'We can't afford it. We're already eating too high on the
hog. I'm sorry, but it was you who wanted to move to a house,
don't forget, and now we've got to pay for it.'

Christine fought against the growing suspicion that Vinson
was mean. You could not think such things about your husband. She would not let herself, but the unacknowledged
thought hung about disturbingly at the back of her brain, like a
child trying to get into a game where he is not wanted.

Some of the curtains from the apartment did not fit the
windows of the house, and those that did were old and not
bright enough for the sunny little suburban home. Vinson,
chewing a pen over the monthly accounts, said that he did not

see how they could afford new curtains yet, so Christine persuaded him that to buy an electric sewing-machine would not be an extravagance, but an investment, because she could then make curtains and slip covers and also clothes for the baby.

They bought the machine on what was called politely the 'deferred payment', or, more excitingly, the 'magic credit' system, to which Christine was becoming accustomed, because nothing of any consequence seemed to be bought in any other way in America. Christine had done a certain amount of sewing at home on Aunt Josephine's ancient treadle machine, which had as much wrought iron on it as an old-fashioned mangle. Although she had never made curtains or baby clothes, she was sure that, with the free lessons given by the sewing-machine company, she would soon be able to make anything on this wonderful machine which ran backwards as well as forwards and had enough gadgets to turn the archaic labour of sewing into a modern sinecure.

Once a week she went down to the sewing shop and sat with five other fidgeting women round the teacher, who was a casual young lady with a polished forehead and straight blonde hair tied back with a bootlace. It soon transpired that the lessons were not really free after all. They got your money by making you pay three dollars for the scraps of cotton and lace on which you practised, and the young lady with the bootlace spent more time unsuccessfully trying to thread her machine than in teaching the fidgeting ladies how to use its gadgets.

One by one the ladies dropped out – the fat matron who had trained her husband to pin up dress hems for her, the woman who boasted that she had a difficult figure to fit, the girl who had been sent to the lessons by her mother because she was going to get married, the breathless young wife who always arrived late and left early, and grumbled under her breath in the back row all the time she was there, like a Communist agitator trying to raise the rabble.

Finally there were left only Christine and the Austrian girl, who could hardly understand anything the casual young lady told her. Then Christine decided that it was too hot to waste a morning watching the young lady with the bootlace trying to thread a sewing-machine, and she, too, abandoned the ship and left only the Austrian girl, presumably sitting out the full course of lessons, patiently trying to discover what bias piping with the multi-slotted binder meant.

Christine abandoned the complicated gadgets for hemming, buttonholing and tucking and just used her machine in the safe old-fashioned way in which she had used Aunt Josephine's. She always put it away before Vinson came home, because he liked her to be ready and unoccupied to greet him, not sitting whirring away, surrounded by bits of stuff and ends of cotton, with pins stuck all over the arm of the chair to spear his hand when he bent to kiss her.

She could often get the machine out again after supper, however, because Vinson, with a basement to use as a workshop, had evinced a surprising interest in home carpentry, and spent many evenings down there in creased linen trousers and a T shirt, banging away at bookshelves or adapting furniture that did not fit. The cost of labour for any home decorating forces every American husband to be a handyman, and Vinson was no exception. He painted everything in or outside the house that was paintable, and when there was nothing left to paint he began to adapt one end of the cellar to be used as a nursery playroom.

He became so absorbed in this that Christine did not see much of him in the evenings or at week-ends, but she rejoiced in his increasing interest in the house he had not really wanted, and in his happy preparation for the baby. When she went down to him with beer or iced coffee, she loved to see him working away there with a cigarette hanging from one corner of his mouth and his brown eyes serious with the concentration of a craftsman. On Saturday mornings she did her washing at the big sink at the other end of the cellar, and they would toss friendly remarks across the noise of the portable radio, which he always automatically turned on but never listened to. It was very domestic. Christine was happy. She was going to have a baby, and she liked her house.

It was not much to look at from the outside. It was merely a little square red-brick box with a steep tiled roof in a row of other little red boxes, with white-painted doors and windows, regularly spaced, with garages between. There were no houses

226

opposite, only thick trees sloping down to an unseen creek which ran brown with mud after the rain.

Her house, like all the others, was built on a bank, so that the small front garden sloped down and the little back garden sloped up, and it was difficult to make flowers grow. Although Vinson said that pushing was bad for her, Christine worked hard on her steep lawn when he was out, with a mower borrowed from a plain but pleasant girl next door, who had two plain children with shaved heads and bandy legs, and a long-nosed husband who was something in insurance and came and went at strange intervals, always in a hurry and always carrying a brief-case.

Christine tried not to borrow anything from the woman in the house on the other side, who threatened to become too friendly. Her name was Mrs Meenehan and her husband was a retired naval officer, which she considered gave her an unassailable entrée into Christine's life. Mr Meenehan, a contentedly hen-pecked man, had risen from the ranks and retired as a lieutenant-commander after the war. The high spot of his naval career had been the command of an elderly tugboat converted for wartime use as a minesweeper. Mrs Meenehan was wont to refer to these days of glory as 'When Daddy and I had command of the *Walrus*'.

Daddy seemed to do most of the work of her house, so she had plenty of time to spare, and was always creeping over the grass at the back of the houses and appearing alarmingly at Christine's kitchen window with a shout of: 'Hi there, Catherine!'

She had got Christine's name wrong the first time she heard it, and even when she heard other people calling her Christine she stuck to Catherine, as if she knew better. Christine wanted Vinson to put up a fence round their garden, so that Mrs Meenehan could not make her cat-footed invasions, but it appeared that you were not allowed to put up fences or hedges on that property. The front gardens must remain just one long continuous slope of community lawn, broken only at mathematical intervals by the neat gravel garage entrances.

The row of houses were alike inside as well as outside, as Christine found when she visited her neighbours, although the plain girl's house was shabbier and more untidy than hers, and the Meenehans' house was an uneasy jungle of travel trophies exemplifying the less-pleasing tastes of countries all over the globe. The front door opened straight into the living-room, which had a pale polished floor and a small fireplace with a white-painted mantel. Since it was summer the fireplace of the plain girl and Mrs Meenehan, and probably every house in the road, had one large, regular-shaped log sitting neatly across the andirons. Christine wanted to have flowers or a plant in her fireplace, but Vinson wanted a log, and so they had a log too.

The living-room narrowed to a small dining space at the far end, and beyond that was the kitchen, which was fitted up like the advertisements in magazines, and was Christine's delight. Upstairs was the tiled bathroom, the front bedroom which Vinson called grandly the Master Bedroom, and a smaller room at the back which he was redecorating for the baby.

Often Christine went into this room with its smell of pink paint and its nursery frieze round the wall and imagined the cot there with the baby in it, and looked down at her barely plumper figure and tried to realize that this was where the body in the cot was now. She had heard people say that when you were pregnant you had a great consciousness of motherhood, but she found that it did not come naturally. You had to make yourself feel like that deliberately, to remind yourself all the time that the life was already created, because it was so hard to believe. Although she felt a deep glow of happiness whenever she thought about the baby, she felt so unchanged that she sometimes forgot about it for hours on end when Vinson was not there to remind her.

He was almost more conscious of the baby than she was. Although he did not like her to mention it in front of other people, he was always wanting to talk about it when they were alone. He was genuinely as pleased as she was, and he took a deep and almost morbid interest in all the symptoms of her condition. She sometimes thought that it was a pity she did not have more interesting things to tell him. She had stopped being sick; and apart from tiring more easily and finding herself suddenly breathless if she talked too much, she felt quite normal. He still treated her with the utmost care. He made her lie

228

down when she did not want to, he rushed out with a hat when she was in the garden, and he always called out: 'Watch it there!' when he saw her feet coming down the steep cellar steps to him.

Because he was so nervous about her he made love to her less often; and when he did, it was almost apologetically, as if he thought that by making her pregnant he had forfeited his right to anything else.

Christine supposed that after the baby was born he would settle down and become a normal husband again.

Christine's pregnancy, combined with her pride in the new house, developed in her a more intense domestic energy. She was for ever cleaning, or tidying cupboards and drawers or moving furniture about. She was like a bird making a nest. Although it would be nearly six months before her baby was born, she was already driven by a restless urgency to get everything in order.

Lianne came to see her one day, and found her standing on a chair washing the kitchen walls, which were perfectly clean. While they drank coffee together Christine took out the table drawer and began to polish the silver while they talked.

'What's the matter with you?' Lianne asked. 'You never used to be so crazily domestic.'

'I can't help it. I just feel like that. I feel there's no time to get everything done. It's because of the baby. Didn't you feel like that with yours?'

'Hell, no,' Lianne said. 'I was worse than I am now. I couldn't be bothered to do a thing except lie around with candy bars and the comic sections. When the apartment got so you could hardly get in the front door, Dick used to have to clean up.'

'That's odd,' Christine said. 'I feel I have to work all the time. I feel like a French housewife. I get terrible urges sometimes to take all the bedding out and air it on the lawn.'

'For heaven's sake!' cried Lianne, startled. 'Do you do it?'

'I have to. I'd worry all day if I didn't. I worry all the time about little things that don't matter at all. I burst trying not to let myself worry to Vin, because it's so boring for him to have me talking all the time about the floor polish and vacuum cleaners. I'm terribly worried just now about my vacuum cleaner. It's old and doesn't seem to suck properly, but we really can't afford a new one. I don't know what to do.'

Lianne laughed at her serious face. 'You sure are in a bad way,' she said. 'If you're going to get like this every time you're pregnant, I hope your family is limited to one. Snap out of it, girl. You're getting like these dreary naval wives who get you in a corner at parties and try to tell you their recipe for corn bread. I haven't come here to shake my head over your domestic problems. I've come here to keep you up to date on the dirt at the apartments. The Deckers have got a new car, and Maxwell is having a hate against them because they won't let him clean it any more since he got water in the glove compartment. He misses you. He told me you were the first real lady he's seen round those parts. And that red-haired girl – the one who was always hanging black lace scanties on the line, remember? – well, wait till I tell you what happened about her . . .'

Mrs Meenehan, however, the wife of the retired lieutenant-commander next door, was more than willing to worry with Christine about her vacuum cleaner. That sort of thing was right up her street. Although she let 'Daddy' do most of the work in her own house, she could not let anyone else alone to run their houses as they liked. She was always telling Christine what brand of soap-flakes she must buy and how she could not possibly get along without this or that cooking gadget. If Christine did not buy the thing she recommended, Mrs Meenehan was quite capable of buying it for her herself and appearing at the kitchen window with the article and a demand for the seventy-five cents she had paid for it.

One morning when Christine was upstairs making the bed she heard Mrs Meenehan yoo-hooing frantically in the back garden. When Christine put her head out of the window, she shouted: 'Come down right away, Catherine! There's something on the TV you must see.'

She never called it television. It was always TV, or even, in her worst moments, video.

Christine knew that Mrs Meenehan would not go away unless she went down, and she could not have her shouting on the back lawn all morning, so she went downstairs with her hair in pins and allowed herself to be hurried across into the Meenehans' living-room, which was arranged somewhat like a cinema, with the mammoth television set as the focal point, and all the chairs placed so that you could not help looking at the screen wherever you sat.

The Meenehans, having nothing much in common except their memories of the days when Daddy had command of the *Walrus*, lived for television. They had another set in the basement room, which they called 'the rumpus room', and which was fixed up with a bar and a pin-table and a juke-box and notices which said 'Gents' and 'Ladies' in foreign languages, and other trophies of the Meenehans' naval travels. They had originally fixed up the basement for their son, but even a rumpus room with funny notices and mugs full of wax beer that looked real until you turned them upside down could not keep him at home. He had gone away from them to marry a girl they did not like, but they kept up the whimsy of the rumpus room under the illusion that they needed it for parties with the crowds of friends they did not have.

The thing that had so excited Mrs Meenehan this morning was a commercial which was advertising secondhand vacuum cleaners. It was still going on when Christine got there, for television commercials were inordinately long and took up almost more time than the actual programmes. The vacuum cleaners were called 'rebuilt', not secondhand, and were selling for merely ten dollars, if only you would call POtomac 8 – 7534 RIGHT NOW.

'Right now, ladies!' shouted the ebullient young man on the screen. 'Don't delay to take advantage of this positively unique offer, which obsoletes any other in the history of rebuilt vacuum cleaners. These machines are going fast! We're getting calls at the studio every minute. Don't miss your chance to get a free demonstration of one of these wonderful, magic, never-before-equalled vacuum cleaners in your home today! Call right now! POtomac 8 – 7534!'

He hammered it at you like machine-gun fire. You could hardly resist. Mrs Meenehan was completely sold on the idea, as she was sold on nearly everything the radio and television

231

commercials hurled at her, as her gadget-cluttered kitchen testified.

'Just what you want!' she told Christine, excited with the lust of buying, particularly at someone else's expense. 'Call that number right now, Catherine honey. You can use my phone.'

Christine hung back. 'I think I ought to ask Vinson first –'

'Oh, shucks. What can you lose? It's only ten dollars fifty. Why, you could pay that out of your housekeeping money and he'd never know it.'

'It does sound a bargain, but I think I'd rather ask him first –'

'You heard what the man said? If you don't call right now you might lose your chance.' Mrs Meenehan took every word that came out of either of her television sets as Gospel truth, although after years of hearing advertising men tell her to call Right Now she should have realized that this was only a device to prevent you thinking better of it.

While Christine still hesitated she took off the Hawaiian doll which covered the telephone, and dialled the number. Before Christine could protest she heard Mrs Meenehan arranging for her to have a rebuilt vacuum cleaner demonstrated that very afternoon.

Well, it was a free demonstration, 'without obligation to buy', the man had said. And although she knew that she would never have the courage to refuse to buy the vacuum cleaner after someone had taken the trouble to bring it out to her house and demonstrate it, it was only ten dollars fifty, and it surely must be better than the old one she had. Had she not seen it on the television screen cutting a swathe like mown grass through a pile of carefully arranged dust on the studio carpet? She was already catching some of Mrs Meenehan's television hypnosis.

The salesman who brought Christine's vacuum cleaner was quite young, a boy just out of college, with a crew cut, a friendly smile and a pleasant, educated voice. Christine felt sorry for him because his four years of youth and glory at college had led only to this, which was precisely why the vacuum cleaner company enployed as salesmen only young men who looked as if they were just out of college. A boy could earn good money in commissions while he was still fresh-faced, but as soon as he began to look too old to make housewives feel sorry for him, then he would probably find himself out of a job.

The rebuilt vacuum cleaner looked rather battered and did not seem to suck any better than the old one which had been worrying Christine, but the salesman was so young and eager that she had not the heart to send him back to the shop with the sale unmade. The cleaner was no worse than the one she had already, and it was only ten dollars fifty after all, so she wrote out the cheque and hoped that Vinson would understand.

The young man had not used any persuasion on her. It had not been necessary; but when she proved herself a serious customer by writing the cheque he suddenly braced himself and began to go to work on her in earnest.

'Just a moment, lady,' he said. 'I'll be right back.' He ran out of the door with his athletic stride and returned in a few moments with a large cardboard box which he set in the middle of the floor.

'What's this?' asked Christine, as she saw a shining new vacuum cleaner being lifted from the box. 'I don't want to see another cleaner. I've just bought one.'

'Sure you have, lady,' said the young man soothingly, 'but quite frankly, between you and me' – his manner was flatteringly confidential – 'that thing you've bought isn't going to last you too long.' He had praised the rebuilt vacuum cleaner while he was demonstrating it, but now that it was sold his manner towards it had changed.

'You're going to realize some day,' he said, still frankly confiding, 'that you're wasting your money buying cheap rebuilt machines when you could get a new one that will last you for years and never give you any trouble. Now, I'm not trying to make a sale. Believe me.' He gazed at her candidly out of his thick-lashed blue eyes. 'I just want to show you our latest model, so that when the time comes for you to realize that you owe it to yourself to buy a new machine you'll have some idea of what to choose.'

'Yes, but –' said Christine. 'I don't think –' But he had already unpacked the new vacuum cleaner, fitted it up with its brush, plugged it in and started away on her carpet with a noise like a jet engine.

233

'I'm not trying to make a sale,' he kept on saying. 'I just want you to see, for your own interest, the difference between this new model and that old thing you've just written out a cheque for.' Now that she had actually bought the secondhand cleaner he began to damn it unmercifully, shaking Christine's confidence in it, as he intended.

The longer she watched the new cleaner working on her home with a suction so powerful that it lifted the rugs off the floor and practically tore the loose covers off the chairs, the more she was convinced that she would never be satisfied with the secondhand one.

After all, as the salesman reminded her, what could you expect for ten dollars fifty? She knew that he was working on her. She knew that he was out at full stretch to make a sale, but she sat hopeless, watching almost dispassionately the mechanics of his salesmanship and the crumbling of her own weak resistance.

He showed her all the gadgets, including the one for spraying paint and blowing moth powder under the upholstery.

'It certainly is a wonderful thing,' Christine said feebly when he had stopped the motor and the rugs had settled back on the floor and there was peace in the house again, 'but I'm afraid I couldn't possibly afford it.'

'With our easy terms? Lady, a pauper could afford it. If you can pay ten-fifty for this old wreck' – he spurned the second-hand cleaner with his crêpe-soled foot – 'you can afford the down payment on this beautiful new one. I can take your same cheque for that if you like. Ten dollars fifty, that's all we're asking as a down payment, and after that you can make whatever monthly arrangements you like. Five dollars, seven dollars, ten dollars – as little or as much as you like. You can take three years to pay if you want.'

'Well, but I'm afraid my husband –' Drowning under his salesmanship, Christine clutched at the straw of Vinson's name.

'Look, lady, if he don't like the idea, why, he needn't ever know. He gives you an allowance for housekeeping? Right. Well, you could pay the ridiculously small instalments out of that and keep the whole business to yourself, hm?' That was what Mrs Meenehan had said. Since she sent for free demonstrations of nearly everything she heard about on the commercials, she was no stranger to American sales methods.

'Oh no, I couldn't do that,' said Christine. 'I'd have to get his consent, though I'm afraid he won't agree.' But perhaps, after all, when she told Vinson about the wonderful cleaner, when she repeated to him what the salesman had said about it being an investment really, because it preserved the life of your house and furniture – perhaps she could get him in a good mood and persuade him.

'I'll talk to him tonight,' she said, 'and let you know.' But the college boy was out to make a sale today or die in the attempt.

'Why not call him now, ma'am?' he suggested. 'And let me tell him about the new model. If he's engineer minded, which I'm sure he is, being in the Navy, he'll appreciate what I have to tell him about the motor.'

'Oh no.' Vinson did not like being called at the office. He did not know anything about engineering or the motors of vacuum cleaners, and she had a feeling that even the expert flattery of the salesman would not make him think that he did. She felt trapped. She wished that the young man would go away and leave her with the secondhand cleaner, although she now despised it.

'I'll have to think about it,' she said, getting up as a sign for him to go. 'I'll think about it and let you know.'

'Now you're letting yourself down,' the young man said, his pleasant face falling in boyish disappointment. 'You had made up your mind, you know you had, that this new machine was the only one for you. Surely you owe it to yourself, lady, to give your house the best. However,' he added sadly, picking up the paint sprayer and looking at it regretfully before he put it back in the box, 'if that's the way you feel about it – O.K. As I told you, we don't go in for this high-pressure salesmanship. We leave that to the firms who can't sell their goods any other way. I sure am sorry, though.'

He looked genuinely crestfallen as he began to pack the new cleaner back into its box. Christine pictured him stowing it into his car again and driving slowly back to the shop, where other young men would be arriving jubilantly, having made sales of the new models, while he had wasted the whole afternoon on her and only got rid of ten dollars and fifty cents' worth of rubbish.

She knew that she was lost. She realized now that she had been lost right from the moment when he had brought out the shining new cleaner and said: 'Now, I'm not trying to make a sale.'

When he had gone away, all charm, and congratulating her on her good sense, she spent the rest of the afternoon cleaning the whole house with the new vacuum cleaner. It really was a wonderful machine. Of course she had been wise to buy it instead of wasting her money on something inferior. Vinson must see it that way.

He did not. She waited until he had had his supper, and then asked him innocently: 'Don't you think the house looks nice and clean?'

'It looks swell, honey. But then it always does. You keep it very nice. You're a good girl, but I don't want you to work too hard and tire yourself.'

Now was the time. She told him about the new cleaner and how much work it would save her. She told him the whole story, about the college boy who looked too good for his job, and about the secondhand cleaner and the difference between the two, and Vinson sat silent and let her talk, but the fingers of one hand were drumming on the arm of the chair and he was biting the nails of the other, and she knew he was getting annoyed.

He said that they could not afford it. She had known that he would say that, but she had not expected him to be less cross about the expense than about the fact that she had been a salesman's dupe.

'I've told you time and again,' he said. 'you should never buy things you hear advertised on the air. The reputable firms don't do business that way. If you wanted a new vacuum cleaner – I don't see why you did, because we had one –'

'Now you're being like the man I heard in a shop. When his wife said: "I'm going to look at some coats", he said: "Why do you want a coat? You've got a coat."'

'If you wanted a new vacuum cleaner,' Vinson repeated when

236

she had finished, 'why in God's name didn't you go to a decent electrical store where you wouldn't be swindled?'

'I haven't been swindled,' Christine protested. 'You're prejudiced. Everybody buys things through commercials. Mrs Meenehan buys all her things that way. She –'

'A very good reason for you not to do it,' he said. 'Isn't there any difference between my wife and the wife of a broken-down old warrant officer who only struggled into a commission because of the war?'

'Vin! Don't be such a snob. Just because you went to that smug Naval Academy –'

'Now, honey, don't try and quarrel with me. You know it's bad for you.' Since she became pregnant this was his new line to stop any arguments.

'Well, it's worse for me to slave away with that old vacuum cleaner you had for years before we were married. And the secondhand one I was going to buy wasn't much better. Honestly, Vin, if you'd *seen* the difference between that and the new one. There was no question of which to buy.'

He laughed, but without mirth. 'To think of you being taken in by that old trick! By God, that salesman certainly had a field-day with you. Don't you know that they only advertise things like cheap secondhand cleaners to give them a chance to get into your home with a new one? And then you know what they do? They bring the old one with a piece of paper or something stuffed into the tube so that it has hardly any suction at all, so of course the new one seems miles better by comparison.'

'Oh no, Vin. He was an awfully nice young man. I'm sure he wouldn't –'

'Sure he was an awfully nice young man. That's why they sent him out to get you.'

Christine was crestfallen. He thought that she had been a fool. Perhaps she had. But she had her new vacuum cleaner. Nothing could take that away from her. Mercifully Vinson did not say that she must send it back. He contented himself with grumbling about the monthly payments and saying that, with the house to pay off and the baby coming, they were living beyond their means.

Presently he went down to the cellar to soothe his soul with carpentry. While Christine was washing the supper dishes, Mrs Meenehan's head, swathed in a mauve hair net, for this was her shampoo night, appeared through the gloaming at the window to ask after the vacuum cleaner.

When Christine told her that she had bought a new one and showed her the treasure, Mrs Meenehan was lavish with approval and borrowed it there and then to try it out in her own house.

Christine went down to the basement, stepping carefully down the stairs with the new deliberate tread she had already acquired, although she was not yet much heavier. She had coffee for Vinson, and an idea.

'If we're so hard up –' she began.

'We soon will be at the rate you're going,' he said, without looking up from his calculations on the drawing-board.

'If you're so hard up, why couldn't I get a job? Part time perhaps. It wouldn't be too tiring. I could easily do something for a bit until I – until I begin to show. I could at least earn enough to pay off the vacuum cleaner.'

'Oh, damn the vacuum cleaner,' he said. 'You're not taking a job.'

'Why not?'

'Because a commander's wife doesn't go out to work, that's why.'

'You're always telling me what a commander's wife does and doesn't do. Why should a commander's wife be different from other women? Lots of wives have jobs.'

'Not mine. Do you think I want people to think I can't support my own wife?'

'Vin, that's archaic. Why, lots of naval wives go out to work. Even commanders' wives. What about Mrs Hollis? She's in the Treasury. And Molly Gregg works part time at that school. You know she does, and her husband's senior to you.'

He could not dispute this, so he tried another line. 'What could you do, anyway? I don't see how you could get a job.'

'Didn't I hold down a perfectly good job at Goldwyn's for four years? The estimable Miss Cope. Why shouldn't I be the estimable Mrs Gaegler in some bookshop in Washington? And I'm a trained nurse. You forget that sometimes when you treat me as if I didn't know how to look after myself. I could be a nurses' aid. I'd love to go back into hospital for a bit.'

He thought of another objection, triumphantly, for it was a valid one. 'You couldn't get a job with the temporary visa you have. The Immigration Department wouldn't allow it.'

'What would I need then?'

'You'd need a permanent immigration visa, the one I've already applied for as a first step to taking out your citizenship papers, and it will take ages for that to come through, and by that time you'll be too near having the baby, so that stops all this nonsense about a job.'

Christine did not argue the point further. The idea of the job was going out of her head, because the discussion about the visa had reminded her of something else.

Weeks ago, Vinson had asked to see her visa, to check when it expired. During the move from the apartment to the house she had mislaid her passport with the visa inside it. She could not horrify Vinson by telling him this. He was always deadly careful about things like passports and permits. He stood in awe of the inclemency of government authority, and would begin to imagine that his wife would be deported or put into prison because she had lost her passport. So Christine had told him that she would check the visa herself, and had then forgotten all about it.

After Vinson had left for work the next day she turned the house upside down to find her passport, and finally ran it to earth at the bottom of a hatbox full of sweaters put away for the summer.

The visa had expired. It had expired more than a month ago, and here she was living in sin, so to speak, an alien without a permit.

She was getting ready to hurry off to the Immigration Office when Betty Kessler came round from next door to ask if Christine would keep an eye on her children while she went to the doctor. Betty was expecting another little bandy-legged Kessler. She and Christine sometimes exchanged symptoms, but Betty was not pleased and excited about her baby, as Christine was. She was a languid, long-faced girl who took life as it came and was never roused to visible emotion about anything, and she

239

accepted this third baby as just another of the tiring things that life with the insurance salesman had brought her.

By the time she had come back and relieved Christine of the two little boys, whose vocabulary did not encompass much more than 'don't wanna', and by the time Christine had walked to the end of the road and taken the long bus ride and then the streetcar, and another bus, the Immigration Office was closed for the day.

It was a branch office out in the northern suburb of Bethesda; a drab and uninviting building on the cluttered main street. It looked the kind of place that would be shut when you most wanted it to be open. It looked the kind of place where all the employees would go off to lunch at the same time, and shut the office to foil anyone who could get there in their lunch hour.

She took a bus back to the District Line, where people were crowding on to the streetcars. Christine had to wait a long time before she could push on to one. She had to stand all the way. Since she came to Washington she had only once been offered a seat, and she had never seen a man stand up for any woman, however old or burdened with parcels. If American women thought they were as good as men – all right, let them stand. Christine wondered whether anyone would give her a seat when she became noticeably pregnant. Probably not, and when that time came she would not feel like risking the jammed and jerky streetcars to find out.

She stood limply, tired and discouraged among the odours of hot and work-stale humanity in the crowded car. She was jerked forwards and backwards and from side to side as the car started and stopped and rocked round corners like an unseaworthy boat. She wished she was back in England where she would not be an alien, but where bus conductors were kind, and she would have a grey expectant-mother's ration book and be allowed to go to the heads of food queues.

When she got off the bus at the corner of her road the heat of the day had drawn itself up into a vast black cloud that brooded for a moment overhead and then suddenly let itself go in one of the drenching, battering rainstorms with which heat-heavy Washington likes to play at being the tropics. Christine ran. Her clothes and hair were soaked, but by the time she had reached home and put on a dressing-gown and pinned up her hair the rain had stopped and she was already as hot again as she had been before it started.

She felt quite exhausted. She lay down on the bed and wished that Aunt Josephine were there to look after her. She found that she was thinking about Aunt Josephine more often these days than she had done immediately after her aunt's death. The shock of Aunt Josephine so suddenly not being there had to a certain extent numbed Christine's realization that she would never be there any more. But since she was married and had begun to settle down to her life in America with Vinson, and particularly since the baby, the thought came into her head time and again: I wish Aunt Jo were here.

Not living with them, of course. It was not disloyal to Aunt Jo's memory to realize that one could never conduct a tranquil married life with her in the house, but living near by, on hand to discuss things and share things, and give, when it was needed, her own brand of wisely irrational advice.

How she would have revelled in this baby! Sylvia had never let her in on her pregnancies. She had not even told Aunt Josephine about Clement until his presence became too obvious, because when she was expecting Jeanette Aunt Josephine had told her she was standing all wrong, and Roger had snapped back at her not to interfere in things she knew nothing about, and there had been a quarrel, which had upset what Sylvia called her nerves, and she had cried on and off for two days, which had been no fun for anyone.

But Christine would have shared her baby, and let Aunt Josephine give advice, and gone to her when she felt tired or ill for the sympathy that she dared not ask of Vinson, because he went into a frenzy of concern if she said she did not feel well.

Christine lay on the bed and wanted Aunt Josephine. When the clock struck six she sighed and got up heavily, pushing aside her sad fancies to reach back to actuality.

She had to go downstairs before Vinson came home. If he found her in bed he would worry and catechize her about why she was so tired, and she could not tell him about the visa. It was one of his evenings when he came home gay and full of energy. He wanted to take her out to supper, so Christine put

241

the food she had prepared into the refrigerator for tomorrow, plodded upstairs to change her dress and went out with him to a hot little restaurant with a television screen nagging at you from the wall, and tried to eat the steak he ordered for her.

She was still tired when she woke the next morning. Her legs ached like weights when she put them to the floor.

'Why are you getting dressed?' Vinson asked when he came back from the bathroom.

'I'm coming with you to the Annexe. I want to have the car today.'

'I'm sorry, honey, but I'm afraid I'll have to keep it there. I have to go over to Main Navy for a conference this morning.' Buses ran from the Arlington Annexe to the Main Navy building on Constitution Avenue, but Vinson never went in buses. 'Did you want the car for anything in particular?'

'Oh no,' Christine said, going wearily downstairs to make the coffee. 'Nothing particular.'

The day was already sweltering with a sticky heat. While she was clearing up the kitchen after Vinson had gone, she heard the radio telling her that it was probably going to be the hottest day of the year so far, and might also break temperature records for that date. The man who gave out the weather forecasts was always very proud and excited when the thermometer broke a record. As he was spending the day in an air-conditioned studio, it did not incommode him.

It was a damp clinging heat that Christine had never met anywhere else in her life. If you moved at all, sweat stood on your skin and could not evaporate, because the air was as damp as you were. It was a limp heat, a clammy heat that seemed to close you round with stifling hands and wring the moisture out of you. If you took a shower you were wet again with sweat before you could dry the water off yourself. Making up your face was a lost cause. Your skin was never dry for long enough to put a foundation on evenly, and beads of perspiration were starting up between the grains of powder before you had put down the puff.

When Christine went out at half past ten the road lay sizzling in the sun like a griddle ready for pancakes. The air-conditioning fan in the Meenehans' top window was making a noise that no one but the Meenehans could have lived with. The Kesslers' dog lay panting on the lawn with no sense or energy to get himself back to the house. As Christine walked down to the bus stop her bare arms burned and she could almost fancy that her brains were bubbling in her head like gravy. She felt sick.

The bus had been standing in the sun at the terminal and its interior was like an oven. The streetcar was slightly cooler, but it was one of those with a radio, and Christine's ride along Wisconsin Avenue was made hideous by hillbilly music and commercials about scouring powder and laxatives.

In Bethesda, she had to walk two blocks in the sun to get to the building which housed the Immigration Office. Going up in the lift she felt dizzy, and trod on a man's toe as she stepped back to lean against the wall. The man took off his hat and apologized, which was unnecessarily civil of him, but his clothes smelled as if he had worn them day and night all summer, and Christine could not summon a smile for him.

The operator directed her to a door at the end of a long passage, where people were going busily in and out of doors with armfuls of papers. Constantly coming and going – out of one door, across the passage, in at another door – they seemed to be the same people, in motion all the time to give the effect of a busy crowd, like stage soldiers marching across the backcloth, then dashing round behind the scenes to march across the stage again and give the illusion of an army out of half a dozen extras in helmets and dusty doublets.

The Immigration Office had nothing in common with the passage that led to it. No one bustled about in there. Nothing seemed to be happening at all. When Christine opened the door on the tableau of quiet figures sitting at desks or on chairs against the wall, she had the impression of stepping into a photograph.

The desk near the door was called INFORMATION. Its chair was empty, although a half-smoked cigarette sent up a straight thread of smoke from a brimming ashtray. Christine stood by the desk and looked around. One of the figures in the tableau came to life and nodded civilly at her from another desk.

'Hullo,' he said. Americans in shops or offices never said:

243

'Good morning', or: 'Good afternoon.' It was always: 'Hullo', or even, in the hardware store: 'Hi there!'

'Mrs Dent has just stepped out for a moment,' said the figure. 'Won't you have a seat, and we'll attend to your business directly.'

Christine sat down at the end of the line of people along the wall, who were waiting to have their business attended to directly. They seemed to have been waiting a long time. Some were reading. Others were slumped in attitudes of hopeless resignation. A small boy was fidgeting and squirming and falling off his chair, and his mother had tired long ago of telling him to sit still. A man in a black felt hat was tapping his foot and jabbing at his chin with the handle of the umbrella which he had unaccountably brought with him on the hottest day of the year.

Although it was a relief to be out of the glaring sun, it was as hot in here as it was in the street; a stale, suffocating heat that sapped the senses and made you drowsy. There was plenty of air space under the high ceiling, but the air had been used up long ago – probably days ago, because the closed windows did not look as if they could ever be forced open without giving yourself a hernia, and none of the Immigration staff looked feckless enough to risk that.

It was a large high room decorated and furnished with a somewhat temporary air, like wartime civil defence offices in England. The windows were dirty, one wall was distempered a different colour from the others, no two desks were the same, and the odd collection of chairs looked as though they had been filched from other offices when no one was looking. The whole place looked as though the Immigration business might come to an end at any moment and the room and its occupants find themselves evacuated.

One corner of the room was divided into a cubicle by plaster-board walls which did not quite reach the ceiling. There was a doorway without a door in both the walls, so that the people sitting waiting to have their business attended to directly could see the man who sat at the desk in the cubicle, and he in turn, by leaning backwards and looking over his shoulder, could see and talk to the occupants of the desks in the main office.

That was what he was doing now. He was talking to a stout

man with a perspiring bald head, who sat in shirt-sleeves and a tie like a Gauguin nightmare at a desk nearest the cubicle. They talked a full ten minutes with the sober intensity of two women discussing a confinement.

Christine could not hear what they said, beyond the fact that the fat man was called Aubrey, and the small sandy man in the cubicle was called Elwood. They finally finished with the confinement, and Elwood turned back again to his desk, on the other side of which a woman in mourning sat in a detached way, as if she had given up hope of ever making contact with him. Elwood looked at her pensively for a while as if he might be going to say something, and then the telephone rang.

The two men and the woman at the desks in the main office looked up eagerly, as if the telephone bell were quite an excitement in their day. Elwood leaned back in his chair and said: 'Shall I get it, Aubrey, or will you?'

'I don't mind, Elwood. Just as you like. Unless Miss Hattie would like to take it?' He glanced chivalrously to the other side of him, where a middle-aged lady in a mauve sleeveless dress, with hair lying in thin coils on her forehead, was studying something which, from the poised pencil and the furrowed brow, might have been a crossword puzzle. She looked up and answered Aubrey's smile. Everyone in that office was as polite to each other as if they were in a quadrille.

'No, no,' she murmured. 'You get it.'

'Well, then, will you, Elwood?' It seemed almost too much to ask.

'Of course, my dear chap.' Elwood let down the legs of his chair and picked up the telephone, which had been ringing merrily all through this little courteous exchange. 'Oh, hullo there! How are you? How have you been coming along?' Christine heard him say. The woman in mourning folded her hands; and her shoulders lifted in the suspicion of a sigh.

The grey-faced man at the desk beyond Miss Hattie's, whose occupation was hidden by a barrier of ledgers, got up with a little cough, tiptoed across to Aubrey and whispered something in his ear. Aubrey closed his eyes and shook his head, and the grey-faced man tiptoed back to his side of the room. As he passed Miss Hattie he murmured: 'Hot enough for you?' and

Miss Hattie said: 'My goodness, yes, Mr Pierrepont', and fanned herself with a piece of blotting-paper.

Mr Pierrepont looked pleased that somebody agreed with him about something and hid himself behind his ledgers again.

Suddenly there was a whirl of activity. Aubrey looked up from his desk and called out: 'Next please!' in a startled tone, as if surprised to find himself still alive. Miss Hattie, catching the infection, looked up from her crossword puzzle and also called out: 'Next, please!' in the loudest voice her muted throat could muster.

Consternation! Everyone sitting on the chairs along the wall stood up, or if they were women, made the motions of collecting handbags and uncrossing their legs preparatory to standing up.

'No, no,' said Aubrey soothingly. 'One at a time please. We must take you all in order or we'll never get anywhere. The people at the head of the lines first, you know.'

The man with the umbrella and the woman with the small boy advanced towards the desks. 'But I was before her,' complained an Italian voice farther down the line. 'Just because I sit in the wrong place –'

He did not complain very loud or very long, however. There was something about the doldrum atmosphere of the Immigration Office which was catching, and stifled rebellion. Everyone sat meekly down again. The woman next to Christine, whose tight head scarf emphasized the dominance of her nose, told her: 'Yesterday I come, I wait two hour. Today I wait already one hour, but what can you do?'

What indeed? Christine sat on her hard chair and felt like a displaced person. Her first irritation was subsiding. It was too hot to go on fuming. She began to drift into a sort of coma of waiting, melting gently in the heat like a forgotten jelly, watching the slow happenings in the room with half-focused eyes.

The man with the umbrella was sitting at Aubrey's desk with the black hat tipped over his eyes and the umbrella held straight up between his knees, like an old gentleman in the pavilion at Lord's. He did not sit there nearly as long as the old gentlemen do, however. He sat there for two minutes. After squaring his shoulders and applying himself with heavy breathing to the form which the man with the umbrella had brought, Aubrey discovered that it was the wrong form, and told him that he must go back to his firm and get another.

The man leaned the umbrella carefully against his knee so as to be able to spread his hands in a Gallic gesture. 'I am waiting here two hours,' he said. 'Two hours I am waiting, and now you are saying I must go away and come back again. It's not O.K.'

'But look here, my friend,' said Aubrey, with a charming smile. 'It's not my fault if you make a mistake. You have the wrong form, that's all. You can easily get the right one and come back.' He spoke as if a second visit to the Immigration Office would be a pleasure.

'But this is the form you were telling me I must have,' the Frenchman protested.

'*I?*' Aubrey leaned back in his chair, shocked. 'I certainly never told you that, nor, I'm sure, did any of my colleagues.'

'Well, it was someone here. . . .' The Frenchman looked cautiously at Miss Hattie and Mr Pierrepont, and craned his neck to peep into the cubicle at Elwood but he lacked the courage to accuse anyone.

'If you don't mind,' suggested Aubrey, all smiles again, 'there are other people waiting to be helped, and our time is precious, you know.'

The Frenchman was beaten. He straightened his umbrella, shifted his grip farther down the handle and went out of the room, with bent knees. The eyes of the people sitting by the wall followed him dully to the door.

A woman in a creased linen suit, who was now head of the line, stood up hopefully, but Aubrey had leaned towards the cubicle and Elwood had tipped back his chair and they were off on another of their chummy gossips. The woman sat down again, moistening her lips and trying not to look as if she had made a mistake.

'Hot enough for you?' Mr Pierrepont asked Miss Hattie, on his way to whisper something to Aubrey.

'My goodness, yes,' said Miss Hattie. Her smile faded as she turned back to the woman with the small boy, who was sitting at her desk. She was having trouble with them. The woman could not speak English, so everything had to be said to the

247

small boy, who then translated it to his mother. It was question-able whether he was translating right, for each of his gabbled remarks brought a deeper bewilderment to the mother's face. Her eyes were troubled. She shrugged her shoulders and said something to the small boy, which might have been: 'If I'd known it was going to be like this in America I would never have come.'

The small boy laughed and looked up at the ceiling, drum-ming his heels against the bars of the chair. He watched a fly. With one of the sudden *ennuis* of childhood, he was bored with the whole thing. He would translate no more.

'You – must – fill – in – this – form,' Miss Hattie told the mother slowly and patiently in her useless little voice. 'Thees form you moost fill een.' Miss Hattie tried it in broken English, but the woman still looked as if she were being asked to explain Einstein's theory. Miss Hattie thrust the form under her nose, and the woman drew back a little as if it were a lighted match. Miss Hattie looked round for help, but Aubrey was still talking to Elwood, and Mr Pierrepont was buried behind his ledgers with only the thinning top of his bony head showing.

'Take this, dear.' Miss Hattie gave the form to the little boy. 'Fill it in for your mother.'

'O.K.,' said the child, very blasé.

'Can you write, dear?'

'Sure I can write. What do you think I am?' The boy's voice rose to a whine. He had evidently been in America longer than his mother; long enough, anyway, to pick up the inflections of his schoolmates. He said something to his mother, and she collected the parcels which she had strewn around her chair, smiled nervously at Miss Hattie and followed her son to a table in the corner, where there were inkwells, and pens on chains. They sat down side by side, the mother sitting anxiously on the edge of her chair, as if her son were a defeated general signing a peace treaty, and the boy twisting his legs round the chair, poking out his tongue, ruffling his hair, and attacking the form with all the manifestations of labour he would give at his desk in school.

The telephone bell set Aubrey and Elwood and Miss Hattie courteously passing the buck again. They finally unloaded it on to Mr Pierrepont, who was not privileged to have a telephone on his desk and had to answer it standing at a window-sill at the back of the room. His legs were crooked and the seat of his trousers was shiny. Christine felt idly sorry for him, but she could not care too much. She was beginning to feel sick again. However, she stood up automatically with the rest when Aubrey, with the air of a man too busy even to look up from his desk, threw out a casual: 'Next, please!'

It was the woman in the creased linen suit. She had a prim, bloodless face and hair cut like a schoolgirl, although she had not been a schoolgirl these twenty years or more. She was English. She was also kittenish. She did some high-pitched giggling with Aubrey, and then he rose heavily and took her over to a recess in a corner of the office, where a table held some mysterious pieces of apparatus. What was he going to do? Everyone turned their heads to look, as if they were at a tennis match. Aubrey said something to the Englishwoman and she took off her scarf. He said something else and she took off the jacket of her suit. He spoke to her again and she shook her head, apparently jibbing at taking off her spotted voile blouse as well.

Aubrey rolled up his sleeves. He took hold of her bare arm above the wrist and the Englishwoman wriggled a little and fluttered her eyes. Was he then going to ravish her in the recesses of the Immigration Office? But no. Firming his grip, he guided her hand on to a pad on the table and pressed down hard. He was only taking her fingerprints, but from the coy way he handled her, pressing one finger after another on to the pad as if he were playing This Little Piggy Went to Market, and from the squirmings and gigglings with which she half acquiesced, half protested, they might have been playing a most daring game between the sexes.

When it was over and Aubrey perspiring with achievement, the Englishwoman was left holding her inkstained hands daintily away from the spotted blouse and looking at him with helpless feminine appeal.

'Where can I –?'

'Just down the corridor on the left,' he whispered. 'Do you think you can find it?'

'Oh yes,' she said, lest he might offer to accompany her.

Gallantly he threw open the door for her, and she tripped out of the room, still holding her fingers delicately extended, as if she were passing the cucumber sandwiches at the vicarage fête.

This little episode seemed to have sapped Aubrey. He sat down at his desk and mopped his forehead and brooded, and would not call out: 'Next, please!'

Christine shifted on her chair, leaned forward and surreptitiously hung her head down, because she was beginning to feel faint. Would they never get to her? Miss Hattie was now occupied with a voluble Austrian woman, who was pouring forth a recital of her trials and tribulations in the land of liberty. Her nerves were bad, she was telling Miss Hattie hoarsely, and no one could understand that sinking feeling which came over her. Miss Hattie listened with fascinated sympathy, although what the Austrian woman's nerves had to do with the business of the Immigration Office it was hard to see.

The cracked, breathless voice seemed as if it would go on for ever. The woman and the small boy were still sitting at the table battling with the form. Elwood was telephoning again. His client in mourning had disappeared. Perhaps she had only been a figment of the imagination in this unreal vacuum of a world. Mr Pierrepont asked Miss Hattie if it was hot enough for her, then he coughed, got up and tiptoed crookedly to the door, murmuring: 'I think I'll be going to lunch.' He said it to no one in particular, and no one answered him.

When Elwood had finished his telephone conversation he tipped his chair so far back that he was in danger of falling and breaking his spine and said: 'I'll go and grab myself some lunch, Aubrey, if that suits you.'

'Fine, fine,' said Aubrey. 'You do that. I'll be following you myself as soon as I'm through with all this.'

But how could he ever be through? He had a young Chinese boy at his desk now. People were gradually being taken off the top of the line, but more people were coming in all the time, all races, all shapes, all accents. Christine was now half-way up the line. If she could hold out, they must finally get to her and she could get the extension to her visa and go home and Vinson would not know that she had ever been an undesirable alien without a permit.

The door burst open and a round, rosy woman with her hair curled like a poodle and odd bits of colourful clothing hung about her pranced in with an exuberance that disturbed the turgid waters of the office like a flung stone.

'Hi there!' she greeted Aubrey and Miss Hattie.

Miss Hattie beamed and Aubrey answered. 'How's it coming, Mrs D.?' and took new life from her vitality. They were pleased to see her. She was evidently the life and soul of the party, the office Merry Andrew, who was everybody's friend. She threw a jolly glance round the room, put a lot of parcels and a loaf of bread down on the desk which said: INFOR-MATION, and began, chuckling, to read a note that some-body had left there for her. Perhaps it was Mr Pierrepont. Perhaps he was secretly in love with Mrs D., but dared not Speak, so he had written her a love-letter and escaped to lunch before she came back.

Christine looked at her watch. It was long after her usual lunch-time. Her doctor had told her to eat at regular hours. Perhaps she felt faint because she was hungry. Conscious of the gaze of the other people waiting in the line, she got up and went over to Mrs D.'s desk.

'I've been waiting such a long time,' she said diffidently. 'Do you think I might get attended to soon? I really am in rather a hurry.'

It was an innocent enough remark, but Mrs D.'s eyebrows shot up as if at an indecency.

'Just a moment, *please*,' she said. 'I've only just come in. I'll see to you directly if you'll just have a seat.'

'I've been just having a seat for nearly two hours,' Christine said. 'I was only asking. After all, your desk does say Informa-tion.'

Mrs D. did not think this was funny. She went to a cupboard at the back of the room and hung up her hat and jacket and began to rearrange her curls in the misted mirror on the wall. Aubrey finished with the Chinese boy and ambled over to in-spect the trophies of her shopping expedition. Miss Hattie, drawn by the lure of parcels, left her Austrian confidante and went over to have a look too. They made a cosy little scene, examining and exclaiming, while the line of aliens waited

251

listlessly against the wall like the debilitated inmates of a concentration camp waiting to go to the ovens.

When Mrs D., revived with fresh powder and lipstick, went back to her desk, Christine went to her again to ask what the chances were of getting a visa before the winter set in.

'All will be attended to in their turn,' Mrs D. said cheerfully. 'We can't see everyone at once, you know. We're very busy.' She made the motions of fluffing up some papers on her desk, but after Christine had sat down she did nothing at all except twist her hair round her fingers, hum little tunes, and throw coquettish remarks across the room to Aubrey.

The door opened and shut, opened and shut. People came and went. White people, yellow people, coloured people. One by one, at deadly intervals, the people in the line were seen by Miss Hattie or Aubrey, or sent about their business because they had the wrong forms. Christine was moving gradually towards the top. The atmosphere in the office was stifling. The heat was unbearable. The woman next to her in the tight scarf had begun to pick at her nails, and the man on the other side was seized with a fit of yawning which sent garlic out on the air every time he opened his mouth. Christine began to yawn too. Her eyes glazed over. She could not focus properly. Her head swam, and she had that terrible heavy feeling as if all the blood in her body was pooling together in the pit of her stomach.

She managed to get up, and walked uncertainly over to Mrs D.'s desk. 'Do you think I might have a glass of water?' she asked. Her ears could hardly catch the sound of her own voice.

'There is a water cooler in the corridor.'

'I wonder – could you get it for me? I feel so queer –'

Mrs D. gave her a penetrating glance which seemed to see right through Christine to the baby within, shrugged her shoulders, got to her feet as if it were a great effort and went to the door, sweeping a look from Christine to Aubrey and back again which seemed to say: 'Whatever next? Whatever will they ask of us next?'

Christine leaned against the desk. She could not get back to her chair. She looked at Aubrey, and as she looked the top of his bald head seemed to lift slightly and float from side to side. The walls of the room swayed and reeled. A mist like a rushing wind swept across her eyes. She thought she cried out, but the roaring in her ears drowned all sense or sound.

When she came to she was lying on the floor surrounded by feet and bending bodies and shrill foreign cries of alarm. It was the most stirring thing that had ever happened in that office. Everybody was giving useless advice. Aubrey was wringing his hands and Miss Hattie was letting out little peeps of dismay, but Mrs D. came back with a paper cup of iced water and set the whole scene to rights.

She pushed back the crowd, helped Christine to her feet and lugged her into Elwood's cubicle. Her blouse smelled hot and unpleasing and her arms were fat and squashy, but she was a solid help and Christine clung to her until she was lowered into a chair with a torn leather seat in the corner of Elwood's little den. Like a policeman, Mrs D. stopped the rabble from coming in after her and got them back in order to their places against the wall. Christine leaned back and closed her eyes. She had never felt so weak in her life.

'What shall we do with her?' she heard Aubrey whisper.

'We must get someone to take her away,' said Mrs D. as if Christine were a corpse or a barrel of garbage.

'Can we telephone someone for you?' Her voice was suddenly close. Christine opened her eyes. Mrs D. was bending over her. 'My husband ...' She forced herself to think of Vinson's office number. Aubrey, chivalrous to the last and anxious to play some active role in the drama, took over the arduous job of telephoning Vinson. Christine heard him at his desk giving the most hair-raising account of what had happened to her: 'Your wife has been taken ill. ... I think you should come at once. ...'

Poor Vin. He would be in a terrible state, would drive much too fast, perhaps have an accident and never get there. Christine closed her eyes so that she could not see the people who sat by the wall staring curiously in at her, and resigned herself to the fancy that Vinson would not come.

She drifted away almost into a faint again. It seemed an eternity, or only a moment of time, until Vinson arrived. As Christine expected, he was highly perturbed. When he had fussed over her for a moment he went out of the cubicle and

253

began to outrage the dignity of the Immigration Office by throwing questions and orders about as if he were on a quarter-deck. Christine was glad that he was in uniform. People did not pay so much attention to him when he was in ordinary clothes. Aubrey was inclined to be huffy with him, but Mrs D. was subdued and Miss Hattie all of a twitter and the line of concentration camp inmates frankly impressed. Christine felt secure and blissfully dependent. Vinson was going to take her home. She had someone to look after her now.

She persuaded Vinson that she was not dying and did not need an ambulance. Mrs D. found her handbag and patted her on the shoulder, with a nod that said: 'We women know what trouble is', and Vinson helped her to her feet and supported her to the door. As they went out she heard Aubrey say: 'And now perhaps I'll get a chance to go to lunch.'

Christine felt much better, but Vinson insisted on almost carrying her along the corridor, so that she could hardly keep her feet on the ground. The people going in and out of the offices stared. The lift man stared. The loungers in the doorway stared, but at last they were in the car and going home. When Christine started to tell Vinson what had happened, he said: 'Don't try to talk now. Just rest', and would not let her say anything.

When they reached home he took her upstairs and undressed her and put her to bed. He sat down on the bed and stroked her hair.

'Why didn't you tell me about the visa?' he asked very kindly. 'I ought to be shot for being so selfish about the car this morning. I'd have gone there with you if I'd known. Why didn't you tell me, darling?'

'Well –' Christine looked down and fingered the sheet. 'I'd forgotten to look at the visa when you asked me, and when I did it had expired ages ago, and I was afraid you'd be cross about it.'

He looked distressed. His black brows came together and his flecked, unblinking eyes stared at her with concern. 'Am I such an ogre? I thought you always told me everything. You know you promised you would.'

That was true. She had promised, the day after they were

married, when they were talking very solemnly. She thought of all the things she had not told him since then. Times when she had wanted him to make love to her, and had been too shy or too proud to say so. Times when she had been bored. Days and nights when America was too big, and she had been homesick for England. Moments when she thought of Jerry, and felt guilty for trying to compare two different kind of love.

How could one tell a husband those things? They would not help a marriage.

'You do tell me everything, don't you?' Vinson persisted, his face close to hers. 'You must, you know.'

'Of course I do.' She looked away. 'I was just silly about the visa. I'm sorry, Vin.'

'Are you afraid of me?'

'No.'

He kissed her. He was sweet and tender and she felt very close to him. It was worth fainting in the Immigration Office to bring them together in one of these brief idylls when she felt that marriage to him was all she wanted in the world.

She would have to faint again some day.

Chapter Six

SHE did not faint again. August was beginning to cool into September, and with the gradual lifting of the sticky Washington heat Christine felt very well. She was well enough to receive with equanimity the news that Vinson's mother had decided that she was able to face the trip to Washington, and was coming to stay with them for two weeks.

Christine took the news better than Vinson did. When he began to read his mother's letter, he said: 'Oh my God', although he hastily amended it to: 'Well, isn't that fine? Mother's coming east to see us.'

He seemed uneasy, but Christine was rather pleased. She was naturally curious to see her mother-in-law, and eager to make friends with her if possible. Vinson did not often speak about her, and when he did it was with no very great enthusiasm. Brought up in a family who loved and accepted each other in spite of irritations and disputes, Christine could not understand anyone not wanting to see his mother.

Vinson did not actually say that he did not want to see her. He was too conventionally well-mannered for that. Even to Christine he did not always say what was in his mind when it was something that had no right to be there. It was obviously with an effort, however, that he said at intervals: 'It will be nice when Mother comes. I'm sure you and she will get on.' Sometimes, when they were planning something for the near future, he said: 'Oh, but of course that will be when Mother's here', and had to brighten his tone deliberately in the middle of the sentence which he had started with inadvertent gloom.

When Christine saw Mrs Gaegler senior she understood Vinson's unease a little better. Mrs Gaegler had said that she would arrive on a Sunday morning, but instead she arrived early on the Saturday evening when Christine and Vinson were changing to go to a cocktail party at Admiral and Mrs Hamer's. That was only the first of many inconvenient things she did. The next was that she brought with her a horrid little dog called

Honeychile. It was a chihuahua, a tiny creature like a spider, with spindling legs, eyes like gooseberries, a rat tail, a skull too narrow to house a brain and a shrieking yap that rent the nerves. It was Mrs Gaegler's pride and joy, the solace of her life since her husband and children had abandoned her to live alone in Kaloomis, Kansas.

That was the way she put it. 'I've been abandoned by my family,' she would say, with the false half-laugh of self-pity. She classed her children's defection with her husband's, although he had gone off with a girl from a drugstore, while all they had done was to go into the Army or the Navy or get married.

The obscene little dog ran into the house before her and nipped Christine on the ankle as soon as it saw her. Vinson raised a foot at it, and it nipped at him too and fell into a paroxysm of frustrated yapping because its futile teeth could not get through his trousers.

'Poor little Honeychile!' People with unpleasing dogs always come in just in time to catch you if you raise a hand or foot to them. 'Vinson, I'm surprised at you!' Mrs Gaegler cried, before she had even said hullo to her son. She bent down and picked up the dog, which went on yapping in her arms as a background to her talk. Looking back afterwards on her visit, it seemed to Christine that all her mother-in-law's conversation had been to the accompaniment of Honeychile's shrill yapping.

There was plenty of it – both the yapping and the conversation. Mrs Gaegler talked all the time as if it were a bodily necessity, like breathing. She could not sit silent in a room for longer than she would have been able to hold her breath without choking. Words rattled from her in a jarring Middle West twang from the moment she woke in the morning to the moment when she had taken her sleeping-tablets and retired for the night with the threat that she would not sleep; and the words were mostly about herself.

She was one of those very ordinary people who consider themselves unique. As a nonpareil, Mrs Gaegler was of vast interest to herself, if to no one else, and the ills and discomforts of her person were her religion. She began to complain the moment she arrived, standing in the hall in her spike heels and extraordinary little pagoda hat, with the dog barking, and

Christine in her dressing-gown, and Vinson in his shirt-sleeves with his tie hanging round his open collar.

Mrs Gaegler was an undersized, short-legged woman, who would have been fat if she had not been held in and pushed up at all the salient points. She wore her clothes well and went in for conspicuous accessories like an outsize handbag in the shape of a fishing creel, and a necklace made of small glass balls in each of which was suspended an imitation goldfish. The gold bracelet flopping at her wrist spelled out the letters I L-O-V-E Y-O-U. If Vinson's father had given it to her, it was hard to believe that she would still wear it after he had transferred his love to the girl from the drugstore. Perhaps she had bought it for herself.

In her youth she must often have been called 'Babyface', and she was trying to perpetuate the attribute into middle-age. Her round face was made up very pink and white, the bow of her lips was painted on outside the natural edge, her eyebrows repeated the round line of her china eyes, and her blue-grey hair was brushed back in a fluff of little curls. Christine had to admit that she did not really look sixty, although there were times when she was complaining when she could look a disgruntled eighty.

Almost before she had greeted Christine and flicked her round eye up and down to sum up her daughter-in-law, she began to tell them about the trip: how tired she was, and how terrible the hotels had been, and how a thousand miles was much too far to drive – as if it were Washington's fault for being so far away from Kansas.

'Matt drives too fast, you know,' she grumbled. 'He always has. I kept telling him and telling him to watch his speed, and finally he side-swiped a truck back there in Zanesville, Ohio, and put a scratch on the car, which just about makes me mad, because I've always been so careful about the paintwork on that automobile.'

Matt was her other son, Vinson's younger brother, who was a captain in the Army. He was on leave now and had driven his mother to Washington, where he was going to stay with an old college friend while she visited Vinson and Christine.

He came in with his mother's bags, smiling broadly. His face looked as if he were more at home with a grin on it than anything else. He was taller than Vinson and more burly, with a wider, larger-featured face. Although they were both dark, they did not look at all alike. They greeted each other with a handshake and a slap across the shoulders, but you would not have thought that they were brothers who had not met for over a year. Christine sensed a certain restraint between them; not quite an animosity, but a certain caution on Vinson's part, as if he were in the habit of expecting his brother to get above himself, and a half-mocking watchfulness from Matthew, as if he had never quite made up his mind whether Vinson was a joke or not.

When Vinson introduced him to Christine, Matthew looked at her contemplatively for a moment with a spreading smile, then put down the suitcases, took a deliberate stride and a firm hold on her arms and kissed her, a little too near the mouth. Christine glanced at Vinson and saw that he did not like it.

Matthew grinned. 'All right, all right, Mother,' he said, for Mrs Gaegler was hopping about among her many bags like a schoolteacher trying to count a picnic party. 'I brought everything in. Yes, your cosmetic bag's there. You don't have to fuss, toots.'

'It appears we've come a day too early, Matt,' she said, opening her eyes very wide, while Vinson and Christine murmured that it did not matter at all. 'Vinson and this lovely girl – isn't she just a darling person? I knew she would be – are just off to a party, so of course there's nothing for us but to put on our party dresses and go along with them.'

'That would be wonderful, Mother,' Vinson said awkwardly, 'but I don't know whether the Admiral –'

'Don't worry,' his mother said. 'I'm not afraid of admirals. I can get along with anyone,' she told Christine, 'because I'm so interested in people. I've studied psychology, you see, so I know what makes everyone tick.' Christine smiled and tried to receive this information well. She was determined to like her mother-in-law, and to be liked.

'I thought you were so tired,' Vinson said, and Christine saw that Matt was grinning at the sight of Vinson trying to persuade

259

his mother out of something she meant to do. 'Wouldn't you rather lie down and rest a while? Christine can get your bed fixed in a moment, and we won't be away too long. If it were anything else we'd cut the party, but since it's the Admiral we can't very well . . .'

'Of course I'm tired,' said his mother. 'Motoring always makes me feel just terrible. You know that. But don't imagine that I haven't trained myself to be sociable when I feel limp as a rag. Every evening,' she told Christine, 'I suffer from Five o'Clock Fatigue. My doctor says it's only my spirit that keeps me going through all the entertaining we have back home. But of course I'll come with you, Vinson. I know you'll want to have all your Washington friends meet your mother.'

'Well –' Vinson glanced helplessly at Christine. She had never seen him so at a loss. His mother seemed to subdue him and sap his confidence. 'You'd better go call Mrs Hamer and ask if we may bring my mother and brother to her party.'

'Not me, Vin,' Matthew said. 'I'm going right on to Bob's. You can have your admirals, but count me out.'

'Just say it's my mother then. And be sure to ask her very nicely, won't you, darling?'

'Why shouldn't I?' Christine was irritated by his nervousness. 'I know how to talk to admirals' wives. I ought to. I've had enough practice with the brutes.'

Matthew laughed and Honeychile barked at him. 'Of course she does,' said Mrs Gaegler, tapping the dog's flimsy skull with her finger. 'She's a very lovely girl. I always know about people the minute I see them. Vinson, you mustn't be so –'

'Oh no,' said Christine instantly on the defensive to stop Vinson's mother trying to gang up with her against him. 'I'm dreadful. I always say the wrong thing.'

As she went through to the living-room to telephone she heard Matthew say: 'I say, though, Vin boy, I like your wife.' Vinson murmured, and then she heard him say to his mother: 'Let me take your bags up and show you your room. I'm sure you'll want to freshen up.' It was not like a son talking to his mother. It was like a host dealing courteously with an acquaintance. He was as unnaturally polite to her as he had been to his sister Edna. Politeness was all right – the Copes had never gone in for it enough – but this seemed to Christine to be an odd way to treat your relations.

Matthew treated Mrs Gaegler less politely and was more successful with her. He treated her like an inconvenient child, and merely laughed at her when she was difficult. He did not look as if he took anything seriously.

When Vinson and his mother had gone upstairs, Mrs Gaegler complaining above Honeychile's yapping that the stairs were too steep and someone would break their neck there some day, Matthew came into the living-room, where Christine was being obsequious to Mrs Hamer, with a sycophantic smile on her face, as if the Admiral's wife could see her. Matthew winked, made a face at Mrs Hamer's voice clacking through the telephone, and gave Christine a casual salute. ''Bye, Chris,' he said. 'Be seeing you.'

Christine changed her sycophantic smile to a friendly one for him. She was glad he had come. She liked him. Perhaps he would become a real brother to her, as Roger had never quite been.

With Matt's inconsequential influence removed, Mrs Gaegler became more difficult. Vinson could not laugh at her as his brother did. He just stood and looked worried while she said that the bed would have to be moved because she would get neuralgia if she faced the light, and might she have another lamp and a cushion for Honeychile – 'She likes green ones best. She's allergic to red' – and she hoped that dog next door was not going to bark all the time and upset poor Honey, who had not fully recovered from her last confinement.

She kept the door of her room open and talked on while Christine and Vinson finished their interrupted changing. Vinson did not answer. He tied his tie and brushed his hair deliberately, plodding about the room with an expressionless face.

Christine felt that she had to say something. When there was a pause while Mrs Gaegler was putting her head into a dress, Christine told her that the room was going to be the baby's, and that Vinson had decorated it himself.

'It's very charming,' Mrs Gaegler emerged through the neck of the dress. 'If you *want* my opinion, the frieze is a little too

261

high, and of course they never use pink for nursery walls now. It's always yellow. It has a definite psychological effect, you know.'

'Well, we like it, said Christine stoutly 'Vinson painted it himself.'

'I know, dear. You told me. And as I've said – it's very charming.'

They had to wait for her quite a long time, and Vinson fussed about being late at the Admiral's. When his mother emerged in a tight black dress with her bosom pushed well up and her smoky hair fluffed out, the question then arose of what was to be done with Honeychile.

She could not be left in the house alone. Mrs Gaegler said that was cruel, and she was funny, but she could never be unkind to dumb animals or children. In Kaloomis, Kansas, Mrs Gaegler said, she always got a dog-sitter when she had to go anywhere without Honey. 'Though, of course, most people are delighted to have her along. Perhaps one of your neighbours would have her?' she asked Christine. 'I'm sure they'd be glad to look after her. She's everyone's pet. Why, back in Kaloomis everyone knows her. She's quite a public figure. When she had her puppies I had it put in the Births column of the *Herald*. Let's take her round to one of your neighbours, shall we, and then get going. I need a drink. I'm a little weak right now. My adrenal glands don't produce enough natural stimulant, you know. It's always the same at this time in the evening.'

'I don't think we could do that,' Christine said. 'Betty is always so busy, and they've got a dog, and I don't think Mrs Meenehan . . .'

'They wouldn't help you out?' Mrs Gaegler raised the arcs of her eyebrows. 'That doesn't sound very neighbourly. Haven't you gotten around to making friends with your neighbours then? Of course I must remember. You're English.'

Christine looked at her and clenched her fists. If Vinson's mother were going to start on *that* line . . . She turned and went downstairs, reminding herself that she was going to like her mother-in-law.

They took Honeychile with them. There was nothing else to do. They left her in the car, yapping frenziedly and scrabbling

262

at the window, and when they came out from the party they found that she had chewed a hole in the leather of the back seat. Vinson was furious. He prized his car next to the Navy, his wife and his house. He sulked while he drove, but his mother did not notice. A couple of drinks had compensated for her defective adrenal secretions and she had had a good time. She had gone round saying to everybody: 'I'm Commander Gaegler's mother. I'm sure you know my son.'

Christine, drinking Coca-Cola and standing unobtrusively in a corner because she thought from Mrs Hamer's glance that her condition must be too obvious, heard her mother-in-law beard Captain Fleischman, who was the chief of Vinson's division, and tell him how lucky he was to have her son working for him.

Vinson finally came back and rescued Christine to take her home. She never saw much of him at parties. He always went off and talked shop with other naval officers, and left her to domestic banalities among the wives. All the husbands did that. At any naval party you would find all the men at one end of the room and all the women at the other, the sexes divided like oil and water.

Knowing him well, she saw that he had had several drinks, but he appeared to be perfectly sober. No one who was looking for a promotion would ever be anything else at an admiral's party. They collected Mrs Gaegler, who had Captain Fleischman hypnotized like a chicken against the wall, and then they said good-bye to the Admiral, who grunted at them, and gave the appropriate effusive thanks to Mrs Hamer, who was standing by the table which held the inevitable cold turkey and ham, so that no one dared to come and eat it.

Christine and Vinson had planned to have supper at home, but there was not enough for three, so they went to a restaurant. Mrs Gaegler said she was not hungry, but she ate quite a large steak, although she complained that it was too rare and no one in the east knew how to broil a steak the way they did back home.

The stimulation of her drinks was wearing off, and evidently her adrenals were not yet functioning, for she began to feel poorly now, and while Christine and Vinson ate their dessert, at which she made a face, she was fidgeting to get back to her digestive mixture.

At home they urged her to go to bed, although she promised them she would not sleep. They shut the door on her and Honeychile at last, and went downstairs to have some coffee by themselves. Vinson looked tired. He seemed depressed. Christine made a little light conversation to him, as she sometimes had to do when she did not know what to say to please him, but she felt silly sitting there in her best cocktail dress that was now too tight, making conversation to her husband, so she gave it up.

'What's the matter, Vin?' She moved closer to him on the sofa.

'Nothing. I'm tired.'

'More than that.'

'Uh-huh.' He shook his head. 'Well,' he began in a brighter tone, 'how do you like my mother?'

'Oh, she's sweet, Vin. I'm sure we shall get on very well.'

'Of course. She's a grand person. It's wonderful to have her here.'

He sounded as if he wanted to be convinced, but Christine could not find the words to back up his attempt.

'I'm sorry, darling,' he said, suddenly relaxing. 'I know what you're thinking. But – look. Every time, I think it will be better, and we shall be like a friendly family. I do try. One must love one's mother, but – I don't know. She's not like other people's mothers. She's so difficult. She always has been. When we were children she –' He shook his shoulders a little. 'Oh, to hell with that. But a mother – you know. It's kind of a let-down when you can't feel about her as you should.'

'You mustn't say that, darling,' Christine said, but she was glad that he was confiding in her. 'After all, your mother isn't very well. She seems to have so many things wrong with her.'

'She's the healthiest woman on God's earth,' he said. 'There isn't a damn thing wrong with her. But she's always been like that. My father was a pill, but I sometimes think he ... Oh, Christine,' he put his arms around her, 'thank God I've got you. I've never had anyone – close, you know. Don't ever leave me.'

'Of course not, darling.' She sat and cuddled him for a while. If he wanted her to be a mother to him, all right, she would be maternal.

Presently she said: 'I like your brother, Vin. I think he's terribly nice.'

She thought that he would be pleased, but if he was he did not show it. He sat up and smoothed his short black hair. 'Matt?' he said. 'He's O.K. Cocky, though. He always was. Come on, let's go to bed.'

They went to their room and heard through the flimsy wall the snuffling snores of Mrs Gaegler, who informed Christine next morning when she tottered down for breakfast two hours after Vinson had left that she had not slept a wink all night and knew she never would in a house that faced north and south.

Mrs Gaegler was full of ills and strange disorders, some of which Christine had never heard of before. She seemed to suffer from a different complaint on every day of her visit. You never knew what it would be. She told Christine all about it when she came down in the morning, and by evening she had fallen a victim to something else, with which she would greet Vinson when he came home.

Her voice went on and on all day. The only thing that could drown it was Christine's noisy vacuum cleaner, which Mrs Gaegler said had an unhygienic dust-bag and should be banned by federal law. When the vacuum cleaner was roaring round sucking up the rugs you could not hear an airplane directly overhead, but Mrs Gaegler went on talking, her lips nimble and her hands idle. She never offered to help Christine with the housework. She was allergic to dust, dishwater, silver polish and hot irons.

She was allergic to anything she did not like, and when she felt liverish from drinking too much rye whisky her quite plebeian symptoms were ennobled with the name of allergy too.

She was adept at aggrandizing minor complaints into full-scale ills. If she was a little tired it was nervous exhaustion, or prostration, or the defective adrenals again. If she had a headache it was a migraine coming on, or even in her wilder flights the threat of a cerebral tumour. If her skin itched she was sure

265

she was in for hives or shingles. Indigestion from over-eating was called gastritis; a cough from over-smoking was a touch of bronchitis. She complained for days that she had sprained her thumb writing letters, and when she was persuaded out into the garden one day to help weed the lawn the slight backache she acquired convinced her that she had slipped a disc in her spine, and she made Christine drive her to the doctor.

She was always wanting to go to the doctor. The opportunity of plaguing a new one was too good to miss. Christine had to drive her there every other day to have injections – no one knew what for – but she had brought with her a selection of ampoules which she insisted on having pumped into herself at regular intervals. Christine hoped that the doctor threw away the ampoules and pumped in sterile water instead, as she had often done with hypochondriacs in the hospital.

One whole shelf in the bathroom had to be cleared for Mrs Gaegler's drugs and medicaments. She took little nips at them all day long, and sometimes at night Christine would hear her patter into the bathroom in her gold kid mules to refresh herself with a dose of this or that. Her craving for penicillin was abnormal. If she pricked herself with a pin she wanted it, and once when she got a rose thorn in her finger she wanted to have an anti-tetanus shot as well.

The luckless Honeychile was also subjected to frequent dosings. She had vitamin pills every morning, cod-liver oil at midday and gland extract at night to compensate for the hormones Mrs Gaegler said she had lost when she had her puppies. Sometimes she spat the pills out, a half-dissolved mess on the carpet, and Mrs Gaegler would fear for her life and want to take her to the vet. The preparation of the dog's food was the only labour she would undertake in the kitchen. Christine had half-heartedly offered to do it, but her mother-in-law insisted on mashing up the tinned chicken and strained baby foods herself, as if she thought – perhaps with reason – that anyone else might poison Honeychile.

Matthew merely laughed at his mother's hypochondria. Vinson was resigned to it, and Christine soon learned not to take it seriously. She would sympathize politely, and would run up to the bathroom for a medicine bottle or drive Mrs Gaegler to the doctor when she wanted, but she was no longer disturbed by the announcements of a gastric ulcer or a perilous blood pressure.

However, if no one in her family would worry about her ills, Mrs Gaegler was compensated by the interest which Mrs Meenehan took in them. On the morning after Mrs Gaegler's arrival she had appeared at the kitchen window ostensibly to borrow a 'drain of salad oil', but really in the hope of meeting the visitor, whose arrival she had watched round the corner of a curtain the day before. Mrs Gaegler was at the sink mixing herself a double bicarbonate of soda, and Mrs Meenehan, who loved other people's insides as much as she loved gadgets, weighed cheerfully into a discussion of Mrs Gaegler's morning symptoms. They took to each other at once. Mrs Meenehan had a floating kidney, which in itself was a passport to friendship.

After this she was always coming round with some patent medicine or unguent, or a newspaper article about cancer, and she and Vinson's mother would stand talking on the porch for hours, with the nodding heads, sucked-in mouths and popping eyes peculiar to clinically minded women. Sometimes Mrs Gaegler would go across the garden to the Meenehans' house and come back flushed with the discovery of a new kind of aspirin she had heard advertised on the television, and want to be driven to the drugstore immediately. Christine always had to take Vinson to work now so that she could have the car, for Mrs Gaegler could not walk anywhere, even to the shopping centre at the end of the road. She had spastic insteps and threatened cartilage in her knee joint.

Christine was pleased that her mother-in-law had made friends with Mrs Meenehan. It took her off her hands and gave her some free moments to get on with her work undisturbed by conversation and the short figure following her about saying: 'Why do you do it that way?', but Vinson was not pleased. He liked having the Meenehans next door no better than he had liked having Mr and Mrs Pitman R. Preedy opposite, and for the same reason. He was more snobbish than any Englishman. If people were 'not quite our kind' he did not want to mix with them, and he did not think his mother should either.

When she was not talking about her own ailments Mrs

Gaegler liked to discuss other people's. She was always boring Vinson and Christine with long stories about people they did not know, who all seemed to have cancer or T.B. or poliomyelitis. It did not make for stimulating conversation. After supper Vinson would usually escape to his carpentry in the basement – he was making a play-pen now – and Christine would be left to hear about that perfectly darling Sally Thorne, who's just riddled with bone cancer, the most shocking thing.

When she had temporarily exhausted her own and other people's insides Mrs Gaegler would turn her attention to Christine's. Never had an expectant mother been given so much advice and criticism as Christine had in those two weeks. It maddened her. Although she was always willing to discuss the baby with Vinson or Lianne or Nancy Lee or even the pessimistic Betty Kessler next door, she found herself reluctant to discuss it with her mother-in-law. Mrs Gaegler's approach was somehow offensive. She was almost ghoulishly curious, and she was full of all the unappetizing old wives' expressions like Quickening and Waters Breaking. She said that Christine was wearing the wrong clothes, doing the wrong exercises, eating the wrong food. Christine was following her doctor's advice and her own instincts, but her mother-in-law, having produced three children – 'and nearly died with each of them, for all the thanks they give me now' – considered herself a sounder authority than any doctor, and certainly than any green wife with her first baby – and an English wife at that.

Although she never openly insulted Christine's homeland, she was always taking little digs at it; and in spite of the evidence of the overpopulated British Isles, she was of the opinion that having a baby in unenlightened England was the most hazardous thing in the world.

She was talking about the baby one evening when she and Christine drove to the Arlington Annexe to fetch Vinson. She always said: 'My first grandchild. Don't let's talk about it; it makes me feel so old', and then proceeded to discuss every aspect of the baby, before and after birth.

She was objecting now to the names that Vinson and Christine had chosen. No Gaegler had ever been called Stephen or Pamela. It would not do. Christine drove in silence. She would not give her mother-in-law the satisfaction of knowing that if the child was a boy she was going to let Vinson saddle him with the unfortunate middle name of Norbert, which was a Gaegler family name.

Mrs Gaegler never noticed if you did not answer. If she asked you a question she was usually saying something else before you could speak.

'Careful, dear,' she said, shrinking delicately back from the windscreen. 'You were too near that green car. I shall come east for the christening, of course. I know you'll want me to, even though I shall balk at the font when I hear the child's name spoken. What kind of church shall you have the christening in?'

'A Catholic one, of course.' Christine was surprised that she should ask.

'Oh, my dear, I do hope you're not getting infected with this popish bug of Vinson's. He got it from his father, and it's stuck to him even after Harry Gaegler managed to throw it off to suit his own convenience.' She always spoke of her miscreant husband by his full name, as though he had been a mere acquaintance.

'I'm not thinking of being converted, if that's what you mean,' Christine said as she drove through the gates of the Annexe and slowed down for the coloured policeman to recognize her and wave her on with a smile. 'But Vin's a Catholic and it's a law of his Church that his children should be too, and of course he wants it.' She looked behind her to back the car into Vinson's numbered parking space opposite the end doors of the building.

'But you're surely not going to sit down under that! Watch it, dear. You're very near that other car. I think it's terrible the way the Romans grab hold of the children before they're old enough to know better, though they have to, I suppose, to save the Church from dying out. I had to have Edna and Vinson baptized Catholics, but when it came to Matt I dug my toes in, and he was baptized a good Methodist. Harry Gaegler didn't mind by that time, because he was already interested in That Girl and beginning to see the disadvantages of his religion.'

'I don't see that it has any disadvantages,' Christine said. 'I

269

often wish I'd been born a Catholic instead of someone who's supposed to be a Protestant, but never learned to do anything about it.'

'You are thinking of being converted!' Mrs Gaegler accused her. 'I wouldn't have thought it of a level-headed girl like you.' She was always saying how sensible and level-headed Christine was, as opposed to herself, who was so sensitive and emotional. 'I despise the Catholic Church. I never would have married Harry Gaegler if I hadn't been an innocent young thing and so mad in love with the guy that I thought it didn't matter. I tell you, it's been a great disappointment to me to see my son grow up in the toils of Rome. It brings on one of my migraines whenever I think of it. I feel I have one coming on right now, if you want to know. Edie was more enlightened, thank goodness. She took my advice and gave it up long before she met Milt, and now she goes to the Episcopal Church with him like a sensible woman. But Vinson's so stubborn and prejudiced.'

'He's not,' protested Christine. She hated her mother-in-law to criticize Vinson in any way. It seemed unfair. She had no right to, when she had done so little for him. 'Not about religion, anyway. He just does what he thinks is right and leaves other people to do what they like. He's never tried to persuade me to be converted. Sometimes lately I've thought I might, because it would be more convenient with taking the child to church and everything, but Vinson says if one's only doing it for convenience it wouldn't be right. They probably wouldn't have me, anyway. The Catholic Church isn't always out to grab people, like you say. You have to work your way in.'

'My, my,' said Mrs Gaegler, raising her eyebrows and patting her fluffy hair, 'you are very much under Vinson's influence, aren't you? More than I thought. I declare, it's quite a change to see a nice old-fashioned submissive wife. Perhaps that's why Vinson chose to marry an English girl. They're not so enlightened as American women in that way.'

Christine said nothing. She was not going to be rude to her mother-in-law. She would not give her that weapon – that English girls were rude, and she was suddenly too tired to talk to her any more.

'I hope Vin comes out punctually,' she said, to change the

subject. 'He promised he would, because I've got a lot to do.'
Milt and Edna were in Washington and were coming to dinner.
Matthew was coming too. It would be a family reunion, and
Christine was determined to have everything perfect in case
anyone felt like thinking that English girls did not make as
good wives as Americans.

Vinson did not come out punctually. At four-thirty the doors
opened and the stream of white, coloured, uniformed, crippled,
old, young, thin, and fat people began to pour out and head for
the cars and buses like lava. She had seen this many-headed
sight often since she came to Washington, but it never failed to
fascinate her. If Vinson came out late, which he usually did, she
was quite happy to sit and watch the throng of released workers, recognising a face here and there among the officers, specu-
lating about the civilian employees, and what their homes were
like and what they were off to do now in such a hurry.

Mrs Gaegler, for all her psychology and her professed interest
in people, did not want to watch the crowd which poured out of
the Annexe for a solid ten minutes. She bent her head and
began to fiddle with the dial of the radio. She did not want to
watch any crowd that had negroes in it. She was allergic to
coloured people. She was proud of that. It was her Southern
blood, she said. She was almost pure Middle West, but she
made great play with a far-away ancestor who had come from
Louisiana, and her eyes misted over if she saw a Confederate
flag.

The last stragglers had come out before Vinson appeared. He
was talking with another naval officer, who wore a ridiculous
plastic cover over his uniform cap, because it looked like rain.
On the steps Vinson waved at Christine and then stood and
talked for a few more minutes, the two of them with brief-cases
under their arms and their heads poked forward seriously, as if
the entire defence programme of the United States was on their
shoulders.

'Sorry, honey,' he said, as Christine moved over and he got
into the driving seat – he would never let her drive him. 'Hope
you haven't been waiting.'

'We have. You know you said you'd come out early, because
of the dinner.'

'I know, but I had to stop back and talk with John Flett about that Japanese business. That's important.'

'So is my dinner,' Christine said, and he laughed and patted her knee to show that he did not think she meant it crossly.

'We waited a full quarter of an hour,' his mother told him, 'and the leather odour of this car brings on my nausea. Honeychile didn't like waiting. She barked at everyone who came out, didn't you, my pet?'

'I'll bet she did.'

'But your wife and I have been having a very interesting talk.' She had taken to calling Christine Your Wife, almost as if she were disclaiming her as a daughter-in-law and reminding Vinson that the responsibility for bringing her into the family was all his. Christine retaliated by calling her Your Mother. Mrs Gaegler had said that she must call her Lucette, but Christine could not bring herself to do that. She could not call her Mrs Gaegler, and she was not going to call her Mother, so she spoke of her to Vinson as Your Mother, and did not address her directly by any name.

'Well, that's fine,' Vinson said. 'What were you two girls gossiping about?' He tried to preserve the illusion that his mother and his wife were the best of friends.

'She was telling me that you intend to bring my grandchild up a Papist,' Mrs Gaegler said.

'I told you to keep off the subject of religion,' Vinson murmured to Christine.

'Oh, you did?' said Mrs Gaegler, who always heard things she was not meant to. 'So your wife is to be told what she can and can't talk about now, is she? My goodness, if Harry Gaegler had spoken to me like that I'd have given him something to remember. I would never have stood for half the nonsense your wife puts up with from you.'

No one said: 'Perhaps that's why he left you.' Vinson swore at a perfectly harmless old man in a panama hat who was trying to cross the road, and Christine turned up the radio with a blare of 'Shrimp boats are a-coming'.

The family reunion went off no better than might have been expected with a family who did not particularly want to be re-

272

united. The evening started unpropitiously by Honeychile refusing to take her gland extract. Every time she was given the pill she stuck out her long tongue and deposited it on the carpet. Mrs Gaegler was in a ferment. She wrapped the pill in meat, and Honeychile ate the meat and spat out the pill. She crushed it with sugar, and Honeychile took the spoonful into her mouth, goggled her eyes and threw the whole lot back on Mrs Gaegler's shoe.

'Open her mouth and put the pill on the back of her tongue and then close your hand round her nose so that she has to swallow it,' Vinson said.

'Oh no, Vinson, that's cruel. You must remember Honeychile isn't like other dogs. She's sensitive. She gets it from me. Why, if I were to force the pill down her she'd never take one again.'

'She doesn't seem to be taking it now,' said Vinson, with the mild sarcasm which was all the impertinence he would allow himself to give his mother.

'She will, she will. It just takes a little psychology. I can always win her round.'

She was still trying to make the rat-tailed dog take its hormones when Edna arrived. She was so busy fussing on the carpet with Honeychile that she hardly looked up to greet the daughter she had not seen for months.

When at last she could be persuaded to stand upright Edna kissed the air near her cheek and said: 'How are you, Mother?' This was rash, because her mother proceeded to tell her just how she was that evening, which was half dead from nervous exhaustion, with a nauseated feeling to her stomach.

'Where's Milt?' she asked suspiciously, as if she thought Edna's husband might have left her.

'Outside fooling with the car. He think's he's got a slow puncture. He never notices these things when we're near a garage. Will you help him he if wants to change the wheel, Vinson?'

'I'd be glad to. But this suit has just come back from the cleaner –'

'Oh, never mind,' said Edna briskly. 'I expect Matt will help him when he comes.'

'I don't know why you're so fond of that gaberdine, Vinson,' Mrs Gaegler said, travelling her eye up and down him as if he were something that somebody was trying to sell her. 'The colour's all wrong. Don't you think so, Edna?'

'But it's an expensive suit,' Vinson said. 'It cost me a hundred bucks.' To the Americans in the room that absolved the gaberdine from further criticism.

Milt came in presently, kissed Christine in his squashy way and told her she was the most wonderful girl he had ever seen, and asked his mother-in-law: 'How are you?' before anyone could stop him. Mrs Gaegler told him how she was, with embellishments on the story she had told Edna and the addition of a pain in her foot from the worry about Honeychile – 're-actionary nerves'. Milt incensed her by saying she looked wonderful, perfectly wonderful. He would have made a good compère on an audience-participation radio programme. Wonderful was his favourite adjective.

Washington was having two days of Indian summer. It was as hot as it had ever been in July, and although there was a storm approaching, it was sucking air into a stifling vacuum before it could bring relief. Everyone felt limp, and Christine saw that she was not alone in having to smother yawns. There seemed to be nothing to breathe in the little living-room where Mrs Gaegler told about the feeling in her stomach and the electric fan whirled the stale air uselessly round and round. When the heat came down Mrs Gaegler had insisted on closing all the windows in the house, to keep the hot air from coming in, although Christine thought that you could argue a better case for opening the windows to let the hot air out. However, her mother-in-law fussed so much if the windows were opened, and slipped so many discs in her spine reaching to shut them again, that Christine was forced to let her have her way and seal the house up like a biscuit tin.

Vinson made the drinks for everyone except Christine, and then there was a jaunty hammering on the door and Matthew came in and broke up the spiritless boredom of the room with his cheerful presence and exuberant greeting of Edna and Milt. He was the only Gaegler who seemed perfectly at ease with his family. Edna and her mother were fairly polite to each other on

274

the surface, but behind their quick, critical eyes they seemed to be sparring in unspoken combat, like two women in love with the same man. Vinson had been quiet ever since his mother came, and he was even more constrained in the presence of his whole family, as if he could not be himself in front of them.

When Christine went to the kitchen to give the finishing touches to the dinner, Edna followed her out, her slight stoop pulling her dress up on one hip. She was wearing the same brown dress – a little uneven now at the hem – which she had worn for Christine's wedding, and a little hat shaped like a canoe on her untidy coffee-coloured hair.

'How've you been, honey?' she asked, putting down her drink and picking up a cloth to wipe some saucepans on the draining-board. Edna was one of the few women Christine knew who would come into a kitchen and do what was wanted without asking.

'How do you get on with Mother?' she asked, polishing a saucepan more brightly than Christine ever could.

'Oh – very well, really.'

Edna laughed, screwing up her monkey face. 'You'll get used to her. You have to know how to treat her. Vinson never did know. He lets it get him down when she fusses all the time about her health. Me and Matt, we just pay no attention.'

'One day,' Christine said, 'she'll have something really wrong with her and no one will believe it.'

'She'll never have anything wrong with her,' Edna said, 'unless it's penicillin poisoning.'

'Why do you always talk about me behind my back?' Mrs Gaegler came round the kitchen door, her round eyes aggrieved. If you were asleep or trying to telephone she could shake the whole house with the noise of her high heels, but at inconvenient moments she could creep up on you like an Indian.

Christine felt guilty, but Edna said blandly: 'I was saying how much I like that gown, Mother. It's very becoming to you.'

'Oh, do you think so?' Her mother twirled around delightedly. She was a sucker for the glibbest compliment. 'But that's more than I can say for your hat, Edie. You're not of an age to wear that kind of frivolous thing any more.'

That came well from her, whose hats were all about twenty

275

years too young for her, but Edna did not mind. She took off the canoe and threw it up on to the top of the refrigerator.

'I hate any hat,' she said, 'but Milt doesn't care for me to go out without one. I guess I'll take my shoes off too if Christine doesn't mind. My feet are always happier when they can feel the floor.' She kicked her shoes into a corner and ambled across the kitchen for her drink, very short and flat-footed in her stockinged feet.

'You'll have to watch yourself, Edie,' her mother told her. 'You've gotten a bit cranky in your forties.'

'I always have been,' Edna said. 'It's inherited.'

'Harry Gaegler,' said her mother, who did not see how this could mean her, 'never took his shoes off until he went to bed, whatever else he may have done.'

'What are you looking for? Can I help you?' Christine asked, for Mrs Gaegler was questing distractedly about the kitchen.

'Yes, dear. I want some fresh newspaper to put down for Honeychile.'

'I can't see why you don't train her to use the garden,' Christine said, encouraged by Edna's presence to voice an irritation that had been with her ever since her mother-in-law started spreading newspapers on prominent bits of the floor.

Edna winked at her. 'Honeychile isn't like other dogs. Didn't you know that?'

'I'm glad you understand that,' her mother said, not seeing the wink, because she was bending down to the cupboard under the sink. 'Some people' – she straightened up and glanced at Christine – 'just don't seem to see that a dog has to be treated with psychology like everyone else. Oh me.' She pressed the palm of her little pink hand to her forehead. 'Bending down that way has sent my blood pressure way up. Thank you, dear.' She took the newspaper from Christine and went out.

Christine and Edna began to dish up the food. Matthew put his curly head round the door. 'Can I wash my hands?' he asked. 'I've been helping Milt change a wheel, and I don't want to muss up your bathroom, Chris. Your house always looks so clean. If I thought Carol could be like you I'd marry her to-morrow, if she'd marry me.' Carol was his girl friend, who played small parts on television and gave him a lot of trouble.

'I wish Milt were like you, Matt,' Edna said. 'When he's been doing a dirty job around the car he leaves the bathroom floor covered with dirty towels and a scum on the basin an inch thick. I get tired of telling him.'

'Milt's henpecked,' Matthew said, drying his hands on a paper towel and throwing it neatly across the room into the waste bin.

'I guess he is,' said Edna equably.

'Do you think they're ready for dinner?' Christine asked Matthew.

'I imagine so. Milt and Vin are discussing economic trends over a Scotch and water and Mother's crawling about the floor with bits of newspaper, but otherwise they're ready. Anything I can do?'

'You can carve the meat if you like.'

Matthew carved very well. He was useful in a kitchen – more useful than Vinson, who used too much finesse and took a long time to get anything done. Matthew had come out to see Christine once or twice while he had been in Washington, and she found him nice to have about, even when she was busy. He was easy and friendly and he made himself at home.

'What goes on?' Vinson came into the kitchen, looking a little put out. 'What's everyone doing in here? This is no sort of a party. I wish you'd learn to organize a little better, Christine. You shouldn't have to spend so long in the kitchen when you have guests.'

'It isn't guests. It's family,' Christine said through a cloud of steam as she drained the peas.

'When I entertain them in my house my family are my guests,' said Vinson pompously.

'Relax, brother,' said Edna, going out with a pile of plates.

'Where are her shoes?' Vinson asked. 'Listen, Christine, I'm always telling you, when you're a hostess you must arrange things so that you're not in the kitchen so much. It only needs a little method.'

'Do it the Navy way,' Matthew said, without looking up from his carving.

'What are you doing with that roast? I told you I'd carve for you, Christine. I wouldn't let Matt –'

'He's doing it very nicely,' Christine said soothingly. 'You were busy drinking with Milt – being a host, you see.'

'Bring the food in and let's eat,' Vinson said. He did not like her to tease him in front of Matthew.

Christine had taken a lot of trouble with the dinner. Vinson was proud of her, and everyone complimented her, except Mrs Gaegler, who would hardly eat anything. She sat bolt upright turning things distastefully over with a fork, as if she thought there might be grubs underneath.

When Milt, who, as usual, was loud in praise of everything, asked her: 'Aren't you glad Vin married such a lovely girl who can cook so wonderfully?' Mrs Gaegler would only say: 'I'm surprised that an Englishwoman can cook meat at all, when they get no practice at it over there.'

'You're eating nothing, Mother,' said Vinson, hastily, afraid that she was going to start on England. 'Try some of this potato salad. You know you like it.'

'I've told you, Vinson,' she said snappishly, 'I feel painfully sick in my stomach tonight. How can you expect me to eat?'

'It's the heat,' Milt said easily, helping himself from a dish. 'No one can eat in this weather.'

'Except you,' Edna said. 'You always break your diet when we come out. You have just no willpower.'

'Don't pick on me, Edie,' Milt said, and Mrs Gaegler backed him up, choosing to side with him against her daughter, in the same way as she often tried to side with Christine against her son.

'You can't object to me eating salad,' Milt said. 'And this is just the most wonderful salad I ever tasted. Christine, you are just the cleverest girl –'

'The salad would be all right if you didn't pick all the eggs out of it for yourself, like the glutton you are.'

'I notice you're eating potatoes, Edie,' her mother said, 'which is much worse.'

'Oh no. Eggs have far more calories than potatoes.' Edna had read many magazine articles on dieting and was as calorie-conscious as any American. She visualized them as tangible lumps of fattening stuff, marching straight to the waistline.

'Ah, but,' said Mrs Gaegler, who knew all about calories too 'eggs consume their own calories. Potatoes don't.'

After this statement, which was too baffling to be contested, she leaned forward and delicately picked a piece of meat off the dish to give to Honeychile, who had been yapping round the table, high stepping like a show hackney, ever since the meal started.

'You shouldn't feed dogs at the table,' Matthew said.

'This isn't dogs. It's Honeychile. There, I was afraid she wouldn't eat that beef,' Mrs Gaegler said as Honeychile spat the meat out on to the carpet. 'She's so very particular about what she eats. When she was expecting her babies she wouldn't take anything but salmon, and towards the end her nerves were so upset she wouldn't touch anything at all. It's a wonder she came through it. She had two veterinaries at her accouchement – Dr Stiegler and an assistant. My goodness, I'll never forget that night. It just *drained* me. I don't think I could go through that again, though I sold those puppies for fifty dollars apiece. Honeychile is too sensitive to be a mother. When she was nursing, you know, I had to stuff paper in the doorbell, because every time it rang her milk went away.'

Vinson was looking uncomfortable. He did not like this kind of talk at the dinner table. He gave Christine his almost inaudible whistle, to indicate that she should fetch the dessert and make a diversion. They were at opposite ends of the table and she was laughing surreptitiously with Matthew about Honeychile's confinement, but she looked up at once and said: 'Yes, Vin?' although no one else had heard the whistle.

'Now isn't that something?' Mrs Gaegler drew everyone's attention to Christine. 'He's trained his wife to answer when he calls her under his breath. Looks as if he's got her just where he wants her, doesn't it, folks?' She laughed affectedly, pretending that she had meant it as a joke.

'Well, I think that's wonderful,' Milt said. 'Simply wonderful. That's just the most beautiful thing –'

'Harry Gaegler used to shout for me at the top of his voice,' Mrs Gaegler said, 'and, my goodness, that man had a voice like a hog caller. But I would never answer. I wouldn't let any man think I was at his beck and call. Do it again, Vinson. I want to see it again.'

Vinson was never averse to showing off Christine's tricks as if

279

she were a trained dog, but she got up quickly and went out with Edna to the kitchen. As she went she heard Mrs Gaegler say: 'You could never teach an American girl that, but English girls don't seem to have the same strength of character.'

'You're mad, aren't you?' Edna said, putting down a pile of plates.

'Wouldn't you be?' Christine threw the silver into the sink with an infuriated clatter.

'Oh, sure. I'd be hopping mad. I've never seen Mother so trying.'

'Nor me. I wonder if there is really something wrong with her.'

'No. She always starts complaining about her stomach as soon as she sees food.'

'I know, but that doesn't usually stop her eating it.'

'She's all right. The day when she doesn't complain of anything – that will be the day we know she's really ill.'

Mrs Gaegler would not eat any of the dessert, which was blueberry pie. 'I couldn't hold it. My stomach feels like it's turned upside down,' she said, as if she were afraid the pie would fall out of it.

'You're missing the most wonderful blueberry pie,' Milt said. 'Best I ever tasted.'

'Is it all right?' Christine asked Edna. 'It's the first time I've ever made it.'

'Don't they have blueberries in England?' Matt asked. 'I should have thought they could.'

'Of course they could,' his mother said, 'but they would never get anyone to pick them. The British just don't want to work. That's why they'll never be anything but a second-class nation.'

Christine felt her face reddening. 'We're not a –' she began, and was near to tears, but Matthew came to her rescue.

'Look, Mother,' he said, 'when we can stand up to what the British took in World War II we might have the right to judge what makes a second-class nation. I was in London the night the City was on fire. I've seen Plymouth. We should judge the British on that, not on whether they want to pick blueberries.'

'What's eating you, Matt?' Vinson said acidly. 'I thought all you Kansas University boys were isolationists.'

When everyone got up to go to the other end of the room for coffee Christine took his arm and drew him aside. 'Vin! You were horrid to Matt. He was only trying to be nice to me by sticking up for England.'

'It wasn't his place. If anyone's going to stand up for my wife, it's me.'

'Well, why didn't you?'

'He didn't give me a chance. He jumped right in with his slick talk. Just like he's been trying to jump in ahead of me ever since we were children. That smarty pants. It's a damn good thing I saw you first, or he'd have jumped in there too.'

'Don't be silly. He wouldn't have been interested in me. He's got a girl.'

'He's always got a girl. A different one every month. You watch out.'

'Oh, Vin, don't talk such nonsense. He's your *brother*.'

'I'd still kill him if he ever tried to make a pass at you.' He gripped her arm and stared at her. Looking into his flecked eyes, strange and bitter with unreasonable jealousy, Christine could believe that he meant it.

'When you two love-birds have finished your tête-à-tête there,' Milton called out, 'come on over, Vin, and pour us a drink.'

Vinson went over to them and Christine finished clearing the table. The kitchen was suffocatingly hot. Mrs Gaegler said that no one should use an oven in this weather, and perhaps she was right.

Christine opened the back door and stepped out on to the grass. It was almost as hot outside. The storm could not be very far away. There was that breathless, suspended pause on the earth and air, when every leaf hangs motionless, waiting for the rain. Thick clouds covered the stars and moon, and away to the left, above the roofs of the town, the black sky was slit by a streak of yellow light. In the night's silence Christine could hear very clearly the sugary throb from one of the Meenehans' television sets and a tap dripping in the kitchen behind her.

The music stopped and the burst of studio audience applause

which followed it almost drowned the first rumble of thunder. Here it came again, like barrels rolling down a distant cobbled street. Christine waited, her face to the sky, longing to feel the first drops of rain. She did not want to go indoors to the cross-currents of the family party. She wanted to stay out here where the night was quiet and smelled of meadows, and the grass and trees were beginning to stir in the first hint of breeze. For a moment, as the breeze blew suddenly into a wind and flung a gust of raindrops against her lifted face, she thought she was in England, and all the summer storms of her childhood came back to her in a wave of homesickness.

She stood tiptoe on the grass as the rain fell drop by enormous drop, ceased suddenly as the wind held its breath in a pause while the thunder rolled, and then came all at once hissing down in a torrent on the earth, on the houses, on the trees and bushes, and sent Christine running indoors.

'It's coming! The storm's coming!' she called. As she ran into the living-room a deafening clap of thunder exploded over the house, and Mrs Gaegler screamed and fell off the sofa on to the floor.

Everyone looked at each other for a moment, and then began to laugh because they had been frightened.

'Come on, Mother.' Vinson stooped to help her up. 'They didn't get you that time.'

'I've been struck! I was struck by a thunderbolt!' she wailed. 'No you weren't.' Vinson settled her rigid body back on the sofa. 'You just got a fright, and so – whoops!' The lightning stabbed, the thunder clashed and Mrs Gaegler screamed and fell against the back of the sofa with her eyes closed.

'I'm in shock,' she announced, opening her eyes very wide and staring round at them. 'I'm in a state of shock. My head ... Vinson, give me another shot of whisky. The thunderbolt must have knocked my glass over.'

'Do you think she should?' Vinson looked at Christine, who was on her knees with Matthew, picking up the pieces of the glass which Mrs Gaegler had broken.

'Of course,' his mother snapped. 'Why ask her? She's always talking about when she was a nurse, but she's never done any good for *me*. I must have a stimulant. I feel that I'm failing.

My heart . . . my nerves. . . .' The storm was a heaven-sent opportunity for her to go through most of the symptoms in her repertoire. Christine had never seen her put on such a good act. When Vinson handed her the glass of rye and water she took a greedy gulp and almost immediately gasped and clutched at her stomach. 'A stabbing pain – right through me! And you needn't all look at each other,' she said, as the family exchanged glances. 'You'll never know the pain I was in there for a moment. I think I'll go and get myself a sedative.'

'I'll get it for you,' Christine said.

'I wouldn't dream of bothering you,' Mrs Gaegler said coldly. She got up with the face of a martyr and went upstairs to sulk because no one believed in her pain.

The family talked desultorily, while the thunder rumbled into the distance and the sheets of rain lifted to a spatter and gradually ceased. Christine opened the window and the cool air came in like a draught of water.

Milt and Edna, who had a long drive home, were getting ready to leave when Mrs Gaegler came down the stairs. 'I've just vomited,' she informed them. 'In the basin,' she added, as if that made it more interesting. They tried to respond suitably to the news, although they only half believed it. She had made herself sick before now by pushing a spoon down her throat.

Edna found her shoes, retrieved the canoe-shaped hat from the top of the refrigerator and followed Milt out to the car over the cool wet grass.

'Let's drive Matt home,' Christine said, as she and Vinson turned back to the house. Vinson always insisted on guiding people down the driveway from the garage in case they cut up his bank.

'Didn't he come in Mother's car?'

'No, it's being mended. He ran into a bus the other day, but don't tell your mother. He came over in a cab tonight.'

'Let him take one back then.'

'He could, but I'd like to go for a drive. The air's so wonderful now.'

'We'd have to take Mother. She won't like being left alone.'

Mrs Gaegler, however, said she felt much too ill to go out. She would crawl into bed – not that she would sleep – and pull the sheets over her head. That was all she was able for. 'But you go ahead and have your fun. Don't worry about me. I don't want to spoil anyone's enjoyment. You go. Leave me. Why shouldn't you? Why should you worry about me?'

Having successfully made them feel bad about leaving her, she made her exit, hauling herself hand over hand up the banisters, pausing on every third step to gasp a little. She looked smaller than usual, and her girlish ankles weakly climbing were suddenly pathetic.

'We shouldn't have left her, Vin,' Christine said as they went out.

'She's all right. I think she's a little tight as a matter of fact. That's all that's wrong with her.'

Matthew wanted to drive, but Vinson would not let him. They all sat on the front seat with Christine in the middle, and Matthew sang 'Allentown Jail'. He had a pleasant, mournful voice. Christine felt cosy driving along with the three of them close and friendly together. Once or twice Vinson glanced across to see how near to her Matthew was sitting.

When they got to the house where Matthew was staying, his friend Bob came out and insisted that they should come in for a drink. Christine had Coca-Cola and Vinson had several drinks and became more happy and relaxed than Christine had seen him since his mother arrived. Bob played the piano and Matthew sang, and Bob's wife, who was half Hawaiian, took off her shoes and danced a hula.

They stayed for quite a while. Every time Christine said they ought to go Bob said he would not hear of it. Christine was quite happy to stay because Vinson was enjoying himself. It was easy, friendly company, and although she was tired she could sit back and dream to the music and nobody bothered her.

Some time after midnight she asked Vinson: 'Don't you think we should ring up your mother and tell her we'll be home soon, in case she's worrying?'

'No, it's all right.' Vinson waved a careless hand from the piano, where he was singing now, not quite sober. 'She's O.K., I told you; it was the whisky. She's probably in a dead sleep by now.'

'But just in case she isn't.' Christine was troubled by the

284

instinct that makes a nurse go back and look at a patient just once more. When she rang her home number, there was no answer. Her mother-in-law must be asleep. No need to worry then. Her instinct had been wrong.

Nevertheless, when they did get home much later, she quietly opened the door of the room that was to be her baby's, and looked in at her mother-in-law.

Mrs Gaegler was not there. The bed was tumbled, but empty. Honeychile jumped yapping off the bed, skittered between Christine's legs and fled downstairs.

'Vin, come quickly!'

'What's wrong?' His voice was vague with drowsiness and whisky.

'Your mother – she's not here.' Christine ran downstairs and met him coming slowly up. They searched the house. There was no Mrs Gaegler, and her dog went leaping everywhere in a frenzy, scattering the rugs, its ridiculous front legs beating the air.

When the telephone rang Christine got to it first. It was Dr Bladen, the doctor who had stuck a hypodermic needle so many times into Mrs Gaegler.

'I've been trying to get you for some time,' he said. 'I've been ringing your home every half-hour since we took Mrs Gaegler senior away.'

'Took her away? What's happened? What's happened to her?' Christine pushed at Vinson, who was trying to get hold of the telephone.

'She called me about eleven o'clock – said she was alone and very sick, and asked me to come right over. When I got there I called the ambulance at once. Mrs Gaegler is in Saint Mary's Hospital. She had an emergency appendicectomy at twelve-thirty. . . . Oh yes, her condition is satisfactory. The appendix was a nasty-looking thing, though. I wish I could have got hold of you before, but Mrs Gaegler said she didn't know where you were.'

'But she did know, Vin!' Christine said when she had rung off and told him what the doctor had said. 'She knew Bob's telephone number. She's often rung Matt up there.'

'Perhaps she was too ill to remember,' Vinson suggested.

They agreed on this, but as they looked at each other they saw that neither of them believed it.

Mrs Gaegler had won. She had triumphed over them. She had something really wrong with her at last. They had not believed her, and so she had ensured that they should feel as bad as possible by letting them stay out drinking and smoking while she was under the surgeon's knife.

Mrs Gaegler lay like a martyr in the hospital, suffering no complications, but behaving as if she were the sickest person in the place and driving the nurses frantic. Whenever Christine and Vinson went to see her a doctor or a nurse would stop them in the corridor and ask them when they were going to take Mrs Gaegler home. Mrs Gaegler, however, did not want to go home. She was enjoying herself, and Christine and Vinson were in no hurry to have her back. She would have to spend a week or two recuperating with them before she could return to Kansas, and they clung to their breathing space of peace as long as possible.

Vinson was going to give Christine an evening out. They were going to the theatre and then out to dinner. To Christine this innocent diversion seemed very exciting. Washington, the capital of one of the largest countries in the world, has fewer theatres than the capital cities of the smallest countries in the world. Vinson said that this was because Roosevelt had ordained that negroes could sit down with white people for an evening's entertainment, and so the white people stayed away and the theatres closed down or became cinemas. Christine only half believed this, because Vinson was prejudiced against both Roosevelt and the coloured race.

Whatever its cause, the dearth of theatres was a sad blot on an otherwise cultured city, and if the touring company of a second-rate Broadway show came to Washington the drama-starved inhabitants rushed as hungrily to see it as if it were a smash hit with an all-star cast.

Christine had booked the tickets weeks ahead and had been looking forward eagerly to her evening out. As she kissed Vinson good-bye on the morning of the day, she made him promise to come home in plenty of time to change and get to the theatre on time. He was not home at six o'clock. He was not home at seven o'clock. At seven-fifteen she had come to the distressing conclusion that he had forgotten. She was just going to ring him up when the telephone rang as she walked to it.

It was Vinson. He was terribly sorry, but an admiral had just flown in from the west coast and had called a conference for eight o'clock. He would not be able to take her to the theatre. Could he take her out to dinner, anyway? No, the conference might go on for hours. He was terribly sorry, but that was how it was.

Yes, that was how it was. The Navy! There were times when she hated it. The Navy came first. She was just a wife, and who was a wife disappointed of her evening out compared with an admiral who had just flown in from the west coast?

Honeychile, who had developed quite a healthy appetite since Christine had taken her off vitamin pills and cod-liver oil and hormones, came whining round her ankles for food. Christine went into the kitchen, fed the dog and was drearily contemplating whether she would boil or poach an egg for her supper when the telephone rang again. It was Matthew. Bob and his wife had gone out and Matthew was alone and bored. Could he come over?

Christine told him what had happened to her evening. 'Why don't you and I go to the theatre instead, Matt?' she said, her spirits reviving. 'If you go straight there and I take a taxi from here we could just make it in time.'

It was a musical show, not outstanding, but Christine enjoyed it more than she remembered ever enjoying a play in the days when she used to go to the theatre nearly every week in London.

'Now let's you and me go find ourselves the most expensive dinner in town,' Matthew said as they came out. 'If you feel all right that is.' He treated her very cautiously. He was afraid of pregnant women, ever since he had once taken the wife of an absent friend out to dinner and she had been assailed by premature labour pains in the restaurant.

'Of course. I feel fine. But I wonder if I ought – suppose Vin got back before we did? He hates me not to be there.'

'He said the conference would last for hours, didn't he? Well, if I know the Navy, you can add a few hours on to that when they get talking. He won't be back. Come on, Chris, this is your night out. Enjoy yourself.'

Christine did enjoy herself. It was fun going out with Matthew. He took her to a French restaurant where she had never been with Vinson, and he knew the right food to order. He liked her as much as she liked him, and they had a lot to talk about. Christine told him about her life in England before she was married, and Matthew told her about his girl friend Carol, who was trying to make him jealous with a television producer. They both agreed that Matthew should give her up, but Matthew said she was the most wonderful thing since penicillin and he did not think he could.

After dinner he took Christine home in a taxi and sang her all the songs from the show they had seen. Christine wished that Vinson could play the piano or sing. He could not keep two notes of a tune together, and the only music he liked on the radio was the hillbilly songs. He hummed sometimes when he was carpentering or painting, but it was a tuneless hum. He never sang or whistled about the house.

Matthew's crooning tenor inspired a mood of pleasing sentimental melancholy. Christine wished that the evening were not over. Matthew was the nicest brother-in-law she could have wished for. He was just what she would have chosen for a brother.

He left her at her home with a light kiss on the cheek, very different from the moist embraces Milt gave. As Christine walked up the path she saw a chink of light between the living-room curtains. Had she left the light on, or was Vinson home? Oh well, he would not mind. He would be glad that his brother had given her a good time. She told herself this to stifle the little qualm of fear as she put her key into the lock. Ridiculous to have qualms of fear about your husband, and to feel guilty because you had gone out when he could not take you. But when she saw his face as he came into the hall to meet her her little qualm grew to full-size apprehension.

It was the worst quarrel they had ever had. They had bickered before, but they had never lost control to the point when they blazed out the most hurting things they could think of. Always before, when anger had sprung up between them, Vinson had said: 'I won't quarrel with you', and made himself annoyingly unassailable. But now he wanted to quarrel. He was out to have a full-scale row, and he made her come into the living-room and sit down opposite him so that he could tell her all the things he had been brooding over while he waited for her to come home.

He was jealous of Matthew. That was the crux of it. Christine was horrified and slightly repelled that he could be jealous of his own brother, who was so obviously not the kind of person to try and step out of line with a sister-in-law.

'Do you think I'd have gone out with him if he was like that?' Christine asked. 'What do you think I am?'

'I don't know. You can't trust any woman. I learned that a long time ago. What you've told me of your past history doesn't incline me to think you're any different from the rest. What about that Canadian – and the man you picked up at that night-club?'

'Oh, Vin, that was nothing. I'd never have told you, but you made me promise to tell you everything.'

'I'm wondering how many more things there are that you haven't told me.'

'You talk as if I were a prostitute. It's a fine way to talk to your wife. Look here, Vin, nobody gets to the age of thirty-four without having *something*. You're such a prude.'

'A prude!'

'Yes, a prude. Where do you think I've been with your brother? To one of those hotels where you can get a room for a couple of hours?'

'Christine, please.' Vinson shifted on his chair. 'Don't talk like that. You know I'm not suggesting –'

'You're suggesting something, whatever it is. Look at me – the shape I am. As if anyone could be jealous about a woman who looks like this. I think it's vile of you when Matt's so nice. Yes, he is. I like him, like him, like him, do you hear? He's a lot nicer than you in many ways.'

'A pity you didn't marry him, instead of me.'

'I didn't see him first.'

This was terrible, hateful. They were saying things they did not mean, but they could not stop. They had to go on finding worse things to say as they sat there, hating each other.

Christine got up, hot and trembling. She could not stand any more. 'I'm going to bed,' she said. 'I feel sick.'

'I'm not surprised, the way you've worked yourself up. Even if you don't care about me, you might at least give some thought to our baby.'

'Don't start on that tack.'

'Why shouldn't I? It's the most important thing in my life, and it should be in yours, but the way you behave makes me think that you're hardly fit to be the mother of my child.'

'Oh, Vin!' A choking sound broke from Christine. She did not know herself whether she was crying or laughing. 'You sound like a character in an old-fashioned melodrama. You're the most ridiculous –'

'If you're going to laugh at me,' he said icily, 'you'd better go to bed.'

Christine went out. When she was in the hall she found she was not laughing, but crying.

Upstairs, Honeychile jumped guiltily off the bed when she heard her step. Christine knelt down and tried to get from the dog the comfort that Timmy had always given her when she was distressed. Timmy used to stand like a rock, eyes soft with concern while Christine clutched and twisted the hair on his neck and told him all the injustices that no one else understood; but when she put out her hand to Honeychile the spidery dog wriggled away yapping. It fled under the dressing-table and cowered there with its legs apart, trembling as if its life was threatened. It was a useless animal.

When she was in her nightgown Christine forced herself to go to the top of the stairs and call down: 'Vin! Have you had any supper?'

He did not answer.

'Have you had any supper, I said.' Irritation mounted in her voice.

'No,' he answered sulkily.

'Shall I come down and get you something?'

'No.'

All right, if he wanted to sulk, let him. Christine got into bed and turned away from the door. When he came heavily upstairs she pretended to be asleep. When he got into bed perhaps, after all, she would turn over and put out a hand to him and he would take her in his arms and kiss her, and she would weep and everything would be all right. It was not too late to retrieve it.

He did not get into bed. He turned out the light and Christine waited, ready to turn over as soon as she felt his weight on the bed; but he went out of the room, and in a moment she heard the door of the other bedroom slam shut.

When the alarm clock woke her the next morning Christine felt as if she had not slept at all. Her head ached and every limb was weary. She combed her hair and powdered her face and went into the room that was to be the nursery. Vinson was lying very neatly in the bed, his face buried in the pillow and his short black hair sticking up like a porcupine. Christine turned his face over and kissed him. He woke frowning, and sat up. He did not kiss her.

'Is it time to get up?' he asked in a completely wide-awake voice.

'Yes. Oh, Vin – look, darling –' She had planned how she was going to say: 'I'm sorry', but he swung his legs over the side of the bed and, without looking at her, felt for his slippers and slouched off to the bathroom.

He ate his breakfast in the kitchen, just like other mornings. Sulking did not impair his appetite. Christine did not know what to talk about, so she did not talk at all, except to ask him if he wanted more coffee.

He held out his cup. 'I don't want you to use the car today,' he said. 'The fluid in the brakes is low and they're not holding properly. I nearly hit a lamp standard coming home last night, in case that's of any interest to you. John Tanner's picking me up this morning and he'll bring me home. I'll take the car to the garage tonight.'

When he had finished his breakfast he got up without a word, went into the hall, put on his uniform coat and cap and picked up his brief-case. Christine followed him, feeling like a child sent to Coventry. When he opened the front door she put her hand on his arm.

'Aren't you going to kiss me good-bye?' she asked.

'I didn't think you'd want to.'

'Do *you* want to?'

'Of course.' He put his head forward. It was the briefest kiss. It would have been better to have had no kiss at all.

Vinson stood on the lawn with his toes turned out, to be ready as soon as John Tanner drove up. He never kept anyone waiting. Christine stood just behind him in the doorway. She wondered if he knew she was there.

From the lawn next door Mrs Meenehan called: 'Hi there, Commander! What do you know?'

Vinson did not answer. Mrs Meenehan went into her house. As soon as Vinson had gone she would be round at the kitchen window to ask what was wrong with the Commander. John Tanner arrived and blew his horn. Christine watched Vinson walk down the path. She always waved him good-bye when he drove off in the mornings. If he turned round before he got into the car she would wave today, but she did not think he was going to turn round. She hesitated, then went inside the house and shut the door. Immediately, she wished she had not. Suppose he looked round and she was not there? As she turned back to the door again she heard the car drive off. It was too late. She would have to wait until tonight. She would make it up with him tonight.

'Had a tiff?' Mrs Meenehan appeared at the window as Christine went into the kitchen.

'No,' Christine said coldly, putting dishes into the sink.

'Oh yes you have.' Mrs Meenehan waggled a finger at her. 'You can't fool me. The Commander looked like thunder. Don't worry, honey. It's because of your condition. I was just the same with young Gary. Daddy and I fought like cat and dog. It's physical. You'll see. Everything will be all-a-hunky when the baby comes.'

Perhaps she was right. Everything would be all right when the baby came. All the little differences, the misgivings, the moments of boredom, the slight disappointments that her marriage had brought – all these would be swept away when their child was born. There would be no time for them.

All morning Christine felt particularly, keenly happy about

the baby. Her self-engrossed happiness drove out the sadness of the quarrel. It was no longer a tragedy. It could be put right in a moment this evening. Christine would find the right thing to say, and they would be back where they were before – two people who were going to have a baby which would hold them together in a bond that no petty differences of character could weaken.

Christine got out the vacuum cleaner. It always did one good to clean the house when one wanted to clean out one's mind. While she was bending to sweep under the sofa she suddenly straightened up and put a hand to her side. Yes! The baby had moved. It kicked.

She turned off the motor to stop Honeychile barking. If anything was making a noise the dog always had to augment it. The baby kicked again. She felt it very clearly. This was the moment for which she had waited so long, this proof that the mystery within her was alive and eager for the world.

Christine felt exalted. She wanted to tell someone. Who? Certainly not Mrs Meenehan, and Betty Kessler would only shake her head and say that now her troubles were really starting. Christine almost rang up Vinson, but the vision of him answering the telephone in a room full of stenographers and electrical typewriters checked her. Besides, he was probably still sulking. He did not know yet that the quarrel was over, that it did not matter, that nothing mattered because her baby was stirring into a new phase of life.

How wonderful it would be to tell him this evening! It would dispel everything else. He would come home frowning perhaps, determined not to make an advance before she did, and she would run to the front door as soon as she heard the car, and tell him about the baby. His face would light up, and it would be as if they had never said those terrible things last night.

When Matthew rang up she almost told him, but remembered his fear of pregnant women, and refrained. It only mattered to her and Vinson, anyway. The news was not for anyone else.

Matthew wanted to know if she had the car at home. He wanted to borrow it for the afternoon.

'Matt, I'm sorry, but you can't. The brakes are bad. Vin said it mustn't be driven.'

'To hell with that, Chris. I'll be O.K. I can always throw it into low gear, or use the emergency brake.'

'No, Matt. Vinson said not.'

'Vin's been saying not all his life. Listen, I have to have it. Carol's in town. She's here to do a show on one of the local stations, and I'm going to take her to lunch and then to the studio for rehearsal.'

'Well, but couldn't you –?' No, of course he couldn't take a taxi. No American could take his girl out without a car.

Christine knew that even if the car had been all right Vinson would not have let Matthew borrow it, but Matthew persisted. He was excited. He was urgent and persuasive. It was his big chance. Carol was here. He had to be with Carol. His leave was up tomorrow and he was flying west this evening. Heaven knew when he would see her again. She might get married or anything.

'Chris,' he said, 'you're my pal. I didn't think you'd let me down.'

'I wouldn't, but Vin –'

'He'll never know. I'll bring the car back before he's due home. Honest. You will? Ah – that's a girl; that's a girl, Chris. I knew you'd come through.'

After Matthew had fetched the car Christine worried all afternoon. She worried that he would have an accident, although he assured her that he had driven a car without brakes all the time he was at college, and she worried that Vinson would come home before Matthew and the car, and all her news about the baby and her plans to make up the quarrel would be as nothing compared to his wrath.

When she came back from the supermarket she took out a canvas chair and sat on the only bit of lawn that was not sloping to watch for the car. Which car? Hers or John Tanner's? It was four-thirty. Vinson might be home at five o'clock if he came out punctually to suit John Tanner. Every car that came along the road brought her to her feet. Here came one much too fast, with another car following it. That couldn't be John Tanner, who was a solid family man, and cautious.

Matthew whipped the car round the corner into the driveway

and pulled it to a slithering stop with the emergency brake outside the closed garage doors. He jumped out as Christine came over the lawn towards him with the slow tread that now was hers.

'Got to run, Chris,' he shouted. 'Bob followed me down. He's driving me to the airport and I'm late as hell.'

'All right. I'll drive the car in.'

'Thanks a million for everything. I had a swell time. Everything was swell. Carol – she – well, I'll write you about it. You're a honey, Chris. Best sister-in-law I ever had.' He kissed her and bounded down the slope and over the side of Bob's open convertible, which jumped ahead like a racehorse at a starting gate.

Christine felt quite breathless. She had to pause for a moment to recover. Then she opened the garage doors and got into the car to drive it inside before Vinson came home and saw it.

There was no ignition key. Matthew must have slipped it into his pocket from habit when he jumped out. She could not start the car. She could not drive it into the garage, and Vinson might be home at any moment.

It did not matter about the key. Vinson had his own, and she could say she had lost hers until she got Matthew to send it back. But the car! She would have to push it into the garage. It was standing on the level where the driveway flattened out. She could do it.

Putting her hands on the fat shiny trunk of the car, she pushed. Nothing happened. She went round and took off the brake and then tried again. Still the big heavy car would not move. No time to go for Mr Meenehan. He would be watching the television in the rumpus room in his slippers. It would take ages to get him organized. She pushed again. If only it was a sensible little English car instead of this gross American monster. . .

Straining with all her might, she struggled, panting. As the car at last rolled slowly into the garage she stood upright, swayed dizzily with a spinning head, and knew that she was either going to faint or be sick.

She never could remember afterwards how she got into the house and on to the sofa, where Vinson found her with the pains beginning when he came home whistling and calling for her to show the quarrel was forgotten. She thought she must have crawled there, because when the nurses washed her in the hospital she heard them exclaiming gently about the grazes on her knees and hands.

Chapter Seven

IT was a rough crossing. The ship rolled sickeningly, unceasingly as it ploughed through the heaving waters, away from the country of Christine's unhappiness; but her unhappiness went with her. She had not left it behind. She could not escape it just by getting on a ship and travelling the slow Atlantic miles to England.

The blanket of depression that had settled on her after she lost her baby was said by the doctors to be a perfectly natural phenomenon.

'Purely a pathological symptom,' they told her. 'Naturally a woman feels sad to lose her baby, but the particular depression she experiences after a miscarriage is a normal physical manifestation – like the after-effects of jaundice, or grippe.'

It annoyed her when they said grippe instead of influenza. Everything annoyed her when she was recuperating, even the Americanisms to which she was accustomed. The doctors annoyed her, the nurses with their red nails and impertinent caps annoyed her, the poor eclamptic woman who shared her room infuriated her. Vinson annoyed her, her house, when she returned to it, annoyed her, but most of all she was annoyed by everyone's insistence that the depression which weighed on her night and day was only an ordinary physical symptom.

What if it was? That did not make it any easier to bear. 'You'll shake it off,' they told her, 'as you grow stronger'; but she grew stronger and she did not shake it off. She began to think that it would be with her for the rest of her life, this hopelessness, this weary spirit.

Vinson's depression was almost as great as her own, but no one could tell him that it was only a pathological symptom. Their common misfortune should have brought them together, and for a moment at the beginning it did, when Vinson was first allowed to see her in the hospital while she was having the second tranfusion, and told her that it did not matter, that nothing mattered as long as she was all right. But when she was no longer in danger, and they both began to think about the loss of their hopes and plans, they each withdrew into an egotistical despondency from which neither could put out a hand in mutual comfort.

When Vinson was ordered to Panama for a few weeks, he suggested that Christine should go to England while he was away 'to try and get over it'. She willingly agreed. It was the one thing she wanted to do. Her family, her friends, the country she knew and loved – all the familiar things that had made her happy before would surely break the thread of her depression and make her happy again.

She had expected to feel more cheerful as soon as she got on the boat, but she did not. She was too tired by the journey to New York and the tedium of the formalities of embarkation, and by the strain of saying good-bye to Vinson, who at the last minute had let his face slip and looked suddenly lost and almost afraid. When she was tired the sorrows came crowding in unopposed. ('Physical, purely physical,' the smooth doctor had said. 'When you are stronger, your unhappy thoughts will leave you.')

It began to be rough on the first day out. Christine took to her bed, because there seemed no point in struggling about when you could not keep your feet and struggling down to the dining saloon when you did not want to eat. She lay in her bunk and dozed and woke and dozed and woke to the creak of the panelling and the hiss of the sea and the crashing of crockery in the stewards' pantry, and with her still was the depression she had thought she could leave behind in the little house in Arlington.

She never wanted to go back to that house, although, of course, she would have to, because Vinson would be in Washington for some time after he came back from Panama. They had both been so unhappy in that house. Could they ever start again there and build some hope into their marriage? They had been happy there when she was expecting the baby, she with her sewing machine and her nest-making domesticity, he with his carpentry and his painting and his home-made nursery in the basement.

After she came back from the hospital he never went into the basement unless he had to fetch something. He did not want to do anything about the house at all, could not be bothered to put a new washer on a dripping tap or repair a loose shelf in a

298

cupboard. He behaved as if the purpose of his home life had been taken from him and nothing was worth while.

In the evenings he was at a loose end. He did not want to read. He did not want to listen to the radio. He went back to his naval technical manuals and his notebooks. He got out the dictaphone again and put it by the bed, and sometimes at night Christine would wake from a heavy dream and hear him dictating incomprehensible things into it. The Navy was the only thing that could console him. If he could not look forward to his baby he would fix his eyes on getting his promotion to captain. He stayed later and later at the office, and when he did come home it was often difficult to find things to talk about now that they did not have plans about the baby to discuss.

The doctors had assured Christine that she could have another child later on, but she did not believe them. She felt in her heart that she was finished as a normal happy woman. She had had her chance and lost it. She had lost weight during her illness and it did not suit her face. She would not be pretty and fresh-skinned any more, and people would not say to Vinson: 'Your charming wife.' She would be just a wife, growing middle-aged in a meaningless marriage, and she often thought of what Stevenson wrote: '*Times are changed with him who marries; there are no more by-path meadows, where you may innocently linger, but the road lies long and straight and dusty to the grave.*'

Long and straight and dusty . . . that was how she saw her future. She was morbid. She knew it, but she could not shake it off, could not laugh herself out of it, because there seemed to be nothing to laugh at.

Her conviction that she would not have another baby was partly due to Vinson. She had not told him or anyone else about pushing the car, and because he knew no reason why she should have had a miscarriage he got it into his head that she was incapable of carrying a baby to its birth. They never talked about the baby which was lost, but if Christine ventured to say: 'Perhaps we'll have another one', Vinson looked gloomy and said: 'I doubt it', and Christine was ready to believe him.

He had been so solicitous and indulgent of her when she was pregnant that it was hard to bear the difference now that she had failed him and no longer deserved coddling. Sometimes she asked for things which he might have granted before, but now he raised objections.

She was so lonely all day. 'I wish we could have a dog,' she said one evening. 'I'd feel better if I had a dog.'

'It would be a nuisance,' he said. 'Look what a pest that little beast of Mother's was.'

'Poor Honeychile. You shouldn't speak of her like that,' Christine said, for while she was in the hospital Vinson had left a window open when he went to work and Honeychile had jumped out and run yapping at the wheels of a car, which had killed her. Mrs Gaegler, coming out of the hospital the next day, had flown back to Kansas in a fury and would probably never forgive Vinson.

'I didn't mean a dog like that, anyway,' Christine went on. 'I meant a proper dog. Like my Timmy. He was a great joy to me.'

'You were a spinster then,' he reminded her. 'Sublimating your frustrations.'

'I wasn't! It's natural to love a dog. I noticed you pretended to like the dogs all right when you were after me. You put on quite a good act, I must say – you and your tins of ham and your candy bars.' They often spoke to each other like this nowadays. They never had another violent quarrel like the one which stormed up after Christine had been out with Matthew, but they did not mind saying caustic things to each other.

'There were far too many animals in that house you lived in,' Vinson said. 'If I let you have a dog, next thing this house will be just the same. You've got the goldfish, and they're bad enough. They stink to high heaven.'

'You always used to change their water,' Christine said sadly. 'Now you don't bother.'

Neither of them seemed to bother about anything very much these days. Some evenings Christine did not bother to come out of the kitchen to kiss him when he came home. He did not seem to notice. At the beginning of their marriage they had always been so conscious of each other's presence, but now Christine sometimes thought that he did not know if she was in the room with him or not. He did not give her his special whistle any more for the pleasure of seeing her look up to a sound no one else could hear.

One morning, when she woke very tired, he said: 'Don't bother to get up. I'll get my own breakfast', and she let him. After he had gone she remembered that she had once thought that when you did not kiss your husband good-bye and hullo, and did not get up to give him his breakfast, it was the beginning of the end. She was only thirty-five. This could not happen to her marriage. After that she always got up when he did and was always punctilious about kissing him in the morning and evening, and he did not seem to notice the difference between a kiss that you wanted to give and a kiss that was a duty.

Ever since they came to the house Mrs Meenehan had been pressing them to get a television set. 'I can't think how you can live without one,' she said. 'I'd just die without mine.' It did not occur to her that she had lived quite happily for many years before television was invented. She was an addict, a fanatic. The routine of her life was geared to the programmes. She could not iron or sew or write letters or read the newspapers unless the television was turned on. She and Daddy took most of their meals at an uncomfortable plastic-topped table in front of the set in the rumpus room, and all their visitors were forced willy-nilly to sit down in semi-darkness and watch the lighted screen.

Christine's experience of television in England had already prejudiced her against it as a time waster and an intruder of homes, and living next door to the Meenehans had done nothing to change her mind. If having a television set meant letting it rule your life, she did not want one.

She was quite happy with the radio. She still listened to the soap operas in the afternoon, although the first novelty of them had long worn off. They were old friends now, coming up as regularly as the milk on the doorstep and the newspaper hurled from the road by a small boy with a hand-cart. The noble young widow, who undoubtedly would get no older or plainer if the programme went on for twenty years, was still trying to resolve the eternal conflict between a mother's duty and a woman's heart. The homey smalltown barber was still giving out a lot of advice which nobody wanted to take. The man who announced the programme about the sage, cosy Mom who was the hub of the household was still saying: 'Imperious man, look in your heart and dwell on this. Without the woman in my house, what would I be?'

It was all just the same. It went on day after day for the comfort of hardworked housewives all over the United States. It was a harmless vice, a drug to stop women thinking too much about their lot.

Vinson, although he had once remarked wistfully that theirs was the only house in the road without a television aerial, had not wanted a set either, perhaps because it would cost too much, perhaps because anything that Mrs Meenehan recommended he automatically rejected.

On Christine's birthday he unaccountably bought her a television set, a mammoth thing of varnished wood with almost as many knobs as a cinema organ. The installation men brought it one afternoon while Vinson was at work, hooked it up, fixed up the aerial and went away, leaving Christine moving the set about the room on its castors, trying to find a place where it would not be in the way.

When Vinson came home she did not know what to say. 'You shouldn't have,' she said. 'It's much too big a present.'

'Well,' he mumbled, embarrassed, 'I thought it would be nice for you. Your life is kind of dull now.'

'Oh no it isn't, Vin.' They never admitted that anything was wrong.

'Yes it is. I know it is!' he burst out, and suddenly he held her very tightly. 'Darling, darling, what's wrong with us? I want us to be happy.'

Now was the time. They could have been close now and drawn some help from each other to get over this bad time together, but Christine, cursing herself as she heard her voice say it, answered: 'Nothing's wrong. We're perfectly happy', and the chance was lost.

Although Vinson had bought the set for her, he was the one who looked at it most. When she discovered that there were other programmes besides the ones the Meenehans liked, Christine began to overcome her prejudice, but she did not want to have the set playing all the time, night after night like an unwelcome lodger.

Vinson, however, took to it like a duck to water. As soon as he had taken off his uniform cap and jacket at night, he would turn on the television and squat in front of it, fiddling with the knobs and making the pictures jitter or chase each other up the screen like slowly wound film. The set would be on while they had their cocktails, and after Christine had wrenched him away to eat his dinner Vinson would go back and spend the rest of the evening in front of the screen, his naval manuals forgotten.

Christine was glad that he had found something to keep him happy, but she hoped that he would get over his enthusiasm when the novelty wore off. Some of the television programmes were very good, with all the top talent that beer or soap or floor wax could buy, but some of the programmes were very bad, and the lengthy commercials that were forced on you in the middle did not make them any better.

All the oldest films in the world seemed to have been gathered together in the studios for the entertainment of an unprotesting public. On the television screen Jackie Coogan was still a small child, and Bebe Daniels was a mere slip of a girl with a sideways ogle and hair pulled low on the forehead. Waists were low and hats were cloche and the worn-out soundtracks grated like an early phonograph. Cowboy films of all vintages filled the screen in the early evening, for the children of America had long since given up going out to play when they could be crouched indoors watching the pintos gallop and the guns snap from the hip and the good cowboy get the sweet young girl from the bad cattle rustler.

The television commercials were far longer than the ones on the radio, and far more irksome, because you could see the eulogizers as well as hear them. On the screen, husbands in tweed jackets came home from work as cleanly shaved as when they had set out in the morning, were greeted with a glass of beer by arch little women in frilly house dresses, and downed the foaming nectar with genteel smacking of lips and knowing winks at the camera. White-capped butchers lectured you about cuts of meat, aproned grocers held up cans of peas and packets

303

of margarine, blonde studio models who looked as if they had never been in a kitchen in their lives took cakes and biscuits out of the oven wearing a delighted air of astonishment, as well they might, cooing that someone else had made them.

When the product advertised was toothpaste or deodorant or headache pills, someone inevitably came on the screen wearing the Cossack-necked white coat peculiar to American medicine, and terrorized you about what would befall you if you did not use the sponsor's product. Cigarettes were also advertised by men dressed up as doctors or pharmacists. The tobacco business seemed to have outgrown the selling point of which cigarette would give you most pleasure. Now it was only which one would do you the least harm. One firm went so far as to claim that their cigarette must be the best, because if you pulled a strip of paper off the side the tobacco would not fall out, which was all right if that was what you wanted cigarettes for.

Christine soon got to know all the television commercial slogans by heart, just as she had learned the ones on the radio, but she did not sing the irritating catchy tunes as she cleaned about the house or worked with her sewing-machine. Nowadays she hardly ever bothered to use the machine on which she had made so many baby clothes. In the evenings Vinson always had the television on, and she would usually sit beside him and watch the wrestling or the quiz programmes or the musical farragos, to save herself having to think of anything else to do.

On the evening before she left for England they were watching a television play, just as if it were an ordinary evening and they were not parting tomorrow. At a dramatic moment the picture went off, the voices stopped, and the announcement of a breakdown appeared on the screen.

Nothing happened for quite a long time. 'Let's try the radio,' Vinson said. 'We haven't had that on for quite a time. Turn it on, there's a good girl.'

'Turn it on yourself,' Christine said, 'if you want it.' She was still a little cross with him for what he had said at supper. They had been talking about her trip to England and Vinson had started to grumble, not about her leaving him – that would have been all right – but about the expense of the fare.

'It was you who suggested I should go,' she had said. 'It's a bit late to think of the expense now.'

'I have to think of these things,' he said. 'It's a good thing someone in this family does.'

'You talk as if I was madly extravagant. I seem to be wasting my efforts trying to be so careful in the shops. Oh Lord, how I wish I had some money of my own! I tell you what, Vin; when I get back I shall have my permanent visa, and I really am going to get a job then.'

'I told you,' he said, putting down his fork, 'a commander's wife doesn't go out to work. And soon I hope you'll be a captain's wife. That will make it even more impossible.'

'I don't *want* to be a captain's wife,' she said sulkily. 'I think it will be hell.'

'Christine,' he said, calmly finishing his food, 'you talk like a child. Compared to American women of your age you're really very immature.'

How could he talk to her like that when she was going away tomorrow? The thought that perhaps he did not mind rankled with her all evening. She would not get up and turn on the radio for him.

When he turned it on it was the 'Stop the Music' programme, on which they played or sang a tune and rang people up anywhere in the United States to ask them what it was. If you could name the tune, you won a first prize and were given a chance to guess the 'Mystery Melody', and if you got that right yours was the earth and everything that's in it. The compère was announcing the prizes: 'Sixteen hundred dollars in cash, an electric clothes drier that leaves your clothesline for the birds, an unbreakable, washable plastic rocking-chair, a super-magnificent broilomatic, boilomatic, bakeomatic kitchen range with a left-off – excuse me, friends – ha, ha! – lift-off oven door, a holiday for two in Nassau. . . .' The list went staggeringly on.

How wonderful to be someone who won a prize like that! Even if you had to pay income tax on it all you would still have a lot to play with. People were telephoned in Alaska, in Montana, in Big Spring, Texas – all sorts of out-of-the-way places – but never in Washington, D.C. It was never you. It was always someone else.

The telephone rang, and Christine went to it. It would be Lianne, calling to say good-bye.

'Is that the residence of Commander Vinson Gaegler, U.S. Navy?' said a professional operator's voice, refining a Brooklyn accent. 'Is Mrs Gaegler home? May I speak with her, please? Oh, hullo, Mrs Gaegler. This is your "Stop the Music" operator in New York calling.'

'Vinson!' Christine hissed. 'It's us!'

'Hallo, hallo! Are you still on the line? Your name has been picked to be a contestant tonight in the "Stop the Music" radio programme. Do you care to participate?'

Did she care! Christine stammered into the telephone. She could hardly hold the receiver.

Non-committally, as if she were used – which, of course, she was – to offering someone the chance of winning sixteen hundred dollars in cash, an electric clothes drier, a plastic rocking-chair, a stove with a lift-off oven door, a holiday for two in Nassau, the operator explained the rules of the contest, asked Christine if she was listening to the programme, and told her to continue to listen to the telephone.

'If you hang up or leave the phone,' she said in her ritual voice, 'you cannot be telephoned again.'

Christine glued one ear to the telephone and the other to the radio. Vinson was leaning forward watching the radio as if it were the television. His face was flushed with excitement, and Christine's was on fire. Sixteen hundred dollars in cash! Now he need not grumble about her fare to England. They were finishing with another competitor – Mr Duane P. Bamburger of Boise, Idaho, who had failed to guess an obvious tune and would only get a few cartons of cigarettes.

Christine pitied Mr Bamburger fleetingly, but hated him for getting a tune she would have known. The one she got might be – 'Vin, listen!' They had started another tune. What was it? It sounded familiar. A girl sang the words, humming when she came to the title line 'Da da da *da* da.' It was a relic from the past. Christine remembered doing homework to it when she was at school. What was it? Something like *I'll never leave you . . . I won't forget you . . . You'll always find me. . . .*

What was it? What was it? Oh, don't ask me, don't ask me

306

this one, she prayed silently. *If you should ask me . . . ? I'll always want you . . . ? I never –*'

'Stop the MUSIC!' bellowed the compère. A telephone bell was ringing through the song. 'Hallo . . . hallo . . .!' she heard him say through the loudspeaker, and then there was a click in her other ear and his voice was coming through the telephone.

'Is that Mrs Gaegler of Arlington, Virginia? Hallo there, Mrs Gaegler! How's everything in Arlington, Virginia? Pretty swell?' he roistered, although Christine had not been able to find the voice to answer. 'Well, that's fine. Just fine.' She could hear his voice coming out of the radio a fraction of a second before it came out of the telephone. 'Now, Mrs Gaegler, we want to give you a chance to win this wonderful jackpot of prizes. Can you name that tune we've just played?'

'I – er – I – er – could you play a bit of it again?'

'Sure thing.' The girl sang a phrase or two.

'*I'll never leave you,*' Christine blurted out. She was sure. The prize was hers. Sixteen hundred dollars in cash, an electric clothes drier –

'I'm awfully sorry, Mrs Gaegler. No. I'm afraid you haven't hit the jackpot this time.'

Christine rang off while he was promising her cartons of cigarettes. On the radio she could still hear him talking to her with undiminished bonhomie. She switched it off, very near tears.

'Oh, Vin –' She turned to him for sympathy, but his voice was angry.

'You idiot,' he said, 'losing a chance like that. Why didn't you get it? I thought you knew all the tunes. You've got all day to listen to that damn radio.'

'I didn't know it,' she said miserably.

'Well, you ought to have.' He stuck out his lower lip.

'Did you?'

He turned away from her as the television suddenly came on again with a burst of sound, just in time for the commercial.

He had no right to be so cross, but he was, and so was she – cross with herself as well as him. The glittering haul that had

307

been dangled before her had been too tempting. It was not fair to tantalize people like that. They were doing it all the time. It was the modern American tragedy.

She and Vinson were still a little cross with each other when they drove to New York the next day. Christine had to keep reminding herself that she was leaving him for several weeks, that she loved him, that he was her husband, that she would undoubtedly miss him as soon as he was not there.

And then on the dockside, as she turned at the foot of the gangway and saw his face left behind among the crowd, and it had the look on it that he had not meant her to see, she did not have to remind herself of these things. She wanted to run back and say she would not go, that she would come with him to Coco Solo, Panama; but her legs took her on up the gangway, and when she went to the rail to lean over and wave, his face was back to normal again.

All these things she thought of as she lay in her bunk and braced her tired body against the rolling of the ship. At night she took sleeping pills to make sure that she would not lie awake and go on thinking, but when she slept she dreamed of Jerry. She had not dreamed of him for months, but on the ship she dreamed of him every night. On the last morning she woke believing that he was still alive. When reality seeped back to her she lay for a while quite still, thinking that she might recapture the dream if she did not move. Then she realized that she was able to lie still, that she was not being shifted from side to side of the bunk. The sea was calm, the boat sailed evenly on, and outside her porthole the early-morning sun glittered on the sea and on an unpretentious coastline of low cliffs and little white houses. She had come home to England.

Roger met her at Waterloo wearing his hairy winter overcoat that made him look like a bison. Sylvia had not come up from Farnborough because it was her ironing day. She also had Mr Cope still in bed recovering from an attack of bronchitis.

'To tell you the truth,' Roger said, as he drove his sedate black family car heavy-handedly along the Portsmouth road, 'the old chap really has been pretty bad this time. Syl didn't tel you just how bad in her letter, because we didn't want to worry you. It was just after you . . . *you* know.'

'After I lost the baby, you mean.'

Roger cleared his throat. Although his jokes were often coarse, he was never free about mentioning the realities of such things. 'Bad business,' he said gruffly. 'Damn bad luck. Awfully sorry and all that.'

'Thanks, Rodge.' Christine felt miles away from him. She was glad to see him. He was uncomplicated and solid and just the same; but if she had thought that by coming back to England she could slip immediately into the familiar pattern of life, she was wrong. She felt out of place, a stranger in the car which was so small and upright and so very different from the one she was used to in America. Although she had been away from England less than a year, driving on the left was just as strange and frightening as driving on the right had been at first.

'I tell you, my old woman and I were quite upset when we got your cable. We were in the garden at the time, putting in some bulbs for next year, and when Syl came back from the phone and told me, I must say it was quite a shock.' Roger remembered with some pride how he and Sylvia had stood among the garden tools and bags of bulbs and been upset.

'Oh, look,' Christine said. 'There's that lovely old pub with the thatch and pink walls. I'd forgotten about it.'

'You talk as if you'd been away for years.'

'I feel as if I had. I'd almost forgotten there were such things as thatched roofs and real beams. And hedges,' she said, as they left the village and the country opened quietly out into its jig-saw pattern of little fields climbing towards the low hills. 'You never see a cut-and-laid hedge in America. Oh, Rodge, how I do love England!'

He grunted. He never responded very well to any outburst of emotion. He picked up his train of thought. 'If only you'd been over here. We didn't like to think of you in one of those Yank hospitals. They tell me all the nurses are blacks.'

Christine laughed. 'Only some of them. As a matter of fact, the coloured nurse I had on night duty was better than any of the others.'

'Well, I wouldn't like one of them to lay her great black hands

309

on me, I know that,' Roger said, with a shudder that ill-befitted the son of an empire-building race.

'Most of the hospitals there are much better than anything we've got over here,' Christine said.

'Oh, naturally, my dear old soul, naturally. It's your country now, after all, so I'm sure everything over there is bigger and better than anything poor gone to seed old England has got.'

Christine looked at him in surprise. It occurred to her that he and Sylvia had decided that she would come back quite changed, praising everything American and belittling everything English.

She was right. Sylvia had a defence mechanism all prepared to take the wind out of any high-flown sails Christine might try to set. She had squandered the whole week's meat ration, had bought vegetables and fruit out of season to make a brave show for the homecoming, but she dispelled Christine's appreciation by saying with a sniff that was part sinus trouble, part sarcasm: 'Of course this won't be anything to *you*. I dare say you can have this sort of thing every day.'

'We can't,' Christine said, 'because we can't afford it', but they did not believe her. She was the American, the visitor from the land of boastful plenty.

She had come back to refresh herself with the familiarity of her own family and country. She wanted everything to be as it had always been. She wanted to slip back without effort into the family group, but Roger and Sylvia held off a little warily, as if they suspected that she had only come back to patronize.

Even the children treated her differently. They were at the age when a year can make a startling change in appearance and behaviour. They were not her babies any more. She could no longer wash their faces and hands for them, or retie the bow that always slipped off Jeanette's forelock. Jeanette was growing her hair now, and wore it scraped back unbecomingly into a slide at the neck which never came undone. She was going to a new school, and had picked up all the high-school mannerisms. She talked very fast. She giggled a lot and hitched up her stockings. She made prissy mouths when anyone said something she thought was 'feeble'. She had taken up tennis and did not want Christine to bowl cricket balls to her on the lawn any more

She and Clement did not want to play any of the games that Christine used to play with them. They did not hang around her and treat her as if she was more fun than their parents. She had gone away from them. She had deserted them, and now they held aloof from her a little as if they did not entirely trust her any more.

She had brought chocolate for them, and American sweaters, and pistols and half a dozen boxes of chewing gum. They stayed with her until everything had come out of her suitcase, and then they went away to mull over their booty, abandoning her when she had no more to give, shamefully embodying the anti-New Dealer's imaginary picture of Britain's reaction to dollar aid.

Sylvia and Roger were more gracious about the presents Christine had brought for them, although Sylvia doubted whether the nylons would fit her now that her feet had swollen from so much running up and downstairs after poor Copey.

Christine heard a lot about how difficult it had been to Manage when her father was ill. The maid had been on holiday, and the daughter of My Mrs Hatchett, the morning woman, had elected to give birth to twins at the most inconvenient time, so that Sylvia had had to Manage on her own, with the erratic help of My Mrs Hatchett's other daughter, who was a little weak in the head and could not be trusted with the children.

You would not have thought that Christine had been away for nearly a year to marriage in a fascinating, unknown country. Sylvia and Roger did not want to hear her news; they wanted to tell her theirs. Christine could have told them things that would make their eyes stand out of their heads, but they were too busy telling her about the crockery broken by My Mrs Hatchett's unmarried daughter, the confinement of the other daughter (rumoured to be also unmarried), the ups and downs of the meat and cheese ration, the improvement of the lawn and the disappointment of the prize gladioli, the contest between Roger and the garage over the price of reboring, and Roger's triumph in the local golf championships, in which he had defeated the famous Henry Slater – 'My good sister, you must remember Slater. You've met him here. Chap with the handle-bar moustache. Real Pilot-Officer Prune type. Hell of a chap.'

Only her father was genuinely pleased and absorbed in

Christine's homecoming. Only her father wanted to hear all that she could tell him about America, and insisted on being assured that she was really happy in her new life.

Since his illness Mr Cope had become less irritable and argumentative. He was much older and more feeble; and although they had been apart for so long, Christine felt a more sympathetic intimacy between them than there had ever been when they lived together at 'Roselawn'.

Mr Cope had grown a short grey beard during his illness, and had not bothered to shave it off when he got better. His hair had become whiter, the smudges round his eyes darker, his mouth more vague and his skin more loose and crinkled as the flesh had thinned away from his sick bones.

Christine got a shock when she saw him, propped up among snowy linen (Sylvia changed all her sheets twice a week and was for ever complaining about laundry bills), his glasses far down his nose, his hands idle on the counterpane, his eyes riveted on the door as if he had turned them there at the first sounds of her arrival.

Christine's first thought was: How could I have gone away? How could I have gone away and left him? Although she knew that if she had stayed he would not have loved and needed her as much as he did because she had gone away. Mr Cope had always been inclined to pin his faith on something that was not there, to think that everything would be all right if only . . . to sigh for the things he had not instead of accepting the things he had.

Christine spent most of her time at Roger's house up in her father's bedroom talking to him. She told him everything about her marriage and her life in America – everything except the most important thing. She did not tell him that she could not shake off the depression that the loss of her baby had stabbed into her, nor that she and Vinson had reached the point when they both tacitly welcomed the opportunity to be apart for a while.

The alsatian lay on the floor between them with his strong head on his black-nailed paws, lifting a yellow eye from one to the other. He had lost the bounce and ferocity with which he had scattered rugs and terrorized postmen at 'Roselawn'. He did not like Farnborough. The rabbit scents of the sandy countryside meant less to him than the more urban trail of smells that other dogs had left for him on Barnes Common. Since his master had been ill nobody would take him out, because he pulled like a plough horse on the leash and there were too many cars on the shiny black roads to take him out without one. When he went into the garden there was always somebody to shout him off the flower-beds. The children were afraid of him, and he of them. He could not tell these things, but he showed them in his dull coat and lazy eye and his listless, almost sheepish manner. He and Mr Cope had both become older and milder, and it made Christine feel closer and more affectionate towards them both.

When she asked her father how he liked living at Farnborough, he surprisingly, with his new gentleness, did not complain, although from a few unthinking remarks he let fall it was obvious that there were many things that did not please him.

Roger and Sylvia, on the other hand, made no secret of the things that did not please them about having Mr Cope living there. Frankly, he and his dog were a nuisance to them, but since there was no alternative to the present arrangement there seemed to be no point in dwelling on its inconveniences. They did dwell on them, however, but in a martyred way, rejecting any alleviating suggestions, such as getting a nurse the next time Mr Cope was ill, as the doctor said he might be if the winter was a severe one. When Christine said tentatively: 'Perhaps I could have him out to stay with me for a while', Roger said: 'God no, that would kill the old man.'

Having a sister who lived in America had in no way mitigated his prejudice against that country. He lost no opportunity to jibe, and Christine found herself defending her adopted country with as much heat as she defended England if any American slighted it.

Roger said that she had acquired an American accent, although she knew she had not. His new joke was to use what he thought was American slang, his idea of the transatlantic vernacular being culled from the earlier works of P. G. Wodehouse. He would say 'Hot dog!' or 'Twenty-three skidoo! – as you say in America', undeterred by Christine's assurances that they did not. He laughed when she said radio instead of wireless, and nearly killed himself when he saw her use her knife and fork in the American way she had learned from Vinson.

He still talked about Vinson as if he were an improbable joke. He insisted on calling him Gaegler, and the children, taking their tone from him, referred to their uncle as Gaegler too.

When Roger asked Christine: 'Where is the great Gaegler now?' and she said 'Coco Solo, Panama', he bellowed with laughter, and the children chanted: 'Coca-Cola! Coca-Cola!' wild with glee.

'Shut up, Champ and Boots,' Roger said. 'Stow it, troops. But I must say, Chrissie, it is a hell of a funny name. No one but the Yanks would have a naval station at a place with a name like that.'

After she had been at Farnborough for several days Christine went up to London to stay with Rhona. Rhona had a new house in Hampstead, which was very grand, with a curving staircase and a manservant to open the door; but Rhona herself was quite unchanged and just as glad to see Christine as Christine was to see her.

'I've sent Dan up to Gleneagles for a few days' golf,' she said. 'I thought we'd have a better time without him. Darling, I *am* glad to see you. And you've got so thin! You look marvellous. I'd know that was an American dress anywhere. I like your hair too. Come upstairs and let's start talking. We've got masses to say.'

They fell back at once, as they always could, into the intimacy of their early youth. They talked for hours together. They went shopping, they went to the theatre, Rhona gave a cocktail party for people Christine knew, and everyone said how wonderful Christine looked, and admired her new figure, which was gratifying, but made Christine think she must have been fatter than she realized before.

Geoffrey came to the cocktail party. He had a white scar across his left eyebrow where the hair would never grow again. It gave him a slightly quizzical air, which made his face look less negative than before. Christine was more glad to see him than she expected. When she had lived in England she had not cared whether she saw Geoffrey or not. He was too familiar, and he

314

was always there for parties if you needed an extra man; but now she was glad to see him just because he was so familiar.

Her life in America had been a succession of new impressions, overstimulating and tiring. Over there the unexpected was always happening. In England you knew what to expect, and could relax. She realized that although she had promised herself before her marriage that she would teach Vinson the English way of relaxing and letting things slide if they could not be helped, he had taught her instead the American way of getting tense and worried over things that did not merit the importance you gave to them.

It was good to talk to Geoffrey in the familiar disrespectful language they had always used. He came to the party straight from the office in striped trousers and a stiff white collar over a blue shirt, and left a bowler hat and a rolled umbrella and a folded copy of *The Economist* in the hall. That was good too. It reminded you that, however far away you went to change and strange emotions, you could always come back and find England just the same.

Rhona was just the same too, although she was full of all the new things that had happened to her. Christine enjoyed her stay in the pretentious comfortable house where a maid ran your bath and ironed your nightdress every day. It was a welcome change from Sylvia's house at Farnborough, where fires were never lit until the evening and Sylvia was perpetually worrying about whether the meat had gone off or the maid had taken umbrage.

Christine missed Vinson often. He had become a part of life that one could not shut out by going three thousand miles away, but at the same time she was glad that she was staying at Rhoda's without him. Vinson would not have enjoyed the luxury. He was unnecessarily impressed by things like manservants and expensive china, but although he had only met Rhona once he had formed one of his censorious opinions about her. If they had been staying in the same house he would have pretended to be more prudish than he was and Rhona would have pretended to be more indecorous than she was, and Christine would have had a difficult time between them. Vinson would have been jealous of her friendship with Rhona, and

Rhona would have been incredulous at her wifely submission to Vinson. It was better to be there alone. They would never have been able to talk like this if Vinson were there.

Gossiping all day and half the night with Rhona, she realised how much she missed an intimate friend in America. Lianne and Nancy Lee had been companionable, but you could not make a real confidante in such a short time. You needed to grow up together as she and Rhona had done.

Rhona was in love again. She had been in love twice since the Hungarian film director, but this time it was the real thing. She never went very far with any of her affairs, and she did not sincerely contemplate doing anything but spend the rest of her life with the complaisant Dan, but Dan annoyed her very much at times, and so she found other men to divert her.

'It keeps you going,' she said. 'Being in love is a wonderful thing to keep you going.'

'Yes, but doesn't Dan –?'

'Oh, he never knows. He's always dashing about on some scheme to make five thousand pounds. He's quite happy as long as I'm happy, and you know, I'm much nicer to him when I've got someone else on the stocks, so I reckon that makes up for it.'

Rhona's ups and downs with the Hungarian and his successors took a lot of telling, but unlike Sylvia and Roger, she was just as eager to hear Christine's news as to tell her own. Christine talked and talked and found that she was beginning to talk herself out of her depression. The things that she had brooded over alone because she could not tell them to anyone – especially not to Vinson – seemed much less when they were voiced and discussed with Rhona's carefree philosophy. She told Rhona everything, and if Rhona did not understand some of the finer points she at least knew how to minimize their significance.

'You worry too much,' she said, 'just like you always did. You're taking this marriage business much too seriously.'

'But, Ro, one must, if one's to make it work.'

'Oh, I *know* – but, all the same, you mustn't mind things so much. Gosh, if I brooded every time I had a row with Dan I'd be broody all the time. Take a little look at some other man, why don't you? I know you say Vin's so jealous, but why not give him something to be jealous about? It would do him a power of good, and you too. A bit of outside attention would set you up no end.'

'Oh, Ro, you know I never would. I don't want to, anyway. That's one of the best things about being married. You don't have to go around any more looking at every frightful man to see if he'd possibly do.'

'You could look just a little bit.'

'You know I couldn't.'

'I know. You're hopeless.' They laughed together. Rhona was absurd. She never gave any advice worth taking, and yet the few days of talking and laughing with her did Christine far more good than any solemn discussion with someone who would take her problems seriously.

Her depression began to lift. She prayed that it would not come back again when she got home to Arlington. She wished that she were not going back to the little house where she and Vinson had been unhappy. It would have been better to go somewhere new and start again. She did not ask herself whether she wanted to go back to America. She was going back. That was all.

After she left Rhona she went to visit the book department at Goldwyn's. She had often thought about going back there as a married woman who had escaped. She had planned how it would be. They would all be pleased to see her, would stare at her new clothes, would tell her spicy bits of gossip that had happened in the store while she had been away, would say: 'Things are not the same as they were when you were here, Miss Cope – Mrs Gaegler, I mean.'

She went there on a busy afternoon, and at first she could not see anyone she knew. They all seemed to be customers. No, there was Miss Burman, just the same as ever, with the same brown dress and the same wisp of grey hair that fell into her eye as she frowned over someone's bill.

Miss Burman was pleased to see Christine. 'Well, look who's here!' she cried, throwing her wall-eye about at no one in particular. 'My stars, you are a sight for sore eyes, Miss Cope – excuse me – Mrs Gaegler. That takes some getting used to. And

317

how's that handsome sailor boy of yours? That's right, that's right. Quite the yankee-doodle, aren't you? Mother? Oh, she's wonderful, thank you, dear. We had visitors to tea last week, and it tired her a little, but otherwise she's Oh yes, certainly, madam. Excuse me.' She blushed, and hurried away to her waiting customer.

Christine stood looking round her and feeling like a customer. The woman with the cut-away nostrils who had taken her place as head of the department sailed up on pointed feet and gave her a brief handshake and said that Oh yes, she liked the department *very* much, although of course she had done a lot of re-organizing since Christine had left.

She went away and Christine stood for a moment vaguely, wondering if she had ever belonged here. Miss Burman had given her a nice welcome. She was just the same, but there was no Mr Parker, no Helen, no Alice, no Margaret, and the cookery books were where the collected editions of poets used to be. She wished she had not come.

When she went to see Margaret she found her engrossed in her baby, and much happier than she had been before. She and Laurie were short of money certainly, as they had expected to be, but it did not seem to matter as they had expected it would. They were still managing to keep the ugly old house going. It was no more or less shabby than before. Laurie looked no more like a patient scarecrow in his clothes than he always had and Margaret looked just as neat and clean as ever.

Christine had almost dreaded going to Margaret's home, partly because she did not want to see anyone else with a baby, and partly because she was afraid that Timmy would not recognize her. She had thought about him so often, and it would be such a snub if he had forgotten her completely.

He knew her at once. He was in the garden, and he heard her step on the pavement and rushed barking to the gate, flailing his tail and giving yelps of joy as Christine fumbled at the latch of the gate in her excitement to get in to him. Then she was in the garden, and Timmy was all over her – his tongue, his paws, his panting excitement – and she had to grasp his fur and hold him still so that she could wipe her silly tears off on his neck.

Timmy never left Christine's side all the time she was in

Margaret's house. 'He's afraid you'll go away again without him,' Margaret said. 'Anyone would think we'd been cruel to him.'

'Oh, Maggie, I know you've been wonderful –'

'But he's your dog,' Laurie said in his slow, pondering way. 'You can never take that away from them.'

'Why don't you take him back with you this time?' Margaret said. 'You could take him on the boat, and I believe they don't have quarantine in America. They give them injections instead.'

'If only I could . . .' Christine thought of how the day before she left she had asked Vinson whether she could bring Timmy back with her. She asked it diffidently, almost timidly. She had thought about asking it for a long time, but dreaded hearing what he would answer.

'I thought we'd settled all that,' he said. 'Do I have to say no to you all over again? What's the point of bringing the animal over here when we may be gone from Washington soon? If they send me to the naval shipyard at Brooklyn we'll probably be in an apartment.'

'Oh, Vin, are they going to send you to Brooklyn? I don't think I'll like that. Nancy Lee says it's horrible. Must we go there?'

'My dear Christine,' he said in his professional naval officer voice, 'the United States Navy assigns its officers where it needs them, not where their wives happen to want to go.'

When the time came for Christine to leave England she did not know whether she was glad or sorry. She wanted to see Vinson, but she did not like leaving her father, who had leaned on her during these weeks she had spent with him as he never had before. He looked so old and heavy-eyed, and she knew he was not happy at Farnborough. He had not been able to work for some time. Sylvia had packed away his dictionaries and manuscript paper and carefully sharpened pencils, and when he was not hunched in bed he pottered purposelessly about the place like a ghost that has lost its way and come to the wrong house to haunt. Christine had promised him that he should come to her in America when he was stronger, but although he said vaguely: 'Yes, yes, I'll do that', she did not think he would

319

ever get there. She wondered if she would ever see him alive again.

It was not easy to leave England. Even a raw drizzly Sunday, with the undersized girls and pimply youths waiting in the rain for the cinemas to open, and the seedy coughing men waiting in doorways for the pubs to open, was a thing to be clung to because no Sunday was like it anywhere else in the world.

At the same time she found she was looking forward to getting back to America. She had accepted it as her home now, and there were many things about it that she had missed. Cold all the time she was in England, she had missed the sensuous pleasure of opening a front door and stepping out of an icy wind into a warm bath of air. She missed her impeccable white-tiled bathroom and the shower which made it so easy to wash your hair. She missed the supermarket, and the man making bacon-and-egg sandwiches at the lunch counter in the drugstore; the friendly familiarity of strangers on trains and buses, and the unrepressed chit-chat of salesgirls and young men who came to mend the refrigerator and told you their life's ambitions. She missed the cars, the sweeping roads, the evening light on the white buildings of Washington, and Lincoln looking pensively into his watery mirror, with the golden reflection of the floodlit Monument coming across to meet him at night.

She looked forward to getting back to Vinson. Without him she often felt alone, as she never had when she was single. His letters said that he missed her, and she knew that he weighed his letters carefully and never said in them what was not true. When they met, everything would be all right again perhaps. She would work to make it so. She wanted to get back to America to start again to make her marriage happy, yet she was half afraid lest she should fail and things should not be any better.

And there would be Timmy to explain – Timmy, who was in a box in the guard's van of the train which took her to Southampton. The last time she had travelled this way she had been crying and too unhappy to look out of the window. On this journey she looked out all the time, her eyes trying to hold the fleeting fields and hedges and naked elms, the garden plots dug neatly for the winter, a boy's bicycle flung down with the wheel spinning, drably dressed people glimpsed on a shopping street as the train rushed over a bridge, because she did not know whether she would see England again.

She was glad that she would have the boat trip before she met Vinson. It would give her time to get her thoughts straight. A nuisance about this friend of Laurie's who would be on the boat.

'He's going to America to teach English,' Margaret had said. 'We've told him to look you up. Do be nice to him. He's rather a dear.'

Christine visualized a wispy professor with hair like candy floss being rather a dear in a soft-voiced unworldly way. She hoped he would not want to settle down next to her in a deck-chair and tap his fingertips together and talk about Coleridge.

In the customs shed a woman porter handled her luggage. She was broad and strong and shiny like the women who had gone out to help the rescue men in the Blitz, and when Christine paid her she tipped her broken-peaked cap jauntily and said: 'Ta, ducks.'

A crowd of boys and girls from some youth movement were travelling with rucksacks and thick clumsy clothes. Christine looked down from the ship and saw them gathered round a flustered woman who was handing out tea and buns from a trolley.

American voices were all around Christine on the boat in the turmoil of embarking. It was the last of England. When would she see another dowdy flustered woman dispensing tea and Chelsea buns, and when would someone call her Ducks again?

Chapter Eight

CHRISTINE did not see Margaret's friend on the ship at first. She did not look for him, for she preferred to be alone, and the middle-aged New England couple who sat at her table with their opinionated teenage daughter were boring enough without having to be bored by an English professor as well.

On the second day out Christine was sitting in her deck-chair trying to read, but lifting her eyes more often to the sun-specked sea that dipped beyond the rail and to the procession of earnest walkers who paced their mile round the deck with their coats buttoned round their throats.

One of the milers, a middle-aged man with a thick woollen scarf and sparse hair that lifted in the sea breeze, looked curiously at Christine every time he went by her chair. Presently he stopped after he had passed her and went to stand at the rail near by. He glanced back at her once and then looked quickly away when he saw that she was watching him.

This must be Laurie's friend. Soon he would summon the courage to come and speak to her, and she would have to be polite. She sighed and closed her book. She would not be polite to him for long, because it was nearly time to take Timmy out of the kennel for his morning exercise.

'Excuse me,' a voice said behind her. 'You are Mrs Gaegler, aren't you?'

Christine turned and saw a man with light-brown untidy hair, a strong English nose and an expectant smile. He wore a turtle-necked sweater under a thick tweed jacket, and flannel trousers that needed pressing.

'The deck steward told me who you were,' he said. 'I hope you don't mind. It's probably a bore, but I'm a friend of Laurie and Margaret Drew.'

'Oh yes,' Christine said, surprised. 'You're Mr Burns.'

He nodded. 'It's funny?' he asked, for her full cheekbones were lifting into a wide smile.

'I'm sorry,' she said. 'But – you see that man over there by the rail? Well, I've been thinking that he was Laurie's friend, and expecting him to come and speak to me. I thought you'd look – well, more like a college professor.'

'I am one, I'm afraid.' He stood and looked at her with his hands in his pockets, resting one leg. Although he had a rather ingenuous face, he had a bold sort of look, as if he did not care what people thought of him. 'I've been teaching English litera ture at Nottingham University,' he said, 'and now I'm going over for a year at a college in Washington under some exchange deal. They offered me the chance, and I thought it couldn't be any worse than Nottingham.'

'Oh, you'll like Washington,' Christine said. 'I like it better than any town – except London, of course.'

'You live there?'

'Yes. I'm married to an American naval officer.'

'I know,' he said. 'Margaret told me.' He studied her face carefully for a moment, as if he was trying to memorize it. Perhaps he was, for on a crowded boat one often meets someone one day and fails to recognize them the next.

Christine looked at her watch. 'I'll have to go now,' she said. 'I've got a dog in the kennels and they only let you take them out at certain times.' She unwrapped her steamer rug and stood up. The middle-aged man by the rail moved away and started once more on his mileage, arms swinging, the slit of his overcoat flapping.

'Could I come with you?' Laurie's friend said. 'I'd like to see the dog.'

Timmy liked everyone, so of course it was not remarkable that he liked Mr Burns, but he did put on a particularly gleeful show for him, and Laurie's friend knew how to talk to dogs.

In the afternoon the ship ran into a small storm. Christine had eaten too much at lunch out of boredom, for the couple from New England were arguing with their fat daughter, who was winning hands down as she always did, because she had the loudest and the rudest voice. When the ship began to move out of its throbbing rhythm Christine was afraid she was going to feel sea-sick and retired to her cabin.

She slept. When she woke and blinked round the cabin, as one always has to on a ship to remember where one is, she saw a note lying just inside the door. She saw the clock as she got out

323

of bed. She had missed her time for taking Timmy out. She would have to try and get round the steward downstairs, who was one of those difficult public servants who said: 'I'd like to, madam. You know I'd like to help you, but if I let you break the regulations everyone else will be wanting to do the same.'

The note said: '*Have taken dog out for you. Tommie Burns.*'

Christine was not able to thank him before dinner. She walked round the deck once or twice, and looking through the smoking-room window, she saw him sitting with three other men drinking whisky in a haze of cigarette smoke. Why should she feel this curious stab of irritation? He was entitled to drink whisky with three men in the smoking-room. She realized that she had been half expecting him to ask her to go to the bar for a cocktail. If she had been single he probably would have, but she was married now and could not go into bars with anyone but Vinson.

She never had the courage to go into a bar alone, so she went into the main lounge and asked the steward to bring her a martini. She had two, so that she could go down to dinner as late as possible when her table mates would be half-way through their meal.

Mr and Mrs Warren, however, were too polite to get up and go before Christine had finished her dinner. Their daughter went, because she had a date with a dreamy boy, but the parents sat on, smoking all over Christine's food and telling her where their ancestors had come from and how long their family had been in Madison, Connecticut.

After dinner Christine sat in an armchair in a corner of the lounge and watched the couples dancing and was bored. If Vinson were here they would be dancing and having drinks together between dances, and looking like any of the youngish unremarkable couples who were scattered about the lounge among the fat and elderly and a few very young people like the Warrens' daughter, who was dancing with the dreamy boy with her bottom stuck out.

Christine sat and thought about how, if she were single, she would be sitting here trying not to look as if she wanted to dance, and yet hoping that someone would come up and ask her. She had told Rhona that one of the best things about being married was that you did not have to look about for men any more, but although that was a relief it did take away some of the excitement of life, particularly on a journey like this. Shipboard life was a great setting for romance. Christine had never had a romance on a ship. Now she never would.

Before you were married a journey like this would be an exciting adventure, just as every party was an adventure, because you never knew whom you might meet. But when you had met the person you were looking for and had married him, then you were out of the running for excitement. One part of your life was finished. There could be no more adventures, and men did not look at you in the same speculative way.

While she was thinking this and looking round the lounge at the people dancing on the floor and drinking at little tables, the corner of her eye was watching the door for Tommie Burns to come in. She knew that the corner of her eye had no business to be doing that. If he should come in and talk to her – what was there in that? Margaret had probably told him to be nice to her, just as she had told Christine to be nice to him.

When he did not come into the lounge all evening, she was disappointed. She remembered being disappointed like that on holidays long ago when she had sat in hotel lounges, wasting an evening in case a young man on whom she had fixed her eye should come in.

She saw the Warrens open the door leading from the library, so she got up and went out the opposite door. As she crossed the space outside the purser's office to go downstairs Tommie Burns came out of the bar. He was wearing a blue suit and a white shirt and his hair was slicked down, showing the square shape of his head, wide at the corners of the forehead.

'I thought you were never coming out,' he said. 'I want to buy you a drink.'

'Why didn't you come into the lounge then?'

'I was afraid you'd expect me to dance with you, and I don't – not properly, that is. Do you want a drink now?'

'Well, I –'

'That's all right. I don't either. Let's go out on deck. I believe there must be a moon. Feverish young women and their escorts have been going out there and not coming back.'

325

'Not here,' he said when they were on the enclosed promenade deck. 'Let's go up top.' Christine walked with him along the deck to the ladder and saw for the first time that he limped slightly. She had not noticed it when they were walking Timmy this morning.

On the boat deck they leaned on the rail between two lifeboats and talked – not about themselves, not about anything in particular. It was just talk. It was cold, but Christine held herself from shivering in case he should take his coat off and put it round her. It was bad enough to be up here with him without that. Heavens, if Vinson had been on the boat and had found her here in such a setting, with the moon scudding in and out of the clouds and the phosphorescence tracking on the cleaved water far below, he –

'I think I should be going to bed,' she said.

'Thinking you should go and wanting to go are two different things,' Tommie said. 'What are you afraid of, Christine?'

'Nothing. Why should I be?' She laughed, but it sounded affected.

'You know what's going to happen, don't you?'

'No –' She tried to push him away, but he was strong: taller than Vinson and much stronger.

She held herself stiffly, her lips resisting his kiss.

'What's the matter?' he asked. He had a shocking air of innocence, as if he were surprised at you for thinking wrong into something he thought right.

'Well, you *know*,' she said crossly. 'I'm married.'

'So I've heard.' He smiled gently. He was so unscrupulous that it was almost funny.

'I ought to slap your face and run screaming for the captain,' Christine said, trying not to answer his smile.

'He'd probably enjoy that. He's youngish and quite personable.' Tommie moved in close to her again, standing so that she was pinned between him and the ship's rail. Below her the sea ran hissing past, back to England.

'Oh, you're quite impossible,' Christine said. 'I thought you were supposed to be just a nice respectable friend of Laurie's. My goodness, if he knew what you were like, he –'

'No, he wouldn't. I dare say even old Laurie behaved like this

326

when he fell in love with Margaret. It's just that things are speeded up on a ship. If you are going to fall in love with someone you do it quicker, don't you? . . . Don't you, Christine?'

'I don't know,' she murmured feebly. 'I don't know. . . .' She felt as if she had fallen over backwards and was drowning without a struggle in the phosphorescent sea.

Christine had expected to wake next morning in an agony of remorse, but she did not. She woke to a tingle of expectancy, wondering for a moment what was going to happen that made it such a lovely day. She remembered waking to just this feeling years ago in one of the chintzy spare rooms at Jennifer's house the night after she met Jerry.

She turned her eyes to the dressing-table, where Vinson's photograph regarded her as sternly as if it knew what had happened on the boat deck last night. No good telling it not to worry, that this was nothing to do with her and Vinson. The photograph had every right to worry. She was desperately worried herself.

She rang for her breakfast – she was never too worried to eat – and took a long time over having her bath and dressing, to put off the moment when she was going to find Tommie and get things straight between them. It was eleven o'clock by the time she came out of her cabin, so she decided to go and take Timmy out first, to delay the meeting a little longer.

Tommie was at the kennels, talking to Timmy through the bars. 'I knew you'd be coming down,' he said, 'so I thought I'd wait for you here.'

'You shouldn't be waiting for me at *all*,' Christine said in the voice which she had made up her mind to use. 'In any case, I'm only going to see you for long enough to say –' The steward came to unlock the kennel, so she had to stop saying it.

When they had quietened down Timmy's first excitement at being free Christine clipped the leash on his collar and they walked briskly up and down the small triangle of deck allotted for the exercise of dogs. Christine began to say what she had planned, but Timmy kept pulling her from one side to the other, and it was difficult to be coherent.

'You keep telling me you're married,' Tommie said. 'I know you are, and it's too bad, but talking about it won't make you any less married.'

'You don't understand! I'm *happily* married, that's the point.'

'Uh-huh,' Tommie looked at her, his eyes remembering last night.

Trying not to remember, Christine assumed a lecturing voice. 'You ought to be safely married too, at your age,' she said. 'Why aren't you married, anyway?' It was a rash question, because you never knew what tragedies or disappointments lay in a man's past, and she got the answer she deserved.

'I've never felt like asking anyone to marry a cripple,' he said. 'I was engaged before the war, but when the Japs locked me up she was told I might be dead, and she married someone else. Just as well, really.'

'Your – your legs?' Christine asked, remembering the scarcely perceptible limp.

'Only got one of 'em.'

Timmy pulled her away at that moment, and when she came back to Tommie they did not talk any more about his having lost a leg. They did not talk about her being married either. Christine did not want to be unkind. She felt sorry for him, and let him take her hand.

When they had put Timmy back in the kennel again and were walking along a white corridor between closed cabin doors, Tommie took her elbow, looked quickly up and down, and kissed her. Christine could not deceive herself then that she was only feeling sorry for him, only wanting to be kind. It was nothing like that.

'We never see anything of you now, Mrs Gaegler,' Mr Warren said, sopping bread in his gravy. 'Where do you get to? Maimie and I were looking for you last night to make up a fourth at bridge, and this morning I tried to find you to introduce you to some very lovely people from Maine I've just met up with. But you never seem to be around.'

'Oh, I know where *she* is,' said his daughter in an offensive singsong. 'She's always around with that English fellow.

Haven't you seen him, Pop? He's dreamy. Looks kinda like Spencer Tracy in his palmier days.'

'No, indeed,' said her father, blinking with pleasure at the idea of a new person to bore. 'I don't believe I have met up with him. I should be very happy to know your friend, Mrs Gaegler. Whyn't you bring him along to the bar for a cocktail tonight?'

'Thank you,' said Christine uncomfortably, 'but I don't know if he –'

'Oh, they won't want to waste their time with *you*, Pop,' said the daughter rudely. 'They've got better things to do, don't you know that?' She leered at Christine with her small ginger-lashed eyes.

'Excuse me,' said Christine, getting up. 'I think I'll have my coffee upstairs.' After she had left them she wished that she had not. It had been bad enough not knowing what to say to Mr Warren to avoid being coupled with Tommie as two people who accepted invitations together, but it was worse that she had shown annoyance at the daughter's crass teasing.

Now the whole family would begin to talk about her. Perhaps they would tell other people, and the other people would talk. How had she ever been foolish enough to get herself into such a situation? She went to find Tommie to tell him that they must not see each other any more.

'Short of one of us jumping into the sea,' Tommie said affably, 'I don't see how we can help it.' He was practising deck quoits by himself on the windy sports deck, balancing himself adroitly with his artificial leg when the ship rolled. His sleeves were turned up and the muscle of his forearm made a beautiful strong shape under the golden brown hairs. Christine took her eyes away from it.

They had two and a half more days together on the ship, and Christine spent quite a lot of time telling Tommie that they must not go on like this, but it made no difference to the behaviour of either of them. It was terrible and it was wonderful, but at New York Vinson would meet her and she would never see Tommie again. She had made him promise not to try and see her in Washington. She did not trust him at all, but she believed that he would stick to that.

329

At New York there was a cable waiting for Christine. It said:
'*Homecoming delayed. Letter explanation at house. Love Vinson.*'

Just 'Love', that was all. Nothing about how pleased he was that she was back in America and how sorry not to see her at once; but Vinson was never any good at conveying loving messages in letters, let alone in cables.

Christine looked for Tommie on the boat and in the customs shed. They could have travelled to Washington together, could have had a few more hours together, but perhaps it was just as well that she could not find him. What was the use of a few more hours? They had said all that there was to be said last night.

When she got Timmy out of the clutches of the authorities and had coped with customs and red caps, marvelling at her assured Americanized self who was so different from the bewildered English self arriving in New York last time, Christine took a taxi to Pennsylvania station and travelled the long train ride to Washington.

When the taxi-driver who brought her out to Arlington had carried in her bags for her and driven away, Christine turned on the heating plant in the cellar and began to go all round the house taking the dust-sheets off the furniture. There was no point in doing that straight away, but she felt that she had to occupy herself with something to try and take away the dead disappointed feeling of her homecoming.

The little house was cold, and at the same time stuffy with disuse. It was very quiet. Still wearing her coat, Christine sat down on the stairs and thought about Tommie. He had fallen in love with her. He had loved her so much that he did not care whether she was married, nor whether she was honest enough to say if she loved him. She had been romantic and exciting to him. Now she was just any tired woman in her own home, taking off dust-sheets and waiting for the radiators to warm up, and she was not exciting to anybody, least of all to herself.

The bell rang. Mrs Meenehan was celebrating Christine's home-coming by a ceremonious visit to the front door instead of one of her everyday appearances at the kitchen window.

'I've got all your mail here,' she said, when she had got over the first exclamations of welcome. 'I got the mailman to give everything to me.'

'Oh, you needn't have –'

'It was no bother, Catherine honey. I knew you'd want me to be in charge while you were away, and there's not a day passed but I've been round the house checking up. You ask Daddy.'

Christine took the letters, wondering how many of them Mrs Meenehan had steamed open and stuck down again.

'No, I won't come inside,' Mrs Meenehan said, making Christine feel that she should have asked her in. 'I'm just dying to hear about your trip and how you found poor old England, but you look plenty tired right now. We'll have a good long gab-fest tomorrow. And where's the Commander? I didn't see him get out of the taxi with you.'

'He's staying in Panama a bit longer,' Christine said. 'I expect there's a letter from him here about it. Oh yes, here it is. Excuse me. I must read it straight away.' She began to shut the door imperceptibly, so that Mrs Meenehan, who was standing on the sill, might be pushed gently outside without knowing it.

Timmy was on the lawn barking at the strangeness of everything. 'I brought my dog back with me,' Christine said, when Mrs Meenehan was safely outside and the door was shut, too far for her to step in again and start talking about the dog.

'Oh yes, I know,' said Mrs Meenehan. 'I saw him. We've already made friends.' You never could tell her anything new.

The telephone rang while Christine was reading Vinson's letter. 'Hullo?' She answered it abstractedly, still reading. 'Oh . . . Tommie. Tommie, you promised you wouldn't ring up. Vin isn't here yet as a matter of fact, but if he had been –'

'Well, he isn't, so why worry? When's he coming back?'

'I'm just reading his letter. Let's see. . . . About two weeks, he says.'

'I see.' The silence on the wire between them was just as if they had looked at each other.

Every day Christine told herself that she would not see Tommie any more, and every day she told him that, but it made no more difference than it had on the ship. She knew that she must be careful in Washington, where the slightest hint of

331

scandal would fly round the Navy wives like a torch set to oil-soaked stubble, but Tommie's rashness was infectious, and time and again she found herself doing the things that she knew were dangerous.

She knew that she should not visit the house where he was living alone, but she could not stop herself going there. He gave her a key, and she was waiting for him every evening when he came back from the college. It was late when she drove herself home. As she turned in at her driveway she would see the light go off in the bedroom where Mrs Meenehan had been staying awake to hear what time the car came back.

One night Christine did not go home at all, and after that she stayed every night with Tommie. It did not seem to matter any more. Nothing mattered, except the diminishing time that was left to them.

Tommie had taken over the house vacated by the American Professor who had taken his place at Nottingham. The house was in Georgetown, the old part of Washington through which Vinson had driven Christine when she first arrived, and wished that he could live at such a good address.

Christine thought what a waste it was that Vinson could never know that she had been living in Georgetown. Under other circumstances he would have been so impressed.

There was nothing impressive, however, about the tiny red-brick house whose flat roof was scraped eerily by the fingers of trees on a windy night. It was the thinnest house Christine had ever seen. It stood alone, looking like a slice cut out of a terrace, with a junk yard on one side and a short alley of consciously 'cute' little houses converted from slave quarters on the other. Because it stood on a slight slope it seemed to tilt a little, teetering in its thinness, as if it would one day fall across the entrance of the alley and imprison the embassy girls and colonels' widows who lived in the cute little houses.

Inside the thin house the hall was narrow, the living-room was too narrow to hold a sofa, the kitchen was so narrow that you could reach the stove, the table, the shelves, the sink without moving your feet, and the bedroom upstairs was not much bigger than the bathroom. French windows only wide enough for one person to walk through at a time led from the living-

332

room to the neglected garden, which was littered with odds and ends thrown over by the negroes in the junk yard. The back of the house looked even narrower than the front, because there was a playground across the street instead of buildings, and so the house stood out insecurely against the winter sky, like those emaciated villas that stand about bleakly on the Belgian coast.

It was a queer, inconvenient house with doors that opened the wrong way and some windows that would not open at all, very different from Christine's neat, scientifically designed home in Arlington. Cramped and awkward and old, the Georgetown house was romantic. At night, when the cars had stopped going by, it was so quiet that you might have been in the country, except when the sirens of ambulances or fire-engines rushed through the narrow streets with their wail of calamity.

The little red house seemed to have been made for a secret love. You could not imagine anyone quite ordinary living there, running the vacuum cleaner every morning, spraying moth powder in the cupboards, reckoning up accounts, entertaining dull guests, or stepping sedately out of the white front door and down the three brick steps to go to a dull party. Christine felt that there must have been lovers there who had left their enchantment imprisoned between the narrow walls, just as she and Tommie would leave some of theirs when they had gone.

When they had gone. . . .

Christine tried not to think about what would happen to her when her foolish romance was over. She would be on the down-hill slope of thirty-five, her last clutch at youth irretrievably loosed on the day when Vinson came back and woke her from her dream to travel the 'long and straight and dusty' road with him. When the future came to trouble her she shut her mind to it, as a sleeper disturbed from a beautiful dream pulls the sheets over his head and shuts his eyes tightly to fight his way back into sleep again before the dream can escape.

Being in Washington with Tommie was like seeing America all over again, in quite a new way. When Vinson had first introduced her to his country he had been so anxious that she should like it, so watchful of her reactions that it had sometimes been a strain to summon enough enthusiasm and to say the right things to please him. But Tommie brought enough enthusiasm for them both, and it was easy to discover in his happy company just how many things one enjoyed about America.

Unlike some of the British who go to America with their backs up and spend their time telling people how much better things are done in England, Tommie had come over with an expectant heart, and he plunged into the life of America looking for enjoyment like an eager dog going after a stick.

With him, Christine went to all the places where she had never been with Vinson. Vinson had taken her sightseeing in the Capitol and the Monument and the memorials and museums and art galleries. He had taken her to Mount Vernon and to the home of Robert E. Lee. He had taken her to the Army and Navy Club among the old generals' and admirals' widows, and to reputable restaurants where you knew what kind of food you would get.

Tommie took her to dark Italian restaurants where the proprietor came and sat talking politics through a toothpick at your table, and you never knew what was in the minestrone. He took her to underground bars where all the men kept their hats on – including once the barman – and to a fish restaurant on the waterfront where you sat at a long table and joked with strangers over the fried shrimps, and out to a 'Hot Shoppe' where you could sit in your car while a Philippino waiter skipped out to you through the rain with a tray of food.

Christine had been wanting to go to one of these drive-in restaurants ever since she came to America, but Vinson liked to get his knees under a table when he ate. He never let her play jukeboxes, but Tommie wanted to play the jukebox wherever he found one. They would sit for hours in a waffle shop or a hamburger joint or a soda fountain putting nickels in the slot and being in love, while the over-amplified music and the chatter of teenagers lapped them round with the unsubtle noises of America.

Tommie said that some of the boys at the college snickered at him because he was English, so he began conscientiously to pepper his speech with what he thought were native expressions. He had a very English voice, unstressed, with the consonants casually slurred, so that words like 'gee' and 'sure' and 'you're telling me' sounded very odd when he brought them carefully out. It made him happy, however, to think that he was talking American, and Americans themselves, always quick to be flattered by imitation, did not laugh when he said to them: 'Look here – er – bud, I surely would be happy to have you have me introduce you to Mrs Gaegler.'

He said that at a cocktail party given by one of the college professors, to which he took Christine. She knew that she should not risk going with him, but she and Tommie were at that stage where caution has no meaning and the egotism of love sees love itself as a talisman against mishap. They had so little time left together. If Tommie must go to the party she could not let him go alone.

He stayed by her side all the time instead of going away and talking to the other men he knew, as Vinson would have done. They behaved very circumspectly, but Christine wondered if people could tell they were in love by looking at them. Once when Tommie touched her bare arm she thought that if she had been someone else watching them she would have known at once.

Tommie practised his American. When they were introduced to other guests, Christine said: 'How do you do?', which she had not given up even after nine months in America, but Tommie said: 'Glad to know you', or 'I certainly am happy to meet you', and repeated people's names, just like an old hand.

However, when a surly-looking man arrived not quite sober from another cocktail party and Tommie brought out his: 'Happy to meet you', the man stuck out his jaw as if he were spoiling for a fight, and said: 'Why should you be? You've never seen me before, and you're never going to see me again. I'm leaving this goddamn town in two hours for Chicago. Why should you be happy to meet me?'

'Well, I don't know – dash it, my dear chap,' stammered Tommie, surprised into being very English. 'Bit of a setback,' he said, as the man stumbled away to the bar. 'I'll have to re-write my lines. Perhaps I – Gosh, darling, look. There's a man wearing my regimental tie. Let's go and talk to him and be English for a bit.'

'Tommie, it doesn't mean that he –' Christine tried to detain him, but he was already half-way across the room, his limp more pronounced, as it always was when he had had a few drinks.

'I see you were in my lot,' Tommie said, holding out his hand.

'How?' said the man in the regimental tie. 'How's that again, sir?'

'Your tie.'

The man's baffled face broke into a beam. 'Smooth, isn't it? My wife bought it for me. The first one she's bought I've been able to wear. Glad you like it.'

'It's a pattern I've grown fond of,' Tommie said, leaning forward to examine the little label on the end of the tie, which said: 'King's Own Yorkshire Light Infantry. Genuine copy.'

Tommie wanted to see Christine's home at Arlington. He said that he must be able to imagine her there after she had gone back. He added also that he wanted to know where to find her.

'Oh, Tommie, don't,' she said. 'Even if you're joking. You know you promised that you wouldn't try to see me after Vin gets back. I won't go on with it. I can't. You must leave me alone – please, darling, or I shan't be able to get along. And something terrible might happen. Vin might shoot you, or shoot me, or anything. You don't know what he's like.'

'Tell me,' Tommie said. 'Tell me more about the man Gaegler.' He was always wanting to hear about Vinson. His curiosity about Christine's husband was unnatural and almost morbid. Christine did not want to tell him anything. What she was doing to Vinson was bad enough without the added disloyalty of discussing him with her lover. Sometimes, when she felt a sudden panic about Vinson's homecoming, she wanted desperately to tell Tommie everything, and to say to him with tears that he was all the things that Vinson was not; but she would not let herself.

'Tell me more about how jealous he is,' Tommie persisted. 'Tell me about the time you went out with his brother.'

'No. I wish I'd never said anything about that. I didn't mean to. You're so unfair, Tommie. You must make things worse this way. I won't criticize Vin to you. I won't, however much your male vanity wants me to. He's my husband and I –'

'The loyal wife,' Tommie said, grinning. 'A charming picture.'

'That's unfair too, but I suppose I deserve it. Please, Tommie, you must help me. I've got to get back to Vinson in three days. Don't make it more difficult than it is already.'

'Why shouldn't I? I may have plans of my own.'

'You promised! You promised me you'd stay away. Tommie, you must. It's the only thing to do.'

'That's right,' he said with his baffling look, at the same time innocent and bold. 'I promised, didn't I?'

'I don't trust you,' Christine said in a small voice.

'Why not?' He opened his eyes very wide. 'I've promised. So let me come and see your house, my darling. If you're going back to get that dress for tonight, I'll come with you. I must know everything about you, don't you understand? How you've got your kitchen arranged, what your dressing-table is like, how the light will strike your face when you open the door in the morning to let Timmy out.'

Christine got up. 'Let's go now then,' she said. She had known all along that she would take him. She had never been able to refuse him anything he wanted, and they only had three more days together.

It was Sunday. With any luck, the Meenehans would be in their rumpus room with the central heating and the television and Daddy's cigar all going full blast. Christine stopped the car at the bottom of the lawn. If she did not take it into the driveway, perhaps Mrs Meenehan would not hear them arrive.

While she was in her bedroom getting her dress and Tommie was roaming round the house with a small smile on his face, Timmy, who had not lived in the house long enough to trust it, began to bark his misgivings on the lawn. Christine leaned out of the window and tried to shout at him in a whisper. He waved his plumed tail and went on barking.

'Darling!' Tommie called up the stairs. 'There's a woman with a face like a sweet potato pounding on the kitchen window. What do I do?'

'Nothing. I'll come down. And don't call me darling, for heaven's sake.'

'I heard the doggie bark,' Mrs Meenehan said, when Christine opened the back door, 'so I came right over to bring you back for some coffee and cake. I have a very dear friend with me I want to have you know.'

'I haven't got very long,' Christine said, 'I just came home to get a dress and then I have to go straight back to the friends I'm staying with.'

'You come right along with me now.' If Mrs Meenehan issued an invitation, there was no getting out of it.

'I have someone with me, though,' Christine said, for Tommie was visible in the hall, inspecting Vinson's ship prints. 'My cousin – a cousin of mine from England. He happened to come to Washington for a few days on business. Wasn't that lucky?' She wondered if her voice sounded as wild and unnatural as it felt.

'Bring him along. Hi there, Mr –'

'Burns,' said Tommie, coming into the kitchen.

'So you're Catherine's cousin. My, my. Well, I'm sure the Commander will be pleased to hear she had someone to look after her while he's away. These Navy men. Always here and there. I know what it is. When Daddy and I had command of the *Walrus* he was never home for but a few days at a time.'

The Meenehans' rumpus room was in semi-darkness, with a variety show on the screen, Mr Meenehan in slippers and a lumber jacket, and Mrs Meenehan's friend, very fat, wedged into an upright canvas chair, head on to the television set.

'I certainly am happy to meet you,' she told Christine. 'Tessie here has told me so many antidotes about you.' She was also happy to meet Tommie, and he said that he was happy to meet her, and asked her where she came from, which he had already discovered was a thing Americans greatly liked to be asked.

'Tuscarawas County, Ohio,' Mrs Grady said with a proud gleam in her protruding eyes. Christine and Tommie murmured unconvincingly – it was always hard to think of a suitable response when someone had told you their home town – and

338

sat down in front of the television set, which was the only place where there were chairs.

Mrs Meenehan climbed up the basement stairs with her slip showing to get coffee and cake, although they said that they had only just had lunch. Mr Meenehan made a little conversation, with half his attention on the television show, and Mrs Grady told them some items about Tuscarawas County, Ohio, with music and song and eulogies about toothpaste sounding through her talk of schools and county jails. No one thought of turning the television down to make talk easier. The Meenehans preferred just to raise their voices.

Mrs Meenehan's coffee was bitter and her cake like a loofah that has been left to dry out on the edge of the bath. Christine and Tommie ate and drank bravely, trying not to look at each other. With the return of his wife from the kitchen Mr Meenehan made no further attempt at conversation. It was Sunday, and he wanted to watch the television, so he went on watching it, chuckling sometimes to himself and slapping his thin knees.

When she had exhausted Tuscarawas County Mrs Grady did not have any more to say either. She preferred to sit and stare, storing impressions away behind her glaucaemic eyes to retail to the folks back home. Mrs Meenehan, however, was never at a loss for talk. Every time Christine was getting up to say they must go Mrs Meenehan started on a new topic and she had to sit down again. Tommie was very polite and patient, but he kept telegraphing looks to Christine which showed that he was thinking as she was, that they had so little time together, and must they waste it like this?

Mrs Meenehan was telling him about the trip she and Daddy had taken in Europe after he retired. 'We rented a car over there,' she said, when she had finished making it quite clear that Daddy had retired as a *lieutenant commander*, 'the funniest little French automobile. You never saw anything like it.'

'Tell about where you went,' Mrs Grady said, nodding her fleshy head. 'They'll admire to hear that.'

'Well, we went just about everywhere, you know. We covered France in five days. Don't you think that was something? Then we went over the Alps to Italy. Quite a climb, though of course nothing to our Rockies. We were quite impressed with Italy. We hadn't been too impressed with France, with all those children going about in black aprons, but when we got into Italy, and the people had some colour to their clothes – why, you might have been in the United States!'

'That must have set you up no end,' Tommie said seriously.

Mrs Grady, who had been looking speculatively at him for some time, shifted her weight in the chair and said: 'You're foreign, ain't you? May I ask where you come from?'

'England.'

'Oh, fancy. And how long have you been over here?'

'Let's see – about a week.'

'I suppose,' said Mrs Grady, 'you studied our language before you came over here. I think it's wonderful that you are able to speak it so well.'

Christine stared at the television set. She dared not look at Tommie. They both stood up and made some excuse to go. When they had had their laugh out, doubled up and gasping behind Mr Meenehan's toolshed, Christine realized that she had not laughed like that since she was married.

When they got into the house they began to laugh again, laughing and kissing each other in the hall. When Christine went to her bedroom to get the dress she had come for, Tommie followed her upstairs.

'Plees,' he said. 'I do not spick the language so well – but I know how to say it in French.' He said it.

'Oh no, Tommie.' Christine backed quickly away from the bed. 'Not here. Please not here. Don't you see, that's the last, most awful thing we –'

He was much stronger. Even with his handicap it was never any use trying to struggle against Tommie. She was lost. This was the worst sin of all, and one that could never be forgotten. How could she ever again lie with Vinson on this bed and not remember Tommie? Was that what Tommie wanted?

'What do people say at a time like this?' It was their last evening together. 'There must be something that people say that makes it easier to bear, or at least makes them able to realize that it really is good-bye. I can't realize it.'

'No, darling,' Tommie said, 'because it isn't good-bye. All right, I know. Don't say it. Don't say: "You promised." I know I did. I promised, and I am coming with you to New York tomorrow to try and persuade that chap to take over my place at the college here and let me have his. I haven't said just how I'll try, but I've said I'll try. Well now, look. If he says yes, I'll be in New York; you'll be in Washington, two hundred and fifty miles apart. Do you honestly think that's going to keep you and me away from each other? How can anything do that? It would be like trying to keep the two cut ends of a worm apart. And suppose the chap says no, then I'll have to stay in Washington. How do you think we can avoid seeing each other?'

'We could. We wouldn't know the same people. We'd move in different circles.'

'Move in different circles!' He laughed, throwing his head back. 'What an expression. My God, you *are* a Navy wife. I suppose the man Gaegler talks about "moving in the right circles".'

'Don't be horrid, Tommie.'

'Never will discuss him, will you? But I gather from things you've let slip that he's a snob. Snobbish and selfish and conventional and jealous – and probably a bore. My God, Christine darling, you got yourself into a hell of a mess that day you sat on a bench in Grosvenor Square.'

'No I didn't. Vin isn't like you think. My marriage isn't any worse than most people's. It would have been all right if I hadn't met you.'

'How can a marriage be all right unless it's perfect?'

'You don't understand. You get fond of a person. You – you get used to them. If they have faults – or perhaps not faults, but things that just aren't right for you – well, you do mind when you first discover them, but after a bit you get used to them and it doesn't matter.'

'It must matter. It must get worse and worse.'

'No. You don't understand. It isn't like that. You don't understand about marriage.'

'I understand about *your* marriage,' Tommie said. 'It's all washed up.'

'It isn't! Be quiet, Tommie.'

341

'Christine darling, don't snap my head off every time I mention divorce.'

'Why not? I've told you Vin would never divorce me. He's a Catholic.'

'But would you get a divorce if you could?'

'What's the use of asking me that? I can't.'

'But *would* you?' Tommie took hold of her shoulders painfully and made her look at him.

'I couldn't. Oh – one can't. You get married, and you have to go on with it. Let me go. You're hurting me.'

She turned away and went to look out of the glass door at the dark bare garden. Above the rooftops the sky was orange in the city's glow, and two shafts of beacon light stood straight up from the airport across the river.

'It's like what Stevenson wrote about marriage,' she said. 'There can be no by-path meadows. "The road lies long and straight and dusty to the grave".'

'A dismal picture,' Tommie said. 'But, anyway, Stevenson didn't mean it. He'd only been married about a year when he wrote it, and he was madly in love with his wife. She was full of sex and mystery, they say. Listen, darling.' He came and stood behind her. 'If it was you and me it wouldn't be long and straight and dusty.' He rested his chin on her shoulder and they looked out at the city night together. 'I know I told you on the ship that I'd never ask a girl to marry me because of my tin leg, but that was just making an excuse. Trying to be noble, or something. If I'd met you it wouldn't have mattered. Would you have married me if you'd met me before Vinson?'

Christine did not want to say yes. She was afraid to say it. But when he turned her round and saw her face he did not need an answer.

Christine was driving along the U.S. 1 highway to New York, where she was going to greet her husband and say good-bye to her lover. It should have been a very poignant drive, but Christine felt dead and without emotion, driving automatically, unable to think about the future towards which she was heading, the end of a dream. Tommie did not talk very much. He behaved as if this were a drive like any other. He played with the

342

radio, trying all the different stations, sang a little out of tune, and seemed quite happy.

He should not have been like that. Christine glanced at his guileless face and was suspicious. Did it mean that to him this drive was not the end of the journey, that he was not going to try very hard to persuade the other English professor to change places with him, or that even if he did, he was not going to let two hundred and fifty miles keep him away from Christine?

Christine was afraid. She did not trust Tommie not to write to her, although she had told him that Vinson was quite capable of opening her letters if his suspicions were aroused. She did not trust him not to ring her up. He might even turn up at Arlington with a charming smile and an innocent alibi that would not deceive Vinson for a moment. It would be terrible, unthinkable. Christine was afraid of what Tommie might do to the lives of all three of them, yet at the same time she could not help cherishing at the back of her mind the thought that he would still be in America and that she might see him again after all.

When Jerry had not written to her for two years, the thought that he was somewhere in the world and that she might see him again had been something to cling to. After he was killed she realized how much store she had set by that hope. She and Tommie were parting, for ever, she thought, but he was not dead. He would still be there, just in case . . .

One side of her was glad of that; the other feared it. She looked again at Tommie, grinning at the mournful crooning of an amateur on the radio. He should have been a pathetic person, a person you could feel sorry for because he had lost a leg and lost a girl who would not wait the war out for him and lost his chance of the Army career he had always wanted, but he was not pathetic. You could not be sorry for him. You could only fall in love with him and be a little sorry for yourself and afraid of his power to complicate the future.

Timmy, who did not like riding in the back of the car, jumped over to the front seat and turned Christine's thoughts to the problems of the more immediate future. She had not written to Vinson that she was bringing the dog over. If he was going to be angry about it, there was no point in letting him foster his anger beforehand. She had not meant to bring

343

Timmy to New York. Vinson would be pleased to see her at the pier, and she was not going to spoil that at least, but when she had shut Timmy in the house he had begun to jump up at the window and knock down plants as soon as he heard the car start up, so she had to go back and bring him with her.

She would not take him on to the dock. That would be too much. Vinson might look for her from the ship and see Timmy and start to get angry before she had a chance to explain. She would leave him in the car and try to find some way of breaking it to Vinson while he was being happy to see her and glad to be home. But however happy he was to see her, whatever words she found to tell him about Timmy, Vinson was sure to be angry. She had disobeyed him flatly, as she had seldom done before. Vinson had told her not to bring the dog from England, and she had brought him. There was going to be trouble.

There was going to be trouble too if she did not get to New York on time. Vinson hated her to be late. He was never late himself. He was always ready much too early and he could not understand that circumstances could ever make anyone else late. He would certainly not understand these circumstances, because she could not tell them to him. She was late because when she had finished getting her home ready for Vinson's arrival and had gone to the little red house to fetch Tommie he had not been ready and he would not hurry.

If she was late in New York and Vinson had to wait for her he would be angry already before she told him about the dog. She must not be late.

'You're driving awfully fast,' Tommie said. 'Do you always go at this speed with this much traffic about?'

'We're late,' Christine said. 'It's all right. I'm a better driver than any man ever gives me credit for. I wish this horrible great truck would let me pass. It's been holding us up for miles.'

'You're thinking about the man Gaegler,' Tommie said 'Hurrying to meet him. Oh well.'

'If I obeyed my instincts I'd be crawling,' Christine looked at him. He was smiling. She would never forget what he looked like. She said: 'You are the most attractive man I ever met.'

He leaned across to see her face in the driving mirror. 'And you,' he said, 'you're beautiful.'

'You know I'm not.'

'You are, and you know when you're most beautiful? It's when I tell you you are.'

If she had not turned her eyes to look at him in the mirror she might have seen a split second sooner the car racing towards her in the middle of the road as she pulled out to pass the big truck. . . . If she had not swerved to the right away from the other car it might have avoided her. . . . If she had speeded up to get past in time. . . . What was the use of these thoughts chasing round in her brain after the truck had crumpled the side of her car like tinfoil, and she stood unhurt by the side of the road, while the clustering aftermath of an accident gathered round her? Someone had kept Timmy alive for half an hour, but there was nothing anyone could do for Tommie.

Chapter Nine

VINSON was very patient, very understanding, very kind, but he could not arouse Christine out of the numb lethargy in which she moved through the long days. He tried. He tried very hard to help her. He had a theory that the best way to get over the shock of an accident was to talk about it, and Christine sometimes felt that she would scream when he talked once more on the subject of the hitch-hiker, and how Christine must not feel responsible for his death, because if a man was foolish enough to take lifts on the highway he deserved all he got.

He was very forbearing. He did not upbraid her for her careless driving – although he would not let her drive the new car – and he never reminded her that she had promised him that she would never stop for anybody on the road. Utterly cast down, guilty and despairing, Christine found herself wishing that Vinson would be cross with her. His tolerance of her reckless mistake, his assurance that he would pay anything to get the best defence for her if she were charged with dangerous driving, his easy acceptance of her story about the hitch-hiker all piled reproach upon miserable reproach into her secret thoughts.

Vinson had come back determined, as she had been when she left England, to start their marriage off again more happily and forget the sorry time they had been through. He was expecting his promotion to come up at the next selection board, and he was always reminding her of that, promising her that she should be a captain's wife, as if he were offering candy to make a child happy.

Christine moved dully and purposelessly through the long days, and the nights when she lay awake, haunted by her thoughts. The only thing she saw clearly was that Vinson must never know about Tommie. It would be the end of even the pretence at marriage that they had between them now.

She did not let Vinson see her cry. She did her weeping after he was asleep, or when she was alone in the house in the afternoon when the day seemed never-ending. The only time she

346

wept before him was one Saturday morning when they were sitting late over breakfast and the letter came from Margaret. Christine opened the letter unthinkingly and had read half through it before she came to the bad part.

'*Did you ever meet our friend Tommie Burns on the boat?*' Margaret wrote. '*I wonder if you heard about the terrible thing that happened to him. He was hitch-hiking to New York – just the sort of crazy thing he would do – and he was killed by some fool of a woman driver who gave him a lift.*'

Christine did not move. She sat stiffly at her end of the kitchen table with tears rolling down her face, unable even to raise a hand to wipe them away.

'What's the matter, honey? What on earth's the matter?' Vinson got up and came to her.

'It's nothing.' Christine crumpled the letter in her lap. 'A letter from Margaret. Somebody – somebody that she and I knew is dead, that's all.'

'Somebody you were fond of?'

Christine shook her head.

'Well, you mustn't cry for that. Your nerves are all upset these days, honey, that's what it is.' Being an American, that was a thing he could understand in a woman. 'I wish you'd go see a doctor.'

If it were as simple as that. If only she were a neurotic woman who could go to a doctor and get solace from injections of sterile water and egotistical hours of lying on a couch and being psycho-analysed.

Once she drove with Vinson past the narrow little red-brick house in Georgetown that looked like a slice of a house instead of a house. Vinson liked to drive through Georgetown whenever he was in that part of Washington. He liked to point out its old-world beauties to Christine and tell her that when they had made their million that was where they would live. What would he have said if Christine had turned to him and said : 'When you were in Coco Solo I lived in that red house with the white door for a week with a man I was in love with'?

The white door had a black-and-white notice on it saying FOR RENT. Down the hill of Thirty-Fourth Street and over the crossing of Volta Place, two fire-engines sped with sirens screaming, as Christine had so often heard them come screaming through the night from the fire station on Q Street.

'When you were in Coco Solo, Vinson,' she would say, 'I lived for a week in that silly red house with a man I was in love with.'

Because she would never say it, it was interesting to toy with the idea of how Vinson would react. Would he really have said and done all the things she had told Tommie he might if Tommie did not stay away from her? She would never know now, any more than she would ever know whether he would have tried to make her give Timmy away or have him destroyed. All her problems had been solved, very neatly, by tragedy.

Admiral Hamer would be on the selection board which would either make Vinson a captain or leave him a commander for another year; therefore Admiral and Mrs Hamer must be invited for cocktails.

'Oh, Vin, why?' Christine said. 'Surely if they want to make you a captain they'll do it whether you pour the old man full of martinis or not.'

'That has nothing to do with it,' Vinson said stiffly. 'It's simply a friendly, courteous gesture that we should make at this time. You ought to get to know Mrs Hamer better. I'd like to have them just sit down here with us and feel at home.'

It seemed an unlikely picture, but Vinson was bent on it, so Christine acquiesced. She would have to make some delicate canapés and polish up the silver tray, but she would not wash the white paint of the mantelpiece as Vinson said she must.

'Why should I? Good Lord, you talk as if they were royalty. A house is supposed to look lived in, and you can't have fires without getting smudge marks. Everyone knows that even Mrs Hamer, I should think, though she doesn't know much.'

'What's come over you, Christine? You used to be so particular about the house.'

'That was before . . . That was when I . . . Well, I felt like it then. Now it doesn't seem to matter any more.'

'It matters very much. I want you to wash the mantelpiece.'

'I've got better things to do.' It would not take her half a hour to clean the paint round the fireplace, but it had now become an issue.

She would not do it, and so on the day the Hamers were invited, when Vinson came home he fetched a bucket of water and a cloth and a tin of scouring powder and went on his knees to wash the paint. He did not do it reproachfully. He did it quite happily, humming tunelessly while he worked, and imagining Mrs Hamer saying to the Admiral what a nice trim house the Gaeglers had, everything spick and span in true Navy fashion.

Christine was in the kitchen in her dressing-gown, putting out the canapés. Mrs Meenehan came in to tell her that there was a soap sale on at the supermarket, and insisted on showing her how to cut radishes to look like little crowns, although Christine preferred to cut them like flowers in the way she knew.

'I had a letter from my friend Mary Grady,' Mrs Meenehan said. 'She sent you her regards, and said how much she'd enjoyed meeting you and your cousin. How is that handsome cousin of yours, by the way? Is he still around? I thought he was just the most *charming* man. It was so nice for you to have him to squire you while the Commander was away.'

Mrs Meenehan had a carrying voice. She could stand outside her back door and talk in her normal tones, and Christine could hear her quite easily from her own house. When she was close to you, she did not bother to turn down the volume any more than she ever turned down the television set.

Had Vinson heard? Was he going to be suspicious now? Frightened, Christine began to think of how she could lie her way out of this.

When Mrs Meenehan had gone, Vinson came into the kitchen to empty his bucket.

'Finished cleaning?' Christine asked brightly to disguise her uneasiness.

'Just about. It looks much better now.'

'It looked all right before, I thought.'

Vinson ignored this. 'What was Mrs M. saying about your cousin?' he asked. 'You didn't tell me a relative of yours had been here.' His voice sounded casual, but Christine was afraid.

'Didn't I?' She tried to speak airily. 'I suppose I must have forgotten. There were so many other more important things.'

'Who was he? Nice guy?'

'Not particularly.' She shrugged her shoulders. 'Why?'

'Oh, I don't know.' Vinson went over to the refrigerator. 'I thought you might like to tell me about him, that's all.'

'There's nothing to tell. He was a bore.'

'Uh-huh.' Vinson seemed satisfied. How easy it was to lie. How frighteningly easy to deceive. Christine hated herself for telling yet another lie, and suddenly she hated Vinson for being so easily deceived. How silly of him to be so unsuspecting. He with his dramatic jealousies over nothing at all could not now recognize it when he had a real cause for jealousy. Now that the moment of danger was past, her relief quickly turned to annoyance. Her nerves were strung up into a hot taut thread of irritation.

Vinson turned and said: 'I wish you'd go up and take off that dressing-gown and get ready.'

'Don't fuss,' Christine snapped. She would have liked to scream at him.

'But you forget,' he said earnestly. 'The Admiral will be here in half an hour.'

'Oh, damn the Admiral!' Christine burst out. She had thought this so many times, but never risked saying it. She would think it many times again. She saw her future in sudden desperation.

'I'm sick of the Admiral!' she cried. 'I'm sick of Mrs Hamer too – and all of them. I'm sick of the whole Navy!'

'And sick of me?' Vinson asked calmly, taking the ice trays to the sink.

Christine drew in her breath. So the crisis was here. For a moment she could not answer; then she said jerkily: 'Vin, it's no good. I can't go on.'

'What's that? I can't hear you with the water running.'

When he turned off the tap, she told him about Tommie. There seemed nothing else to do. It was the time now to finish everything.

Vinson listened without a word until her degrading story was done. It was degrading now. The romance and the glory were faded, dead as Tommie was dead. It was just the sorry little story of an unfaithful wife.

Vinson was sitting at the kitchen table, tracing the pattern of the plastic cloth. Christine went and stood before him at the end of the table, like a prisoner before a judge.

'Well,' she asked wearily, 'now what?'

'Nothing,' he said without looking up. 'I knew this already.'

'You *knew*?'

'Yes, I knew. Chet Staples, a civilian who works in the Navy Department, told me he'd seen you with this man at a party, and – oh, some of the things he'd heard. Chet's the kind of guy who likes to break that sort of news.'

'Why didn't you tell me you knew?'

'I was waiting for you to tell me about it.'

'And if I never had?'

'I knew you would, Christine. You're honest.'

'I'm not honest!' she said passionately. 'How can you say that after what I've done to you? How can you be so – so calm about this, Vin? What's wrong with you? Don't you *care*?'

He looked over her head out of the kitchen window where the tulip tree held out bare branches to a cold drizzle of rain. As if he were speaking to himself, he said: 'I'll leave it to you to guess how much I care.'

'This is the end then – isn't it? We can't go on together with this between us.'

'We couldn't have gone on with this as a secret between us. I don't know what I would have done if you hadn't told me. But you have, and so – no, this isn't the end. Could be it's the beginning of something a bit better for us?' He put it as a question, looking at her with a shy pleading, like a child that does not know if it is going to be praised or scolded.

'Could be?' Christine felt her face lifting in a smile. As Vinson rose to move towards her, the front-door bell struck him rigid, his kiss arrested in mid-air.

'My God – the Admiral!'

'Let them ring. Let them think we're out, or dead, or –'

'For Christ's sake, Christine!' Vinson gripped her arm hard and turned her towards the door. 'Get upstairs at once and make yourself look like something. Don't you understand? It's the Admiral!'

Christine kissed him lightly and picked up the skirts of her dressing-gown 'Yes, dear,' she said, and ran upstairs smiling, as the bell pealed again, and a hand that could be only Mrs Hamer's pounded the brass knocker on the door.